THE HIDDEN
GIFT

IAN SOMERS

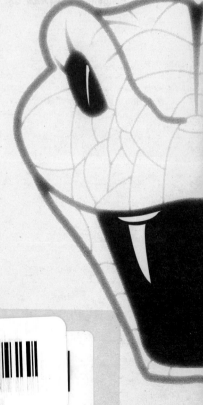

Ian Somers lives in Dublin and works as a graphic designer. His first book about Ross Bentley, *Million Dollar Gift*, is also published by The O'Brien Press.

SOMETIMES REVENGE IS NOT ENOUGH

THE HIDDEN GIFT

IAN SOMERS

THE O'BRIEN PRESS
DUBLIN

First published 2013 by
The O'Brien Press Ltd,
12 Terenure Road East, Rathgar,
Dublin 6, Ireland.Tel: +353 1 4923333; Fax: +353 1 4922777
E-mail: books@obrien.ie.
Website: www.obrien.ie

ISBN: 978-1-84717-308-9

British Library Cataloguing-in-Publication Data
A catalogue record for this title is available from the British Library

1 2 3 4 5 6 7 8
13 14 15 16 17

Printed and bound by CPI Group (UK) Ltd, Croydon, CR0 4YY
The paper used in this book is produced using pulp from managed forests.

The O'Brien Press receives assistance from

Dedication

For Edyta and my family.

You are my inspiration.

Acknowledgements

A big thank you to Helen Carr and all the staff at The O'Brien Press

for their hard work on this project. It's been a wonderful adventure.

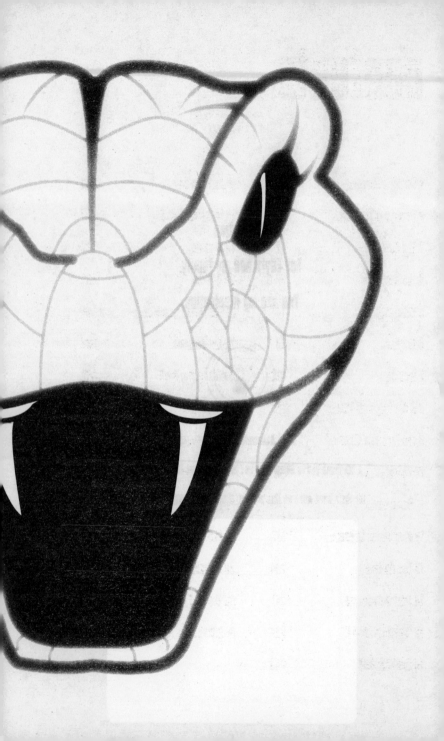

contents

From the journal of Jonathan Atkinson

'*T here are fifteen True Gifts. Each is both wondrous and terrify-ing in its own way. The nature of these gifts will always be determined by the individual who possesses them. The gifts can be used for the bet-terment of mankind or for its destruction.*'

The Prophet
The Psychokinetic
The Pyrokinetic
The Precognitive
The Metallisir
The Ink-Seer
The Warper
The Emotomagnet
The Spacerupter
The Electro-psych
The Mageleton
The Light Tuner
The Siren
The Mind Switcher
The Time Scanner

CHAPTER ONE

Smoke & Mirrors

Night was fast approaching and I was running out of time. I'd spent over ten hours wandering through the forest, unable to find a way out and it would be an impossible task once the sun set. I wasn't afraid of the dark, but at the same time I didn't want to spend an autumn night out in the Scottish wilderness, and certainly not in that particular wooded area; someone had been following me all day and despite my numerous attempts at an ambush they had evaded me time and time again.

I was beginning to think my pursuer was a figment of my imagination until I heard the footsteps once more. I dashed down a slope then sprinted for the cover of a fallen tree. I crouched low to the ground and watched from behind the twisted branches for any sign of life. The forest had fallen silent again and after ten minutes I rose despondently from my hiding place and continued my search for an escape route from the dreadful woodland. The footsteps were not the only things that had me on edge. The forest itself was unsettling. At times that day the trees on the periphery of my vision seemed to move. Something very unusual, and sinister, was going on around me and I was convinced I had been led into a trap that morning. One that I would not easily break free of.

The sun was low to my right and I figured I was heading south. That was the direction I needed to be going if I was to make it back to the road that I'd foolishly left that morning. I set a strong pace and kept to that direction for more than twenty minutes. I stopped when I came to a felled tree – the very same one I'd hidden behind twenty minutes earlier. I kicked up some loose dirt and roared in frustration.

How was this possible? I'd kept the sun to my right the whole time yet I'd walked in a circle. It went against all logic and I'd wasted too much time. The sun was slipping behind the labyrinth of pines and the sky was dimming rapidly. I'd never make it out in darkness and I accepted I was sleeping rough for the night.

I sat down on the trunk of the withered tree and rubbed my face. It was getting cold now the sun was fading and I could see faint trails of mist every time I exhaled. This was not going to be a pleasant experience. It was made ten times worse when I heard the sporadic tapping sounds from the branches above me – the first and unmistakable signs of rain. Within minutes it was a good old-fashioned Scottish downpour. I pulled up my hood and pushed my hands into my pockets and cursed under my breath. I should have been searching out shelter but I was too irritated to concentrate on anything apart from my aching legs; I'd been marching through woodland all day and my thighs and calves were throbbing.

The scar on the back of my leg was acting up too. It had been seven weeks to the day since Marianne Dolloway fired a white-hot arrowhead into my leg and it still dogged me when I over-exercised. Seven weeks since that awful evening when my mentor and friend, Marcus Romand, was killed. I'd escaped the attack with my life, but the scars from the fighting would be with me for the rest of my days. I'd suffered injuries to my legs, ribs and face, however the emotional scars were the hardest to overcome. I hadn't managed one good night's sleep in those seven weeks.

I hung my head and rubbed my hands together vigorously as the rain got heavier. I should have moved to a more sheltered spot but I remained in the open as the rain lashed my shoulders. I didn't move because out of the corner of my eye I could see the trees were shifting around again. I *had* to get to the bottom of this little mystery before I settled down for the night.

Everything was static for a few moments and I remained seated, with my head bowed. I was ready to make my move and once I noticed the trees far off to my right moving again I sprang off the fallen tree and forced psychokinetic energy out of my arm. I whipped the energy through my hand and sent the wave shooting across the forest at the trees that seconds earlier had been floating from side to side.

The energy sliced through the woodland, downing branches and there was a loud blast as one tree took the brunt of the wave and was shredded into a million splinters. As the tree fell I glimpsed a figure moving away into the shadows. I summoned my power once more and fired a spike of energy out of my index finger. More branches crashed to the forest floor, but the figure was gone. Or was it?

Suddenly the trees to my left were shaken by a mysterious force and I threw myself to the ground to avoid it. The pine just next to me bent violently as a psychokinetic wave swept over me. I *had* been followed, and it seemed I'd ruffled my pursuer's feathers!

I scrambled along the damp woodland floor on all fours and

crept into some bushes. The rain was coming down heavier now and it was impossible to listen out for footsteps. I'd have to wait until my attacker revealed himself. I had gathered a lot of energy and was ready to strike at the first sign of movement.

A shadow moved across the pines and I looked left to see a man moving to a thick tree trunk and using it as cover. I sprang from my hiding place and released the energy from within me. The trees swayed before me and the man was knocked off his feet. I moved forward, with the intention of hitting him even harder as soon as he got back to his feet, then I was sent reeling backwards by another wave of energy.

I crashed into the undergrowth and my head bounced off the ground. My blood was boiling as I clambered to my feet and fired an immense wave of power across the forest. The mysterious attacker should have been broken in half by my attack, but he appeared again, as a shadow deep in the forest.

I felt a sudden surge of anxiety creeping into my chest and knew my precognitive gift was warning me of an imminent attack. I moved to the side and an invisible bolt that made a sharp buzzing sound whizzed past my ear. Something struck the tree right behind me and it was instantly set alight. The flames spread across the branches and a bright yellow light shone across my face. I was a sitting duck.

Yet another shot was fired at me and I only managed to avoid it thanks to my precog gift. It had been a close call – the loud buzzing had come so close that it left my right ear ringing. I tried my best to counter the attack by forcing out a broad wave of energy to hold off my foe.

I then saw many shadows moving through the trees. There wasn't just one person following me, it seemed there were scores of them hunting me down! I knew I was outmatched and decided on making a hasty retreat. I fired out a wild blast of energy then turned and ran. To my surprise I saw a gap in the trees ahead of me leading to an open space. I had found the way out and just in time. I ignored my aching legs and sprinted for the opening. I ran as fast as I possibly could, hoping I could reach the open field that would surely deliver me to safety, or at least to a place where I could *see* my enemies.

Something hit my face with an almighty crack. I was knocked off my feet and came down on my back. I rubbed my face to find a trickle of blood from my nostrils, but thankfully my nose wasn't broken. My eyes had filled with water and it took a moment to clear them enough to see what had hit me.

This wasn't making any sense at all. I thought at first that something had hit me; as I gazed upward I saw that it was the other way around. There was no gap now, just another wall of pines and I had run straight into one at full tilt. I recognised the deep rolling laughter that was coming from behind. I didn't need to turn around to know it was Mike 'Hunter' Huntington. I pushed myself off the sodden ground and leaned against the tree, still rubbing my nose. Hunter was sitting on a tree stump nearby.

'You're a horrible person,' I shouted at him. 'What on earth did I do to deserve being sent out here to live with you? This is like a prison sentence! Actually, it's not – it's like being trapped in a lunatic asylum.'

'You're the only crazy one here, Bentley,' he chuckled. 'Look at you, running face-first into a tree. That looked mighty painful by the way.'

'Funny,' I sneered. 'Did you have this whole thing planned?

'It's part of your new training regime.'

'Training regime, my eye!'

I snapped my hand forward and fired a shot of energy at him. The blast shook some long grass at the foot of a tree. Hunter was not there. The tree stump was not there either. Had it been a figment of my imagination? Was I going nuts? I had been through hell and back in recent months and perhaps it was finally taking its toll on me psychologically.

No! This was another illusion. This was Hunter's latest effort at unnerving me. To run away. To have me wandering aimlessly through that damned forest.

I wasn't playing his game any longer. I sat down on the grass and folded my arms. No matter what he tried I was not going to be drawn into this ridiculous game again.

I'd spent seven weeks living in the isolated cottage with Hunter – I called him that because it seemed to irritate him – and he was supposed to be teaching me how to improve my gifts. But in all that time he hadn't taught me a single thing, except how to lose my temper. The man had barely talked to me the first four weeks and he still hadn't even told me what gifts he possessed. When he did start talking to me all he did was order me about and give me *exercises* to do each day. Within a week it became clear that the exercises were only chores and had nothing to do with my gifts. My time in Scotland was becoming a nightmare and all I wanted was to either get back to London to see my girlfriend, Cathy Atkinson, or to kick Hunter's ass!

Chores were difficult enough to deal with but now it seemed my tutor was moving to another level of antagonism by playing mind games. He'd told me that morning that I was about to get a chance to prove my power. We got in his 4x4 and he drove along the border of the forest for an hour before telling me to get out and find my way back to the cottage. And with that he drove off and left me standing in mud up to my ankles by the edge of the darkest forest I'd ever seen.

I shouldn't have been surprised at all; I'd already discovered that the gifted, mostly the older ones, were an eccentric lot. They never did what you expected them to. This also made them very dangerous when they weren't on your side, which I'd found out in such tragic circumstances at the Atkinson house seven weeks earlier.

'Do you always give up so quickly?' Hunter asked in his deep Scottish accent. He was standing only a few yards away and was leaning against a wide tree with his muscular arms folded across his chest.

'Do you always sneak up on people like this?'

'Never answer a question with a question,' he said as he left the tree and strolled towards me. He sat close by and grinned at me, almost as if he were gloating. 'I'm quite skilled at sneaking, aren't I?'

'You are,' I replied as I watched him carefully.

He looked older in the dim light than he had earlier that day. The lines on his face were deep and rigid as if he'd endured a hard life. My Dad would have described it as a face that was well lived in. I guessed he was about forty years old but he was quite athletic and could probably outrun me. He had a fast temper and knew little of fear. Hunter wasn't the type of man you'd want to get into a fight with.

'How did you do it?' I asked.

'You mean follow you without you seeing me?'

'Yes.'

'I thought you might have guessed that by now.'

'I'm too tired to guess.'

'One of my gifts is light-tuning. It's the pure form of the gift and I've mastered most of the techniques developed over the centuries – and I also have a few tricks of my own design.'

'I saw Romand use that gift a few times. He was very skilled.'

'He was. Alas, Romand did not have a pure gift.'

'Someone with a pure gift can draw in energy from their surroundings, right?'

'Exactly. It makes them extremely powerful compared to those with gifts that can only use the residual energy in their own bodies, which is limited. Unfortunately, Romand's gifts were not pure ...' A sudden sadness fell over Hunter's expression and he became distant. It was hardly surprising, as Romand had been his friend for many years.

'It's a shame Romand wasn't more powerful,' I said.

'Indeed,' Hunter nodded. He looked at me and smiled. 'Despite his shortcomings, Romand made the most of his abilities and was a fine warrior. But he could not do some of the things that *I* can do. Romand could only cloak himself using body refraction for a couple of minutes. I have remained cloaked for the entire eight hours that we've been in these woods.'

'You've been on my heels that long?'

'Yes, ever since I left you by the side of the road. I drove on for a couple of hundred yards then pulled over and followed you. I can remain cloaked for days on end, but that isn't the only way I tune light. This woodland for instance, it stretches for only a mile and a half between the road and my cottage, yet you have wandered around for eight hours without finding your way out.'

'That's impossible. If this forest was that small I would have definitely found the road or the fields leading to the cottage by now.'

'I'm not lying. I have shielded the way out from you with my gift.'

'I don't understand.'

'I have been bending light rays around you all day, which has prevented you from seeing the way out. This is one of my own techniques. I came up with the idea when I was a boy. My aunt brought me to a carnival – ever been to a carnival?'

'Yes.'

'Then you must have been in a house of mirrors?'

'Yeah, hate those bloody things. I banged my face off a mirror one time.'

'It seems nothing has changed since then,' he chuckled. 'This technique is very similar to the house of mirrors, which is a series of mirrors strategically placed at conflicting angles so that you can't clearly see the way out. This is the same. You were standing at the border of the forest many times today – you were looking into a mirror which was reflecting trees before your eyes. This has basically trapped you in this woodland for an entire day.'

'How the hell do you make these mirrors? It's like you create them out of thin air. That doesn't make any sense to me.'

'It doesn't make any sense to you because you don't think of light in the way that I, and other light-tuners, do. I think of light as if it's a tangible substance. One that can be captured, gathered, and moulded in whatever manner I choose. Light is everywhere. It is constantly surrounding us. I have the ability to trap it then transform it into any shape. One way of doing this is the creation of a mirror – just a simple shape that reflects the light that hits it. Another way I use light-tuning is to shape light into an orb that sucks in light that surrounds it – it gets brighter and brighter until it's blinding to look at.'

'I saw Romand creating light orbs before.'

'Yes, he was cunning in his use of light. Psychokinetics, like you, must deal with kinetic energy in the same way that light-tuners deal with light rays.'

'I don't understand.'

'You must think of kinetic energy as a substance. One that is invisible yet surrounds us at all times. When you've trained your mind to think of it in that way you will become exceptionally powerful.'

'That's all very interesting but this morning you said we were going to be training. I fail to see how trapping me in a forest is improving my gifts.'

'I said *training*; I didn't say we'd be improving your gifts. I don't think I could teach you how to be a better psychokinetic or time scanner or precog. Perhaps you don't need to improve those skills. After all, you fought Marianne Dolloway and managed to survive.'

'She was about to kill me when she was shot by a police officer.'

'Nevertheless, you're here. By all accounts you held her at bay for quite some time.'

'That still doesn't explain how this is training.'

'Your gifts are strong and you use them well, but you must learn to sharpen your mind and not depend solely on your gifts to survive. If you're to take Romand's place you will need to act fast and decisively. You were able to contend with Marianne because she fought in a way that your mind could easily understand; she used psychokinesis against you. It's a gift you are very familiar with. If you are to be a member of the Guild, though, you will certainly come up against people who have different gifts. Obscure gifts that are more subtle, harder to comprehend and in their own way more dangerous than psychokinesis. You will need to understand these gifts if you are to defend yourself against them. We will start with light-tuning. I will train you by helping you to understand a gift you know little of and how to counter it or, if possible, avoid it.'

'How about we come back to this tomorrow?' I asked. 'I've had enough for one day and I'm wrecked.'

'No. Will you say that to an assassin when he is trying to kill you? "Oh, sorry, Mr Assassin, I'm in need of my beauty sleep. Can you come by tomorrow and try to kill me in the morning?"'

Hunter laughed wildly at me.

'I don't find you in the slightest bit funny.' I said

'So what? I'm not here to entertain you. Besides, I like my own jokes.'

'Nightmare,' I sighed. 'This is an absolute nightmare!'

'It's only a game, Bentley, so stop your whining.'

'It's a very annoying game, *Hunter*.'

'Don't call me that.'

'Why? Does it bother you, *Hunter*?'

'You're only making things harder on yourself.'

'It doesn't get any worse than this!'

I couldn't help thinking of my dad in that moment. I remembered how, only months before, I was so desperate to leave him and the gloomy housing estate we lived in. How foolish I had been. I'd have given anything in that moment to be able to return to Ireland, and to my family home. I would have loved to be sitting watching a football match on the TV with him, and not trapped in a freezing forest.

'Of course it can get worse,' Hunter said, snatching me from my thoughts. 'Imagine I disappeared and left you out here to find your own way home ...'

'Don't you dare! Listen, I've failed this test. I admit it. You've won this round. Just don't leave me here. It's impossible to find a way out in the dark.'

'Darkness doesn't make this test any harder.'

'Oh, really?'

'Remember to use your mind. This is a simple puzzle and like all puzzles there is always a solution.' He swiped his hand in front of his chest and he became cloaked once more. 'I'll see you when you get back to the cottage.'

'Hey, you're not gonna leave me out here, are you? Hunter ...?'

The forest had fallen silent. I couldn't tell if he was still standing in the same spot or if he really had gone off back to the cottage. It didn't matter, he wasn't going to show me the way home either way. This was a problem I would have to solve for myself.

I clambered off the damp ground and looked at the surrounding trees. The forest was filled with darkness, and I had no idea of what direction to take, but I paced forward just to get myself motivated. Two hours later I was sitting on the ground again. I remained trapped.

Hunter had said it was a simple puzzle and all puzzles have a solution. But how could I find my way out? I realised that I could not trust my eyes and that what I was seeing was what was tricking me over and over again. I considered closing my eyes to remove the chance of being fooled by trickery, but the woodland floor was far too unpredictable for that; I'd end up falling down a ravine and breaking my legs or something equally as painful. There *had* to be a way!

'I am being fooled by what I see …' I said to myself. 'The trees are not real, but I cannot distinguish which are the real trees from the reflections that he is creating … I need find and follow something that he cannot distort.'

There was no moon in the black sky above the forest and the mountains nearby were out of sight. There was no landmark to follow, and it probably wouldn't work anyway. After all, Hunter had reflected the sun when I tried using that as a guide hours earlier. It was only now, after his explanation, that I realised he'd used his weird gift to prevent me from seeing the real sun, and to trick me into using a reflection of it as a guide.

I was growing extremely frustrated by the whole situation and the rain was coming down even heavier than before. I bowed my head to hide my face from the torrent and stared at the ground, hoping that a solution would present itself.

'Damn it!' I shouted out. 'How did I not think of this earlier?'

I'd been pacing that opening for quite a while and my footprints were clearly visible on the damp earth. All I had to do was find Hunter's foot prints and follow them home.

I went to the place where I'd ran into the tree and just a few yards away were a number of larger and deeper prints, obviously made by Hunter's heavy boots. The tracks went in circles at first, but soon they led me out of the trees to the grassland that stretched out to the foothills of the mountains, where the cottage was. I trudged through the waterlogged fields and I finally made it to the cottage around midnight.

I had to concentrate hard to stop my body shivering when I got inside. I caught my reflection in the mirror in the hallway and I looked like a half-drowned rat. I didn't want to give Hunter the pleasure of seeing me shaking from the cold so I straightened up and put a brave face on.

I kicked off my runners in the hall then paced through the sitting room to see him sitting, in the only chair there was, by the fire with a cigar in one hand and a glass of whiskey in the other. The cloud of smoke that slowly swirling around him didn't hide his grin. I felt my temper boiling over and I wasn't going to let him get away with leaving me out in the rain for the night.

'What's your problem with me?' I snapped. 'You've treated me like a leper since the day we came here.'

'I don't know what you're talking about, Bentley.'

'I hope you choke on that whiskey!'

'You're making a mess,' he said, pointing his cigar at the expanding pool of water at my feet. 'And I'm sure you don't want to be mopping the floors at this late hour.'

'Mop them yourself. I'm outta here first thing in the morning.'

'Grow up, Bentley.'

'Grow up? You're the one who's acting like a child with all these games and stupid remarks. I'm telling you now, I've had enough of this and I'm leaving tomorrow. You can stick your Guild and your smart remarks where the sun don't shine.'

'Do you always run away when times get tough?'

'I certainly do not but I won't remain here unless I'm shown some respect!'

'Respect is earned not demanded.'

'Respect is a courtesy that should always be given.'

'I think you should take your own advice and lower your voice while you're in my home.'

'I'd show you some respect if you stuck to your word.'

'I have broken my word?'

'Yeah, you have. You told me I was here to learn and all I get is abuse and stupid chores to annoy me. When does the *real* training start?'

'All in good time, Bentley.'

'Stop saying that. You always bloody say that.'

He turned his chair to the fire and took a sip from his glass. There were no more words between us that night.

CHAPTER TWO

Secrets in the Dark

My room was a cramped space with blank walls and no decorations of any kind. There were only two pieces of furniture: the ridiculously narrow bed and a flimsy chest of drawers. The only distraction from the monotony of the room was the clock hanging on the wall. There was no TV, no radio, no games console, no laptop, no phone, no nothing. The bedroom lived up to its description: a room with a bed. It fitted perfectly with Hunter's simple view of life.

The light went on once I opened the door and my saturated clothes proceeded to peel themselves from my quivering limbs as if they had a mind of their own. Most of the time I didn't even need to concentrate on using my gift to do small things like turning on lights and getting undressed. My control over the gift had improved tenfold since I'd left my home in Ireland – probably because I no longer needed to hide it from those around me – practice makes perfect, and all that.

The towel hanging on the back of the door floated across the room into my hands and I dried myself off as best I could. I should've jumped straight into a hot shower, but the plumbing in the little cottage was prehistoric and it took hours for the water in the tank to heat up. Instead I settled for some dry clothes and the hug of the duvet.

I was still fuming after my confrontation with Hunter and I cursed him for playing such a cruel trick on me that day. If I caught pneumonia I'd make sure the Guild found out it was his fault before I died. I rubbed frantically at my ribs in an attempt to generate some heat and I scratched my feet across the mattress cover to warm them. Sleeping in that sorry excuse for a bedroom was bad enough without being frozen half to death.

'Dear Lord!' I breathed. A terrifying idea had just popped into my head. 'I hope the Guild sends for me before winter sets in. I couldn't handle three or four months in this frozen hell of a place.'

When would I return to the world of the living? It was a question that often preyed on my mind. I understood why I had to disappear, after everything that had happened, but I didn't want to be isolated for too long. I was lonely, worried about my dad, I missed Cathy and most of all; I didn't want to end up like Hunter by being exiled to the Scottish wilderness for too long. If I spent many more months with him I'd even develop his thick Scottish accent – not that there was anything wrong with it, I just didn't want to have anything in common with that impossible man!

The rain dashed the window above the bed and the wind rattled the walls of the little cottage. It was a miserable abode and I couldn't wait to get away from it. I told Hunter I was bailing out first thing the next day. It was an idle threat and we both knew it; there was no way I could leave. My face would still be recognised after what happened at The Million Dollar Gift and there was also the looming threat of Golding Scientific and its many minions who were probably still keeping an eye out for me. I was stuck with Hunter for the time being and there was absolutely nothing I could do about it.

I focused on the light switch across the room and used my psychokinetic power to flick it down. The room was cast into shadow and I pulled the duvet up over my shoulder. The worst part of living in the countryside was trying to get some sleep when there was nothing to distract my thoughts from that dreadful place they kept returning to.

I tried to focus on something positive until sleep came, but everything I thought about led to the same subject: Marianne Dolloway and Marcus Romand. And when I thought about what happened I was led back to my darkest memory: I had led that murderous woman to the Atkinson's house, which meant *I* was responsible for Romand's death. It was a fact that I would never escape from.

'Damn,' I whispered. 'I wish I had a TV.'

I always found I could watch some mindless garbage on the tube and easily drift off. It had worked wonders in the year following my mother's death, when there was so much confusion in my mind and so much emptiness in my heart. This was similar, though I didn't have familiarity as a crutch to lean on this time. All I had were my thoughts, and the occasional confrontation with Hunter, who was now pacing along the hallway outside my bedroom.

The door to the next room slammed and a second later the springs of his bed bungeed. It was the same every night. He just closed his door and jumped onto the bed without even getting undressed. He was a right weirdo! At least he didn't snore like Romand ... And so I was back to thinking about *him*, and contemplating the costly mistake I'd made. The one that had alerted Marianne to our hideout.

27

The memories of what happened next were etched into my mind. The fear when I hid with the Atkinsons in the attic, the adrenalin rush when I faced Marianne, the shock of the gunshot that grounded her, the look on Cathy's face when Romand died. I doubted I would ever be able to banish those images.

The night went by slowly; sleep just would not come. My train of thought had paused at that point when Marianne was gunned down by the police. What had happened to her after that? I remembered Peter Williams saying that she had not shown up at any hospitals or police stations, which meant she must have been scooped by Golding's people. Was she dead or alive? Was she lying on a bed in a dark room right at that very moment and plotting my demise?

I thumped the pillow with my fist and scolded myself for being so neurotic. The most likely scenario was that she had died from the gunshot wound. After all, it had blown half her shoulder away and even if she did live, Marianne wouldn't pose much of a threat to me or the Guild.

I forced the sinister thoughts from my mind and focused only on Cathy's face. That was the one thing that filled me with contentment. I nodded off around 4am.

🖜🖜🖜

The bed was kicked at 6am, like it was every single morning. I'd only had two hours sleep and wanted to complain, but I didn't utter a single word in protest. There'd been countless sleepless nights followed by the usual rude awakening, followed by an argument that I lost every single time.

'You look like crap, Bentley,' Hunter pointed out as he walked to the door. 'You really should be getting to bed at a decent hour and not hanging out in the forest until after midnight … Teenagers.'

'Just what I need first thing in the morning, a dose of your special brand of humour.'

'Just trying to get the day off to a good start.'

'Sparing me your jokes would make for a better start.'

He paced out of the room and left me to clamber out of the bed and shuffle to the drawers to find some clothes for the day. I didn't pay much attention to what I put on; we never had visitors and I didn't care what Hunter thought of my dress sense.

I went to the kitchen and sat opposite him at the small, square table. There was a bowl of porridge in front of me and a cup of black coffee. I could not think of a less appetising combination, especially while having to watch Hunter suck up his own porridge. He also stank from smoking cigars the previous night.

I pushed my bowl into the centre of the table and took my cup to the back door and gazed out at the grey clouds gathering at the peaks of the mountains. It looked like a repeat of the previous day's weather and I was hoping Hunter wasn't planning on another excursion into the wilderness.

'What's on the schedule for today?' I asked without turning to him. 'And I want an umbrella if it involves outdoor activities.'

'You have a hood. What do you need a brolly for?'

'The hood is cotton. It soaks through in five minutes.'

'Linda Farrier left her pink raincoat here when she visited last year. I can fetch it for you if you want.'

'That would be swell.' I turned to him and he was grinning ear to ear. I couldn't help but crack a smile. I swiftly turned away from him before he noticed it.

'No chores today, you'll be happy to hear.' He got up and dumped his bowl and cup into the sink, without rinsing them off - that was my job - then walked out onto the back porch before lighting up a cigar. 'I have to go to town in a few hours.'

'Why did you wake me up at six in the morning if you had nothing planned for the day?' I asked through gritted teeth.

He turned to me and blew a cloud of smoke in my direction. 'Because it's healthy to keep a routine.'

'You woke me up, so you'll have to suffer me for the day.'

'What are you yapping about?'

'I'm going with you. I've been holed up here for far too long. I'll go mental if I don't get a break from this place.'

'Out of the question,' he said with a sharp shake of his head. 'It's far too dangerous.'

'What do you care if I'm in danger?'

'I care because if you're spotted they may come here looking for you, then *I* might be in danger. I'd rather that didn't happen. Don't worry, Bentley, you've only got another eight months before you can return south.'

'What did you just say…? *Eight months?*'

'That was the agreement I came to with Peter Williams, to keep you out of sight for a minimum of ten months. You've been here for two, so that leaves eight. Don't get your knickers in a twist about it because you have no say in the matter.'

'Why didn't you tell me it was ten months before I came up here?' I followed him as he re-entered the kitchen. 'I never would have agreed to this if I'd known.'

'You're giving me a headache, Bentley.'

'You're giving me a bigger headache, *Hunter*.'

He spun around and grabbed me by the throat then backed me up against the wall. Within an instant he had raised his other hand in front of my face. His index finger was pressed to my forehead and I felt a sharp tingle against my skull as his entire hand was surrounded by tiny flashes of electricity. I'd heard about electropsychs from Romand and I knew they could kill a person by firing bursts of electricity.

'First of all,' Hunter snarled, 'I didn't want to take this responsibility on for that amount of time. Secondly, I would prefer to be out chasing down Romand's killers rather than babysitting you. Thirdly, *stop calling me Hunter.*'

'Mr Williams calls you that. Why can't I?'

'Williams is an old friend of mine, that's why he can call me that. You, on the other hand, are *not* my friend and you don't get the privilege of referring to me by that name. Are we clear?'

'I'm not scared of you. You think you have me all figured out, don't you?'

'I have you by the throat and I can send a small electrical current into your brain and send you into a coma. I think I have you figured out quite well enough, Bentley.'

Thanks to my precognitive gift, I had sensed his initial attack before he even turned, and by the time he'd thrown me up against the wall I had reached out with my psychokinesis and lifted a knife from the pile of cutlery in the sink. It had been hovering behind his head up until now. I eased the sharp point forward and it prodded at his scalp.

'I'll sense your move before you even decide on it,' I said. 'And if you do I'll push this knife right through your brain. You haven't gotten me completely figured out just yet, *Hunter*.'

Hunter held his stare for a moment then released his grip on my neck. He walked across the room and dragged his coat off the rack and stormed out into the hallway. When I heard his 4x4 rumbling off into the distance I sent the knife back into the sink and pushed myself from the wall with my elbows.

What on earth had convinced Peter Williams to send me away with this madman? Hunter was a complete and utter lunatic, I was convinced of it. Worse still, he was a violent lunatic! I wasn't afraid of him – I reckoned I could beat him in a fight – but I didn't feel comfortable being cooped up with him in the middle of nowhere. And now it seemed I had another eight months of this impossible situation to endure.

There was no way I was going to last that long. We'd surely kill each other if this went on any longer. Someone would come knocking at the cottage next summer and find us both dead, our decaying hands still wrapped around each other's skeletal necks.

I sat on the table and rubbed my throat. The big brute was seriously strong and had almost choked me half to death. He was faster than he looked too. Not quite fast enough to get the jump on a precog like me, but fast nonetheless. He was also very gifted. At least I now knew exactly what his gifts were. He was, on his own admission, a light-tuner, and a very powerful one at that, judging by the prison of mirrors he'd created in the forest the night before. He was also an electropsych because he'd threatened to kill me with that gift just moments earlier, *and* he had psychokinetic skills, although it wasn't clear how strong this gift was; he'd created a wave when we sparred the previous evening, but it wasn't strong, at least nothing compared to what I could do.

Hunter had three gifts, though, and that made him just about as dangerous as any person could be. I also had three gifts, but one of them, my time-scanning power, was of no use in combat. I still believed I could beat him in a straight fight. Although that wasn't a terribly attractive proposition.

It was foolish to leave two people, who both had three of the true gifts and obviously hated one another, alone in a rural cottage together … for the best part of a year! People die when the gifted fight. I had to avoid another confrontation, if I could, until I created a plan of escape. I wasn't spending eight more months with him. I wasn't even going to spend the winter with him. No way was I staying in the drafty cottage during the coldest months of the year in the Scottish wilderness. How the hell was I going to convince him to bring me back to England? Or even to allow me to return to my dad in Ireland?

I walked outside and looked out over the lonely landscape. I had a very boring day ahead. There was quite literally nothing to occupy my time with, unless I wanted to take a leisurely stroll around the woods, and there was no a chance I was ever doing that again.

I stood there feeling sorry for myself until the rain came lashing down from the deep grey sky that churned above the cottage. I went inside and locked the door then wandered from room to room as my boredom grew. I ended up sitting in Hunter's chair by the fireplace and looking at the half full bottle of whiskey on a shelf nearby. Now I understood why he drank each night; the isolation drove him to it. To his credit he didn't overdo it. He never had more than two measures in a single night.

I watched the clock above the mantelpiece as the hour struck seven. He'd probably be gone all day, which should have been a relief, but being alone was a worse prospect. That meant I had to deal with the dark memories that were haunting me relentlessly.

'Damn it!' I shouted. I forced myself out of the wooden chair and stomped around the room. 'There has to be something to do in this bloody hellhole!'

Suddenly a thought came to me – *Hunter's room!* I wondered what secrets he was keeping in there. I knew he wouldn't return until late afternoon, which meant I had hours to battle the temptation to go snooping through his stuff. I'd eventually give in to my curiosity and decided not to bother fighting it.

I walked through the hall and used my psychokinesis to create a small vortex of energy that turned the doorknob anti-clockwise. The door swung open with a creak.

What I saw was hardly surprising. Hunter's room was a carbon copy of my own. The walls were plain white, there was one single bed, a clock on the wall and a small chest of drawers in the corner. How could anyone live like this? Monks had a more extravagant lifestyle than Hunter.

I walked to the chest and pulled open the drawers but there were only clothes inside. Each of the drawers slammed shut when I sent out a small burst of energy from my hand. I could have continued rummaging around the room, but I was beginning to feel guilty for going through his stuff.

I shut the door and went back to the sitting room and sat looking at the rain running across the window in little streams. This really was an empty house. No entertainment. No happiness. No possessions. Well, apart from the pink raincoat that was allegedly stored in the attic ...

'Hello,' I said, looking up at the ceiling.

I'd never been in the attic and my body began to tingle with excitement at the prospect of nosing around up there. This was how bored I had become; I was excited about looking around a dusty old attic. It was about the most intriguing prospect that I had for that day so I practically jumped out of the seat and went to the hallway. I looked at the hatch then nudged some energy upward. The hatch door swung slowly open then I sent energy downward which propelled me into the air, just high enough to grab the sides of the gap.

I pulled myself up and was consumed by the shadows. As soon as I stood upright there was a cord tickling my face and I yanked it down. The attic was filled with light that sparkled across the maze of cobwebs hanging from the rafters. The attic was a polar opposite of the ground floor and was stuffed full of old junk. There was the usual crap like a tool box that was rusted shut, an old mountain bike missing its front wheel, mounds of old books that stank of mould, and there were an inordinate amount of old boots lying around. I even spotted Linda Farrier's raincoat, covered with fine layer of dust. It looked grey at first, but when I swiped my hand over its glossy surface I saw it was indeed pink.

At the other end of the attic was a large wooden box with a canvas sheet covering it. It hadn't been touched in a long time judging by the thick layer of dust on the cover. Much thicker than that on Farrier's raincoat. If her coat had been there since last winter I guessed the canvas cover hadn't been touched in five years or more.

I focused on my powers for a moment then lifted the sheet into the stale air of the attic, gathered more energy around it and rolled it up tightly, then took it in hand and placed on the floor next to the large box. I cautiously lifted the lid, half expecting a colony of rats to be disturbed. Instead I found items that seemed oddly out of place in Hunter's home.

There were some child's clothes neatly folded into a bundle, strangely they all had burn marks on them. Who on earth would keep charred clothes in their attic? Not even Hunter was that strange. Was he? He obviously was. There were a few picture frames too. There was a very fine layer of soot covering them, but I could make out some faces behind the darkened glass. They were family portraits mostly and were quite old. I spotted Hunter in one; at least I thought it was him. He looked no older than ten or eleven and was standing next to a haggard looking woman. There was another photograph showing a slightly older Hunter, this time he was sitting bedside a different woman who was smiling and had a pleasant face. I guessed it was his mum. It was hard to imagine Hunter having a mother. I didn't really think of him as a normal human being, more like a cyborg that had been grown in a test tube someplace.

I came across another picture that was not as pleasant. It was Hunter, a little older than in the other pictures, and he was standing between two police officers. It had been cut from a newspaper and there was no headline or writing of any kind on it. I was starting to feel uncomfortable snooping around his stuff and pulled the lid of the box back down.

A piece of metal caught the light just before I closed the lid. I opened the box again and took a closer look. It was a metal rendering of an emblem that was very familiar to me. It was the wolf head logo that Romand had used in some of his writings – it was the symbol of the Guild of the True.

At first I thought it was just a medallion, but on closer inspection I saw it was actually attached to the front of a book. I freed it from the dust at the bottom of the box and found it to be a journal, rather than a book. It had a leather cover and was about three hundred pages long. I opened it and read the inscription on the inside of the cover: 'The Journal of Jonathan Atkinson 1988-1992'.

Jonathan Atkinson was Cathy's father! What on earth was his journal doing in Hunter's attic? Surely its proper place was with the author's wife and daughter.

There was a more pressing question to be answered: should I read it?

I was starting to get nervous all of a sudden, thinking Hunter could arrive back at any moment and there would be ugly scenes if he caught me reading this journal. I'd wanted to know more about the Guild for some time, though, and this journal would most likely supply me with a lot of the knowledge I craved. Could I not read it?

I decided to flick through the pages and saw they were organised into long entries, each about five pages in length and all had headings along with specific dates. I paused about halfway through and read one of the headings: 'Changing the leadership of the Guild, 1988'. This sparked my curiosity. I simply had to read through the entry.

*I*t has become clear to me, and to many of my colleagues, that a change in leadership is required. The Guild has grown complacent and almost redundant over the course of the last decade. Much of this stems from our well-respected, but aged, leader Theresa Monroe. The blame for our failings is not hers alone. We all had a hand in allowing the Guild to fall into decline.

The death of a gifted child in Spain last month has roused many of us and there are heated discussions in the hallways of the Palatium. The jostling for power has begun.

The common consensus is that Monroe must be forced to relinquish her control immediately and that a more proactive member must take up her position. Herein lies our problem. There are three contenders and all have strong support throughout the Guild.

Clarissa Yenver would be the natural replacement because she has been second-in-command for many years, but she is getting on in years and the feeling is that she lacks the vitality required to bring about significant change. She will have the support of many of the senior members and could possibly gather enough votes to be successful.

I also have much support in the ranks of the senior members and I will put myself forward for the role. I have a vision for the Guild, one that could restore it to the greatness of bygone times. We must build for the future, but learn from the past. I believe we should be more active in the search for gifted youngsters and that they should be taught to use their powers by those with a lifetime of experience. We must not engage in open warfare, as some would advocate. My belief is that we must remain a clandestine group. Our greatest strength throughout the centuries has been to trick the world into believing we don't actually exist.

The third candidate is Brian Blake. It is my opinion that under no circumstance must he be allowed to take control of the Guild. Blake has long lobbied for a more militant approach to our work. This has gained him support from the younger agents within the Guild, but his leadership could transform us into that which we seek to destroy.

I refer to the four organisations that actively search and use gifted people for the pursuit of wealth or military strength or political gain. These organisations have grown in power in recent years, and much of it is our fault for taking a passive stance in the struggles of the gifted.

Our immediate and most deadly opponent is **Armamenti Tal-Future** (Malta). They are currently our most active opponent and have been seeking to destroy us for a number of years. They have snatched many gifted youngsters from their homes throughout this decade and they are training them for use in warfare. Essentially, they have been building an army of gifted mercenaries and have been hired by governments and big business to win wars and to conduct coups in the developing world. They have committed numerous atrocities in recent years, and have tipped the balance of power in trouble spots around the globe in favour of their employers. Their wealth is increasing at an alarming rate and they must be stopped at all costs.

JNCOR is a modern cover front for the old Jin Assassins (Hong Kong). The Jin Assassins were founded in thirteenth-century China to help protect the empire from the invading Mongol forces. Some time in the fifteenth century they broke their ties with the empire and began recruiting other gifted people from around Asia. JNCOR are not as openly malicious or aggressive as Armamenti-Tal-Future, but they are just as dangerous because of their ultimate goal. Their plan is to control the primary governments in East Asia who can then enforce their extreme right-wing views. They almost achieved this in the early twentieth century, but were significantly weakened during and after the Second World War. They have now rebuilt much of their strength and will pose a serious threat to stability in Asia in the coming decades.

The S.P.D. *(Soviet Union) has been our most persistent enemy over the last decade. Their role is to help impose communist ideals around the world and to eliminate anyone who seeks to destroy the Soviet Union. They are active in recruiting gifted youngsters who they use as assassins and spies. Any gifted person who refuses to work for them is murdered.*

The S.P.D. is a repulsive organisation and we have worked tirelessly to ensure that they do not recruit outside of the Soviet Union. Our struggle with them has cost us dearly in the past, but it is possible that they will not continue to be a thorn in our side. Our sources based in Moscow seem to believe that communism in Russia may collapse in the coming years, and this would remove almost all of their financial support. I can only pray that this information is accurate.

Golding Scientific *(USA) is the latest threat to emerge. Most in the Guild do not see them being able to compete with us, or the other organisations, and have ignored them for the most part. I disagree and having conducted a private investigation into its founders, Paul and Sarah Golding, I think they must be dealt with sooner rather than later. Their influence is growing steadily and they should be dealt with before they are strong enough to compete with us properly.*

The big four represent a threat to all humanity if they continue to go unchallenged. The Guild has become too passive under the leadership of Theresa Monroe and has allowed them to recruit and use gifted people to murder political figures, to commit mass killings under the guise of terrorist attacks, to influence wars, and to attain massive wealth for unscrupulous corporations. The Guild must be more proactive. We must strike back.

*The most pragmatic way to hurt these organisations is to cut off their supply of gifted youngsters, by recruiting them into our own organisation before the others can snatch them. This will be a difficult task as our current resources are limited. But with the help of other, benign groups such as **Der Orden der Befähigten** (Germany) and **Os Especiais** (Brazil) I believe we can eliminate the threats that face us.*

I was about to turn the page, instead I snapped the journal shut. I held my breath and listened. I'd heard something from downstairs. Had Hunter arrived home early? If he caught me up here I'd be a dead man.

I threw the journal back into the box and flung the canvas sheet over it. I yanked the light cord and sent the attic into darkness and prepared to dive through the open hatch to the hallway below.

I paused. There was a sharp tapping coming from below. It sounded like someone frantically knocking on one of the windows. It wasn't Hunter; he never forgot his keys and besides, he could easily use his gifts to unlock a door.

The tapping got faster and louder. Someone wanted into the cottage and wasn't going away.

CHAPTER THREE

The Messenger

I channelled a low intensity cushion of energy beneath me and then practically floated down into the hallway without making a sound. I looked up and used my power to draw the hatch down softly. All the while the intense tapping continued at the back of the cottage. Terrible scenarios ran through my mind as I tip-toed along the hallway to the kitchen door. Was it the police? Golding's assassins? Had Marianne Dolloway somehow returned? I regretted reading the page from the journal now because my imagination was running wild with all sorts of horrible possibilities.

I forced a weak wave of energy ahead of me and the kitchen door swung lazily open. I'd half been expecting the door to be blown apart as soon as it moved, but the cottage had fallen silent and I became very aware of how fast my heart was beating.

I took a wary step inside and looked to the back window, there was no one there. I took a few steps forward and leaned on the sill and looked out onto the porch. It was empty. Was my mind playing tricks on me? Was Hunter playing tricks on me again? I'd kill him if he was.

I paced to the sitting room and hid behind the curtains as I gazed out at the front garden. No one there either. This wasn't Hunter's style and no Guild member would be foolish enough to visit us. A sense of foreboding took me and I felt my powers rising from the intense emotions that were running wild inside me.

The tapping came from the back of the cottage again - louder this time. I shot out of the room and went to the kitchen. I raced to the window but could see no one. What the hell was going on?

I'd had enough of this game and pulled the door open. I could see no one at first, but when I looked down I saw that I had a most unusual visitor. There, standing on the wooden porch before me, was the biggest bird I had ever seen. It was about three feet tall and almost as broad. Its sharp face was turned up at me and its yellow eyes were fixed on my own.

The bird came waddling forward and cawed loudly at me, as if telling me to get out of its way. I thought about giving it a kick or nudging it backward with my psychokinesis – it was already in the kitchen before I had time to act.

'Get the hell out of here, stupid bird!' I shouted. 'Go on! Get! There's nothing for you here. There's no food for you.'

It suddenly spread its enormous wings and rose up off the floor. The kitchen was too small for the bird to fly, but it tried and made a right mess of the place in the process. Chairs, cups, plates, pots and pans were knocked off the counters and clattered onto the floor before the bird eventually came to rest. It stood proudly – if a little flustered – on the kitchen table and watched me as I edged to the door leading to the porch. I didn't fancy having my eyes pecked out by this giant hawk, or whatever it was, and I thought it best to give it some space until it decided to bugger off.

'This day is just getting stranger and stranger,' I said, looking at the feathered beast. 'First I get into a fight at 6.30 in the morning and now my home has been invaded by a big ... *vulture*!'

'It's not a vulture. It's a Steller's sea eagle.'

I almost jumped out of my skin and I spun round to see Hunter standing behind me on the back porch.

'Hunter, you nearly gave me a damned heart attack. Why are you always sneaking up on me?'

'A precog should never be surprised,' he said, rolling his eyes.

'That's not entirely accurate,' I replied. 'Precogs can only sense imminent physical danger. They can't predict people sneaking up on them and making smart remarks!'

'How very enlightening,' Hunter snorted as he brushed past me. He stood in the kitchen with his hands on his hips and he looked the bird dead in the eye. 'The stupidity of some people never ceases to amaze me.'

'What are you on about?'

'The Siberian coastline is the natural habitat for these birds so I would deduce that it hasn't simply happened past our home and decided to come in for a nose about. The only logical explanation is that this bird is being controlled by a mind-switcher. It is a rare creature and the only person I know of that has one is Peter Williams. And the only people I know that hang out with him and have the gift of mind-switching are the Atkinsons. And Cathy Atkinson happens to be your sweetheart. It's a good guess that it's her, in an elaborate and *flamboyant* disguise.'

The bird cawed at him before it turned to me and inclined its head slightly. It *was* Cathy, using that weird gift of hers. It had been ages since I'd seen her and we'd had no way of communicating up until now.

'Cathy,' Hunter said to the eagle. 'Using a bird to come up here is one thing. I don't even blame you for that, but couldn't you have picked a more inconspicuous animal? A Steller's sea eagle! One of the largest birds in the world and we're supposed to be in hiding.'

'Look,' I said. 'There's a roll of paper looped to its leg. It must be a message from the Guild.'

'More likely a vomit-inducing love letter to you.'

He stepped forward and tore the roll from a nylon strap that was looped around the eagle's leg. He quickly unravelled it then handed it to me. My name was scribbled on the front of the envelope.

'It's a letter,' I said, examining the envelope. 'This is the best postal service ever! It's like getting invited to Hogwarts.'

'Hogwarts?'

'Hunter, you really need to get out more.'

'I get out enough.'

He turned to the eagle and ordered it out. I still couldn't get my head around the mind-switch gift. I knew Cathy was controlling the bird, but it seemed such a cold and emotionless creature and its eyes betrayed no feelings at all.

'Thank you,' I said, just before it sprang off the table and swooped through the open doorway. I walked out to the porch to see it rising fast and soaring over the forest nearby. It was out of sight within a couple of minutes.

It was the first positive thing that had happened in my life since the battle at the Atkinson house and I wanted to enjoy it alone. I sat on the swing chair out on the porch and pulled open the envelope to find a letter and a photograph inside. I glanced at the picture, but it stirred up some uncomfortable emotions so I slipped it back into the envelope and unfolded the letter that accompanied it. I wanted to lose myself in Cathy's words for a while.

Hello again, handsome!

I'm so sorry it's taken this long to get in touch with you. When we last saw each other I thought I'd be able to write you every second day but it's taken eight weeks for me to convince Peter Williams to let me send you this message. I hope you're not angry, Ross. There's been so much trouble down here since you left and everyone is on edge. Nobody is allowed to travel alone and public meetings are out of the question. Even sending letters has been prohibited by the Guild. Can you believe that??

It was only late last night that Peter told me that it was okay to send this letter. Then he said I couldn't use the regular postal service, and would have to deliver the message personally. I hope the eagle doesn't scare you! I've been spending a lot of time at Peter's wildlife sanctuary (isn't that cool!) and the only bird he had that was capable of a long flight was the Steller's Sea Eagle. I've been practising the mind-switch with the bird all week and I'm really starting to get the hang of it. Learning to fly as an eagle takes a lot of practice. It's not like a kingfisher.

You do remember when I controlled the kingfisher, right? I'll never forget that day, Ross. Our first kiss will stay with me forever and all I think about is seeing you again. I've asked Peter when you'll be allowed to return, but he won't give me a straight answer. I really hope it will be soon!!

It's been a crazy two months since you left. Dreadful, but exciting too. Mum is showing some signs of improvement though she's still not back to her old self. Romand's death has really hit her hard and she spends a lot of time on her own; nobody's allowed mention his name in front of her. That just sets her off crying, and it's very difficult to get her to stop once she starts. What happened with Romand has made life harder for everyone who knew him. I'm sure you miss him too. I know I do. I spend a lot of time by his grave, thinking back to the good times we had with him. I'm almost crying writing this. I still find it hard to come to terms with how he died. It makes me angry and confused. Sometimes I can't talk to anyone about it. I know you probably feel the same. Maybe it will be easier when you come back to England and we can spend time together again ...

There have been some good times recently, though. Peter Williams has a private animal sanctuary near his home. He rescues exotic animals that foolish millionaires bought but couldn't look after once they'd grown up, or weren't permitted to have and the authorities removed them. You should see the animals he has, Ross! I still miss Bebe and Pepe but I'm learning so much by interacting with so many new and weird creatures. I've spent a lot of time with the eagle and I've also switching my mind into a python that he has here. I was always scared of snakes but not any more. They really are incredible creatures – although their minds work very differently to ours and it was hard to learn how to move without limbs!

The animal I've spent most time with is Nightshade. He's a three-year-old black panther rescued recently from a billionaire playboy who had him locked in a cage out his back garden (how can some people be so cruel??)

I've perfected the mind-switch with Nightshade and I'm pushing the limits of my gift by following the work of Miriam Tompkins, the woman who used her gift to tame wild animals. I've come a long way in the last two weeks, and Nightshade is already capable of being around other humans without showing any sign of aggression.

Right, I'm probably boring you now! What exciting stuff have you been up to? I'm sure you and Hunter have been working on loads of cool new training techniques. I hope the two of you have become friends by now. I know he can be a bit cranky when you first meet him, but he chills out after a while.

Please write back soon. Hunter knows the address for the Williams Estate and he'll make sure your letter arrives.

Missing you loads!

Cathy

PS Don't go falling in love with any Scottish girls!!

I read over the letter three times before I folded it over and placed back in the envelope. Reading Cathy's words made me feel close to her again. The one thing I wanted more than anything. I just wanted to kiss her again. To touch her. To hold her. The world sure was a brighter place when Cathy Atkinson was around. I had many more months of Hunter's company ahead of me, but the promise of being with Cathy again made it seem less daunting.

I plucked the photograph from the envelope and gazed at it for a time, then my heart felt heavy and I put it away. I didn't want to feel sad in that moment, I wanted to keep feeling loved and wanted. Reality was never far away, though, and Hunter quickly brought me back down to earth.

'Looks like a cold spell is headed our way,' he said. He was standing in the doorway and looking at the bleak landscape. 'I want you to go get some firewood.'

'All in good time, Hunter.'

'You can take your time, but make sure you do it before sundown. Otherwise you might find yourself trapped outside again.'

'Anything to be away from you.'

'You won't think like that once the temperature drops. We're also due heavy rain. It's your choice, you want to stay outside for the evening then go right ahead.' He disappeared inside the cottage and left me to ponder the letter once more.

I was getting more and more frustrated by my exile. Cathy's letter had accentuated my loneliness and I was jealous that she was having fun and learning to improve her gift. I wasn't much of an animal lover, but spending time in a reserve for exotic creatures in the south of England sounded a lot more appealing than being trapped with Hunter by the side of a cold mountain in the north.

I ignored Hunter's warnings and decided to go to my room and pen a reply to Cathy's message. It took a couple of hours and I scrunched up more than a dozen attempts before I was happy with my written response. It was full of lies. How could I tell her the truth about my time away from her? I simply said that Hunter and I were getting on like a house on fire and I was learning to control my powers and so on. Nothing could have been further from the truth.

'Bentley!' Hunter shouted from his room. 'Don't forget the firewood.'

'Bentley, do this. Bentley, do that,' I moaned to myself. 'Bentley is slowly going nuts.'

At 3pm I passed my letter, sealed in an envelope, to Hunter and told him I wanted him to send it to the Williams Estate. He said he would, although he was hardly convincing. I took one of his coats from a hanger in the hallway and I left the cottage then trudged across the sodden fields to the forest.

Getting firewood wasn't exactly a straightforward chore. Especially as there was no axe at the cottage. I had to use my gift to down a tree then divide it up into small logs. That sounds easier than it actually is.

First I had to create a downward wave – a very precise one. I created a ceiling of energy at the top of the tree then pulled it down along the trunk. It had to be powerful enough to strip away all the branches, yet not so potent as to destroy the trunk itself. It took time to get it right but after an hour or so I was successful and a tree bare of branches was before me.

Cutting down the branchless tree was simple. I gathered my power and sent a slice towards the tree - this was a technique I'd learned from reading the notes of Ala-Qush. The disc of energy cut the tall pine down and it swung lazily before falling to the ground with a loud thump. The next step was to create very precise slicing techniques to cut the thick trunk into blocks that were small enough to throw into the hearth of the fireplace, or into the furnace at the back of the cottage. By the time I was finished chopping up the tree my power was waning. It needed a lot of concentration and I found it hard to use emotion, which fuelled my powers.

I stacked some of the logs together and levitated them a few feet off the ground, then marched back to the cottage with the bundle of logs hovering in front of me. I dropped them on the back porch then tossed a few into the furnace before sitting at the kitchen table, exhausted. Hunter was at the stove and didn't acknowledge me as I sat. I sniffed and wrinkled my nose, realising he was making that awful stew of his again. I was starving, but the thoughts of it were making me queasy.

I managed to down a few spoonfuls of the stew. It tasted even worse than it smelled. Hunter on the other hand lapped it up, then took mine and ate that too. He was a repulsive man when he was eating. A horse would have better table manners. He flung the bowls into the sink when he was finished then went to the sitting room for a cigar, which he always did after dinner. I was glad to be left alone.

🖛 🖛 🖛

The sun was setting and there was just enough light in the kitchen for me to see the faces clearly. The photograph was a little tarnished but as I held it up against the fading light from the window I could see every detail and line on Romand's face. He was sitting in the back garden of the Atkinson's house and had his arm around Cathy. They were both smiling and the evening summer sun cast a warm hue on their faces. I remembered that evening quite well. Romand and I were sitting outside discussing the day's training when Cathy emerged from the house with her camera and started taking snaps of us. She'd said she wanted one of her and Romand and I had volunteered to be the cameraman. It took eight snaps before Romand finally smiled.

I rubbed my thumb over the image of the two people I missed so much. I felt like crying, but knew it wasn't the thing to do. What would Romand say if he saw me weeping over an old photograph? He'd probably curse in French then tell me I was a sissy.

He looked so happy in the photograph, which was a stark contrast to my final memory of him. I shuddered when I pictured his broken body and the demented look in Marianne's eyes when she tried to kill me. The emotional and physical pain was still close, still tugging at my heart whenever I had a quiet moment to myself. I remained angry with myself for allowing Romand to sacrifice himself for me. I should have reacted quicker that night. Perhaps he'd still be alive if I hadn't hid in the attic like a coward.

The letter had eased my worries a little, though, and I knew Cathy remained safe. I wouldn't be able to live with myself if any harm came to her. In fact, I felt guilty that I'd left and she remained in the centre of the trouble. Not that I'd had much of a choice. I would have opted to stay had it been my decision.

'You been reading that soppy love letter again?'

I looked over the photograph to see Hunter standing in the doorway to the hallway. His cold eyes were fixed on me and his broad arms were folded over one another. That mocking smile was on his face again.

'Why are you so cruel?' I replied as I folded the letter and placed it back into the envelope. 'I've never done anything to you.'

'I have to share my home with you. That's reason enough.'

'It wasn't my choice to come here. I'll gladly leave in the morning and go back to living a normal life.'

He stepped into the kitchen and flicked on the overhead lamp. 'Give up on any hope of a normal life, Bentley. This is your life from now on.'

'This isn't a life, *Hunter*.'

'I told you not to call me that, *Bentley*. Only my friends call me that.'

'Don't call me Bentley.'

'I'll call you whatever I like. This is my home and I say what goes.' He pulled a chair from the under the table and sat facing me. He pressed one elbow on the table top and outstretched his other arm towards me. 'Give me a look at that picture.'

'Why should I?'

'Because it's my house and I—'

'Oh, suit yourself.' I slid the photograph across the table. 'It won't cheer you up. It's put me in a right horrid humour.'

He held it up and stared carefully at it for a long while before a smile pushed at one of his cheeks. I knew he and Romand had been close friends for many years and was expecting a different reaction. I certainly didn't think it would bring any warmth to his cold heart.

'Why the smile?' I asked.

'Why not? I have so many fond memories of Romand. Pictures of him will always make me smile.' Hunter's face went blank then, as if he was unsure of how to act in front of me. It was almost as if he was afraid, or embarrassed, to reveal his true emotions to me. I guess that was normal. I was practically a stranger to him, and he didn't seem like a man who was comfortable sharing his feelings. It was in that moment that I realised that Hunter had never been able to properly grieve for his friend because I had been imposed on him immediately after the funeral. I suppose I wasn't the only one who was finding the living arrangements difficult to deal with.

'I'll miss him,' Hunter finally said, 'as will the Guild miss his support.'

'I hate the way you mention the Guild, but never actually talk to me about it. If I didn't know better I'd be starting to think that it's a figment of your imagination. On the first morning that I was here you asked me to join and ever since then you've practically ignored me. You only gave me the vaguest possible description of this Guild. Not a word on who else is part of it, what gifts they have and what members of this group actually *do*.'

'All in good time.'

'And you keep saying that! *All in good time, Bentley*,' I tried to imitate his Scottish accent and did a terrible job. I leaned across the table. 'Tell me, who's in charge of this Guild?'

He leaned forward and his face was very serious. 'All in good time, Bentley.'

I slapped the table top and sighed as he erupted into laughter. Hunter was infuriating and I was trapped in the middle of nowhere with him. I was imprisoned in a tiny cottage with him for eight more months. I needed to escape to situation soon or I'd surely crack up.

I stood up and stuffed the envelope in the back pocket of my jeans. I'd had enough of Hunter's strangeness for one day and I needed to get away from him.

'I'm off to my room,' I told him.

'Not before you do the washing up.'

'You think I'm some sort of slave? I'm sick of this bullshit. Chopping wood and washing dishes and mowing the lawn. I deserve better than this.'

'You think you're too good for chores, Bentley, is that it?'

'What's that even supposed to mean? You make me sound like some rich kid who's never gotten his hands dirty. I used to clean a supermarket for a living before I came here.'

'Oh,' he said in a mocking voice, 'it must have been a tough life for you.'

'I'm a hard worker.'

'You have the look of a grifter not a grafter, Bentley.'

'That's it,' I snapped, 'I want to leave here tomorrow. I'll find my way to the nearest town and catch a bus back down south.'

'That's what you said yesterday. *And* the day before that.'

'This time I mean it.'

'You probably wouldn't make it across the border.'

'I think I can manage to get a bus on my own.'

'You'd probably be dead or arrested before you reached the border.'

'What are you talking about?'

'There are people out there,' he pointed aimlessly, 'who are working around the clock to find you. Some want you dead. Some want you locked up. Others want to use you and your powers for some *very* sinister activities.'

'Who are you talking about?'

'Anyone who doesn't mind taking human life for money.'

'How would you know that?'

'Because I've been in the middle of this conflict for near twenty years and I know what way Golding, and others like him, work. If he can't get you on his side he will put a contract out on your head. The more powerful you are the bigger the contract will be. The bigger the contract is, the more skilled assassins it will attract.'

'I'm trapped then.'

'Only for another eight months. I'm going to toughen you up while you're here. You'll need to be stronger before you enter the fray once more.'

'And chopping wood will make me more capable of fighting people like Marianne? Don't be ridiculous!'

'Healthy body, healthy mind. You need to be in good physical shape before you can push your gifts to the limits again.'

'I'm in good shape.' I shot out a few fast jabs and hooks at thin air just to demonstrate my fitness. It only seemed to amuse Hunter and chuckled to himself as he lit a cigar.

'You're a hypocrite, Hunter,' I said, shaking my head. 'You preach to me about having a healthy body yet you smoke like a chimney.'

'I don't inhale,' he said after a blowing a cloud of smoke over his head. 'I just like the taste of a fine cigar.'

'Give me a break,' I scoffed. 'You also go through quite a lot of whiskey.'

'I'm Scottish. Whiskey's like hot chocolate for me; it helps me sleep.'

'First sign of an alcoholic is denial.'

He laughed out loud at my attempt to antagonise him.

'You should save your energy for your chores and not for inventing baseless accusations, Bentley.'

'I don't need chores to help me fight the likes of Golding. My desire for revenge will be enough. I can't wait to get my hands on that monster.' I turned to him and shook my fist. 'And any assassin that's sent after me will regret they ever heard the name Ross Bentley.'

'That's the spirit,' Hunter said with a genuine smile. 'But Golding isn't the only shadow that has been cast upon the world of the gifted. Believe me, boy, you'll need your strength to take Romand's place.'

'Tell me about these other enemies, Hunter.'

'All in good time, Bentley.'

'I hate you. I really hate you.'

Hunter simply laughed and left the room as abruptly as he'd entered. He really was an odd person, but that was hardly a surprise; almost everyone I'd met since I entered The Million Dollar Gift was mental. I was starting to think that Cathy and I were the only sane people in the Guild. I longed to be with her again.

'Eight more months,' I muttered to myself. 'Eight more months and I can live a normal life again. Just have to hold out until then.'

I stood by the back door and watched the mountains swallow the sun. I was champing at the bit to get back into the conflict with Golding. I knew there was a lot more to the Guild than its vendetta with Golding Scientific. Hunter's mentioning of other enemies within the world of the gifted scared me a bit. I still wanted to know what was lying in wait for me. I needed to know more of the malevolent side to the world of the gifted.

Perhaps there were clues in Jonathan Atkinson's journal. I had to read more of it if I wanted to know what I was really getting myself into. And even if there weren't any clues in it, the journal would surely keep me occupied throughout the long, sleepless nights in the cottage.

Later that night, when Hunter had gone to bed, I sneaked out of my room and used my gift to silently levitate into the attic to retrieve the journal. I floated back into the hall then quietly went to my bed to read more about the Guild of the True.

CHAPTER FOUR

The Inevitable

I sat and continued through the entry that I'd started reading earlier that day. It appeared that the Guild had taken a vote on who the new leader would be and Atkinson had lost out to Brian Blake, the man he had serious reservations about. Under this new regime the Guild had been much more active in its fight against the evil organisations that had risen to power in the 1980s, but the manner of its activities was worrying. Many of the older, and more sensible, members had been forced into retirement because they voiced their concerns about the Guild becoming too aggressive. Even Atkinson had been pushed into the background and expelled from the Council. Blake had filled this inner circle with his closest associates so that he could never be voted down on any issue and no one could propose another change in leadership.

Atkinson's account of that time was rather laborious and I was about to close the journal and get some sleep when I came across a familiar name. It was at the top of the next entry on the opposite page.

Reclaiming our
Guild – 1989

*I*t has finally happened. Blake has gone too far and faces open revolt from the ranks of the Guild. Under his leadership there has been much violence, mostly directed against our enemies, but many of us have grave concerns about collateral damage. A number of innocent civilians have been hurt during the struggles with our foes. The majority of this has been unintentional; that has now changed. A teenager from Scotland, Michael Huntington, was targeted directly by Blake and two of his cohorts. The young man was not acting against our Guild and was not part of any group or plot against us. He had simply made the mistake of using his gift in public, as many teenagers have been known to do.

Blake saw him as a threat. His opinion was that any gifted person who openly displays their powers must be punished. In this case Blake deemed execution to be a fitting punishment for young Huntington.

The majority of Guild members were unaware of Blake's murderous intent until we came across news reports centred on a council estate in Glasgow. It appears Blake travelled north and tried to kill Huntington in his home. The teenager managed to fight off his attackers for a while, but during the struggle Blake used his pyrokinetic abilities to set fire to the house. Huntington's aunt was killed in the ensuing blaze.

Huntington escaped, as did Blake and his men. The teen showed up the next morning at a police station seeking help. He was subsequently arrested for starting the fire that claimed his aunt's life.

I held a secret meeting a few hours ago and it has been decided *that Blake and those loyal to him must be expelled from our Guild immediately. We expect it will be violent and lives may be lost. This is a price we are willing to pay to ensure he can do no further damage.*

We have also reached an agreement that Michael Huntington must be freed from his incarceration and brought into our group and protected. I cannot imagine the pain this young man must be suffering at this very moment. To have a relative murdered right before his eyes is one thing. To be held responsible for her death is another thing entirely. He must not be forsaken to this awful fate. I will gladly risk my own life to secure his freedom.

I was totally stunned. I'd wanted to know more about the Guild for some time, but I also wondered about Hunter; who he was, where he was from, why he was so cold towards me and the world in general. I had just gotten answers to most of my questions. I hadn't been expecting this at all, and I felt sorry for Hunter now. I knew the pain of losing a family member, but to have one murdered was unimaginable.

This story also explained why the old knick-knacks in the attic had scorch marks on them. They must have been the only belongings he salvaged from his home after the blaze. What I had earlier thought of as junk were all that he had left of his family and childhood.

I continued reading and Atkinson explained how he'd led a rebellion against Blake and his supporters. There were deaths on both sides during the fight to control the Guild, but in the end Blake was driven out of the group. When the dust settled Atkinson and Peter Williams broke Hunter out of jail and hid him from the authorities.

It was an exciting end to a tragic and sickening tale. It gave me an understanding of why Hunter was such a grouchy man and I sympathised with what he had endured all those years before. It still didn't excuse his attitude towards me, but perhaps it explained why Hunter and the others in the Guild had been so wary of me contacting my father back home in Ireland. They obviously didn't want the same thing happening to *my* family.

My mind was racing and I couldn't sleep. I decided to flick through the journal again and see if there were any other revelations about the Guild and the gifted who opposed them. There was a lot of personal stuff, which I didn't feel very comfortable reading, so I skipped past a number of entries. I then found a short extract that shed more light on the inner workings of the Guild. In fact it gave me my first real insight into the size and nature of the Guild of the True.

The Nine-Level System

I took control of the Guild some months ago, after successfully expelling Blake and his cohorts. I have studied countless documents on the history of the Guild of the True, and have decided to mould the modern Guild on its nineteenth-century predecessor – The nine-level system.

All 492 members of the Guild are to be split into nine categories – or ranks – depending on their gifts, personalities and their experience. They are as follows:

Primicerius (The Head of the Guild)

The Primicerius is elected by the nine members of the Council, and remains in the role for a maximum of ten years.

Ministers (The nine members of the Council)

The Council is made up of nine influential members from the Guild. They each have powers to conduct their own investigations. Many decisions are made solely by the Council, though the most important are still put to the Primicerius for a final decision.

Senior Agents

Veteran Guild agents who are in line to become Council ministers are often promoted to senior status. While they are awaiting a vacancy on the Council, they act as advisors and managers for the lower-ranking agents and assassins.

Guild Agents

The soldiers of the Guild. They serve as spies, investigators, trackers, bodyguards and killers. Most live in solitude and are only seen when they are given a case to work on. Mostly, they are involved in tracking down and recruiting gifted people. Much of their work is non-violent, however they have licence to kill if they, or the Guild, are under threat.

Specialists

There are never more than a handful of specialised agents. These are agents who are assigned to a specific ongoing investigation, and they are in full control over that investigation and do not report to senior agents or the Council.

Mentors

The mentors foster gifted youngsters and teach them how to come to terms with their gifts, how to improve their skills and how to live as an agent. The majority of mentors are supremely gifted, but are not cut out for the work, and life, of an agent. Others are former agents, in semi-retirement, who have a wealth of experience that they can pass on to youngsters.

Assassins

These are members of the Guild who are most suited for killing, when there is need for it. They carry out assassinations called for by the Council. They also take over investigations that have become too dangerous for normal agents to deal with. Occasionally, they can act as investigators; their main role is as killers.

Thieves

The Guild needs constant investment so that it can compete with the likes of JNCOR and Golding Scientific. We attain our wealth through numerous businesses dealings, but at times we employ gifted members (Thieves) to steal money so the Guild can remain properly financed. The thieves are usually space-rupters or light-tuners.

Moles

The majority of Guild members are 'inactive' and are classed as moles. They are contacted by the Guild and are taught to use their gifts and are protected by the agents. They occupy roles in everyday life like teachers, plumbers, accountants and carpenters. They remain under the protection of the Guild their entire lives and are rarely called upon to get involved in dangerous missions. They provide the Guild with information relating to their gifts, but some are placed in positions of influence (police, politics, big business) and they provide the Guild with important information and help cover up the activities of the Guild.

This single page from the journal had given me more knowledge of the Guild than I'd gathered from the months I had spent in the company of Hunter and Romand. The group was certainly bigger, and better organised, than I first thought. There were hundreds of members all with specific roles.

I flicked through the next few pages, but Atkinson had not gone into more detail about the structure of the Guild. I stopped turning pages when I came across a short entry with a rather dramatic heading. This entry showed how Golding Scientific became the Guild's primary enemy.

The New Generation of Enemies – 1989

After the assassination of the board members of Armamenti Tal-Future we expected their organisation to collapse. This is exactly what happened, but it has presented a new problem. One which may be more perilous than we ever expected.

We were swift to react when the company shut down and convinced almost all of their gifted recruits to join us and help us with our work. We found that the vast majority had lived much of their lives in fear of the organisation (we have learned that many of the gifted members who tried to resign from the organisation were murdered. This kept the existing members from displaying any dissent). These gifted people were only too happy to become part of the Guild. A few openly refused, as was their right, and opted instead for retirement. We were comfortable with this, but there has been another issue that has caused me great concern.

Two of the young gifted mercenaries have disappeared. One was familiar to us: Jermaine Scott – also known as 'Boxer'. There is also Melissa Nijinska – who we were not previously aware of.

Boxer has a lot of us worried because of his violent nature, but also because of his apparent indestructibility. However, it now seems our concern should also have been directed towards Nijinska.

Gareth Kennedy, one of the mercenaries who joined us recently, has provided the Council with some information on Melissa Nijinska. He claims she is a mageleton – a master of one of the rarest of the true gifts. It is also possibly the most dangerous if used against others. Kennedy claims that her gift is pure and that she has been trained to use it in combat.

She represents a great threat to humanity if this is true. I cannot believe that those at Armamenti Tal-Future could have been so reckless. Mageletons can be exceptionally dangerous if they learn to fully develop their gift. The Guild has always been very cautious in the training of Mageletons, because that gift can be almost limitless - they can control entire oceans if they reach their full potential and this power in the hands of a malevolent person can pose a threat to millions of people. With this in mind, the Guild banned the writings of Penelope Gordon, who wrote an in-depth study on this gift and how to maximise it. It appears, however, that Nijinska has learned the techniques invented by Gordon. This represents too much of a risk and the Council ruled that this girl must be tracked down and eliminated without further delay. It is a dangerous task, but one we cannot shy away from.

This mission has become doubly dangerous, though. I received word this evening that Nijinska has been seduced by the riches of Golding Scientific. She is now their chief assassin. This is a new and terrible threat to the Guild and to the world.

I remembered a discussion I'd once had with Romand. He said

that Golding once had a mageleton as his assassin and that it was she who had caused a tsunami in the late 1980s that claimed many lives. It had to be Nijinska.

I turned the page, then I heard Hunter stirring in the next room and decided it was best to hide the journal for now and to get some sleep. The struggles of the past filled my mind and it was deep in the night when I finally drifted off.

🖝 🖝 🖝

I forced myself to eat the porridge. I don't know if it was through near starvation or because I felt sorry for Hunter after what I'd read in the journal the night before. I watched him slurping up his porridge across the table and saw him in a slightly different light. Now I could see there was a real person under that rough exterior.

'What's on the cards today?' I asked as I pushed my bowl away. I took a sip of coffee and winced at its bitterness. 'Chopping wood again?'

'We have enough wood to last us a few days.' He leaned back in his chair and lit a cigar with a match. His face was consumed by smoke and as it snaked over his head I saw he was staring right at me. 'What would you like to do?'

'Am I dreaming? Hunter asks *me* what *I* would like to do?'

'Not out of kindness,' he said with a grin. 'I just can't put up with another day of your constant bitching.'

'I'd like to go to the nearest town to buy a laptop,' I said. I'd been cut off from the outside world for so long and having internet access would have been like winning the lottery. It would also provide me with a means to listen to music again. That was something that I found hard to be without. 'I'd like to buy an iPod, too.'

'I don't know what an *iPod* is, but you're not getting one.'

'Why can't I get one if you don't even know what it is?'

'Firstly, you're not allowed near civilisation. Secondly, you have no money.'

'I have a million dollars, remember?'

'You honestly think that money is waiting for you in a bank account?'

'Probably not.'

'Definitely not.'

'You have money,' I said. 'You could buy me some stuff that would make this exile a little more bearable.'

'I don't have a lot of money, Bentley, and I'm certainly not spending it all on you.'

'Right, how about practising my gifts … properly.'

'You sure you want to do that?'

'Why wouldn't I be?'

'Because you might end up being embarrassed.'

'I know you see me as a spoiled teenager – you shouldn't underestimate what I'm capable of.'

'Oh, I know full well what you're capable of, Bentley. You're capable of being a great liability to those around you.'

'What the hell do you mean by that?'

'Meet me down at the forest in twenty minutes. I'll tell you exactly what I mean.'

He took his bowl and dumped it in the sink before storming out the back door. I felt like a fool for being nice to him! Despite his tragic past, Hunter was an arrogant git whose sole purpose in life was to bully me. He'd been going out of his way to annoy me for weeks. This challenge was a little more than the usual smart remarks; behind his words was an intense hatred of me. Why on earth did he loathe me so much? I had to find out what was behind it. I was going to straighten this out before the end of the day!

I went to the rear porch and watched him storm across the field and disappear into the shadows of the nearby trees. I had no idea what he'd have waiting for me. He'd probably set me an impossible task, but I also had the feeling that it would turn nasty and end up in a confrontation. I wasn't going to chicken out either way.

☞ ☞ ☞

I pulled my leather jacket on and stepped onto the back porch. I was growing anxious about what lay ahead of me; after what happened the day before I knew Hunter could turn violent very easily. But I was no coward. I had faced one of the most dangerous people in the world and survived. I would never back down from a fight again. I had to show Hunter that I was unafraid, and that I would be capable of facing the difficulties of being an agent of the Guild. My life had been a painfully lonely one and being part of this noble group would give my life the direction and meaning that it had always lacked. I could not fail. I even felt as if I owed the Guild because they had risked a lot to save me from Golding Scientific. I wanted to repay that debt to them by helping them to save others like me.

I zipped up my jacket and stepped off the porch. It was a cold morning and waves of drizzle were carried across the field on constant wind that rolled in from the north. I was soaked by the time I got to the forest. The pines offered a little shelter. Getting my clothes wet was the least of my worries. Hunter was somewhere in the forest waiting for me.

There was no sign of him. This was no surprise. I was expecting him to be hiding. That's what he was best at. I didn't bother searching for him and I leaned on a tree and watched the forest carefully. He was purposely making me wait in an attempt to get me agitated. I remained calm. I needed a clear head if I was to be ready.

'You've learned patience,' Hunter said. He'd appeared out of thin air and was standing a few yards in front of me. This didn't come as a surprise to me either, but I'd never fully get used to the light-tuning gift. It was something alien to human nature, just like the mind-switch power that Cathy had.

'I'd have gone insane if I had no patience,' I replied evenly. 'The wilderness life is impossible for an impatient person. I've changed in that regard.'

'Good. As an agent of the Guild you have to choose your moment carefully. Know when to hide. Know when to strike. Know when to run.'

'I'm not one for running away.'

'You're going to learn that you have to retreat when the odds are not in your favour, Bentley. Otherwise you'll wind up dead before long.'

'Enough of the philosophy lesson, Hunter. What do you have planned?'

'A simple exercise.'

'Oh? I thought you were going to give me a challenge.'

'A simple but challenging exercise.' He took a few steps forward and stood right in front of me. 'I want you to hit me. If you can.'

'That's easy.'

'Show me how easy it is. You can try with your fist or foot, but I suggest you try it with your gift, seeing as though you're so determined to improve your control over it.'

I didn't bother continuing the conversation. I stayed perfectly still for a moment then lashed out with my fist without any warning. My hand went straight through his face and I tumbled forward and landed on my knees. His light-tuning gift was tricky. He hadn't been standing in front of me at all. It had been a reflection of him created by bending light; probably through a number of those mirrors he was fond of creating.

'Whoops,' Hunter laughed. 'Doesn't seem so easy now, does it?'

I got to my feet – I couldn't see him. He was close, judging by his voice, but I had no idea where he actually was. I had been foolish when I tried to punch him. We had been talking about patience then I reacted without first considering that he might be using his power to deceive me. I wouldn't be so careless again.

I stood there waiting for him to reappear. I tapped in to my precognitive power and tried to determine his next move. The rain had eased off and the forest was totally silent now. I would have heard his footsteps if he'd been moving around.

Suddenly I felt a stinging anxiety in my chest. My precognitive gift was telling me that I was about to be hit. I sensed it would come from behind and I spun and lashed out.

Hunter had outsmarted me and simply dodged my strike. He

lifted one leg and kicked me full force in the chest, sending me off my feet and crashing down on the sodden woodland floor.

'Hunter, you asshole!' I groaned. 'That was out of order.'

'I did say I'd embarrass you.' He smirked as he looked down on me. He extended his arm towards me. 'Do you want a hand up?'

'You're too busy to help me to my feet.'

'Busy with what?'

'Busy dodging the tree that's about to hit you.'

I had taken control of a nearby tree and used my gift to wrench it out of the ground. As soon as it was free I made it swing through the air at Hunter. It crashed on the ground before me and he dived for cover just in time. He wasted no time getting to his feet and then sent a burst of energy across the forest. He hit nothing. I had used the time while he was distracted to float off the ground and I'd climbed into one of the trees.

I looked down at him as he slowly backed away, looking right to left and back again. From the higher level I saw the mirrors he was creating to try and trap me, or to shield himself from my eye. It was a very complex arrangement of mirrors that would have had me dumbfounded if I was still on the ground. He had not considered that I'd got up a tree and probably thought I was hiding in one of the bushes. I was amazed by his ability, but I remained focused and kept my gaze firmly planted on him. Look beyond the magic to see all magicians are just like any other man. I watched him moving into a thicket of trees then crouch down. He was waiting for me to reveal myself so he could launch an attack. He was in for a big surprise.

I fired a slice of energy across the opening and chopped a couple of branches that came crashing down on him.

His response came quickly as he fired shot of electricity in my direction. It was merely a spark when it left his body, by the time it reached me it had expanded into a cloud of crackling tendrils. There was no avoiding it and I was consumed by the cloud that zapped at every inch of my body. I lost control of my limbs momentarily and came hurtling to the ground with a painful whack.

I'd sensed the attack, but simply couldn't defend myself. It was the first time I'd encountered the electropsych gift in a duel. I fought through the pain that was surging through my body and climbed to my feet. I had to be ready to defend myself because I was sensing yet another attack.

I looked around and saw shadows fleeting amid the boughs of the forest. It was a light-tuning trick and I tried my best to ignore it. Hunter was trying to distract me from the real attack.

I summoned all my power and created a sphere of energy around my body to protect myself. I stood within it and peered out at the forest. It was a house of mirrors I was looking at. He had me trapped and I could not see him. He was going to wait it out. Once I dropped my guard he would strike.

I held the shield for as long as I could. After fifteen minutes my power was drained and my protective cocoon gave way. I made a quick dart for the cover of a ditch, but was zapped in the back. The worst part of it was not the initial hit, it was the spreading shock around my body that lasted a few seconds that really hurt. It delayed me too. I was exposed to further attacks and Hunter took full advantage of my vulnerability.

By the time I got to one knee he had emerged from the trees and fired a volley of electricity at me. I managed to defend myself with an outward wave that deflected the electricity over my head. Hunter continued his attack with a psychokinetic spear that took my lightening reflexes to avoid.

He was bearing right down on top of me, but I nudged him off course with a modest blow of energy. It sent him crashing down in front of me.

'Enough,' I panted. 'This is getting out of hand.'

'I knew you'd give up. Coward!'

'I'm not giving up!'

'Hit me then.'

'Why should I hit you, Hunter?'

'To give me an excuse to hit you back.'

'Why do you hate me so much?' I shouted at him. 'What did I do to deserve this?'

'You got Romand killed!'

At last, he'd come out and said what I knew he was thinking! A mixture of insult and rage took control of me. My powers went into overdrive and I launched everything I had, blasting him into the air. I didn't think he could withstand such an attack but he was back on his feet immediately.

Suddenly there were tiny light orbs all around me and they were growing fast. Within seconds there were as big as beach balls and too bright to look at. I lifted my arm in front of my face and snapped my eyes shut.

I was so tired that my precog gift didn't kick in and I failed to sense the punch he hit me with. I crumbled to one knee from the force of it striking me in the gut. I lashed out wildly before I crumbled completely and caught Hunter across the jaw and his legs gave way.

We both dived at one another and tried our best to strangle the life out of the other.

'I don't know what you did, Bentley, but I do know you led Marianne to that house.'

'I made a phone call. They probably tracked it. I've been kicking myself every second since that night. You think I need you blaming me too?'

'I *knew* you led her there.'

'So did Romand! I told him before she broke in! He didn't blame me for it, though. And when I knew he was in trouble I put my life on the line to protect him. What the hell did you do? You and your powers? You and all these friends in the Guild? Where were you all? You left us there to die. You knew that evil bitch was working night and day to find us yet you didn't intervene. You don't have the right to blame me. *You're* the damned coward here.'

He pressed his knee against my chest and pushed me away then swung his boot and caught me in the side of the head. We both sat there panting and watching each other. Both of us unable to muster the strength to continue the fight. Or perhaps we'd both used up the anger we felt since Romand's death.

'Why was he left alone to deal with Marianne?' I panted.

'He refused to let anyone else get involved. Romand saw her as his own responsibility. He blamed himself because he couldn't bring himself to kill her when she was a child. His compassion allowed her to reach adulthood and that resulted in hundreds of people becoming her victims. That's why he was alone to deal with her.'

'But didn't you know it was getting too dangerous? Why didn't you come and help him?'

'I was in Italy the week it happened.' He let out a deep breath and hung his head. 'I was tracking down a gifted youngster who was in trouble.' He shook his head despondently. 'I couldn't do anything to save him.'

'And I tried my best to save him.'

'You led her there.'

'And I'll live with that burden for the rest of my life. I didn't ask for any of this. I just want to be left alone, Hunter. I want to go home and see my dad. I want all these assassins and corporations to forget I ever existed.'

'They won't. That's why we're both on our own. That's why we're trapped out here.'

'I don't want to be trapped here any more than you do, Hunter. But can't we see out the next few months without trying to kill each other?' I extended my hand towards him. 'Please. I'll even call you Huntington.'

He reluctantly reached out and shook my hand.

'You can call me Hunter from now on. You've earned it.'

CHAPTER FIVE

Midnight Caller

We didn't talk much for the rest of the day even though an unofficial truce had been called. This was hardly surprising. We'd beaten the crap out of each other and were both tired and bruised. I think Hunter came off worse than me. Not physically, although he did have a budding black eye, however his ego had taken a knock now that a teenager like me had been able to contend with him in a duel. The cottage was quiet in the evening, but the charged atmosphere that had filled it recently had evaporated and I was able to relax properly for the first time in many weeks. Hunter had stayed in the sitting room the entire evening and drank more than his usual allowance of whiskey. I'm sure it dulled the pain of his injuries and it also sent him off to bed earlier than usual. By 10pm I was sure he was asleep and pulled the journal from under my bed and went to the entry I'd been reading the night before.

Atkinson went into a lot of detail on how Armamenti Tal-Future had been dismantled and wrote about the restructuring of the Guild after Blake's defeat and also the search for the two mercenaries that had his colleagues so preoccupied. He went on to write about the rise of Golding Scientific. Atkinson explained how the

Guild thought they had made the world a safer place by destroying Armamenti Tal-Future, actually though Paul Golding had swooped in and taken over all the contracts that had been vacated when the Maltabased company crumbled. Within the space of a few months Golding Scientific went from being a nuisance to becoming the Guild's main adversary.

Paul Golding's activities were causing a lot of strife, but the search for the two mercenaries was their immediate problem, and apparently over thirty Guild agents were scouring the globe for them. The man known as *Boxer* kept cropping up. Whenever they closed in on him he evaded capture and moved on to another country.

As for the mageleton, Nijinska, they had searched far and wide but no trace of her could be found. There were echoes of Marianne Dolloway's story here. Just like Marianne, she'd been the number one enemy of the Guild, and proved elusive until the very end.

According to Atkinson's text, the Guild never actually located Nijinska alive. Her body was discovered in the autumn of 1989. She was mentioned in a series of short entries in the journal that also hinted at the beginning of conflicts that would go on to threaten all who had true gifts.

~~~~~~~~~~~~~~~~~~~~~~

*D*espite *the upheaval of recent times and the ongoing search of Melissa Nijinska, we have still found the time to search out gifted youngsters, which is always our main objective. Under my leadership, the Guild has reverted to its old policy regarding recruitment:*

When the Guild learns of a gifted person, we will make contact – usually when the person is in their teenage years. When the gifted person comes to adulthood, they are invited to live with a mentor to learn about their gifts, and to train for a specific role in our group.

When the Guild learns of a supremely gifted child, we will assign an agent to watch over them closely. If the child is in danger or comes to the attention of the authorities, the agent will remove them from their home and bring them to a mentor. This is obviously a traumatic experience for a child, and is usually avoided at all costs.

In the last three months we have identified four teenagers who showed signs of the true gifts and have sought to take them under our wing. Three of them have joined us and are proving to be most impressive and will surely go on to become invaluable in the coming years. I regret that one has slipped from our grasp.

An exceptionally talented teenager from Australia, who goes only by the name Barega, was convinced to join Golding Scientific. We do not blame the young man as he was probably lied to by Golding and his staff. It is a great shame that the only living warper has sided with our main competitor. Barega could become a thorn in our side when he reaches adulthood. I fear that he will cause much suffering and that the Guild might have to assassinate him.

🐾 🐾 🐾

The most promising lead we've had in decades has come to my attention. There is a young man who is said to have incredible powers and has to date avoided all known organisations who seek out gifted people. His name is James Barkley and I have recently been told that he is searching for others like himself. One of our people in the United States has made contact with him and asked if he would become a Guild member, but Barkley has refused our offer. He remains determined to live a life free of rules and constraints. This is admirable and the more I know of him, the more respect I have for his pursuits. He wishes to do good and is trying to understand the origins of the true gifts and where they will ultimately lead mankind. His is a quest for knowledge and he could go on to forge his own Guild, perhaps one that is more relevant than our own. He is gathering like-minded people to him and by all accounts they are a truly wonderful group of youngsters who wish only to make this world a better and more enlightened place to live. My only concern is that he will become a target for Paul Golding. I know the way Golding works: if a gifted person refuses to join him, he usually has them killed. Barkley deserves a better fate than that. I only wish that everyone was like him, and not like Golding or Nijinska.

I was left stunned by the news I received three days ago. It is a dreadful blow, not for the Guild, but for the future of gifted people, and for people of all walks of life.

It appears that Barkley and his troupe were travelling south-east Asia and had found their way to Bali. No doubt they were enjoying the tropical climate and each other's company. Young and free. Their lives full of adventure and exploration. A future of immense possibilities.

That future has been erased. A tsunami struck a small island off the coast of Bali and almost everyone was killed. It is believed that Barkley's group has been decimated, along with many people who were native to the island. At first it seemed like an unavoidable tragedy, but yesterday I learned that no earthquake took place in that region, and that the destructive wave seemed completely unnatural. As soon as I heard this I had an awful feeling that a mageleton might have been involved. Nijinska is the only living person, that we know of, with that gift.

One of our members, Fiona Taylor, flew out to the island yesterday and delivered her report by phone a couple of hours ago. It was one of the most bizarre conversations I have ever had.

There was indeed a group of westerners on the island before the wave struck and there were sightings of their bodies in the immediate aftermath, but their remains have now disappeared. Only one Caucasian body was discovered, and Taylor has confirmed it is that of Nijinska.

The entire incident is baffling and neither I, nor Taylor, could make any sense of it. We are quite sure that Barkley and his friends are dead, but we do not know what led to the demise of Nijinska.

￼ ￼ ￼

I have just received a fax from Fiona Taylor, who has been continuing her investigation into the incident off the coast of Bali. The message was only a single line but it was enough to force me into planning a trip to south-east Asia. My flight leaves in six hours. I do not know what awaits me out there. A deep fear in me swells every time I read her message.

"You must come here ASAP – there are rumours of undead stalking the islands."

I recognised this as the story of how the Kematian came to exist. Romand and June Atkinson had told me about it when I was living with them. It was the darkest tale from the history of the Guild, and one that was rarely discussed. It was the most terrifying story I'd ever heard and the mere mention of it sent a shiver over my skin.

I was surprised to read that James Barkley had started out as a good and honest person, one who was committed to helping others like himself. It was hard to believe that he became the monster that Romand had described. It was yet another example of how decent people could be twisted by the interference of those like Paul Golding.

Nijinska, Barkley, Dolloway, Barega and probably many others had all been corrupted by him. I considered myself very lucky that Romand had saved me before Golding and Shaw poisoned my mind. To think they could have destroyed my life, and forced me into destroying the lives of others. It was sickening to imagine that I could have become like Nijinska.

The story of the Kematian and the disaster that struck in 1989 could wait until tomorrow. I was battered and bruised and my eyes were growing heavy. I slipped the journal under the mattress and used my gift to turn out the light. One good thing had come from my fight with Hunter: it had sapped my energy and I would get a good night's sleep for the first time in months.

☙❦❧

The slamming of a car door snapped me from my dreams. The moon was strong that night and there was enough light in the room to see the clock reading 4.20am on the opposite side of my bedroom. What on earth was Hunter doing up so late? And what was he doing outside?

I sat up and looked out the small window to see a dark coloured saloon parked outside the cottage. I didn't recognise the car and was reminded of Marianne arriving at the Atkinson's place. My nerves went wild and I was about to jump out of bed and alert Hunter when I heard voices coming from the front porch.

'What in God's name are you doing here?' It was Hunter and he sounded aggravated rather than fearful. 'This place is strictly off limits. I thought everyone in the Guild was aware of that?'

'I've been on the road for five hours, Hunter,' a man with a continental accent replied. 'The least you could do is invite me inside.'

They continued talking for a moment, but they'd lowered their voices and I couldn't hear what was being said. I crept out of bed and went to the door and listened to them enter the cottage and go to the sitting room. I wasn't letting the opportunity to eavesdrop on a secret Guild meeting pass me by. They were probably talking about some of their missions! After all, they'd only send someone all the way out here if it was something really important. Hunter never told me much, and despite the truce, he would probably keep the subject of the conversation to himself. I had to get closer to hear what they were saying.

I gently pulled the door open, then stopped before I entered the hallway. The floorboards were well worn and made loud creaks whenever anyone stood on them. I couldn't risk putting my weight on them because the others would hear me then send me back to my room. I had to get creative if I was to go unnoticed.

I used a technique I had practised when I first went to the cottage. It was a rolling cushion of energy that I could balance on top of as it moved over ground. It would allow me to levitate a couple of inches over the floor boards and the others would be unaware that I was spying on them. I created the cushion and rose off the floor then moved slowly, and a little unsteadily, down the hallway without making the slightest sound. I gently dispersed the energy under my feet and eased down to the floor.

Hunter was stoking the fire and throwing a couple of logs into the hearth. He made quite a bit of noise which allowed me to quietly push the sitting room door open slightly, just enough so I could see who was with him.

The late night visitor was Dominic Ballentine – I recognised him from Romand's funeral. He hadn't said much when I'd met him but he gave off an air of authority, as if he were one of the highest-ranking members of the Guild. He was average height, had wide shoulders and was wearing dark clothes that had seen better days. He had that same hardness to his face that many of the senior members of the Guild had. He looked like he'd seen a lot of fights throughout his life and his brooding eyes were surrounded by a tangle of sharp wrinkles.

He sat on the chair next to the fire and Hunter leaned against the mantel on the opposite side. The lights were off and their faces were lit with the orange hue of the flames and I could tell immediately from the intensity of their expressions, and the hushed voices, that something very serious was going on.

'You look like you've been in a fight, Hunter. That black eye could do with some ice.'

'I'll live.'

'I do hope so. So, how has your *vacation* been?'

'Listen, Dominic,' Hunter said sharply. 'We've been colleagues for a long time but let's be honest, we've never been friends. I know you haven't come all the way out here just to be sociable so why don't you save us both some time and get to the real reason for your visit.'

'As forward as always, eh.' Ballentine took a cigarette from a silver case and lit it with a glowing iron poker that had been resting in the flames. He puffed a cloud of smoke over his head and turned to his host. 'Fair enough. I need you to track someone down for me.'

'*You* need me to track someone or the *Guild* needs me to track someone?'

'This request has come direct from the top. The Guild needs you to locate a child who has shown signs of a true gift.'

'I already have a job on my hands: babysitting the superstar. I'm gifted, but I know of no gift that allows me to be in two places at the same time.'

'I'm aware that you are busy, Hunter.'

'Why don't you find this person yourself or get one of the junior agents of the Guild to do it?'

'This one is important and there can be no mistakes. We need someone with experience to pick up the trail.'

'There are plenty of experienced people in the Guild.'

'They will be busy for the foreseeable future.'

'Busy with what?'

Ballentine sighed and flicked some loose ash into the flames. He had a very troubled look about him now and he took a heavy pull on the cigarette before finally answering his colleague.

'There's been an *incident*. It requires a full investigation and many of the senior members of the Guild will be involved.'

'What sort of incident?'

'The home of one of our mentors has been attacked.'

'Which one?'

'It was old Rudolph Cramer's place in Switzerland.'

'I know Cramer. He's a good man, but he's hardly on the frontline. Who the hell would attack *him*?'

'Unknown.'

'Anyone get hurt?'

'Cramer and his wife have had five kids living with them, all with true gifts. The Cramers have been taking care of them and teaching them to develop their powers for the last two years. There was also an agent of the Guild stationed there just for security purposes; it's been protocol for quite some time ...' He took a deep smoke and I noticed his hands were trembling. He wouldn't make eye contact with Hunter for a moment, and I even thought he might break down in tears before he eventually finished what he was saying. 'All eight of them are dead.'

'What?' Hunter asked incredulously. He stepped off the fireplace and began pacing the room. He furiously rubbed the palms of his hands together; something I hadn't seen him do before. 'How did it happen?'

'The house was burned to the ground. It's in a pretty isolated spot so there were no witnesses; therefore we have no clue as to who the perpetrator is.'

'Perhaps it was just a normal house fire?'

'Come off it, Hunter. We both know that's unreasonable. And besides, one of our moles in the Swiss police has informed us that two of the deaths were not caused by smoke inhalation or burns.'

'How did they die?'

'Inconclusive.'

'Who in God's name would do such a thing? To murder five children!'

'We first suspected Golding's people, we don't think he has anyone like that on his payroll though; it would have had to be someone very powerful … and extremely ruthless.'

'Who was stationed there as security?'

'Edward Zalech.' They exchanged a long stare. 'I know you weren't very fond of him, but believe me, he would have fought tooth and nail to save those people.'

'Why are you so sure?'

'His younger sister was among the victims. They were practically inseparable. It's the only reason he took on that job, so that he could be close to her.'

'He never struck me as a particularly affectionate person.'

'He was loyal to his sister and was loyal to the Guild.'

'I didn't doubt his loyalty. I was thinking about how powerful he was. Zalech wouldn't have been easy to take in a fight. He was one of the strongest people I've ever come across. If they could get the better of him, and Cramer at the same time …'

'Not to mention Cramer's wife, Lorena, who was a talented siren *and* the five children. They were only young, but they were all gifted and could have put up quite a fight on their own terms.'

'Who could it have been?' Hunter hissed in frustration. 'Dolloway?'

'Haven't you heard?'

'Heard what?'

'Our moles based here in Britain have finally tracked her down.'

'Where is she?'

'Six feet under.'

'Are you positive about that?'

'We're confident that it's her. That means we have a new killer on the loose.'

'Someone that twisted and powerful could endanger the Guild. You'll need me on this case. I *must* be involved in the investigation!'

'No,' Ballentine insisted. 'You have a duty to watch over Bentley and find this gifted child I spoke of earlier.'

'Who's heading up the investigation?'

'Sakamoto.'

'Sakamoto is an assassin, not an investigator.'

'He's the best man for the job and I've assembled a solid crew to assist him. Listen, Hunter, if we need your help we'll let you know. For the moment, you would be doing us a great favour by finding this kid.' He took a newspaper clipping from his pocket and handed it to Hunter. 'I'm sure you can track her down easily enough.'

Hunter read from the clipping then sighed and stared at the ceiling. 'Are you for real? I've lost count of the times I've searched for prophets, and every single time they turn out to be frauds. This,' he waved the clipping at Ballentine, 'will be nothing more than a wild goose chase.'

'That is a definite possibility. There is always a chance, though, that this lead is genuine and you know full well we cannot ignore it. Our enemies will try to find her too. And you know what they'll do to her if she is just a troubled kid, don't you?'

'I do,' Hunter said glumly.

'Either way, she's in for a very nasty surprise if Golding or some other scumbag gets hold of her. I think it would be better if we reached her before they do. Don't you agree?'

'You any clues to where she is?'

'She's somewhere down near Newcastle. The paper didn't give her name, address or anything like that, and her face is blurred in the photo in the article. I have this,' he handed Hunter another scrap of paper. 'It's the names of the journalist, the photographer and sub-editor who were involved with the article. The office address is there too. It's just a provincial rag and we should be grateful for that; if it had been a leading tabloid you'd have to get on this right away.'

'I'll leave tomorrow. With a bit of luck I'll locate her within forty-eight hours.'

'Good. That settles it.'

'Not quite,' Hunter said, raising his hand at Ballentine. 'You're forgetting one thing.'

'Which is?'

'Bentley. Should we trust him to be left on his own? I could be gone for a few days and he could get himself into a lot of trouble if he decides to go wandering the local towns.'

'Is he that stupid?'

'Quite possibly, yes.'

'What's he like? I mean, what's he *really* like?'

'He's an arrogant little shit, he doesn't do what he's told, his powers are out of control, he hates authority, he has a bad temper – I like him.'

It was a pleasant surprise to hear this from Hunter. In spite of everything, it meant a lot to me that someone like him liked and believed in me.

'Is he up to going out on a mission? This could turn out to be dangerous, and you never know, you might even come up against some of Golding's people. Is he capable of holding his own if it comes to that?'

'He is. I thought the Guild didn't want him near civilisation for a while?'

'Believe me, the Guild has far more serious things to worry about now.'

'I'll bring him with me. I'll be on the road early in the morning,'

'Contact me directly if you run into any outside trouble. Here,' he passed a mobile phone to Hunter, 'I know you don't carry a mobile when you're off duty. My number is saved into the contacts. Oh, one other thing: Linda Farrier is based in Manchester at the moment and I'll send her to assist you if needed.'

'Farrier!' Hunter moaned. 'No, thanks. We don't work well together.'

'Hunter, you have to put personal feelings aside and be professional in circumstances like this.'

'What are you talking about?'

'We all know that you and Linda were … whatever it was that you were.'

'We were working together and that's as far as it went. We have conflicting styles when it comes to investigations and I'd rather not be partnered with her again.'

'Tough. She's the only one available.'

'Bentley and I can handle this on our own. Farrier can stay in

Manchester *forever* as far as I'm concerned.'

'She could be very useful on a case like this.'

'No,' Hunter demanded. 'Linda Farrier is an assassin. I don't particularly like working with assassins.'

'Listen, if you don't want this investigation then just say so. I have another case that you might prefer.'

'What's that?'

'Our old friend Boxer has been sighted in Brazil. If you want a real challenge, we can have someone else take care of Bentley while you can go to Brazil alone, and try to apprehend Boxer.'

'No way. That's one I'd rather avoid. I'll head to Newcastle tomorrow and find this kid – on one condition.'

'Shoot.'

'That I get transferred to the investigation in Switzerland after I bring her in.'

'You can't travel overseas with Bentley.'

'I'm not married to Bentley! He can go live with his girlfriend for a while.'

'I'll discuss it with the Council tomorrow. The faster you find the girl, the more willing they'll be to let you join Sakamoto and the others.'

Ballentine didn't hang around and wanted to get back to London without delay. Apparently there were some important meetings that he could not miss. Hunter walked outside with him and once I heard the car engine start I went back to my room and climbed into bed.

I felt a strange mixture of excitement and fear when I thought of going on my first mission for the Guild. Excitement that I was to leave the isolated cottage and to have an opportunity to save someone from the clutches of Golding. Fear that it might result in combat. Fear also in that I might let the Guild, and Hunter, down. I hadn't always seen eye to eye with Hunter, but I always desired his respect. It felt great that he told Ballentine that I was ready to go on a mission – and also that he liked me despite my problems with authority – and that made it more important that I shouldn't fail him.

After a while I focused on what Ballentine had said about Marianne Dolloway. He'd told Hunter that the Guild was confident she was dead and buried. That felt like a giant weight off my shoulders. The psycho who was responsible for so much destruction – as well as Romand's death – was no more. The world was now a much safer place.

CHAPTER SIX

The Road

I slept for no more than an hour and was out of bed just after 6am. The prospect of leaving the cottage for a week on a mission for the Guild had me bursting with enthusiasm and I couldn't wait to get the day started. I found Hunter sitting at the kitchen table sipping a mug of coffee and there were two packed sports bags by the back door. I pretended I hadn't overheard the conversation he'd had with Ballentine and glanced nonchalantly at the bags before turning to him.

'What's with the bags?' I asked with a casual nod. 'Going somewhere?'

'Yes, and you're coming with me. We leave in an hour.'

'Well, this is a surprise,' I lied. 'Where are we going? Butlins?'

'You wish. We're headed south to Newcastle.'

'What's in Newcastle that's so important?'

'I've been asked by the Guild to find some kid who might have a gift. I don't trust you to stay here on your own so you'll have to tag along.'

'Cool!'

'There's nothing cool about it, Bentley. You'll be stuck in the 4x4 for most of the trip and it's likely that the kid is just some fake who

93

likes attention. But if she is gifted we might run into trouble so you'll need to have your wits about you.'

'What kind of trouble are you talking about?'

'The kind of trouble that will try to snatch the girl and kill us both if we get in the way. You're about to go on your first official duty as an agent for the Guild and that means your life will be in constant danger. Does that sound cool to you?'

'It does actually. I like a bit of danger.'

'Me too,' Hunter replied with a dry smile. 'I'm going to give the 4x4 a once over before we leave. Make sure to have a breakfast because it might be a long time before we have another opportunity to eat a square meal.'

Some of my anticipation had been quashed by how stern Hunter was and I quickly realised that this wasn't a simple adventure I was about to embark on. This was a mission that could turn into a life or death situation in the blink of an eye. I managed to force down a bowl of porridge and I had some toast with goat's cheese on it; this was about the most appetising dish I could create using the meagre contents of the fridge and cupboards.

It was an unimaginative meal, but it would set me up for the day ahead and by 7am I grabbed the only thing I was taking with me: my jacket. It was a little reminder of how basic my life had become. It still felt a bit strange not having a phone or cash or a laptop. I had more or less adjusted to life without those things. I was now free to be myself and not dependent on technology or the media to tell me who I was meant to be, and how I was supposed to live my life.

In truth, I'd been forced to cast aside all belongings by Hunter and Romand before him. This was the way of the Guild. It was never openly talked about, but I knew the reason they didn't permit their members to have much in the way of possessions was because if a member was killed in action the authorities wouldn't be able to link them to any other members of the Guild. It made perfect sense. We were meant to be like phantoms who came and went without anyone being able to track us or to know our business. While the rest of society was becoming more and more traceable because of their mobile phones or email accounts or social network profiles or banking details, we remained clandestine. We were shadows that crossed the world and could never be captured.

Though the mission could turn out to be perilous my mood was as bright as it had been for months. I was no longer confined to the wilderness and I was about to take my first step to becoming a proper agent of the Guild of the True. I was also chirpy because Hunter had said to Ballentine that he liked me. I wasn't an attention seeker, but it was always nice to be liked, and despite the rocky relationship I had with him, I did want Hunter to believe in me and to deem me a worthy successor to his old friend, Romand.

Hunter had been a mystery to me for so long and now in the last twenty-four hours I'd discovered he wasn't the selfish creep he'd first appeared to be. He was now almost human in my eyes. He even had a fling with Linda Farrier – who was rather hot as far as I could remember. I don't know why he denied it to Ballentine; any man would be proud to be associated with her. Maybe he was just shy. That meant I would have to take a sly dig at him about it. We were no longer enemies, but I was still going to wind him up from time to time and this tidbit of information would provide me with a lot of ammunition.

He was gaining my respect too. He'd obviously had a tough life and he was also proving to be exceptionally brave. He'd actually requested to be sent to Switzerland to hunt down the person who murdered all those people. Ballentine had said the murderer must have been extremely powerful yet Hunter didn't hesitate to volunteer to find this person. I'm not sure I would have been so quick to put myself forward for such a task.

I stepped outside and shielded my face from the rain that was carried on a steady breeze. Did it ever stop raining in this part of the world? I really should have brought a hoodie or a hat with me, but there didn't appear to be time enough to go back inside. Hunter was hanging out the driver's window and staring at me.

'Get a move on, Bentley! You're worse than a woman!'

'Nag, nag, nag. I don't see why you're in such a big rush because you drive like a granny.'

'You've got a real smart mouth for someone who hits like a granny!'

'You weren't saying that yesterday when I gave you that black eye.'

'You weren't too clever when I electrocuted you in the forest. It looked like you were doing the moonwalk!'

'The moonwalk! Jesus, you're really showing your age. I'm surprised they haven't offered you retirement from the Guild by now.'

'All right, any more of your lip and you can stay out here on your own.'

I sat into the passenger seat and pointed at the driveway. 'I thought you said we were in a rush. Let's get going.'

'I hate teenagers.'

With that he floored the accelerator and we were soon speeding along the lonely road that led from the cottage into the open countryside. It was a sombre looking place, lifeless fields on either side that stretched out to the highlands, a faint mist was weighing down on the land and a bruised sky hung above the distant mountains, and the rain never ceased. It was the quietest and most isolated place imaginable. There wasn't a house, other than Hunter's cottage, for many miles. Only a member of the Guild would choose to live in such a place.

Within twenty minutes I was getting bored. Hunter hadn't said a single word since we left the cottage and was probably mulling over his strategy to find the girl and we couldn't tune in any radio stations on his prehistoric car stereo because no signal could find its way through the mountains. I wondered what he was planning and couldn't resist being nosey. It would be interesting to see how he worked. Despite being around many of the Guild members, I was yet to witness how they conducted their investigations.

'How long will it take to reach Newcastle?' I asked.

'This road will lead us close to Sterling. We can get onto a motorway from there and it should be about four hours to Newcastle. I'm hoping we'll get there by midday.'

'Thanks for keeping me in the loop, Hunter. I know you could have kept me in the dark and I appreciate you being candid about this whole thing.'

'Don't get carried away, Bentley. We're not going to be holding hands on this trip. We're partners for the next couple of days so I'm cutting you some slack until we have the girl and have her delivered to the Guild. The more you know about this case the more benefit it is to me. So, I'm not doing you a favour by giving you information, I'm doing *me* a favour.'

He reached into his coat and handed me the newspaper clipping that Ballentine had given the night before. I took it from him and unfolded it on my lap. It said that the girl had recently been taken into state care and while she was at a temporary foster home she had made two predictions: the sinking of a trawler in the North Sea that killed five fishermen, and a bus crash in Wales that claimed the lives of seven people. The article didn't name her and there was one photograph where her face was blurred out. It went on to explain that her foster parents couldn't handle her unruly behaviour and that she had recently been moved to a new home in Newcastle. It was a big city and there were no real clues to her exact whereabouts. To me this would be a virtually impossible task.

'How on earth are we going to find her?' I wondered. 'It says she's in care which means she could be anywhere.'

'We won't be able to locate her through conventional methods. The social services go to great lengths to keep this information protected. We have someone working in that area who usually helps us out in situations like this, but she's ill at the moment – perfect timing! The only option we have right now is to question the newspaper people responsible for that article. That will have to be our first port of call.'

'But they're not going to be willing to tell you where she is.'

'We'll get the information one way or another,' he assured me. 'Let's go to the newspaper offices first and we'll see how it goes from there.'

'No master plan?'

'We'll have to think on our feet. This is usually the way investigations go; we never have clear leads and we have to improvise in any way we can. Sometimes it's better not to have a set plan because it can lead to complacency, which can lead to sloppiness which can lead to us getting killed.'

'I was thinking … Wouldn't the work of the Guild be made a lot easier if we just killed Golding?'

'You think we haven't tried before?' He shook his head and snorted.

'Does an agent or an assassin have to get clearance from the Guild before they can kill someone?'

'Not exactly. If an agent is working on a case and their life is in danger then they have the freedom to protect themselves. That often means killing. But you only kill if there is no other option. You can't just go around killing anyone who doesn't share your point of view. On the other hand, an agent cannot make a decision to hunt and kill someone because they see them as a threat. Those decisions are made by the Council, and trained assassins normally do that type of work.'

'Why hasn't the Guild sent assassins to snuff out Golding?'

'Golding rarely appears and when he does he's usually being followed closely by the media, not to mention his own assassins, and the police like to have a presence when he's out and about.'

'Where does he stay when he's not *out and about*?'

'He used to have a big facility in the US but it was more secure than Fort Knox, we could never get near him while he was there. When Marianne started threatening him he moved his operation.'

'Where to?'

'I don't know. Finding Golding is often like chasing your own shadow.'

'Now that you mention shadows, how did you create those shadows in the forest? It was like fifty people were running through the trees.'

'I'm a light-tuner. I can create light, I can alter light, and I can remove light. That's how I made those shadows; I simply created a space that was emptied of light. It's taken many years to perfect the technique so that the shadows appear humanlike.'

'I don't like giving you compliments, Hunter, but it was fairly impressive. It had me dumbfounded for a while.'

'That's the best use of light-tuning: distraction. Remember that if you ever come into conflict with someone who has that gift. They will distract you using light, just remain focused and remember it's nothing more than an illusion.'

'There are so many different gifts and each have so many applications. It's impossible to create defences against each one. It would take a lifetime!'

'True. It's healthy to have knowledge of each of the true gifts because it gives you a fighting chance.'

'Which is the strongest of the true gifts?'

'Hard to say.'

'In your own opinion.' It was hard to believe I was having a coherent conversation with Hunter for the first time. Within the space of a single day he'd been transformed from my tormentor to someone I could relate to. 'Come on, you have to have an opinion, Hunter.'

'Psychokinesis is very effective when a person has precise control over it. Mageletonia is devastating when someone has a pure from of it. Mind-switching is less flamboyant, but is just as deadly – they can transport their minds into someone else's body and use them to kill.'

'What about the Seductor Mortis, isn't that the strongest?'

'What are you talking about?' He straightened up at the mere mention of the fabled sixteenth gift, almost as if he were frightened. I had been expecting a reaction but not like this.

'Romand told me the story of the Kematian. I'm pretty sure you know all about it, Hunter.'

He gave me the 'don't-ask' look then turned back to the road without making comment.

'Pretty creepy story …'

'No one knows what really happened, Bentley.'

'I thought there was talk of people rising up from the grave?'

He let out a snigger with a slight element of nervousness in it.

'What's so funny?'

'Nobody rises from the grave – thankfully. Most of the stories about the Kematian are nothing more than urban legends. Barkley was a good man who was twisted by the deaths of his friends. He wasn't the first to go that way and he certainly won't be the last. It was said he had some higher power, but I never really believed that. He was most likely a raving lunatic who drew up enormous amounts of power because he was so severely deranged.'

'Romand believed otherwise.'

'Romand also drank too much wine when he was telling stories.'

'You *did* go looking for him. You admitted that at Romand's funeral.'

'I've been on a lot of wild goose chases over the years. I just hope we're not on one right now.'

'You want me to change the subject?'

'Please do.'

'All right. What's the deal with you and Linda Farrier?'

'How did you know about that – I mean, what are you talking about? There is no deal with me and Farrier!'

'How come her raincoat is in the cottage then?'

'We were working together. She left some of her stuff behind. There's nothing more to it than that.'

'I believe you.'

'Bentley, shut up!'

'What? I'm just saying that I believe you. I also believe that's why you were so angry that I was sent to stay with you. It meant you couldn't sneak old Linda to your lair for a cuddle.'

'You think you're funny, don't you?'

'I do.'

'We'll see how funny you are when I tell Farrier that you were making fun of her. I've seen her beat the crap out of grown men for less.'

'Stop it, you're scaring me now!' I laughed. 'What gift does she have?'

'The same ability that you have.'

'Which one?'

'The ability to drive people insane by never shutting up!'

'I see. She talks too much which doesn't fit in with your strong, silent type routine. I can see how that could create problems in your relationship.'

'Talking about relationships, I had a good laugh when you were leaving little Cathy Atkinson a couple of months ago. I really thought you were going to cry that morning. Poor Bentley ... Poor, poor little Ross.'

Hunter laughed out loud and I couldn't help joining him. I thought the journey to Newcastle would have been a boring one but I was starting to enjoy it, and the banter with Hunter was becoming more and more amusing the more I got to know him.

When we cleared the mountains the radio static cleared up and an echo of music came from the crackling speakers. Hunter reached out to the stereo and used his electropsyching powers to clear up the reception. I was hoping it would be some decent music – a bit of hardcore or indie rock – it turned out to be traditional Scottish music, which didn't agree with me. Hunter loved it. He whistled along to the tune and I didn't complain. It was quite an experience to see him happy for a change.

I lifted my feet onto the dashboard and got comfortable. Despite being on official Guild duty for the first time, I was more relaxed than I'd been since I left my home in Ireland many months earlier, or since the evenings with Romand and the Atkinsons ... before Marianne found us. I rested my head on my shoulder and soon drifted off.

🐗 🐗 🐗

I had a crick in my neck when I woke up and I thought there was something wrong with my eyes for a second; everything was blurry and grey and I found it hard to focus. When I was fully awake I realised there was nothing strange going on at all. Hunter was smoking a cigar and hadn't bothered opening any of the windows.

'Oh, come on!' I bawled. 'You're killing me with all this smoke.'

'Stop being a baby.'

I rolled down the window and sucked in a deep breath of fresh air and then noticed we were heading towards a city.

'Newcastle?'

'Yeah. The place where we're headed isn't too far from here.' Hunter had a map stretched across the steering wheel and was running a finger along one of the little grey lines. 'Won't take us more than twenty minutes if the traffic's in our favour.'

'Don't you think we should have a plan of action decided on before we get there?'

'Leave that to me. I've done this a thousand times before.'

'You're not going to beat someone up, are you?'

'No … that's plan B. There'll be no violence as long as they play ball.'

'Is plan A to go in and ask for the address of the reporter?'

'Yes.'

'I think that's too obvious. Do you have a mobile phone?'

'I do.'

'Is it as old as this 4x4?'

'No. It's fairly new. The Guild insisted I have one while on the mission. I don't like it very much. Not as easy to use as my old phone.'

'Does the old one have the internet on it?'

'No. I use phones for making calls, Bentley, not surfing the web.'

'Give it here.' I held out my hand impatiently. 'Come on. I'll find out where this guy is.'

He handed it to me and I quickly accessed the web browser and went to Twitter. Just on the off chance that the journalist liked tweeting about every single little meaningless thing he did from day to day. I was in luck. It seemed Peter Lambell had a Twitter account and he liked telling the world all about his day to day business.

'Lunch with friends – pasta and dolcetto. Delish! Back to covering the motorcycle convention now. Zzzz!'

'Right,' I said, 'he finished lunch twenty-five minutes ago and is off to report on a bike convention for his newspaper. *And* I now know what he looks like.' I showed his profile photograph to Hunter, who was quietly impressed by this modern, and more efficient, form of investigatory work. 'Now to find out where the convention is.'

I googled the convention and it led me to the homepage of the company that was promoting the two-day event. It was taking place at a hotel, and the address was just below the header. There was even a link to location on Google maps.

'Take the next exit,' I told Hunter. 'It's only a few miles west of here.'

'Keep this up and I might bring you along to Switzerland with me next week.'

My heart seemed to freeze in my chest. The mention of going to look for the gifted killer was the last thing I wanted. I liked my freedom, I also valued my life.

'What's in Switzerland?' I faked an excited smile. 'Another of your girlfriends?'

'Oh, nothing. Just some friends. Forget I mentioned it.'

I was glad to drop the subject and I kept my mouth shut except to give him to directions to the hotel.

We drove round the back of the main building to the car park and Hunter wasn't too pleased when a security guard told him that he had to pay to park. He handed him a few pounds then drove into the maze of parked vehicles.

'You stay here,' he said as he turned off the engine. 'I'll have a look for him then follow him back to his car.'

'It would be better if both of us went looking for him. We could split up and—'

'This isn't the movies, Bentley. I don't want anyone recognising you so stay here until I return. Do not leave this car no matter what happens.'

I didn't have much of an argument to put to Hunter and I watched him pacing away into the crowd of people. This was the worst part. I really didn't know what Hunter was going to do next. He had a fierce temper and didn't seem to have any problems with being violent towards total strangers. I just hoped he wouldn't drag the journalist back to the 4x4 kicking and screaming.

It was the most excruciating wait of my life. Hunter didn't reappear for ages and I got more and more agitated as the minutes ticked by. How long was I to wait before deciding that something was wrong? The least he could have done was left the phone with me.

People occasionally brushed past the 4x4 and I slid further into the seat and bowed my head in case any of them decided on looking inside and recognised me.

At 4.30pm Hunter finally emerged from the crowd and I watched him following a tall, thin man with a cigarette hanging from his mouth. It was Lambell – I recognised him form the twitter profile photo – and he sauntered through the sea of vehicles before getting into a dark coloured hatchback. Within seconds the car was headed under the barrier and out onto the road.

Hunter jumped into the 4x4 and started the engine. He didn't say anything and barely acknowledged me as he reversed from the parking spot and drove to the exit. I thought we'd lost Lambell's car, but we caught up with it once we got onto the first main road. Hunter's 4x4 looked like a bucket of bolts, but it was a real flier once it hit the open road.

Lambell led us towards the city centre and we soon sank into rush-hour traffic. We were a few cars behind him and I was sure he didn't notice that he had a tail. All had gone according to plan so far, the problem was the lack of any strategy once Lambell reached his home.

'What's our next move?' I asked Hunter.

'We don't have many options,' he shrugged. 'We can only follow him until he goes home then after dark we must confront him.'

'This is going to get messy.'

'Only if he puts up a fight.'

'What if he pulls a gun on you?'

'You watch too much television, Bentley.'

'He *might* have a gun, though.'

'He won't have a bloody gun. This guy is just a features writer for a small newspaper – he doesn't even write crime reports. He's simply unfortunate that he wrote the wrong type of article and has gotten caught up in this. He won't be expecting anyone to hunt him down or to threaten him in any way. He will not have a gun, and I don't expect him to put up much of a fight.'

'If you say so.'

CHAPTER SEVEN

Trouble

Lambell parked his car in front of a three-storey apartment block near the city. He hadn't noticed us and we watched him entering the building from across the street. Hunter waited a few moments to switch off the engine then sat smoking a cigar as he watched the glass door that Lambell had gone through moments earlier. There were a few people on the pavements, none of them paid any attention to us as they strolled past; most were probably on their way home from work and were thinking only of their dinner.

'I wonder if he lives here in one of those apartments,' I said, 'or is just visiting.'

'We'll wait for two hours. If he doesn't come out by then I think we can assume this is his home and we can pay him a visit. I'd also prefer to do this under the cloak of darkness so it's in our interest to wait a while.'

'What if he has a wife? Maybe he has a family. You can't go barging in there if there are children in the apartment.'

'Don't tell me what I can and cannot do, Bentley. I am in charge here and you'll be doing well to remember it.'

'Chill out, will you. It was just a figure of speech.'

'He doesn't have a wife or kids so don't get your knickers in a twist.'

'Charming phrase.' I chuckled at Hunter's crass manner and gazed at the building across the street, wondering what was in store for us. 'How do you know he's single?'

'I followed him around the convention for well over an hour. I watched his every move and I noticed a habit that rules out the possibility of him being a family man.'

'What habit?'

'He was flirting with other men, which means he doesn't have a wife and kids.'

'Perhaps his boyfriend lives with him.'

'Perhaps you're going out of your way to annoy me again.'

'I wasn't trying to annoy you.'

'It doesn't matter if you're trying to or not. You are succeeding in annoying me which is what's important.'

'I'm just trying to present an alterative opinion. It helps to keep an open mind.'

'I don't need an alternative opinion when I've already got a situation figured out. Now please stay quiet.'

The sky gradually dimmed and a rough autumn wind shook the leaves from the trees that lined the street. The lamps warmed up and painted the road and pavements with an amber hue. The street became quiet and lights in the apartments came on. There were no distractions and we kept watching for any sign of Lambell, but he didn't re-emerge from the apartment block. Hardly anyone came out during those two hours, apart from a cuddly couple, an elderly man, and a kid with thick glasses and a guy with a hood up.

None of them fit Lambell's description and at 7pm Hunter ran out of patience. He pulled on his green Parker jacket and stepped from the 4x4 then slammed the door shut. I watched him walking around the front of the vehicle before stepping out into the road. He paused and looked impatiently at me.

'What are you waiting for?'

'I didn't know if you wanted me to come with you or not,' I complained as I left the 4x4 and followed him to the opposite side of the street. 'I'm new to this, remember?'

'I don't particularly want you getting in the way, but you have to learn how to extract information from people. I know you don't like being violent towards *civilians* however it's often necessary. Beating someone up to get answers can save someone else's life. It's the lesser of two evils.'

'What if he feeds you false information?'

'He won't. People tell the truth when they think their life is on the line.'

'You've definitely decided on beating him up?'

'I'll try asking him politely first. Is that all right, Mary Poppins?'

'I'm not totally against violence, Hunter. I just object to the gifted beating the crap out of a normal person who doesn't deserve it.'

'Objection overruled.' He smiled over his shoulder at me. 'Hang back for a moment.'

Hunter walked to the door, keeping his face low, and then pointed at the small camera in the corner of the porch. A shot of electricity left his hand and surrounded the camera for a couple of seconds and the little red light on its side flickered and was extinguished.

'What did you do?'

'I shorted out the CCTV system. It's always best to keep your face hidden from cameras ... a lesson you should have learned before you entered The Million Dollar Gift.'

'That wasn't my fault. How are we going to find out what apartment he's in? Surely you're not planning on knocking on every door in the place?'

'Watch and learn, boy.'

'Don't call me boy.'

'Sorry, *man.*'

He went to an aluminium panel by the door that had the apartment numbers etched next to individual buzzers. He pressed one and moved his face close to the speaker unit above.

'Yeah?' a cranky voice came through the speaker. 'Who's that?'

'Hey there, Lambell,' Hunter put a disturbingly feminine voice. 'It's Cyrille. Aren't you going to let me in?'

'You've got the wrong number, dumbass. Lambell lives in 208.'

Hunter turned to me with an arrogant grin and winked. 'You see that, Bentley. Sherlock Holmes would have been proud of that.'

'Pure luck. That guy could have just have easily told you to bugger off.'

'Maybe so,' he tapped the buzzer panel, 'I had thirty-six other shots to get it right though. Now hop on up here and open this door without making any noise.'

I paced up the steps and pushed out some of psychokinetic power and seized control of the locking mechanism. I remained very calm because I didn't want to exert too much energy which might have cracked the metal lock or even the glass panel and alert someone to our presence. I pulled the metal tongue back and pushed the door open with a secondary wave of energy.

I held it open for Hunter and curtsied. 'Age before beauty.'

'Beautiful people don't have scars like you do, Bentley.'

'Thanks for reminding me.'

Hunter stomped inside the brightly-lit hallway and headed straight for the staircase. I followed a few paces back and watched him rolling up his sleeves and cracking his knuckles as he climbed the steps. I knew he had no intention of asking politely for the information we needed. He had the look of a man who was preparing for a fight – a one-sided fight.

We reached the first floor and looked left and right before stepping into the corridor. 208 was only a few doors down from the entrance to the stair and my nerves spiked as we moved forward. My emotions were stirred which always filled me with energy, I just hoped I wouldn't need to use it.

Hunter stopped dead in his tracks and stared ahead. His entire body had tensed up and his breathing quickened. At first I didn't know what was wrong, but then I saw the door to 208 was ajar.

Hunter pushed me towards the wall and told me to stay put then edged along the wall to the doorway. He sent out a modest burst of energy to push the door fully open but remained with his back against the wall for almost a minute. When it was clear that there was no danger he scouted forward and entered the apartment.

He stuck his head a few moments later and whispered at me to follow him inside.

'What's going on?' I asked quietly when I shut the door behind me.

'It appears we've got trouble.'

I followed him through the cluttered sitting room to a short hallway. The door to the kitchen was open and I could clearly see

Lambell lying spread-eagled on the floor. His face was deathly pale and his eyes were wide open. It was obvious from the instant I laid eyes on him that he was dead. He was a relatively young man, in his mid-thirties, and it was unlikely that he'd died suddenly in the early evening while making his dinner.

'This isn't just a coincidence, is it?'

'Not likely.' Hunter entered the cramped kitchen and stooped over Lambell. 'There are no wounds that I can see, but gifted people don't need to inflict obvious physical injuries in order to kill.'

'But we were right across the street this whole time. How could assassins have slipped in and out without us noticing?'

'The killer could have been waiting for him when he got home. They still managed to slip past us, though.'

'Only five people exited while we were parked outside.'

'Yeah,' Hunter muttered thoughtfully. 'I think we can rule out the elderly man; he looked on death's door and was having a hard time walking never mind killing. And the little kid could barely see where she was going.'

'The killer could have been a mind-switcher and used the old man's body to carry out the hit.'

'Unlikely,' Hunter said. 'A mind-switcher would use a normal person, and a normal person would leave a visible wound on the body.'

'That makes sense,' I said. 'That leaves the lovebirds and the hooded guy as possibles. I know who my money is on.'

'No point in trying to figure out which of them it was. Not yet anyway.' He returned his attention to the body and examined the face and neck then ran his hands through Lambell's hair to check for any hidden head wounds before lifting the jumper to inspect his chest and stomach. 'Nothing. No clues. His death could have been caused any number of ways.'

'Let's check his back,' I suggested. 'He might have a cut or a bruise or something.'

Energy seeped out of my body as I used my psychokinetic power to lift and turn Lambell over, so that his face was to the floor. We scrutinized his back and shoulders and ribs, but again there were no marks of any kind. I was thinking an electro-psych could have stopped Lambell's heart or a psychokinetic could have ruptured his lungs or made mush of his brains or even crushed his throat from the inside. And those were only the theories that immediately came to mind. It would probably be impossible for us to determine the cause of death in the little time that we had.

'Looks like we've drawn a blank,' Hunter sighed.

'Is that normal when someone dies?' I asked, pointing to a pool of fluid coming from the dead man's mouth and forming a circular pool on the tiled floor.

'Depends on what it is.' Hunter dipped his finger in the pool and scooped up a glob and sniffed at it. He frowned then dabbed the liquid on his tongue, which was quite disgusting.

'This is strange,' he breathed. He narrowed his eyes on the liquid slowly sprawling out over the floor tiles. 'Or perhaps it makes perfect sense.'

'What is it?'

'Water.' He turned to me and raised his eye brows. 'Just normal water.'

'What does it mean?'

'It might mean nothing.' He wiped his hand on Lambell's jumper then stood up. 'There's no point in drawing conclusions at this point. There's no obvious cause of death, but I'm guessing this is murder. It's too much of a coincidence. We have to assume that someone else is searching for the girl – that's not totally unexpected – and that they have a head start on us.'

'Do you think Lambell told the killer where the girl is?'

'Impossible to say. What's important is that *we* don't know where she is.'

'We should call the police. They might be able to save the girl *and* Lambell's colleagues.'

'Cops!' Hunter snorted. 'We're the cops in the world of the gifted, Bentley. This is our job.'

'But-'

'But what? You could be sending two, three, five, *ten* cops to their deaths by alerting them to the killer. Take a good look at this body. Whoever did it is very skilful and comfortable with taking human life. It takes practice to kill and leave virtually no trace. We are dealing with a lethal adversary here, Bentley, and if an individual like that is cornered by *normal* people there is only one outcome.'

'Cops will have guns.'

'They still won't stand a chance. I'm not going to risk even more lives because you're too scared to continue this investigation.'

'Don't call me a coward, Hunter. I may be many things, but I'm not a coward.' I was being honest with him when I said I was no coward, however fighting another gifted person couldn't be taken lightly, and there was a growing fear inside me at the prospect.

'You have to stop thinking about leaving our work for someone else to do. We need to locate the photographer who took the pictures for that article. We have to find her as quickly as we can.'

'All we have is a name. It could take hours to find her.'

'She was friends with Lambell. There may be some clues in this apartment. Let's tear this place apart. You take the sitting room and I'll check the other rooms.'

I went to the room and it was a total mess. Newspapers, magazines, empty pizza boxes, clothes, dirty socks everywhere. The man lived like a total slob. I sifted through the junk and heaped it into the corner then went through the cabinet and book shelves but there was no link to any of his colleagues. When I'd gone through all the obvious places I decided to use my gift to levitate the chairs, TV and sofa then flip them upside down. I gave them all a shake by fluctuating my control over them and every stale crisp, half-eaten chip, coin, cigarette butt, scrap of paper and dust particle fell to the floor. There was still nothing of any use to me.

I circled the room over and over until I was all out of ideas and sat on the coffee table by the window. Hunter was really tearing the rooms apart and creating an almighty racket. I walked to the hallway and hissed at him to keep it down; we didn't want the neighbours realising a couple of strangers were tossing the apartment.

He didn't reply and didn't take heed of my warning. He was pulling out drawers from a cabinet and chucking the contents onto the bedroom floor. As I was looking along the hallway I focused on the bundle of coats and scarves that were hanging from a rack on the wall. I noticed the coat I'd seen Lambell wearing at the motorcycle convention and there, as clear as day, was a thick diary sticking out of the pocket.

I went and pulled it out and began flicking through the pages, but found it to be just as untidy as the living space. There didn't seem to be any order in his writing whatsoever - odd considering he made a living from writing. The text didn't seem to be inline with the dates on each page and most of the handwriting was illegible.

'What have you got there?'

'A diary *of sorts*. Can't read most of it.'

'Check the front few pages for names and address. There has to be some sort of list in there.'

I went to the front but there were only empty sheets, apart from doodles. I kept going, trying to figure out anything from the innumerable scribbles. Then a sequence of entries jumped out at me.

HANNERS

283

CHESBIT R

–

BECKY

41

CHILLINGTON A

'Hunter, what was that photographer's name?'

'Rebecca Dunlow.'

'And the editor?'

'Christopher Hanley.'

'Give me that phone again. I think we might be in business.'

I went online and typed in *Chesbit R* into a search engine and it predicted that what I ought to have been searching for was Chesbit Road. I tried again, this time typing in *Chillington A* and it gave me the option of Chillington Avenue. I quickly looked up the addresses and they were both in suburbs outside of Newcastle.

'Dunlow lives on Chillington Avenue and Hanley's on Chesbit Road.' I looked to my colleague and raised an eyebrow. 'Who do we go after first?'

'Who's closest?'

'Dunlow is about five miles from here. Hanley lives maybe ten miles further to the north.'

'We go after Dunlow and pray this murderous swine hasn't reached her first.'

We didn't waste any time and quickly exited the apartment. We kept our heads down as we made our way outside and across the street to the 4x4. No one had taken any notice of us although we had left forensic traces of ourselves behind for the authorities to uncover, but that didn't seem to be of any significance in that desperate moment. The only thing that was on our minds was preventing the killer from claiming any more lives. We got into the 4x4 and Hunter fired the engine. He didn't turn the headlights on until we'd turned off the street. The sky was pitch black and an uncertain night lay ahead.

CHAPTER EIGHT

A Race Against Time

I thought about Lambell as we drove through the suburbs. He was an ordinary man going about his life, probably never wronged anyone, and was likely to be looking forward to spending the weekend with his friends. Then his life was snuffed out just because he knew the name and location of a girl that he probably met only once and for a brief moment. He was just another innocent person who had lost their life because they'd unwittingly gotten involved with the gifted. It was yet another example of how dangerous my world was.

My thoughts then turned to the murderer. What gifts were we facing? Who was the killer working for? Would we come face to face with this abomination before long? Was it an abomination or was it someone just like me who had been seduced by money or twisted by revenge?

This would end in violence and death either way. Hunter had been right when he said our lives were on the line once we took on an investigation for the Guild.

'Hunter, who would want the girl? I mean who would want her enough to kill innocent people?'

'Anyone who could profit from being able to predict future events.'

'Great. That narrows it down to a few billion suspects.'

'It could be a company like Golding Scientific. That seems most likely at this point.'

'So there are other organisations trying to find people with the true gifts? Golding Scientific is only one of many possibilities?'

'Yes. Golding is the most prominent of them but they all pose a threat to us. It may not be the case; it could simply be a gifted person who recognised the girl's power and has decided she would be very valuable if there was a ransom for her.'

'It seems like a lot of trouble to go to considering there is no proof the girl even has a true gift. You said it yourself; this could simply be a child who likes attention.'

'Prophets are rare. Anyone who shows the potential is worth the risk.'

'Is it always like this?'

'What do you mean?'

'Is being an agent for the Guild always this dangerous? Are there always killers lurking about? Evil corporations trying to snatch gifted kids?'

'Let's just say it's never peaceful for too long.'

We reached Chillington Avenue at 8.30pm and slowed the car across the street from number 41. It was a small terraced house with a car parked in the narrow driveway at the front. The lights inside the house were off. That either meant Rebecca Dunlow wasn't at home or she'd also fallen victim to the prophet's pursuer.

Hunter turned off the engine and lifted the handbrake. He watched the house for a few moments, but there was no movement inside and the street was quiet but for the odd car that droned past.

'Be ready for a fight, Bentley. We have no idea what's waiting for us in that house. When we get inside you may sense an attack because of your precog gift, but you'll only have a split second to react. We cannot hesitate if the killer is inside that house. An instant of indecision and we could both wind up like Lambell. You understand?'

'Strike first and ask questions later?'

'Exactly. Let's just hope Dunlow is off out having a night on the tiles.'

We left the 4x4 and quickly crossed the road and leaped over the wooden gate into the front garden. Once we rounded Dunlow's car we both realised that we were already too late. The lock on the front door was busted. How late were we? Could the killer still be inside?

'Get behind me,' Hunter ordered quietly, 'and stay behind me. If I'm attacked you better strike without a second's thought. Otherwise you'll be dead.'

'Let me take the lead,' I argued. 'I'll create a shield in front of us. That should protect us from any surprise attacks.'

Hunter wanted to be the first one in, because he was the more senior of us, but he knew I was right and allowed me to pass to the front.

I moved in front of him and my body tingled as I drew energy in from my surroundings. I allowed a wave of kinetic energy to pass out of my body and form an invisible wall in front of me, which I moved towards the front of the house. The energy pushed the unlocked door open and filled the tight hallway inside. When I was confident that it covered us from all angles I cautiously entered the dim hallway and made the lights switch on. I paused at the bottom of the stair and listened out for any sound. Nothing. The house was silent and there was an odd smell in the air.

'Dunlow must really like garlic!' I grimaced. 'Christ! It's making my eyes water. Must have been frying chicken too. This is the vilest stench I've ever come across.'

'That's not chicken you're smelling, Bentley.'

'What is it?'

'Let's comb the rooms and make sure our murderous friend isn't still hanging about.'

We searched the living room, kitchen and the study before creeping up the stairs and checking each of the three bedrooms. All were dark and empty and the house remained silent. The only place we were yet to look was the bathroom. Hunter walked ahead of me and slowly turned the door knob then pushed the door open. The room was dark, but we had discovered the source of the curious odour; the stench was overpowering now.

Hunter pointed into the room and sent a bolt of electricity inside that crawled the walls until it found the overhead light and a wall mounted lamp above the sink. Both bulbs were ignited by his gift and the small room was suddenly filled with stark white light.

We moved forward together and the stink was making my lungs convulse. I pulled my jacket up over my nose and winced as I took my first step inside. As we rounded the open door we saw what was creating the terrible odour. We had found Rebecca Dunlow and her lifeless body was slumped in the corner, her head and shoulders leaning against the side of the tub. I'd handled the last dead body quite well but this was altogether different. I couldn't focus on what was before my eyes and turned to the wall and hunched over, retching wildly.

'Dear God!' Hunter cursed. 'What on earth is this?'

'It appears the killer doesn't mind leaving marks on the body after all.' I sucked in deep breaths – the stench made water gather in my mouth and I fought the urge to vomit. 'How could anyone do that to another human being?'

'We are obviously dealing with two separate killers.' He turned to me and patted me on the shoulder. 'You don't have to look at it again. Go downstairs and have a glass of water. This would be quite a shock even for the most experienced agents.'

'I've seen it now and there'll be no way I'll ever be able to forget it.'

'Are you sure you can handle this, Bentley?'

'Yeah.' I straightened myself and ran my sleeve over my mouth. 'I'm all right.'

We approached the body and stood either side of it. Dunlow was in a seated position, was wearing a charcoal coloured skirt and black shoes with a dressing gown.

'She was probably getting ready to go out for the night,' Hunter said as he leaned over her.

'How do you know that?'

'Looks like she was in the middle of getting dressed. Fancy shoes and skirt. Look, there's a blouse on a hanger. Make-up by the sink.'

I forced myself to inspect the body. There were circular wounds across her arms, shoulders, chest, neck and face. At first I thought they were simply burns, but on closer examination the flesh looked melted and each wound was very deep – some were right to the bone. There was very little left of her face and strands of her hair were white and curled up like they'd been too close to a fire.

'Was this caused by one of the true gifts?' I wondered. 'Maybe a fire-starter?'

'Yes, a pyrokinetic could be responsible, but the wounds are unusual.' He pointed to the marks in Dunlow's flesh. 'Look here, it's almost like a chemical was used on her. If I didn't know better I'd say these are white phosphorus burns. Some militaries use white phosphorus as weapons … but that would make no sense… it has to be the work of a pyro … I don't know what happened here, I'm sure we're dealing with two separate killers.'

'Working together or both acting independently?'

'I don't know, Bentley. I just do not know.'

'Should we contact the Guild? It's starting to look like we're outnumbered.'

'There's no time to call in help. We have to find the editor of the newspaper.'

'I don't feel right leaving her,' I nodded at the body, 'just lying on a cold floor like this. We should lift her out of here or something.'

'She's dead and the only thing we can do for her now is to catch the person who did this awful thing to her.' He took a towel from a chrome rack above the bath tub and gently placed it over Dunlow's face. 'We have to get moving, Bentley. There's no time to waste.'

I nodded without saying a word and within minutes we'd left the house and were on the road again. I felt guilty walking away and leaving the body of that unfortunate woman slumped on a floor as we skulked away into the night. She deserved better than that and we probably should have called 999. That was out of the question and I knew it; we couldn't notify anyone that we'd discovered the body because that would complicate the hunt for the gifted child. It was already complicated enough.

Hunter drove hard across the suburban streets. I watched him as he drove and noticed an angry determination grow into his face. He was obviously as livid as I was that two people had been murdered in such ghastly ways.

There was a lot I wanted to discuss with him but I said nothing. He didn't have the look of a man who felt very talkative.

A deep fear was rising from my stomach into my chest since we'd found Dunlow in such a dreadful state. To my mind she'd been tortured to extract information out of her. Whoever had done it was a total lunatic and was using methods unfamiliar to us. If we stumbled onto this person it would be difficult to defend against whatever the strange weaponry they were using and it was becoming obvious that human life meant little to those who were also searching for the little girl.

🖙 🖙 🖙

We reached Chesbit Road before 9pm and Hunter parked the car right outside the garden gates. We looked at the house and a few of the windows were illuminated, but there wasn't any movement inside. There was nothing too suspicious about the place, but I knew that anything could have been going inside those walls. My hands had started shaking and I couldn't make them stop. I didn't allow Hunter to see how nervous I had become.

We both left the 4x4 without speaking. There was no need to; we both knew what was to be done. We used the same tactic that had worked when we infiltrated Dunlow's house, and I used my powers to create a wall of energy that moved ahead of us and swept the hall door open as we took to the threshold. I was the first to step inside and I was half expecting that same acrid odour to be sucked into my lungs when I took my first breath of the atmosphere of the house. There was no foul stench though, just the scent of air freshener, or wood polish, I couldn't figure out which it was.

'You take the ground floor,' Hunter whispered over my shoulder. 'I'll take a look upstairs.'

I nodded and made my way into the large dining room to my left. There was no one in sight yet a TV was on, with the volume muted, and a cup of tea was standing on the table with steam still rising from it. The walls on all sides were stuffed with portraits of Hanley and his wife and their two young children.

Where were they? Who'd been drinking that cup of tea? Had the mysterious murderer arrived before us yet again?

I moved back into the hallway and treaded along the glossy wooden floor to the kitchen area. The lights were on, nothing was out of place, and a pot on the stove was bubbling. I checked the back door and it was locked from the inside. There was no sign of any disturbance. But where were Hanley and his family?

'Bentley,' Hunter shouted from above. 'Get up here fast.'

I raced up the staircase to find him standing by the door to the back bedroom. I went to his side and looked into the room, expecting the worst.

We were too late. Hanley was sitting on a chair with his head bent back. He had that same blank look in his eyes that Lambell had. I took a step forward just to be sure that he was dead and placed my fingertips against his neck. There was no pulse, but he wasn't cold yet. That meant he was only killed moments earlier. I looked at his face and the horror was still in those eyes, a Polaroid of his final terrible moment in life. I then looked at his mouth and saw it was full of water; when I lifted his head forward it poured down his chin onto his chest and thighs.

'Our first killer is back in the lead,' Hunter said as he examined the body. 'Lambell's killer surely did this. Identical *modus operandi*.'

'A nasty way to go, though not quite as excruciating as the death Dunlow was given.'

'Indeed. We must have just got here minutes after they left. We should look the place over and try to find some clues if we can.'

'We won't get lucky again. I doubt Hanley left the girl's name and address lying around.'

'It's unlikely, but we have no other options. We can't give up. That's not the way the Guild works. Did Romand give up on you, even when you were surrounded by Golding's people?'

'No. I'm sorry, Hunter. It's just this is all very hard to deal with.'

'I know, lad. If it's any consolation, you've handled it very well.'

'It's not.'

We both spun around to the doorway. A sound was coming from one of the other upstairs rooms. A voice. Someone was whispering.

Hunter pushed me aside and sprang towards the door. I saw him create one of his light mirrors to render himself invisible to anyone in front of him. As I stood behind him I saw small tentacles of electricity flowing out of his fingers as he paced out onto the landing. He was ready to give someone the shock of their life.

There was silence again but we hadn't imagined the voices. Someone else was in the house. My heart began to pound as Hunter slowly made his way to the next door over. My mouth was going dry at the prospect of all hell breaking loose once he opened that door. He used his psychokinetic ability to turn the door handle then to force the door. It swung open and we looked into the modest bedroom lit by a single lamp on a stand beside the bed. Sprawled across the bed was another body, this one a middle aged woman. She was lying on her side and there was a dark stain in front of her face. It seemed she'd met a similar fate to her husband.

There was another whisper from behind the only unopened door on the landing. Hunter and I exchanged a long and very tense stare. He nodded at me to get ready then went to the door. I summoned my power and was ready to send a volley of energy at whoever was hiding in the bedroom. I used all the anger that had been building up inside of me that evening and it would be enough to kill an elephant.

Hunter kicked the door open and I retracted my power as I got my first look inside. I recognised the two children from the portraits in the dining room. The girl was probably around three years old and her brother was two or maybe three years older than her. They were huddled close to one another under the sill of the room's only window.

'Calm down,' I said, stepping towards them with my hands raised. 'We're not here to hurt you. We're here to help. Just try to calm down.' I only realised how stupid I sounded when the words had left my mouth. Their parents had just been murdered and I was trying to get them to relax.

'Where's my mum?' the boy asked, as he put himself between me and his sister. 'Is she all right?'

'She's …' I looked at Hunter and he gave a slight shake of his head. 'She's gone out. I'm not sure where…'

'The man hurt my daddy, didn't he? Will he be OK?'

'I don't know.' I went to him and put my hands on his shoulders. 'I really don't know what's going to happen.'

'Who are you?'

'We were trying to find someone,' Hunter said as he entered the room and stood next to me. 'Your father was supposed to help us.'

'The other man was looking for someone too.'

'The other man?'

'I heard him talking to Daddy. He was angry and told him that he had to know where the girl was.'

'Did you see this man?'

'No. I was hiding in here the whole time. He was shouting and my dad was scared. I was too frightened to leave the room to help him.'

'What did your father say to this man?' Hunter asked. 'Did he give the man an address?'

'I can't remember.'

'Bentley, I need you to use your time-scanning power.'

'What good will that do?'

'It works on humans as well as objects. Scan the child. Look into his past and you'll be able to hear what he heard.'

I stood and whispered in his ear, 'Wouldn't it be better to scan his father?'

'No,' Hunter whispered back. 'Never scan the dead. If you scan through their death you can die yourself from the shock. Scan the boy, Bentley. We're running out of time.'

'Will you hold my hand?' I asked the boy as I knelt before him. We were eye to eye and I felt guilty that I was using him in this way. I had no other choice, though. 'It will help me to find this man who likes to hurt people.'

'Will it make him stop being angry? I don't want him to come back here.'

'Just hold my hand for a moment.'

The boy reached out and I wrapped my hand around his. I wasn't very well versed in time-scanning but I had used it before when I was doing the tests in The Million Dollar Gift. I shut my eyes and awakened the gift from deep within. This power was much more difficult to control than psychokinesis, and harder to summon than my precognitive skill, that seemed more instinctive. I concentrated on the physical connection with the boy and after a moment I felt as if my mind was separating from my body. I was surrounded by darkness and was floating aimlessly through it. The time-scan had begun and I saw and felt what the boy had. I scanned into the past and as he clutched his sister tightly while Hunter and I were in the other room talking. I went further back and the boy had been hiding under the bed and was holding his hand over his sister's mouth. There were footsteps outside the door. I gathered all my strength and forced it into the gift. Time spun past me and I watched his movements in reverse. I stopped when he was standing with his ear to the bedroom door. I rolled the scan forward and I felt the deep fear that the boy had experienced when the intruder had dragged his father up the staircase.

'I have already killed Lambell.' The man had a foreign accent, but his English was perfect, almost better than most people who classed it as their native tongue. 'You see, killing is not a problem for me. Death and murder have been a part of my life since childhood. Ending your life means nothing more to me than swatting a fly.'

'What the hell do you want from me?'

'I only want information, Mr Hanley. Your newspaper ran an article three days ago about a girl who could predict future events. According to Lambell her name was Sarah Fisher.'

'And?'

'And I want to know where that girl is.'

'She's just a disturbed child. We run articles like that all the time. People seeing the future, people who talk to animals, kids who make things move without touching them. It's just a joke. No one really believes it.'

'Call me a believer.'

'What do you want with the girl?'

'That, Mr Hanley, is my own business. You should be more concerned with your own safety and that of your wife.'

'Please don't hurt her.'

'Take a seat before I break off one of your arms. There, you seem much more comfortable now. It is like this, Mr Hanley: tell me the girl's address and I will only kill *you*. If you lie, I will return and murder your wife.'

'Please don't do this. I'll tell you where she is but spare my life.'

'No. You have seen my face and that means you must die. Look on the bright side, your wife can still live a fulfilling life. Maybe even remarry.'

'You sick bastard. I'll kill you!'

There was a loud bang followed by a hissing noise and I could hear Hanley moaning and struggling.

'This pain you are experiencing,' the killer said in a calculating tone of voice, 'is nothing compared to how I can make you suffer if you choose to resist me. Tell me where the child is and I will bring your torture to a swift conclusion.'

'She lives in the Highlawn Estate,' Hanley panted. 'It's a few miles outside of the city.'

'The exact address.'

'I can't recall ...'

There was silence for a moment before furious shuffling and a loud bang.

'The address!' the stranger shouted at Hanley. 'Tell me or I will make your lovely wife suffer in ways you cannot imagine.'

'77...' Hanley, who sounded like he was in agony, said. 'It's 77 Highlawn Estate. She lives there with a young couple who take in troubled kids.'

'Good. If you had only been so helpful at first I would have spared your wife.'

'But you said–'

There was a struggle and muffled screams from Hanley.

'I am sure you would like to kill me, Mr Hanley, but you cannot beat the devil at his own game. You see, *I* am the devil and killing is my game.'

I broke off the time-scan and crumbled to the floor. An intense pain drove into the back my skull and I could hardly breathe.

'Bentley!' Hunter lifted me from the floor. 'Are you all right?'

'I'll be fine. I just scanned too far into the past. It leaves me very weak when I do it.'

'Did you get the girl's address?'

'77 Highlawn Estate. It's somewhere north of here'

'Good work, lad. Now, we have to be on our way.'

'What are we going to do with the kids?' I lowered my voice. 'We can't let them see their parents' bodies. I won't allow them to experience that.'

'We can't take them with us either.' Hunter looked past me at the two terrified children. He went to the boy and looked down on him sorrowfully. 'Are there any friends of your parents living on this street?'

'Mary Barton. She lives across the road. She's Mum's best friend.'

'Listen, son, you did a very brave and clever thing tonight. Now that you're safe I want you to get out of this house and don't come back. I want you to take your sister over to Mary and tell her that a bad person broke into the house and that you don't know what happened to your parents. Do you understand?'

'Where's my mum?'

'I don't know, kid. You have to do as I tell you. Go to Mary's house and tell her what I said.'

'OK.'

We couldn't allow them to see what had really happened to their parents so Hunter went and closed the doors to the other rooms before I led the children out of the room and down the stairs. As I brought them downstairs I felt an uncontrollable anger rising in me. These two innocent souls just had their parents, their protectors, and their futures stolen from them. And for what? *Information*? To know the whereabouts of some kid who might not even have a gift?

When we got outside we sent the two youngsters racing across the street. We quickly climbed into the 4x4 and were off within seconds. I'd never felt so bitter in all my life. All I could think of was the voice I'd heard talking to Hanley. How cold and emotionless it had been, how wicked the person behind it was once Hanley had tried to withhold the girl's location – he'd tried to protect her, but it was just too much for him.

'I'm going to kill this man,' Hunter snapped as he thumped the steering wheel. 'I'm going to kill him and I'm going to make him suffer.' He thumped the dash board and a spark of electricity rebounded into the air. 'He's dead whoever he is!'

He was echoing my own sentiments. This was no longer about solving a crime or finding a prophet. This had turned into a revenge mission. The killer could not get away with what he'd done, and Hunter and I were the only ones who could inflict an appropriate punishment upon him.

Hunter was furious and hissed some very colourful language under his breath. I just sat there motionless, stunned by all I had seen that evening. The last vestige of innocence I had as a teenager had been eradicated. It had been killed just like the staff of the newspaper.

I caught my reflection in the passenger window as a streetlight lit my face. I had the same stern expression that Hunter and Romand and Ballentine always had. I now shared that hardness and cynicism that most of the Guild agents had. I was probably destined to be like my mentors, probably had been since the moment I left London with Romand. I should have found that deeply disturbing but in that moment I wanted to be like them.

I couldn't get the sound of Hanley's voice out of my head. His stuttering and pleading. The weeping. It was such a dreadful and tragic night.

The one good thing that came from it was the killer was in such a hurry that he didn't search for the children or hadn't noticed the photos in the dining room. At least the kids could have some chance at a future. That didn't lighten my mood much.

Hunter never slowed the 4x4 as we headed for the council estate on the northern end of the city. He didn't take his eyes off the road for a single second and determination was written all over his face. I gave him directions and he just grunted and occasionally slapped or punched the steering wheel or dashboard. I remembered what Atkinson had written about Hunter's aunt being killed by Brian Blake. The murders must have struck a chord in him. How could it not? Maybe what had happened to the Hanleys had brought it all back to him.

I couldn't blame him for being so furious. I was just as angry, and as willing to use my gifts to put an end to the killer's rampage through the suburbs.

At 10.30pm we were nearing our destination and the tension in the vehicle was palpable. Surely we'd beaten the killer to the girl or at least we'd catch him in the act this time.

We entered Highlawn estate and Hunter released his seat belt, ensuring that he was free to react if needed.

'You ready?' he asked. 'No second guessing yourself if we stumble on him. Kill first, ask questions later. You got it?'

'No problem. My dislike for violence has faded as this night has gone on.'

He turned the vehicle onto the road and I caught sight of flames swooping from the windows of a house near the opposite end. Hunter suddenly spun the steering wheel and turned the car around and back towards the exit of the estate.

'Where are you going?' I shouted at him. 'Didn't you see the fire? That had to be the house the girl is living in'

'I saw the fire. I also saw that car there.' He pointed ahead at a car speeding away into the night. 'He beat us to the girl, but he won't be getting away this time.'

'Hunter, I know you're dying to get your hands on this creep, but it would be best to keep your distance.'

'I will. We'll have to wait until he stops before we make our move.'

The most intense hour of my life followed. We kept our distance from the silver saloon but it never got far enough in front that we lost sight of it. Who was the driver? Who was this man that spent an entire day killing total strangers? How could we defeat him when the time came? Would he claim one of our lives before the other could execute him?

CHAPTER NINE

The Face of a Killer

We tracked the car until after midnight when it cut off the motorway towards one of the small satellite towns. The driver made no stops as the car passed along the main street then through the many rows of terraced housing. My nervousness grew as each second passed and at times it seemed the car would never stop rolling onward. I simply wanted this excruciating chase to end.

It did. The car turned off the winding road into a spacious car park outside a tall apartment block. Hunter reacted quickly, driving our 4x4 onto a nearby street with houses on either side of it. He killed the headlights and we both looked back over our shoulders through the rear window.

The car park was well lit and we both got a good look at the driver when he left the car. He was average height and had an athletic build. His hair was cut tight, shaven at the sides with the top slightly longer, like a marine's haircut. He was much younger than I'd expected – probably in his late twenties. He had very pale skin and there were deep shadows beneath his eyes.

He lingered beside the car and surveyed the car park before ushered two youngsters out of the back seat. The first to step out was a girl who looked about eight years old and fitted the description of the troublesome prophet who had caused all the bother. She was followed by an older girl, maybe twelve or thirteen years old with hunched shoulders, long black hair and a surly expression on her ghostly-white face.

'Well, well, well,' Hunter said shaking his head. 'Look who it is.'

'You recognise him?'

'I certainly do. He's a Guild assassin – one who's supposed to be dead.'

'Don't you mean a Guild *agent*?'

'No. We have a special branch of the organisation that deals with the hottest situations. Anyone who is part of it is known as an *assassin*, not simply an agent. I have been part of it from time to time. So has this dirtbag.'

'Who is he?'

'His name is Edward Zalech. He was meant to have been killed in a house fire in Switzerland a few days ago. The older of the girls is his sister, Ania - she was also meant to have lost her life in the blaze. Seems we have solved two separate investigations. These two are now responsible for ten or more deaths in three days.'

'Maybe Ania isn't responsible and is just following her older brother. She only looks about thirteen! I can't believe she's a cold-blooded killer.'

'We'll find out in due course.' He took the mobile phone from his coat and punched in a number. 'We'll need back up. Zalech is a very powerful mageleton and we'd be taking a major risk tackling him by ourselves.'

He held off putting the call through until the Zalechs and the young prophet had gone inside the apartment building. I remembered the passages in Atkinson's journal concerning mageletons and how the Guild didn't like them to be fully trained because of how destructive they could be. I once thought that I would never face an enemy as powerful Marianne Dolloway again, but now it appeared I was on a collision course with a foe who was just as deadly.

'Ballentine, we found the girl.' Hunter announced when the call was connected. 'Yes, it does have something to do with the spate of murders in Newcastle that's all over the news. We've come up against a most unexpected adversary. We've also solved the case in Switzerland for you … Oh, I'm not talking rubbish at all. Edward Zalech has the prophet and I've just followed him to an apartment block a few miles out of the city … Yes, his sister is with him. They obviously set up the fire in Cramer's house and they're definitely the ones who killed the newspaper people … Don't worry I won't do anything rash. You better send a team here as soon as you can … I'll text you our location.'

'Is he sending help?'

'Yeah, a team will arrive tomorrow morning. He'll notify any other Guild agents based in northern England to see if they can reach us earlier. Linda Farrier might be the closest - no smart remarks, Bentley.'

'I don't feel like I have a sense of humour anymore, Hunter.'

'That's understandable,' he replied. 'You did well tonight. Much better than I thought you would.'

I'd been desperate to prove myself to Hunter and his praise should have made me feel good, but I felt empty after the night's events.

'It's hard to make any sense of this,' I said. 'There are too many bad memories in my mind to focus on anything.'

'Try not to concentrate on it too much. We're still in the middle of a deadly situation. If they try to move the girl again we'll have to intervene. We can't risk Zalech escaping us.'

'I know. I've seen what that monster is capable of doing in the space of a few hours. I can't imagine the carnage he could create if he gets away. Who do you think he's working for?'

'Maybe he's working for himself. Zalech is a clever man and doesn't need the likes of Golding to corrupt him.'

'How could the Guild employ someone like him? Surely they would have known what he's really like!'

'Sometimes it's better to have people like Zalech as close as possible so that you can keep an eye on them.'

'Obviously they didn't watch him carefully enough.'

The hours slipped by and the night grew cold and rain pelted the roof and bonnet of the old 4x4. Hunter had turned the vehicle around and parked it closer to the building so we wouldn't miss the Zalechs if they tried to slip away into the night. It was an uncomfortable time and we took turns to keep a lookout while the other slept. I woke at 3.30am and Hunter was smoking the end of a cigar and blowing it out the open window. It was freezing but I didn't complain; it seemed petty to be bothered by a chill after what had happened a few hours earlier.

'You want to get some sleep now?' I asked Hunter as he threw the cigar butt into the road. 'I don't think I'll sleep again tonight.'

'Neither will I.'

'Tell me about Zalech.' I said to break the silence of the night. 'How did he get into the Guild in the first place?'

'It's a long story.'

'We've got all night by the looks of it.'

'There was once a secret agency within the USSR called the SPD. They were closely linked to the KGB and they searched out and recruited gifted people from across the Soviet Union. They were a nasty bunch and used the gifted to assassinate politicians and business leaders around the world, and also forced them into the conflicts the communists got involved in like Korean War in the 1950s, Vietnam in the 60s and the war with Afghanistan in the 80s. They were a major thorn in the side of the Guild until the fall of communism in 1991. After that the SPD was disbanded along with the KGB and we thought we had one less enemy to deal with.

'Alas, we weren't so lucky. In the mid-1990s a man called Viktor Yeleshev, who was one of the main recruiting officers in the SPD, reappeared. He'd spent the intervening years trying to rebuild his old agency, but he kept getting blocked by the new democratic government in Russia. He got lucky in 1995. One of the new billionaire oligarchs, Boris Komolov, had heard of what Yeleshev was trying to do and decided to bank roll his project, which became known unofficially as 'The Eastern Shadow'.

'Yeleshev had the experience and contacts, Komolov had all the money in the world. It was a match made in hell. Within a few short years Yeleshev had hired many of the gifted who had formerly been in the employment of the old SPD – most had fallen on hard times and were lured in by Komolov's riches. He was also hiring new and promising individuals from Russia and the Balkan states. The Eastern Shadow had become a great threat and the Guild grew increasingly fearful of the power they had attained in such a short period of time. Even Golding was afraid of them and tried to have Yeleshev assassinated a couple of times.

'The Eastern Shadow had been mostly confined within the borders of the former Soviet Union, but in 2001 they branched out and began operations in Pakistan, Finland, Holland and Poland. This is when they came into direct conflict with the Guild and there were deaths on both sides. One of their operations, or should I say hunts, that year took place in Zory, a small city in southern Poland. The story will seem familiar to you: a boy in his early teens had been reported as having a supernatural ability. This came to the attention of Yeleshev and he sent a team to snatch the kid.'

'That boy was Zalech, right?'

'Right,' Hunter nodded. 'He was thirteen at the time and had been witnessed raising droplets of water from a lake near his home. Mageletons are rare and both the Guild and the Eastern Shadow went looking for him. It's a tragic story and one that is sadly repeated all too often. He was a loner and often got into trouble with the authorities. When Yeleshev's people found him he saw them as no different from the police or the teachers that he'd been rebelling against. He told them he wasn't interested in working for them. They weren't, however, taking no for an answer.

'The Shadow's methods of recruitment were crude but effective. Yeleshev ordered his team to murder Zalech's parents and then told the youngster that if he didn't join them they would torture and kill his sister, Ania, who was only an infant at the time. Edward had little choice but to give in to their demands.

'While they were trying to smuggle the Zalechs over the border into Ukraine one of the Guild agents, Sebastian Kowalski, intercepted them. He killed Yeleshev's team and hid the Zalechs at his home near Wroclaw for a few months. Yeleshev didn't give up easily and eventually he located Kowalski and tried again to snatch the talented young mageleton. Kowalski was killed in the ensuing struggle, but he'd been teaching Zalech how to use his powers and it held him in good stead when the fighting took place. Zalech managed to fend off the attackers and escaped with his sister. He found his way to Wroclaw city centre and was soon picked up by another agent of the Guild before being brought to Nuremberg, Germany, where we had a safe-house. He spent a few years there before being moved to London. I met him a few times and I can't say I ever liked, or trusted, him but I never believed he'd be capable of the crimes he's committed over the last few days.'

'How come you didn't like him?'

'Because he's like a damned robot and shows no feelings at all. He never once revealed what he was thinking and never had much of an opinion – or at least he never voiced one. He was also too enthusiastic about killing people. The worst thing about him was that I always had a nagging suspicion that one day he would explode into a rage. That somehow the emotions he held back were building in some dark corner of his mind and would eventually escape.'

'How strong is he?'

'Too strong. Mageletons are a bloody nightmare for us because their gift is almost limitless. They also seem to have a propensity for violent behaviour which means they should not, under any circumstance, be trained to maximise their powers.'

'What's the deal with his sister? Is she as bad as him?'

'Yeah, she's a bit odd too – hardly surprising seeing as she's been shifted around from one home to another since she was a toddler.'

'She's gifted, right?'

'A pyrokinetic – a pure form of the gift. It's likely she's just following her big brother around because he's the only family she has. Still, she could do a lot of damage if she feels threatened. You've never encountered a pyro before, have you?'

'No.'

'They have bad tempers and can't be fought in any conventional way. You have to make sure you strike first – before they flare up.'

'They can set fire to anything?'

'They can. With a little training they can even set human flesh alight. That's why you can't allow them to attack you; it's difficult to fight back if you're on fire.'

'I'll take your word for it.' My thoughts then turned to Sarah Fisher, and what she must have been going through in that very moment. She'd probably witnessed her foster parents being murdered and was now in the hands of a gifted psychopath. 'That prophet must be freaking out.'

'Of that I have no doubt.' He shook his head and snorted. 'This situation is ridiculous. We don't even know if she's gifted.'

'You ever met a prophet before? You know, a real one.'

'Yes, I knew one quite well actually. We were once good friends, but that was before his visions had driven him to the brink of insanity. It's a curse more than a gift. Imagine every time you go to bed wondering if you're going to see the end of the world or a murder or a train wreck. It's no wonder most of them commit suicide.'

'They only predict the bad stuff?'

'As far as I know, yes.'

'Can they be trained to predict certain events?'

'Why do you think they're so valuable?'

'Golding would probably offer a lot of money for someone with that gift. Do you think he's the one behind all this?'

'Possibly. If he is I'll be more concerned that Zalech is in his employment than this girl being under his influence.'

'Why?'

'Zalech has the potential to be more destructive than Marianne Dolloway.'

'I thought Golding valued psychokinetics more than anything else.'

'He does. Zalech also has that ability.'

'He does? He's a mageleton *and* psychokinetic! That would make him…'

'About as dangerous as it gets.'

'How on earth are we going to capture him?'

'Capture him he says!' Hunter laughed. 'You can't capture someone as strong as him. There's only one outcome here, Bentley.'

'He has to be killed?'

'Yes, and even that won't be easy. All the strongest Guild agents and assassins that are usually based here in Britain are currently overseas, on the continent trying to capture a killer that doesn't exist.'

'So, who is Ballentine sending then?'

'I have no idea.' He pulled back his sleeve and read his wristwatch. 'But we'll find out soon enough.'

CHAPTER TEN

Reunion

I t was past 4am when Linda Farrier parked her car on the opposite side of the narrow street. She took her time getting out then stretched her limbs before casually stepping into the road. She was a tall woman in her early thirties with dark skin and silky black hair tied tightly behind her head. She strode confidently to the 4x4 and climbed into the back. Hunter had gone quiet as soon as he saw her car approach and didn't even acknowledge her when she joined us, which I thought was rather rude.

'Hi,' I said as I turned to her and smiled. 'Nice to see you again.'

'Hello, Ross,' she replied. Her voice was husky and she had a very thick London accent. Listening to her talk was like scratching your back with a velvet glove; you'd never tire of it. 'Feeling any better? You were head to toe in bandages the last time I saw you.'

'I'm feeling a lot better thanks. Hunter here has been nursing me back to health. He's like the big sister I never had.'

'Put a cork in it, Bentley,' Hunter growled. 'I'm too tired to listen to your wisecracks.'

'Someone's in a good humour.' Farrier rolled her eyes. 'How have you been, Michael?'

'Never mind how I've been. We've much more important things

to be discussing.'

'Fine,' Farrier snorted. 'What's going on then? Ballentine said you might need a hand.'

'*Might need a hand*!' Hunter jabbed the steering wheel in front of him in frustration. 'How has that blithering idiot lasted so long in the Guild? Didn't he tell you what we were up against?'

'He said someone had kidnapped a kid and that you and Ross would need some help. Nothing more than that.'

'We need help all right. Edward Zalech and his sister are the ones who kidnapped the kid and they're holed up in that apartment block over there.'

'Edward Zalech …?'

'Yeah.'

'I thought he was dead.'

'He's very much alive and he's been leaving dead bodies all over the place for days on end.'

'The three of us can't handle this,' she insisted – the mere mention of Zalech had scuffed her confident sheen – 'It's a suicide mission if it's left up to the three of us.'

'Ballentine said he was sending a team. They should be here soon.'

'Hey,' I interrupted. 'With all this going on I almost forgot there's still another killer on the loose. The person who murdered Rebecca Dunlow.'

'There's another killer?' Farrier was incredulous. 'What on earth has been going on?'

'One of the victims was killed in a different manner to the others,' Hunter sighed.

'In what manner?'

'She had some strange burns on her body. It's most likely that Ania Zalech is responsible.'

'But you said they didn't look like Ania's work ...' I said

'Can you elaborate on why these burns were *strange*?' interrupted Ballentine.

'I'm not a pathologist,' grumbled Hunter, 'Maybe Ania is more dangerous than I thought.'

'They were strange because they didn't look like they'd been caused by fire,' I said. 'Hunter might be right about Ania being responsible, but I have my doubts—'

'We have enough on our plate without hypothesising over this crime,' Hunter interrupted. 'When Zalech is out of the way we can look into Dunlow's murder. Will that satisfy you, Detective Bentley?'

'Hunter, that woman was tortured and murdered less than twelve hours ago. It's a little hard to simply forget about it.'

'I'm not saying you should forget about it. Just put it to one side until we deal with the matter at hand! I don't want to hear another word about Dunlow until we have Zalech out of the way. Are we clear?'

'Whatever you say.'

There was a long silence after that, but Hunter's strong words helped us all to calm down and that's what was required of us. We would have to outsmart Zalech rather than try to outmuscle him, which wouldn't be very wise judging by the way others spoke of him.

I started to ponder Edward Zalech and what he was capable of.

Could he really be more powerful than Marianne? Romand talked about her from time to time and according to him she was the greatest threat of all. Maybe that was because she had a fourth gift and the potential to turn out like James Barkley. Still, I found it hard to imagine anyone being as psychotic and gifted as she was. Marianne had been virtually indestructible. If Zalech was stronger than her we would require a whole team of gifted agents backing us up before we even contemplated tackling him.

'How is Zalech so dangerous?' I asked the others. 'We're not near a river or a coastline. Seriously, what's he going to do? Spit on us?'

'Didn't you see the bodies of Lambell and Hanley?'

'Yeah, but they weren't gifted like us.'

'What's on the windscreen, Bentley?'

'Hmm?'

'The windscreen – look at it. What's on it?'

'Rain droplets.'

'Indeed. Now, imagine someone who can control every drop of rain within a mile radius. Imagine every drop for a mile hitting you at the same time. Imagine them hitting you as fast as bullets. Imagine that he could bring every drop of rain together into one single body of water that he can control entirely. Imagine it hits you. Imagine you get trapped within it. Imagine he surrounds himself with it - how are you going to hurt him if he's surrounded by a ton of water?'

'I could cut through it with a psychokinetic slice.'

'Kinetic energy doesn't travel well through water,' Farrier argued. 'And let's not forget it's not only water that he can control. The most powerful mageletons can control fluids. They can turn a bottle of lemonade into defensive shield or a deadly weapon.'

'And don't forget, Bentley,' Hunter added, 'the human body is full of fluid that a mageleton can manipulate. If you're not careful you can end up drowning in your own saliva or he could stop your blood from circulating around your body.'

'As far as we know, Zalech hasn't been taught those techniques,' Farrier pointed out. 'The Guild has always kept his skills at a basic level. But Hunter's right, his powers make him a deadly opponent and we shouldn't take him lightly. I almost forgot that he has psychokinetic powers too.'

'And they are both pure gifts,' Hunter pointed out.

'All right,' I sulked. 'I get the point.'

Farrier leaned forward and squeezed my shoulder. 'We're not trying to belittle you, Ross. I, for one, feel a lot safer because you're here. After all, you're the one who beat Marianne Dolloway. There's not many who I'd rather have by my side in a fight.'

'Marianne was shot by a police officer. I didn't beat her.'

'Ross, you fought her and survived even though you only had a few weeks training. The entire Guild has been buzzing for months because of you.'

'Don't tell him that!' Hunter groaned. 'He already has an ego problem! Bentley, don't believe the hype. You're no better or stronger than the rest of us.'

'I don't believe I'm better than anyone else. I just don't want to let anyone down.'

'You won't as long as you do as I tell you. Just follow whatever–' he went silent and leaned forward then wiped the condensation from the inside of the windscreen.

I looked up at the tower block and there as clear as day was Ania Zalech on one of the balconies. She was leaning her elbows on the rail guard and looking over the small town. Oddly, she looked like any other teenage girl who hadn't a care in the world.

'You think she knows what her brother has been up to?' I asked. 'She looks pretty relaxed to me.'

'I don't know.'

'I didn't hear her voice when I scanned Hanley's son which could mean she wasn't in the house and didn't take part in the murders.'

'She sure knows about what he did in Switzerland!'

'We don't know that,' Farrier intervened as she leaned into the front to get a better view. 'Edward might have moved her off the property before he set the fire.'

'The house burned down,' Hunter said. 'My bet is that she used her gift to do it.'

'Always so quick to judge, Michael.'

'Give me a break, *Linda*. Why do you always see the worst in me?'

'I don't. I just don't like you to go unchallenged.'

'There's no fear of that, seeing as though I'm stuck here with you and Bentley.'

A heavy shower broke out and I watched Ania slowly receding from the balcony into the shadows. The night rolled on, as if it would never end.

🕶 🕶 🕶

We sat there watching the building as the last of the nocturnal hours drifted by and sunlight gradually seeped into the sky. By 8am I was delirious with hunger and so was Hunter. He asked Farrier to continue the vigil while we walked to a nearby service station where we picked some packaged sandwiches and snacks. It wasn't wise for us to linger in the open so we ate on our feet and were back sitting in the 4x4 by 9am. Farrier had nothing to report.

The morning turned out to be as excruciating as the night that preceded it; all we did was sit there watching the apartment block, but nothing happened and neither the Zalechs nor Sarah Fisher appeared. I was considering a nap when a transit van slowly turned the corner and parked across the street. Hunter seemed to recognise the driver and gave him a nod.

'About bloody time,' he said under his breath. 'I better go over and talk to them. You two stay here.'

He walked to the rear of the van and banged on the back doors. They were opened for him a few seconds later and he climbed inside.

'Did you know you left your raincoat at Hunter's place?' I asked Farrier. I couldn't think of anything else to say to break the uneasy silence. I just blurted it out not realising that it might seem like I was implying something.

'I was aware of that,' she said evenly. 'I used to visit him quite a bit.'

'Oh … you two must be good friends.'

'We used to be.'

'Not anymore?'

'It's not easy being his friend.'

'You should try living with him,' I laughed. 'He is one seriously grumpy man.'

Farrier went quiet. Whatever had happened between them had probably ended badly, not that relationships ever ended any other way. Just when I thought she wouldn't say another word to me, she climbed from the backseat and sat in the front.

'Tell me, Ross,' she said shrewdly, 'does he ever talk about me?'

'He told me you can beat the crap out of a grown man.'

'Yes,' she giggled. 'I can do that, even without using my gifts.'

'Best not to get on your bad side, eh?'

'Don't worry, Ross. You haven't given me a reason to kick your ass yet.'

I didn't like the way she ended her sentence with *yet*. I liked her smile even less. When we locked eyes I knew this was Linda Farrier's way of giving me a little warning not to be prying into her private life. Even the women of the Guild were hard as nails!

After a few moments of awkward silence Hunter emerged from the van and waved at me then pointed at the van. I gave Farrier another rather nervous grin before slipping out the door and quickly jogging over to the van.

'Now I know why you dumped her, Hunter.'

'Did she give you *the smile*?'

'Yeah.'

'Terrifying, isn't it?'

'It sure is.'

'Oh, speaking of girlfriends, get in the back of the van. Someone wants to talk to you.'

He opened the rear double doors and there were two lines of people sitting down on rows of seats. The passengers, six of them in all, turned to me in unison. Cathy was the only one I recognised.

'What are you doing here?' I asked as I stepped forward and grabbed her hands. 'Damn, it's good to see you.'

She leaned forward and kissed me passionately.

'Hey!' Hunter hissed. 'Get in the van, Bentley, and control your hormones!'

'All right, all right.'

I jumped up and almost landed on what I first thought was a black sack lying between the two rows of feet. It was only when the dark object turned and looked at me that I jumped straight back out onto the street. It was a black panther and its pale green eyes were fixed on me as if I was a juicy pork chop.

'Ross, get back in the van,' Cathy laughed. 'He won't hurt you. His name is Nightshade; he's one of Peter Williams's animals. I've learned to tame him since you went away.'

'Oh, that's the cat you told me about in the letter.' I climbed back inside and cautiously manoeuvred around the large feline and sat next to Cathy. 'He's bigger than I expected.'

'Enough about the cat,' Hunter snarled as he climbed inside and slammed the door. He switched on the interior light and sat opposite me. 'I'm sure you all know this is Ross Bentley.'

They stared at me and smiled, but there was an air of tension and I didn't know if it was because of me for some reason or the situation with Edward Zalech. Either way it killed the enthusiasm I got from seeing Cathy, who was now squeezing my hand very tightly.

Hunter went on to introduce me to the Guild members. First was Imelda Chapman, who was a thin woman with cold eyes; I thought she was a bit old to be engaging in combat – she looked about sixty! Then there was Steve Barker who was a jittery guy in his twenties who wore thick spectacles. To my right was Janice Powell who was younger than the others – maybe a year older than Cathy – and hers was the only smile that was genuine. There was also John Adeyemi who was the toughest-looking of the lot and made a point of shaking my hand. And last was Robert Motson, a middle-aged man wearing a very formal suit. He didn't offer his hand and barely made eye contact with me. I took an immediate dislike to him.

These people were different to the likes of Ballentine and Hunter and Farrier who were battle-hardened agents and seemed able and willing to walk into any situation, no matter how perilous it might be. They seemed more like people who worked in an office, all getting ready for a night out together. I had the feeling they'd be terribly outmatched by someone as vicious as Edward Zalech, but I couldn't openly say this, and after all, they didn't need to look tough to be very powerful. Still, I didn't want my life, or Cathy's, depending on any of them.

'Right, before we go any further I want to make it very clear that I am in charge of this operation.' Motson almost boasted, as if anyone in their right mind would want to be one making the decision to go head to head with the Zalechs. 'And I have a fair idea of how we should proceed.'

'What are you on about, Motson?' Hunter sneered. There was bad blood between them already and my companion was making it very clear he had no respect for the older man. 'You're not an experienced agent. You're only a mole. You work as an accountant for God's sake!'

'Mr Ballentine asked me to take control of the situation. I have some experience in hostage scenarios and he felt that it would best that an even-tempered person be in charge.'

Adeyemi nodded despondently at Hunter and it was obvious he'd had the same argument with Motson, and lost.

'This is totally unacceptable,' Hunter said. He rummaged in his trouser pockets for his phone then punched a number on the screen. 'Ballentine,' he bawled when the call was connected. 'What the bloody hell is going on? Did you put Motson in charge of this mission?'

'Yes and no.' Hunter was sitting close enough for me to hear what Ballentine was saying. 'I told him to take charge, but it wasn't my decision.'

'What fool made the decision?'

'The decision was made by the Council. They didn't want you taking control after what happened in Finland.'

'That was ages ago!'

'It was twelve months ago and the Council ministers have good memories. I suggest you obey this order. Otherwise you'll end up being struck off the list of agents. Got it?'

Hunter ended the call and stuffed the phone into his pocket. He leaned back and folded his arms then stared at Motson. 'So, fearless leader, what do you suggest we do?'

'I thought that would have been quite obvious: we must kill Edward. The two girls should be taken alive, if circumstances permit.'

'Hold up,' I butted in. 'One of those girls has been kidnapped and she's done nothing wrong. You can't just kill her!'

'Bentley's right,' Hunter said. 'We can't sacrifice the kid. That's out of the question.'

'We don't have a choice,' Motson replied. 'We cannot, even

though we have superior numbers, get drawn into a battle with a mageleton.'

'I agree,' Chapman nodded. 'It's a fight we cannot win.'

'You want to go up there and attack the apartment?' Hunter asked. 'Is that it?'

'No,' Motson shook his head. 'We wait until they leave then strike while they're in the car.'

'What if someone comes to pick up the girl?'

'Then we allow them to leave with the girl and we can follow them while the second group prepares an attack on the Zalechs.'

'We're to split up into two groups?' I asked. 'Wouldn't we be stronger together?'

'We *are* stronger together, but there must be two groups in case there are two objectives.'

'I reluctantly agree,' Hunters said. 'Splitting the group in two is the wisest course of action. Not only if someone shows up to collect the girl, also in case the Zalechs split up for some reason.'

'I want to be in Ross's group,' Cathy announced, squeezing my hand when she said it.

'No,' Motson replied. 'Ross will remain with Hunter and Farrier and I would like Janice to join them.'

'Why her?' Cathy frowned.

'Because we need you with *us*. Or should I say, we need Night-shade with us.'

'Right,' Hunter said. 'Edward might leave the apartment if they need something. If he does, which group gets the job of tackling him?'

'My group,' Motson replied. The others looked at each other

with concerned eyes. They sure weren't confident that they could take Edward Zalech on. But Motson had made up his mind and Hunter wasn't arguing with him.

'That settles it,' Hunter announced. 'We'll go after the prophet.'

'Very well,' Motson said. 'Try not to mess it up.'

'I've never failed the Guild,' Hunter boasted as he stood and moved to the door. 'I don't intend to start now.'

'You be careful,' Cathy whispered to me. 'Don't do anything stupid.'

'I can look after myself. I'm more worried about you. This Zalech guy is a serious nutcase, Cathy.'

'You don't have to worry about me, Ross. Nightshade does my fighting for me. I'll be sitting here the whole time.'

'Good.' I leaned over and kissed her on the cheek then whispered in her ear, 'Hunter said I might not have to stay in Scotland when all this is over. We might be able to spend some time together again.'

'I want nothing more.'

'Bentley, get a move on.' Hunter shouted. 'We don't have time for canoodling!'

I turned to him and smiled. 'There's always time for canoodling.'

Hunter and I returned to our seats in the front of the 4x4 and Janice sat next to Farrier in the back. There was very little said and each of us was feeling the pressure of the situation. Motson didn't inspire confidence at all and none of us truly approved of his plan. It was a dangerous state of affairs to begin with, but having a fool like that in charge made it doubly so.

The rain cleared up as the afternoon wore on and I struggled to fend off tiredness. My eyelids were growing heavy and all I wanted was a comfortable bed and a few hours sleep. Nothing broke the monotony of the stakeout and eventually I nodded off, only for Hunter to nudge me with his elbow seconds later.

'Stay awake. Our enemy could emerge at any moment.'

'Sorry,' I grumbled. 'I'm not used to this sort of thing.'

'You can't get used to it, believe me. I've been doing this for twenty years and I still have trouble keeping my eyes open on stakeouts.'

'Hunter,' Janice spoke up finally. 'We won't really have to kill that little girl, will we?'

'I'd like to say no.'

'It doesn't seem right that harm would come to her. Aren't we supposed to be rescuing her?'

'Edward Zalech's betrayal has made this more than a rescue mission, Janice. This is one of the lessons you learn when you join the Guild: innocents who get in the way often end up dead.'

'That's not what I was told when I was training in Holland.'

'They don't teach you how to kill in school, Janice. It's not something you can be taught in a classroom.'

'Why don't you stop scaring her,' Farrier snapped. 'Don't worry, Janice, we'll do everything we can to get that girl out of there safely.'

'I'm not trying to scare her. I'm getting her ready to deal with the reality that faces us. They might use the girl as a shield. It's not the first time that's happened.'

He was obviously referring to something that they had experienced in the past and Farrier fell silent as soon as he mentioned it and slumped back in her seat. I tried to lighten the mood by turning to Janice and asking where she was from and what gifts she had.

'I'm from Belfast originally, we moved to Birmingham when I was very young. Can't say I was ever happy at living at home with my parents – not because of Birmingham, I quite like the city actually – but I always knew I was different to everyone else and some people treated me really badly. When I was fourteen I ran away from home and made my way to London. I don't know what I was thinking. I had no plan at all. Eventually I started begging outside a café; I wasn't earning enough to eat. I decided to use my gift to entertain people and I started making a tidy sum.'

'What is your gift?'

'I'm …' she broke off eye contact and started fidgeting with the end of her jumper. 'I'm … er …'

'You don't have to tell me if you don't want to.'

She looked back at me and smiled, but her eyes were full of uncertainty. 'I'm a space-rupter.'

'Wow,' I breathed. 'Isn't that the rarest gift of all?'

'That's what they say. I can make myself disappear, and then reappear in a different location. I can also make objects disappear – that's how I made so much money entertaining people.'

'You can slip right out of reality into some … alternate place, right?'

'It's more complicated than that.'

'Uncomplicate it for me?'

'Bentley, don't harass the girl,' Hunter said. 'Janice, ignore him. He's a pest.'

'I'm just curious, Hunter.'

'I can cut through the fabric of time and space,' Janice said unexpectedly. 'I go to a place where there is no time, where there is no substance or life. It is a place that is not a place.'

'Doesn't sound very nice.'

'It's calm, as long as I can keep a doorway open to this universe.' She smiled nervously again. 'And as long as doorways to other places don't open.'

'Other places?'

She nodded then looked out the window. Whatever Janice had seen was not easily shared and it opened up all sorts of crazy ideas in my head. I started thinking about alternate universes and alien invasions and I quickly decided that I didn't want to know anymore about the gift of space-rupting.

The afternoon became evening and the sun slowly fell to the horizon. It looked like we were in for another night of watching the apartment block and I doubted I could keep my eyes open for much longer. It was then that we all leaned forward in unison, as if the earth beneath us had tilted.

Edward Zalech was walking towards his car.

CHAPTER ELEVEN

Fire & Water

We watched Zalech climb into the silver saloon and drive through the car park onto the main road. The car was followed seconds later by the transit carrying our colleagues from the Guild. Hunter waited until both vehicles were out of sight before starting the engine of the 4x4. He took a deep breath before turning to us.

'I'm going to park outside the apartment block. Linda and I will go in and try to smuggle the girl out. If we're not out of there in five minutes …' There was a long pause and I was expecting him to order us to drive away and not look back, '… you two have to follow us in and finish the job.'

'What the hell does that mean?' Janice asked.

'Bentley knows what to do.'

I knew exactly what he meant, without him saying it. If he and Farrier were killed then I would have to go into the building and try to save the child. But if Ania attacked me I would have to use my gift to destroy everything inside the apartment. There could be no caution – that would be suicide. Sarah Fisher's life was no more important than mine or Janice's. It was a dreadful mission to have and I was starting to question if I really wanted to be an agent for the Guild. It meant I had to be an indiscriminate killer and that was not in my nature.

'I could get into the apartment,' Janice said as Hunter drove towards the building. 'I can make a jump though time and space and land inside that apartment.'

'I know you can,' Farrier said, turning to her. 'But you don't have the skills to fight a pyrokinetic once you reappear.'

'I can grab hold of her; drag her out of this universe. I'm well able to handle myself.'

'No,' Hunter demanded. 'Ania will set you alight the instant she sees you. Linda and I can handle this.'

'There is another way,' I interrupted. 'It might be safer and it wouldn't put Ania in a position where she feels the need to attack us.'

'Make it fast, Bentley.'

'I can scale up the balconies and sneak into that apartment. I might be able to get the child out without Ania noticing.'

'You're not one for stealth, Bentley.'

'Doesn't matter. I'm a precog. I'll sense an attack before it comes.'

Hunter looked in the rear view mirror. 'Linda, what do you think?'

'I'm not sure. Ross, you do realise how dangerous this will be? You've never fought a pyro before.'

'I know – I've fought worse.'

Hunter drove through the car park and brought the 4x4 to a halt near the building's main entrance.

'We need to make a call on this,' he insisted. 'Fast!'

'I can do it, Hunter. Let me try.'

'I don't know if you're brave or just stupid,' he replied. He turned to Farrier and nodded. 'I'm willing to let him try.'

'It's as good a plan as any.' She leaned forward and clapped me on the shoulder. 'Good luck, Ross.'

I opened the door and stepped out into the cool evening air. My heart was pounding like never before and my hands started shaking at the prospect of a gifted duel. I was determined to get this right even though I was nervous. I was going to rescue that kid, even if I had to fight Ania Zalech to the death. Ania was young – just a child – but I knew what she was capable of, and I wasn't going to make the same mistake that Romand made with Marianne.

Hunter left the vehicle and walked by my side as I approached the foot of the tower block.

'Just try to remain as calm as possible.' He sounded almost like my old football coach. 'Don't let your emotions rule your powers. That's when things get messy.'

'I know. Thanks for letting me do this.'

'Thank me when it's over. Time to get moving.'

I shook his hand and walked towards the wall. I craned my neck and focused on the balcony on the seventh floor; the one we'd watched Ania standing on the night before. I took a few steps forward and prepared myself to make the first jump.

'Bentley!'

'Yeah?' I asked, turning back to Hunter. 'What is it?'

'Don't fall,' he smirked.

'You're an asshole, Hunter.'

I looked up at the first balcony which was about fifteen feet above me. I took a few fast breaths before I forced a powerful burst of energy downwards that propelled me up into the air, just high enough for me to grab hold of the guard rail of the lowest balcony. I gripped it with both hands then pulled myself up before blasting out another wave of energy which sent me shooting upward again. Within a minute I was hanging off a fourth-floor balcony and there were only three more before I reached my destination.

I took a moment to compose myself then pushed another burst of energy down at my feet and I leaped up to the next balcony, this time adding a somersault just for good measure. I stood on the railings of the fifth-floor balcony and prepared my next jump but paused. There was a small child standing by the window in front of me and was waving furiously. I gave him a wink then fired myself up to the next floor where I took another few seconds before making the final jump.

I had no idea what was waiting for me up there. There was a good chance that death was anticipating my arrival and that this was my final moment in life. I couldn't delay any further, I had to throw caution to the wind and make the final leap.

I sent out a pulse towards my feet and I was lifted into the air. I reached out with both hands as I levitated upwards and snatched at the rough ironwork of the balcony railing. I hung there for a few seconds then slowly pulled myself up until I could peek into the apartment.

Ania was sitting on the other side of the glass door watching TV and combing her long, black hair. She was a very thin girl with pale skin and a gaunt face. Her large green eyes were glazed over as if she was in a trance and I noticed a few strands of grey in her raven hair. I knew she'd had a very difficult childhood, and in any other circumstance I would have said the poor girl looked traumatised. But the word that came into my mind while I watched her was 'demented' – she looked demented.

I looked around the room, but there was no sign of Sarah Fisher. She had to be in the next room over, which had a separate balcony. I quickly shuffled across the ledge then fired a modest amount of energy to my side that forced me out into the air, just far enough that I could catch the rail of the next balcony.

This time I simply climbed over the railing onto the narrow balcony. Sarah Fisher was sitting on a bed and staring right at me. She was small for her age, and had short blonde hair dangling either side of her round face. Her brown eyes were large and filled with terror. Somewhere deep inside them I caught a glimmer of relief that I had appeared.

I raised a finger to my lips then stepped forward and tested the glass door. It was unlocked and I gently pulled it open, without making a sound.

'I'm going to get you out of here,' I whispered to the child. 'I'm with some people who can protect you.'

She slowly stepped off the bed and nodded at me without saying a word.

'I want you to get up on my back and hold on tight. We have seven floors to climb down so don't let go no matter what happens. Do you understand?'

'Yes,' she said softly. 'I just need to bring my diary.'

'Hurry,' I whispered back.

I don't why I allowed her to retrieve the diary when we were in such precarious situation. It turned out to the biggest mistake I would ever make.

Sarah tip-toed across the room and reached for thick diary that was on top of chest of drawers in the corner of the room. She slid it off and when she did, the diary nudged a glass jug filled with water that was next to it. Even my lightening reflexes weren't enough to stop the glass from smashing on the wooden floor. It was loud enough to be heard over the TV in the next room and I would soon be under attack from a demented young girl who just happened to be a pure pyrokinetic.

I grabbed hold of Sarah and threw her over my shoulder then ran for the balcony. I stepped outside and was ready to climb over the railing but halted and looked right to see Ania standing on the next balcony over, her big, crazy eyes fixed on me.

'Bring Sarah back inside,' she said very calmly. 'She has to stay with us.'

'Ania, I think *you* should go back inside before there's any trouble,' I replied, doing a good job of hiding my fear. 'You don't want trouble, do you?'

'You're the only one here who's in trouble.'

It felt like my brain shivered when I sensed the attack was coming. I leaped up onto the railing with Sarah over my shoulder. I sent out a burst of kinetic energy at Ania – she was quicker than I expected and spun out of the way then countered my attack by reaching out and screaming at the top of her voice. Suddenly there was cloud of fire around her and it came flowing at me. I ducked and it went rushing over my head and dispersed into the evening air.

Before I knew it, there was another wave of flame rushed at my face and I lost balance. I fell backward and the firebolt swept over my head as Sarah and I went toppling over the railing, with a fall of over one hundred feet below us.

Paranoia was a ghost that haunted me for most of the twenty-seven years of life. It became somewhat overwhelming when The Eastern Shadow murdered my parents, and were threatening to kill my sister, Ania.

The torturous feeling left me temporarily – while I was working as an assassin for the Guild of the True. It then returned with a vengeance when I killed the Cramers and those children of theirs. I was constantly looking over my shoulder, expecting a trained killer to be bearing down on me. I did not know if they were already searching for me. Eventually they would come after me ... and probably find me.

I was extremely paranoid after I left the apartment that night. I did not want to leave the girls alone, but I had little choice. There was not enough food in the apartment to last us for more than a day. The short drive to the shopping centre was a necessary one.

I had kidnapped Sarah Fisher for money. Somehow JNCOR had picked up on the article written by that little coward, Lambell. Apparently they had been without a prophet for decades and would not allow this opportunity pass them by. But there was a problem: they had a truce with the Guild for years and did not want to break it. The agreement between the two groups was simple: The Guild had to stay out of Asia; JNCOR had to stay out of Europe. That meant JNCOR had to hire someone from the Guild to kidnap Sarah Fisher. I gratefully accepted their generous offer.

Finding her was simple though I had to kill people along the way. I had expected the body count to be higher. The waiting was the difficult part. Yanhao – my contact in JNCOR – could arrive at any moment to collect the child. But there was an equal chance that I could be kept waiting for a number of days.

I had been given keys to the apartment when I arrived in England after my escape from Switzerland, by a woman who worked as a spy for JNCOR. She said she had left enough supplies for at least three days. She had lied; I found only mouldy bread and sour milk when I arrived at the apartment. The two girls and I had gone over twenty-four hours with only water and I could not allow myself or my sister to grow weak. We needed our strength now more than ever.

I would have felt more comfortable if I had kept Ania close to me, but I could not risk taking Sarah Fisher out of the apartment. It was likely that she had been reported missing and had probably been mentioned on the news. It was too much of a risk to take. I had no choice but to leave Ania alone to watch over her.

I stopped the car in the centre of the car park. I had

a clear view of the building in front of me, and I could monitor the car park entrance from the road through the rear view mirror. The Guild had taught me such tactics while I was training to be an assassin. 'Always have your back covered.' It was one of the first things they told me.

I sat there watching the building and the road in the mirror for more than fifteen minutes before I turned off the engine and stepped into the chilled air. I stood next to the car for a few minutes more then made my way to the building. I scanned every face as I passed through the electronic doors to the brightness inside. There were lots of people hurrying about – something that irritated me about the non-gifted – they were always in such a big hurry. I watched everything and everyone around me.

I had to be vigilant at all times. The Guild would eventually find out that I faked my own death and would put out a contract on me. It was unlikely they had uncovered my ruse yet, but there were other potential dangers: Golding Scientific was watching everything that happened in the world of the gifted and it was likely their many assassins were searching for girl. JNCOR also represented a threat; it was easier for them to kill me and my sister than pay the ten million pounds ransom for the girl.

I walked the aisles of the supermarket and loaded bread and tinned foods into a trolley that rolled ahead of me all by itself. I was no longer afraid to use my gifts in public. I did not care what the non-gifted thought of me. They were maggots, nothing more. They had taunted me so much when I was a child. 'Freak!' they called me. It was strange thinking back on it. I had wanted nothing more than to be normal. To be like those jeering children – who were most likely jealous or afraid of me. I was a fool to be envious of normality. I no longer envied them. When I became an adult I saw how superior I was. I became confident where once I had been frightened. I remained a quiet person, though. I did not like to share my thoughts and feelings with others. I learned a long time ago that shared feelings can be used against you.

It was best to be a quiet man. A man who never *ever* reveals his true emotions. A man who never allows his strongest desires to dictate his actions. Cramer said I was repressed and needed help. He was saying something very different before I killed him! I took some pleasure in that. He thought he knew everything. He said I was nothing more than a novice. He deserved to die for that alone. He said I was not right for the Guild of the True. That was the only thing about me that he got right.

Killing people, particularly the non-gifted, always gave me immense pleasure. The non-gifted were so feeble that I found it difficult not to toy with them before ending their miserable existence. I had also taken pleasure in killing other gifted people, like those in Switzerland, but all gifted people are dangerous, even in their final moments, so I had to be clinical and efficient when killing them. I had taken no chances when I murdered the Cramers. After that I drowned the children and then allowed Ania to burn the house down to hide any evidence, and to burn beyond recognition the bodies that would pose as our own.

The two reporters and Sarah Fisher's foster parents had been so pitiful when they faced death and I teased them before I finished them off. That was fun. Particularly the foster parents, they had both cried and begged me to spare them. I dismissed their pleas and murdered them both while Sarah Fisher watched. I wanted her to feel the same anguish that I had felt when *my* parents were killed. I wanted *everyone* to share the pain I had endured.

'Do you have a club card, sir?' The checkout girl asked when I wheeled the trolley up to the till. She was young and pretty, but her smile was false. I hated that type of plastic pleasantness that normal people seemed to think was necessary.

'Do I look like someone who has a club card?' I asked. I purposely made my voice sound strict. Most people found it intimidating. 'Well?'

'I guess not.'

'Why do you guess? Are you unable to form an opinion?'

'I have opinions,' she said sheepishly.

'Oh, you do? What is your opinion of me?'

'I don't have one.' She began swiping the items over the laser as quickly as she could. 'I'm not paid to have opinions on customers.'

'So, they pay you not to have opinions or they pay you to adopt *their* opinions?'

'I'd rather not give my opinion, sir.'

I was using my mageletonia to stifle the blood circulating around her body. The girl's heart had to beat faster to compensate. It was a little trick I had learned when I was a teenager and I enjoyed seeing the flustered expression on people's faces when I used it. It could only be used on the docile, non-gifted. The technique takes time, which you rarely get when you are dealing with another gifted person.

If she only knew how close she was to death. I could have stopped the blood from passing through her heart at any moment. I could have ended her life without raising a finger.

'You seem to be in some discomfort,' I said to her, feigning concern. 'Was my questioning so difficult for you?'

'Leave me alone, you jerk!'

A security guard had noticed the girl's unease and stood near the till and folded his thick arms over his barrel chest. He fixed his dull gaze on me. I returned his stare.

'Everything all right here?' he asked the girl, nodding towards me with his flabby chin.

'Yeah. It's nothing I can't handle,' she replied.

'You just watch yourself, pal,' the guard told me.

'I will,' I tittered. 'I will watch myself.'

The checkout girl dragged the last of the items over the scanner and the total blinked on the screen next to her.

'Forty seven pounds fifty, sir.'

I handed her a fifty pound note and told her to keep the change; she did not thank me. I dumped the shopping into plastic bags and grinned at the security guard as I walked towards the entrance.

'You seem to be good at your job, but your *heart* is not in it.'

'What did you say?'

'Nothing of consequence.'

I continued towards the exit while I was using my mageletonia to control the guard's blood flow. Slowly the blood in his veins slowed and became stagnated. The burly guard hunched over clutching his chest. He crumbled to his knees and gurgled out a breath as his heart failed.

I continued to the exit at an even pace. I had done that dozens of times before and no one ever guessed it was murder. I believed I was the most prolific serial killer in the history of the human race. I liked that idea. It was a curious sensation to feel special. Yes, that idea gave me great satisfaction.

The paranoia returned as I crossed the car park.

🖛 🖛 🖛

Sarah was knocked free from my grasp when we toppled over the balcony. I reached for her, but she was out of range and we were plummeting to the ground at speed. I had to create a cushion of energy to break my fall. I couldn't be sure it would also save Sarah. I only had a couple of seconds to figure out what to do.

'Save yourself, Bentley!' I heard Hunter roar from the car park below. He was directly below us and I had to trust that he meant *he* would save Sarah from the impact.

I reached out and channelled energy out of body as I came hurtling towards the ground. It felt as if I was physically throwing the panic out of my body and using it to form a cushion that would stop me from hitting the ground. I formed the bubble of energy just in time and I spun high into air when I bounced off it. I tumbled back down to earth at high speed and crashed onto the bonnet of a parked car.

The deafening scream of the car alarm did not distract me from the stinging pain that was pulsing from the top of my arm. I had dislocated my shoulder when I landed on the car. I couldn't let this slow me down and quickly used my psychokinesis to pull the bones in my upper arm back into the socket. It went in with a loud *clunk* and I cut my lower lip from biting down on it so hard.

I climbed off the car and staggered forward to see Sarah Fisher uninjured, in Hunter's arms. He must have used his gift to cushion her before she fell into his grasp. We'd managed to save her and no one was hurt.

Farrier took the child and climbed into the back of the 4x4 while Hunter got into the driver's seat. I practically dived into the vehicle, but I jumped out as quickly as I got in. The upholstery was aflame and Hunter screamed at everyone to get out.

'Run. She's using her gift to burn the 4x4. Once the flames reach the engine it'll blow.'

Janice disappeared from the back of the vehicle and reappeared half way across the car park. Farrier and Hunter got out and led Sarah from the burning vehicle.

I looked up expecting to see Ania staring back from the eighth-floor balcony, but she was nowhere to be seen. That meant she was coming after us. I thought it best to stay and fight her off while the others escape then Hunter shouted at me to follow him.

'Bentley, don't be a hero. Come on, let's get to Linda's car and get the hell out of here!'

I raced after them, as I entered the street my hoodie caught fire and I barely managed to untangle myself from it before the flames burned through to my skin. I didn't dare look back and threw the burning hoodie to the ground and kept running.

I watched as the others climbed into Linda Farrier's car. I was almost there but was brought to a halt by a ball of fire that shot in front of me and surrounded the car. I spun round and Ania was standing in the road behind me. Her demented eyes were glowing with rage.

'Burn!' she screamed.

Panic overcame me. I knew she meant to set me alight and the mere thought of burning alive sent a tremor of terror through me. I lashed out instinctively, trying to create a wave to knock off her feet before she could produce another fireball, but I had sucked in too much energy from my surroundings. I swung my arm to create the wave and an unbelievable force was released; a car parked on the side of the road was struck and launched into the air. It spun like a skittle through the air and landed on Ania Zalech.

Time seemed to slow down when I realised what I'd done. I stood there hoping that she would somehow creep out from beneath the overturned vehicle, but I knew that was impossible. No one could survive a blow like that.

'Bentley, get in the car!'

I ignored Hunter. I had to be sure she was dead. I jogged across the street and around the wrecked vehicle to see it was lying on right top of Ania. All that was visible was her head, chest and arms.

She'd looked so insane and terrifying when she was alive. Now she looked nothing more than a helpless child, her frozen eyes staring sorrowfully at the sky.

I'd killed a child.

I spent more time looking at the mirrors than the road ahead as I drove from the shopping centre. No one was following me, but I would have to make another stop before returning to Ania; the petrol light on the dashboard was blinking bright orange and it is never wise to have an empty tank when you are on the run.

I parked the car next to the nearest pump to the road and switched off the engine. I looked along the road, across the forecourt, at the small store, and at the windows of the houses nearby. All was as it should have been. No one was following me.

I checked the contents of my trouser pockets as I left the car and found only some loose change and a few notes. I could not afford to fill the tank, but there was enough to buy me a few miles on the open road.

I looked at the meagre sum in my hands. It was all the money I had in the world. I was currently poorer than a beggar, but that was unimportant; I would have millions of pounds once I handed Sarah Fisher over to Yanhao.

The sum was a mere drop in the ocean for those who bankrolled JNCOR, but it would make a world of difference to my life. Not that I intended to live the life of luxury with the ransom money. No, I planned to use much of that sum to set up a stable life for Ania, one that was far away from the grasp of the Guild and other groups like them.

I would then use the rest of the money to exact my revenge against the people responsible for murdering my parents. Yes, once Ania was safe I would hunt down and punish Viktor Yeleshev and those who had aided him. Perhaps when I finally faced him I would be able to reveal my true self. Perhaps when we were eye to eye I would be free to release the anger and hatred and the violence that had been raging inside me since the night he shot my mother and father.

I leaned against the side of the car and slotted the nozzle of the petrol pump into the tank. The numbers on the digital screen climbing hypnotically. Fatigue was finally setting in. I badly needed sleep, but could not rest until I had offloaded the girl and received the money from Yanhao.

As the screen flicked to twenty I released the handle and returned the pump to the stand. I did it casually. I did it as if everything was normal. As if I had not noticed the man standing close to the streetlight across the road from the forecourt of the service station.

I recognised him immediately even though I had caught just a glimpse of his face. It was Motson – a mole who worked for the Guild. I had no idea how they had found me. That no longer mattered. I now had a fight on my hands. Not from of Motson – he was nothing – I was most likely surrounded by Guild agents.

I screwed the petrol cap back on and stared across the street at Motson. Out of the corner of my eye I saw other figures slowly approaching. They were closing in on me.

I took a step away from the car and looked at the four of them standing just beyond the boundary of the forecourt. I recognised Chapman, who was a mole like

Motson, and Adeyemi, an agent who was long past his prime. I had never seen the young man with glasses before, but he looked frightened and timid. I was confident that none of them posed much of a threat to me. This was not going to be the ferocious battle I had been expecting when the Guild finally caught up with me.

'You should have killed me while my back was turned,' I called out to Motson. 'Your only chance of victory is gone.'

'We are the Guild of the True. We don't need to shoot our enemies in the back.'

'You do when you are facing a foe more powerful than yourself. I am stunned that they only sent the four of you – and two of you are washed-up cowards who have spent your lives avoiding the dangerous missions. I would have thought they would send Hunter or Ballentine or perhaps even Armitage. Do they think so little of me that they believe idiots such as you can contend with me?'

'You underestimate us,' Motson smiled. 'I think four of us can handle one delusional young man who doesn't have a clue how to use his gifts.'

'I have a very good knowledge of the true gifts. I will show you once you have told me one thing.'

'And what might that be?'

'Why did you not kill me when you had the chance?'

'We want to know who you're working for, Edward. Tell us and we'll end this quickly.'

'We can't let you live, Edward,' Chapman added. 'You have become too much of a liability to us, and to the non-gifted.'

'Your crimes cannot go unpunished!' Adeyemi shouted across the street. His tone was far more aggressive than the others. 'You're sick in the head! How could you kill those children? Coward!'

'They were in my way. They had to be removed.'

'Speak like a man!' Adeyemi bawled. 'Fight like a man! Come on!'

I remained calm. Losing my temper and meeting them in a straight fight was not a good idea – it was exactly what they wanted. I decided on a more subtle approach. I began to use my gift of mageletonia.

Using this gift allowed me to sense and then control all liquids in the vicinity – as if they were part of my own body that I could control. It took only a couple of seconds to isolate the weakest of my adversaries by using the gift. Motson's blood was thick and full of toxins; his heart was working very hard to pump it around his body. He was not a healthy man. I chose him as my initial target.

'Motson, you smoke too much,' I said. 'Your blood is all *gooey*.'

Motson began to tremble as I seized control of the blood in his body.

'Such a nasty habit. One I am glad you indulged over the years. It has made killing you a lot easier than

I thought it would be.'

I took full control of the blood in his body and pre-vented it from passing through his heart. Motson tum-bled forward and was dead before his face smacked the pavement. I wasted no time in launching an attack against the others.

I spun round and used my psychokinetic power to yank two of the petrol pumps free of their stands and then quickly switched gifts and used my mageletonia to control the petrol pouring out.

Within a split second there was a funnel of petrol that whipped through the air and created a barrier between me and the agents of the Guild.

Adeyemi was first to react. He sent a precise pocket of kinetic energy that pierced the liquid shield. It was not strong enough to penetrate the inner shield – I had also created a thin cocoon of kinetic energy as back up. I was pleasantly surprised at how feeble the assault was. This emboldened me to go on the offensive and I pinpointed the most immobile of the three remains agents: Chapman.

I allowed the petrol to disperse from the orb and it shot forward and doused Chapman. The impact was powerful enough to knock her to the ground and send her skating across the road.

Suddenly there was a bright flash and I threw my arms over my face and ducked behind my car. One of them was obviously a light-tuner and was trying to blind me. It was an old and common trick, but one that was quite effective when used properly. I remained hidden and used my power to gather up all the loose petrol on the roadside and mould it into a spinning ball of fluid that hovered across the forecourt.

My attackers had fanned out when they should have combined their powers to attack. It gave me enough time to recreate the cocoon of energy that would protect me as I restarted my assault. I stood up from my hiding place and scanned the forecourt.

I noticed Adeyemi using a parked van as cover and fired the ball of petrol as fast as I could. It struck the van, missing the actual target. That did not matter. The force of the impact had created a spark than consumed the floating mass of petrol and there was a tremendous explosion that surrounded the van and Adeyemi. My most imposing of opponents had been dealt with. Now all I had to do was eliminate the other two and I could be on my way.

There was blue flash in front of me as Chapman shot a bolt of electricity across the forecourt. It had not been strong enough to penetrate my shield and Chapman – without knowing it – had made her final mistake. She had revealed herself. I gathered the flaming petrol and weaved it into an immense whip of fire then I lashed out at the old woman.

She tried to run, but the flames slashed her back. Her clothes, already soaked with petrol, caught fire. I watched her running aimlessly and screaming in sheer terror as her body was consumed with flames. For a moment I considered ending her misery by shooting a kinetic slice at her ... I quickly decided not to. Her wailing would surely distract the last of my enemies: the young light-tuner.

I could not see him. I knew he was most likely cloaked and cowering in a corner of the forecourt. There was no time to track him down. Instead I decided to allow nature to do my work for me. I paced away from the petrol station onto the road and then sent the last of the burning petrol towards the bank of pumps. The blast was awesome and rumbled the ground under my feet. The fearful light-tuner was most likely barbequed and I could now slip away into the night.

Some locals had left their homes and were standing at the far end of the road, watching the inferno. Others were pressed against the windows of the little houses, their frightened faces painted orange in the glow of the roaring blaze. I kept my head bowed as I walked, not wanting these maggots to give my description to the authorities. Police posed no threat to me, but were an annoyance I could do without.

The battle had been so easy. I loved that I could now dominate not only normal people, but those with gifts. Even the mighty Guild had now failed in trying to kill me. I wiped the perspiration from my brow as I quickened my pace. I had broken a sweat, but that was only because of the heat from the flames and not because of the meagre challenge the agents had represented.

I stalled on the pavement and spun to my left. The sinuous black shape was so fast I could not focus on it. I could not even identify what it was. Only when it had leaped into the air and was coming straight at my face did I identify it as a panther.

My reflexes were lightning fast, but the shock of seeing such a beast bearing down on me meant I hesitated in the most pivotal moment. The large black feline smacked me flush in the face with one of its powerful paws and I felt my teeth rattle out of my gums into the back of my mouth.

I fell back onto the ground and before I could get up the cat dashed across the pavement from behind and latched onto either side of my face with its claws shredding deep into the flesh. It then wrapped its jaws around my neck and its fangs sank into my throat.

Blood was fizzing out of my neck and was pushing up into my mouth. In that last moment I gathered my psychokinetic power and launched the cat into the air. It landed in the middle of the road and an oncoming vehicle struck it before it could attack once more.

The panther was dead yet I was no better off. I could not move and just lay there in an ever widening pool of my own blood. I heard the chatter of the locals along with distant sirens before life finally drained out of me.

CHAPTER TWELVE

Prophecies of Doom

As I sat slumped in the back seat, all I could think of was the empty stare in Ania's eyes. I would never forget her lifeless expression and the shock of realising I had killed her. She was nothing more than a child and I *killed* her. I had joined the Guild to protect gifted youngsters and on my first mission I killed one. I felt like a monster for what I had done. All I wanted to do was throw myself from the car and die.

'Hold it together, Bentley,' Hunter said over his shoulder from the front passenger seat. 'You did the right thing.'

'That wasn't the right thing to do,' I replied instantly. 'Killing someone is never right.'

'She would have burned you alive,' Farrier added, as she steered the car into corner and shifted gear. 'You were backed into a corner and did the only thing you could. No one will hate you for this. Everyone will understand.'

'I don't care what everyone thinks. Everyone doesn't have a young girl's death on their conscience.'

'Don't they …?' Farrier said distantly. 'A lot of us have done worse in the past.'

'Well, maybe I'm in the wrong profession.'

'You're not in the wrong profession, Bentley,' Hunter interjected. 'What happened back there proves you're perfect for this line of work. That girl would have killed us all if she'd been given the chance. You saved people's lives and acted when you needed to.'

'It doesn't feel very heroic.'

'Heroes only exist in fairytales. I'll talk to you about this when we reach safety. Just try to keep it together until then.'

'Where are we going?' Janice asked – the first words she'd said since the fight.

'Good question,' Hunter replied as he turned to Farrier. 'We'll have to get the girl to Peter Williams.'

'I know. We can get there in five hours if we don't make any stops.'

'Sounds like a plan.'

'Are you all right?' Janice asked the young girl, who was sitting in the centre of the backseat. 'Are you hurt at all?'

The child looked dazed at first, then she shook her head and lurched forward. She sucked in a deep breath then vomited at my feet. Janice patted her on the back and pulled her hair away from her face. I turned to the window and ignored the puke on my runners. I couldn't even take pleasure from knowing that I had saved Sarah Fisher. I had traded the life of one child for another's.

The first bang sounded like a firework in the distance. It caught our attention, but didn't set off any alarm bells. The second was like thunder and I felt the force of it rumbling my stomach.

'What the hell was that?' Janice asked. 'Sounded like a bomb or something.'

'It's going to be the big fire,' Sarah said quietly.

'What?' Farrier asked.

'Ignore her. We can't be wasting any more time,' Hunter demanded. 'Linda, we have to get out of this town as quickly as we can.'

'That might have been the others,' Janice continued. 'They could be in trouble.'

'We can't forsake them, Hunter,' Farrier insisted. 'That's not the way the Guild does things.'

'Damn it,' Hunter said after a moment of deliberation. 'Take the left turn up ahead, it'll lead us towards the town centre.'

As soon as the car banked left we saw a great orange glow rising above the rows of houses. I couldn't imagine what had caused such a fire but all I could think of was Cathy. Was she caught up in it? Was she still alive? Losing her would make life unbearable.

We turned onto one of the main streets and saw the fire in full flow. A petrol station was consumed by the immense blaze that was spilling out on to the road and snatching at the roofs of nearby houses. There were scores of weary people wandering the street and police officers were rushing here and there and pushing them back from the area. Smaller, secondary explosions erupted from the epi-centre of the fire and thick black smoke was belched out over the crowd. It looked as if we'd driven to the gates of hell and at any moment the devil would appear before us.

Farrier slowed the car to a halt as pyjama-clad youngsters flooded past us on the pavements and we all stared ahead at the rising flames.

'Move back!' a police officer, who appeared out of nowhere screamed at Farrier. 'Get this car out of here!'

She didn't argue with him. It was best not to draw attention to us and she swung the car onto an adjacent street and picked up speed. As we got to the end of the street a figure emerged from a doorway of a grocery store and flagged us down. It was Cathy and she appeared unharmed.

I pushed my door open as the car slowed and she dived in and sat in the middle next to Sarah Fisher, who had drifted back into that daze she'd been in since the fall from the seventh floor of the apartment block.

'Are you all right?' I asked her.

'I think so.'

'What happened?' Hunter asked. 'Where are the others?'

'Dead. They're all dead.'

'And Zalech?'

'He killed them one by one. He was escaping so I switched my mind into Nightshade and tried to stop him. My head is so sore – Nightshade was killed and I switched out of his body just in time. A second later and my mind would have died too.'

'*Zalech*?' Hunter turned to her. 'Did you kill him?'

'I tore his throat out …'

'That settles it then,' Farrier said. 'Let's get the hell out of here.'

'Not so fast,' Hunter replied. 'They are too many of us to travel in one car and we'll be running the risk of getting pulled over by the police. I think we should split up.'

'You're probably right. We should borrow another vehicle.'

'Now is a good time to steal one, while the cops are distracted with the fire,' said Hunter.

We drove slowly around the streets looking for an appropriate vehicle and my nerves were choking me. Ania's lifeless face in my mind again and I was finding it hard to catch my breath. The only thing that got me through the dreadful hour was Cathy, who never let go of my hand. When we finally found a suitable car, Hunter used his gift to bypass the lock and he got it going within a few seconds. Linda Farrier and Janice switched over to the stolen car and she said she would head to Manchester and lie low for a couple of days.

Cathy sat up front as Hunter drove, and I remained in the back with Sarah who was mumbling quietly to herself. As soon as we reached the first motorway I capitulated to fatigue – or perhaps it was shock – and was out cold.

❧ ❧ ❧

I woke to see the sun rising over the horizon with a blue and pink sky overhead, a welcome change to the grey skies and the rain that had lasted for many weeks. The car was parked outside a roadside diner, an all-night place for weary travellers and truckers to take rest and fill up on cheap grub. Sarah was sleeping next to me, still clutching that accursed diary of hers. I looked at the glass front of the diner and saw Hunter and Cathy inside, standing by the counter. I caught Cathy looking back at me and smiling. She was so beautiful. I was reminded of the first time she smiled at me, when I was staying at her home and had shot her with a paintball. It seemed a lifetime had passed since that day. So much had happened and I had gone through so many changes and tragedies.

I was cast into a dark place when I thought of Ania Zalech crushed under the car. That same shock I felt when it happened kept repeating inside me every time I pictured it. It would take a long time to banish that image from my mind and even longer to cleanse my soul of the guilt. I had robbed her of so much. At least I'd saved the others from harm. Knowing that I'd saved them from hideous burns or worse made the guilt *almost* bearable.

My gloomy thoughts were chased away when Cathy pulled open the door next to me and plonked a brown paper bag on my lap.

'Chips, cheeseburger and nuggets,' she said with a tired smile. 'Eat it before it gets cold.'

She sat in the front next to Hunter, who was chomping into a chicken burger, and looked back at Sarah.

'I got her some too. Should we wake her?'

'I think you better,' Hunter said with his mouth full. 'I doubt the child has eaten since she was abducted.'

I reached over and nudged her, but she didn't stir.

'Leave her, Ross,' Cathy said. 'She looked tormented a few hours ago and I think the sleep will do her good. The last thing we need is her in hysterics while other people are around.'

'She did look a bit wired, didn't she?'

'So would you if you'd been abducted.'

'At least she's safe,' Hunter said as he finished his meal and wiped his fingers on the lapel of his jacket. 'And those two lunatics are dead which means she can sleep soundly from now on.'

'Have some respect for the dead,' I said to him.

'Respect,' he spat. 'Edward Zalech killed more than a dozen people in the last week, most of whom were gifted and valuable members of the Guild. There were also children amongst his victims and you think I should show him respect? Should I *mourn* his passing?'

'Just didn't sound right the way you said it.'

'Bah! He can rot in his grave now.'

'That's if he's dead,' Cathy said as she picked her at the basket of chips on her lap.

'What did you just say?' Hunter leaned towards her and his eyes looked ready to pop out of his head. 'I thought you said that you killed him?'

'Well … he was dying. I presume he's dead, but I didn't actually see him die.'

'Marvellous.' Hunter gave a weary sigh and rubbed his face. 'That's just marvellous.'

'Lay off her, Hunter. Cathy's been through the mill and she doesn't need you interrogating her now.'

'Bentley, you would want to alter the tone of your voice when you speak to me because that sounded almost like you were telling me what to do. There was even a hint of a warning there.'

'Hunter, you seem to forget I'm not afraid of you. I wasn't giving you a warning; I was simply telling you to ease off.'

'It's my job to ensure that psychopath can't hurt anyone else. I need to be certain he's not still wandering around the north-east of England drowning people in their own juices!'

'When I was fighting him, through Nightshade's body,' Cathy said, 'I managed to bite into his neck. That was a fatal injury in itself. Just before the end he managed to use psychokinesis to throw me into the road, but when he did I tore out a large part of his throat. There's no one who could survive that.'

'You sure?'

'No, I'm not *sure*. I'm simply telling you what happened. You can draw your own conclusions.'

'I doubt he could have lived after that,' Hunter admitted after a moment. 'How did the others die?'

'Horribly. He was in control of a petrol spillage and used it to shield himself and also used it as a weapon. At some point the petrol ignited and he used this flaming rope like a lasso that wrangled the others so easily. He wiped them out in a couple of minutes.'

'Lucky we have you on our side then, isn't it?'

'No. Lucky it was dark and I chose a black cat. It *was* pure luck that he didn't see Nightshade approach. I can only imagine what he could have done if he'd managed to escape. He was so strong, Hunter.'

'I know. Be thankful he was never trained to maximise his gifts. You cannot imagine how dangerous a fully-trained mageleton can be.'

'I don't want to imagine it,' Cathy said, shaking her head. 'I still don't feel good about killing him … it makes me *sick* every time I think about it.'

'Cathy, he had to be stopped before he could murder any more people. God knows he killed enough. Can't say I was too fond of Motson, but he didn't deserve to die at the hands of that maniac. Neither did the others … Christ, two of them were only weeks away from retiring from the Guild altogether.'

'Some times I don't think I'm cut out for this,' Cathy said before she turned to look at Sarah. 'I hope she was worth all this.'

'Me too,' I said. I thought back to how Ania was alerted to my presence and started to wonder why Sarah had insisted on bringing her diary. 'I wonder what's in that journal. She grabbed hold of it like her very life depended on it.'

'Most likely it's important notes on how fluffy the clouds are,' Hunter snorted, 'or how the colour pink is prettier than blue.'

'Or they could be a record of her premonitions.'

'We'll know soon enough. I'm sure Peter Williams will sniff out if she has a true gift or not.'

'Will you be staying at the house too?' Cathy asked him. 'You could probably do with some sleep.'

'No. I'll drop the three of you off then go straight to the Palatium to speak with the Council about what happened last night.'

'You think they'll be ticked off?' I asked.

'Not half as ticked off as I am, Bentley. I want to know what they were doing sending lightweights like Motson and Chapman to assassinate Edward Zalech. Believe me, Ballentine has a lot of explaining to do.'

He lifted the handbrake and reversed out on the road before shifting into first and flooring the accelerator. The car jolted when it hit the road and Sarah lurched forward, her eyes wide open and her hands clutching her diary so tight that her knuckles were white.

'It's all right,' I told her. 'You're safe.'

'We're not safe.'

'What do you mean?'

She sank slowly back into her seat and a deep frown fell over her face.

'Those two won't bother you again, lass,' Hunter said from the front. 'They won't bother anyone again.'

'That's what you think.'

'What do you mean?' Cathy asked, turning quickly and fixing

her gaze on the young girl. 'Have you seen them in the future?'

'I'm not sure. There's a lot of darkness ahead and it's hard for me to see anyone clearly.'

'You think we're in danger?' I asked her.

She nodded slowly.

'What have you seen?'

'There's a big shadow spreading over the world.'

'What's casting such a big shadow?'

'Bad people,' she said. She looked away from me and her grip on the journal tightened.

'Who are these bad people?'

'Bentley, you're giving her an audience,' Hunter said. 'Leave it to Williams to figure out what she's capable of.'

The car fell silent after that. I guess no one was in the mood of talking, and each of us had a lot on our minds. The journey to the Williams estate was a long and very uncomfortable one.

I experienced a strange mix of emotions when we turned off the narrow road and through the tall gates of the Williams' estate. I felt secure coming to this place, but also felt great sorrow when I remembered the last time I drove away from the house and left Cathy and her mother behind. And there was also the memory of bringing Romand here only a few months before, dragging him out of the car onto the lawn and trying to revive him to no avail. Romand had been a tough mentor but I missed him a lot, especially in times of trouble. He'd have made some sense of the regret and confusion that filled my heart.

Mr Williams was standing in the shadows of the front door-way when we left the car and stepped outside to greet us as we approached. He kissed Cathy on the cheek then shook my hand before stooping to talk to Sarah.

'Well, well, well,' he said. 'Who do we have here?'

'Sarah,' she replied. 'Sarah Fisher.'

'Pleased to meet you, Sarah Fisher. My name is Peter and I'm hoping I can help you to cope with all that you have had to endure throughout your short life.'

'I don't know what you mean,' she said, wrinkling her brow.

'I'll explain it all after you've had some rest and gotten used to your new surroundings.'

'I get to stay here?' she looked up at the tall and rather grand façade of the house. 'It's much nicer than the last place I lived.'

'Safer too,' Hunter added.

'Indeed,' Mr Williams smiled. 'Let's go inside, shall we?'

Cathy took the girl inside the house and brought her through to the kitchen while Mr Williams led Hunter and me into the sitting room; he said he needed to know what happened up north right away. His mood went very sombre once inside and he told us to sit down while he remained on his feet near the window.

'I've heard some rather disturbing reports from the north-east this morning,' he said as he clasped his hands behind his back. 'I take it all did not go according to plan?'

'You can say that again,' Hunter laughed, although there was no hint of amusement in his voice. He looked very tired and his eyes were circled with shadows; I don't know how he managed to stay awake because he hadn't had a wink of sleep in over two days.

'The rescue was an unmitigated disaster,' Hunter went on, giving the arm of the couch a tired slap. 'I've never been involved in such a mess in all my years with the Guild. We should be thankful that young Bentley here was involved. He was the one who saved the kid.'

It should have felt good to get praised by Hunter, but it simply reminded me of what had happened after I rescued Sarah from the apartment.

'Well done, Ross,' Williams said. He gave me a smile that disappeared when he saw how dejected I was. He didn't question me and returned to his conversation with Hunter. 'I've heard Edward Zalech remerged.'

'Yeah. He was the one behind the killings in Switzerland and he was the other person searching for Sarah. He murdered those newspaper people and he also managed to kill Motson and his team.'

'Dear God,' Mr Williams breathed; he seemed to shrink right before our eyes at this news. 'Chapman and Adeyemi were friends of mine … They were ready for retirement … And Motson … he had three young children.'

'A tragedy,' Hunter said quietly. 'No doubt about it.'

'How did it come to this?' Mr Williams said. 'I had hoped Edward had conquered his demons and would become a decent man and a valuable member of our group. He had made so much progress in recent times …'

'He was a bloody psycho.'

'I only spoke with him a few weeks ago. There was no hint that he could commit such atrocities.'

'I saw what he did,' I said, leaning forward in my chair. 'He had no regard for human life and he had to be stopped. If you'd only seen what he did to the newspapers editor and his wife you'd realise how twisted he really was.'

'And what has become of Edward?'

'Most likely dead,' Hunter answered. 'Cathy switched her mind into Nightshade's body and attacked him as he fled.'

'*Cathy* killed him!' Mr Williams gasped. 'How has she been coping with this?'

'Been pretty quiet the whole way down here. She's doing fine, though, as far as I can tell.'

'I'll speak with her shortly, to be sure. This has not turned out to be the simple rescue mission we thought it would have been.'

'It certainly didn't,' Hunter nodded. 'I'm going to kill Ballentine for leaving Motson in charge of the operation. He sent civilians into a war and there's only one outcome when that happens.'

'There was no one else to send, Hunter. All our British-based operatives have been flown to the continent to track down the Cramer's murderer. Ballentine had no one other than Motson and his team to call on. At least the two of you and Cathy survived. What of Linda? Is she alive?'

'Linda is fine,' Hunter said. 'She returned to Manchester with Janice Powell. They'll lie low for a few days.'

'Good,' Mr Williams nodded thoughtfully. 'That's the wisest course of action. So, were there any clues as to *why* Edward Zalech turned?'

'None. But I find it hard to believe he was acting alone. He must have been working for someone, or at least planning to sell the girl to one of our competitors.'

'That would make sense. I wonder who got to him.'

'Probably Golding,' I said. 'He seems to be everywhere.'

'He would top the list of suspects.' Mr Williams agreed. 'Oh, and Edward's sister? Where is she?'

'Dead,' Hunter said with no emotion. 'Bentley killed her.'

'I was acting in self-defence – not that it makes me feel any better about it. Jesus, I feel like getting sick every time I think about her.'

'It's never easy to kill,' Mr Williams said as he turned to me. 'I understand what you must be going through, Ross. We should talk this over, you and I, at great length.'

'I don't want to talk about it.'

'Trust me, Ross. You cannot continue in the Guild if this incident makes you hesitate in the future. There will always be threats to the gifted and we need agents who can deal with killing, if it's needed.'

'I didn't turn into a sissy all of a sudden. It's just … if it had been Edward that I killed I'd probably feel proud of myself, but Ania was just a kid. We don't even know she was involved in the murders. Edward could have told her that *they* were rescuing Sarah and that *we* were the bad guys who were trying to harm her. Maybe that's why Ania reacted so violently.'

'You're making up excuses for her,' Hunter argued. 'She didn't seem to have the child's wellbeing at heart when she shot fire at you both and sent you tumbling off that balcony.'

'I suppose – even so, she was only twelve or thirteen. I wouldn't have wanted to die for things I'd done at that age … '

'There's no supposing! Those two snatched the girl for money.

End of.'

'You think we'll find out who was behind it now that they're both dead?' I asked. 'I'd sure like to see the people responsible punished.'

'Unlikely.'

'There will have to be an investigation into what happened,' Mr Williams added. 'There always are in such circumstances.'

'Hopefully it will be a proper one this time,' Hunter said under his breath.

'It will be,' Mr Williams snapped. He was obviously tiring of Hunter's abrasive attitude. 'We will have a meeting at the Palatium about this.'

'I'm going there as soon as you make me a cup of coffee.'

'No, Hunter. Stay the night; you look dead on your feet.'

'I'll live.'

'Sleep on it, old friend. You're tired and cranky and will only be going there looking for a fight. Best not to argue with the Council. You know this better than anyone.'

'What are they going to do? Kick me out of the club? They need me now more than ever.'

'They can have you working on the worst investigations imagina-ble if you alienate yourself further. Remember the suicide missions they used to send you and Romand on? They only did it because the two of you constantly bickered with them.'

'All right, all right. How about that cup of coffee?'

'I'm not the butler here, Hunter. Get it yourself!'

Hunter pushed himself off the couch with a groan and sauntered out into the hallway. Mr Williams took Hunter's seat when he left and focused his studious gaze on me.

'I can see by your face that you've found these last few months very arduous.'

'That's one way to describe living with Hunter. He's a very difficult man, you know.'

'There's a warm heart under that prickly exterior,' he smiled. 'I am glad to see you, Ross. I want you to know we took no joy in exiling you to the wilderness. We did it for your own safety.'

'I understand that. But I don't want to go back there, Mr Williams. I've spent too much of my life hiding and I don't want to do it anymore.'

'I'll accompany Hunter to the Council tomorrow. I will speak with them about your situation and ask if you can remain here for the time being.'

'Thanks, Mr Williams.'

We went to the kitchen to find Hunter raiding the fridge. I was famished and started stuffing my face. Mr Williams made a pot of tea and then the three of us went to sit on the benches outside on the patio overlooking the grounds. The mighty oak that stood over Romand's grave was a couple of hundred yards down the sloping lawn and they had a wooden bench next to it. Cathy was sitting there watching Sarah running around chasing, then being chased by, a Jack Russell puppy.

It was almost like I had returned to the summer at the Atkinson house. There was a feeling of normality in simply watching the two of them in the shade of the old oak. It had been so long since I'd seen people smiling and a child playing innocently. Finally there were no monsters lurking around the corner. No back-breaking chores. No depressing silence. I'd spent far too long in isolation.

I made up my mind right then and there that I would refuse to go back to the cottage with Hunter. No matter what the Council decided. Hunter's place wasn't good for my soul. *He* was well able for the solitude, but I was different.

'How is Cathy's mum?' I said to Mr Williams. 'I heard she moved to France for a few months, with your wife.'

'June is steadily improving, but not quite back to her old self just yet. I'm confident she will make a full recovery in time. Romand's death, along with the destruction of her home, was too much for her mind to deal with. There was a breakdown. Slowly I have helped her to rebuild and to recover. My holiday home in France is a very peaceful place and it should be the perfect environment for her.'

'And Cathy? How has she been?'

'Cathy is as strong as any person I have ever encountered. You don't need to worry about her.'

'I wonder if the kid really does have a true gift,' I said as I watched Sarah running around after the puppy.

'We'll know soon enough,' Mr Williams replied. 'I have a lot of experience with prophets and I know how to weed out the fakes.'

'I hope she isn't genuine.'

'Why's that?'

'Because she said something rather disturbing on the way here.'

'Tell me.'

'She said there was a dark shadow spreading across the world.'

Peter Williams said nothing, but looked deeply troubled.

CHAPTER THIRTEEN

The Tin Man

Mr Williams started preparing dinner and soon after that Hunter grumbled that he didn't want any fancy food and went upstairs to get some much-needed sleep. Cathy and I stayed out back and kept an eye on Sarah, who was already very attached to the puppy, that she'd christened 'Hopper' on account of his ability to hop off the ground without ever getting tired. Cathy and I chatted very much like we had that summer, as if everything was right with the world. Everything had changed though, that much was obvious in her eyes. She had become a killer, just like I had, and there was no way of recapturing the innocence we once had. It still felt like heaven being close to her. I had missed that long red hair, the freckles on her nose, her emerald eyes, her smile, the way she laughed, the way she talked, the way she liked to hold my hand. It wasn't difficult to miss perfection.

'Still thinking about what happened?' she asked after a moment of silence between us.

'Hard not to,' I said, rolling my eyes. 'Still can't believe I killed her.'

'Did you mean to do it?'

'No. I lost control and my powers increase tenfold when that happens. I worry what might happen if I ever lost my cool when people I care for are in the way.'

'We all lose our temper, Ross, and according to Hunter she was preparing to kill you and the others! Look,' she nodded at Sarah running across the lawn with Hopper right behind her, 'she's here and safe because of what you did. Ania chose her own path. She didn't have to chase you into that street. She didn't have to try and kill you. You did the only thing you could.'

'I've come to terms with that. But it's just that she was so young …'

'I know what you mean.'

'How do you feel about what you did to Edward Zalech?'

'It makes me feel sick that he forced me to kill him. I realise his actions led to it, not mine.' She moved close and rested her cheek on my shoulder. 'I'm just glad that he's gone and I hope we won't have to deal with people like him and Marianne again for a long time.'

'Me too.' I kissed her forehead and wrapped my arm over her shoulder. I couldn't shake the feeling that we would soon be up against another psychotic killer. The world of the gifted seemed littered with them. It was only a matter of time before the next one emerged from obscurity.

'I don't think this is the life for me, Ross. I'm not a killer. I don't ever want to take another life again.'

'I know, Cathy. Hopefully they won't send us out to fight again for a long time.'

'I hope not.'

I watched Sarah playing with the puppy and she looked like any normal kid, but there was something sinister lurking in her mind. Although the others were uncertain of her gift, I was sure she had caught a glimpse of the future, and according to her it was very, very dark. I didn't really want to know what she'd seen. I didn't want the others to know either. That would mean we would have to deal with it.

At 7pm we were called inside and sat at the long and rather formal-looking dinner table. It was a contrast to what I'd gotten used to while living with Hunter and I felt a little awkward in such fine surroundings. There wasn't much said over dinner, and there was absolutely no talk of Guild business. I think we were all glad to have some time away from it.

Hunter still hadn't appeared as we were cleaning up. I was hoping Sarah and Mr Williams would go away so I could spend some time alone with Cathy, but Sarah had grown quite attached to her and followed her wherever she went. It seemed like we were in for a night of babysitting until Mr Williams suggested that the three of us go with him to his private animal sanctuary which was only a twenty-minute drive away. Cathy, an animal lover, jumped at the chance, and Sarah seemed excited by it too. I wasn't all that crazy about animals, but I needed a distraction so I went along with them.

Mr Williams took us there in one of his cars, a Mercedes, that he described as 'vintage', but it was just an old banger to my eyes. It was a short trip, thankfully, and he parked in one of three spots outside a property surrounded with tall fences. We passed through the entrance and a security guard gave Mr Williams the keys to get into the main area.

We went strolling around the pathways as the flood lights powered up for the night. I'd been expecting it to be like a zoo, however there weren't too many enclosures and I didn't see any animals in them either, which made the visit seem a bit pointless to me.

'Where are all the animals?' I wondered. 'Are they light-tuners?'

'Very funny,' Mr Williams replied. 'Most are watching you as if you were a giant, walking hotdog.'

'Yeah, right.'

He whistled as we neared one of the plexiglass barriers and within a flash there were three grey wolves only yards away sniffing at the air and staring back at us.

'Where the hell do you get these from? Aren't there laws banning them?'

'There are, but many wealthy and bored people flout these laws and when the animals reach maturity they realise it's too dangerous to keep them and they disregard them. Most end up in zoos, but some come my way and I am glad to look after them.'

'And then they come under my control,' Cathy laughed wickedly. 'I spend endless hours here. My control over my gift has doubled in the last three months. You should see the tricks I can do with the spiders!'

'I like spiders,' Sarah said. I got the feeling she didn't and just said to impress Cathy.

'Come on,' Cathy said taking her hand. Obviously dying to show off her new skills to an eager audience.

Peter and I continued along the path and we caught glimpses of a number of his exotic animals. There were hyenas, vultures, black bears, lions, jaguars, and I even spotted the familiar feathered pattern of the Steller's sea eagle that had delivered Cathy's letter to me while I was in Scotland.

'You know, I was about your age when I joined the Guild,' Mr Williams said, as we admired the eagle. 'It was way back in 1957 and it remains crystal clear in my mind – for many reasons.'

'Damn, that's a long time ago. I'm surprised you can remember anything about it.'

'I remember it like it was only yesterday. I joined the Guild in March of that year, I met my lovely wife, Maria, in June of that year, and I went on my first official duty in December of that year. I also killed for the first time in December 1957.'

'Sounds like a familiar story.'

'Yes. The similarities between my youth and yours have not been lost on me. I know of the remorse – the shame even – in taking a human life. Particularly the first human life you take. I tormented myself for many months after it happened until in the summer of 1958 I saw what happens when you hesitate in a life or death situation. That took away a lot of the remorse.'

'This a pep talk?'

'No. Just talk.'

'Who was the first person you killed?'

'I don't know his name, and never will. He was a young man – similar age to myself – but he was on the enemy's side.'

'Which enemy? There seems to be many.'

'They were based in Czechoslovakia at that time but were founded in Germany before the Second World War. They were known as '*Gotteskrieger*' – roughly translated as 'The Warriors of God'. But they were not doing the work of God. Far from it. They had infiltrated the Nazi party during their rise to power in the late 1930s and had worked their way into various positions of influence. They had an even more warped view than most Nazis: they felt that *all* humans were inferior to them, and that after the war, if Germany had won, they could seize control of the third Reich and then dictate to the world of the non-gifted.

'They vanished after Germany lost the war, only to appear yet again in 1952 in Czechoslovakia under the guise of the *Bojovnici Lidi* – Czech for 'The Warriors of the People'. The plan was a similar one: they would infiltrate communism, rise through the ranks and then in an unstable moment they would seize control. They never got that far, as their plot was uncovered in 1955 by the *Statni Bezpecnost* and they were chased out of Eastern Europe altogether. The Guild was aware of them for a long time. However they posed no threat to us until in the late 1950s when some of their operatives arrived in London. I was one of the younger agents in the Guild and I took part in the quest to hunt them down.

'We'd gotten a tip-off that one of them was renting a flat in Tottenham and I was sent with my mentor, Kevin Watts, to *remove* him. I was to wait at the back of the block of flats in case the man made a run for it. He did. And I panicked and killed him as he tried to get past me. Panic is often a gifted person's worst enemy. Later I learned that hesitation is even worse. I had to be sent away from London after what had happened. I spent six months in Devon with some Guild retirees as I struggled to come to terms with what I had done. When I was back to my normal self I was drafted back into the fight and on my first outing we came up against Lucas Skala, who was the last, and most desperate, member of the *Gotteskrieger*.

'I was part of a four-man team – that's what we called it but we were actually two men and two women – and we tracked Skala down to the docks. A colleague of mine, Stephen Kenny, had Skala cornered, but hesitated and was killed, as was one of our female colleagues, and seven civilians. I found Skala two days later and assassinated him. It could not bring back my colleagues. I'd learned the hard way how destructive hesitation can be.'

'I won't hesitate if I find myself in a scenario like that, Mr Williams. I'm not comfortable with killing, and I'm deeply sorry for taking the life of that girl, but if someone like Marianne or Zalech were to cross my path in the future I would not hesitate, not for an instant. I know they have to be stopped. And I know it's my job to do it.'

'You are a wiser man than I was at your age,' he gave me a pat of approval on the shoulder. 'I do hope you will have time to reflect on the matters in the north-east before the Council allows you into a situation like that again. I also hope you will welcome the time to be an ordinary person again, and not throw yourself into one conflict after another, in the way that Hunter has done. I won't like it if you become as cold and solitary as him.'

'I can't be solitary. I love Cathy too much for that.'

'And she feels the same, I'm sure. You're all she ever talks about.'

'Can't blame her really,' I joked. 'I am pretty awesome.'

'Cocky too!' He smiled.

'I'm modest really.'

'Your powers, though, are not. How have you been dealing with them? Have you noticed increased control or levels in the effectiveness of your gifts?'

'I had more control until I killed Ania Zalech. They certainly are more effective and they seem to be increasing all the time. I've also learned about other gifts from Hunter.'

'You need to learn *more* about them. I will give you some books that should help you. It will also help to take your mind off more sombre matters.'

'Are you talking about Romand's paper that I brought to your house after he died?'

'No. I have an old book that was written by a talented psychokinetic who had mastered all the known techniques in combat, and also invented a few of his own. You'll find it invaluable.'

'I'll look forward to it, I learned loads from the Ala Qush writings Romand gave me before,' I said. 'Mr Williams, can I ask a favour of you?'

'Of course you can.'

'When you visit the Council tomorrow, tell them that I didn't set out to kill Ania Zalech. I want them to know that I'm not a maniac who can't control himself. I want them to realise that I'm not another Edward Zalech.'

'There's no need for me to convince them of your sanity or motives, Ross. They have very high hopes for you.'

'They do?'

'Ross, I and those on the Council have precious few years left. And many of the active agents like Hunter and Ballentine have spent too much of their lives isolated or traversing the world in search of enemies. Hunter can barely use a mobile phone and Ballentine is not much better. They tend to act like cavemen at times. The Guild must have a secure future, and it needs bright young people like you and Cathy to take over so that it can keep up with the advances that society is making. Our enemies are innovative and evolve with the world around them. The Guild must do the same in order to survive. The Guild needs a future. Many of us believe that you are an important part of that future. We are passing through a violent time right now. It's not always this way. It's only in the more peaceful times that the real spirit of the Guild comes to life.'

'What do you mean?'

'Right now we must appear to a youngster like you to be a horde of gifted soldiers who bounce from one conflict to another. That is not what the Guild is intended to be. Our community is about knowledge and understanding. It is about preparation, too … one day the gifted will have to reveal themselves to the wider world. We must take a natural place in society – not as rulers or killers or thieves. One day we should become a foundation for mankind to better itself. That is the goal of the Guild of the True.'

In that moment Mr Williams convinced me that my future was with the Guild. I believed the Guild could achieve its ultimate goal and I wanted to be a part of that achievement.

We strolled around for almost an hour and he told me some of his old war stories before we reunited with Cathy and Sarah. The young girl was now full of chatter about dancing spiders. The excitement seemed to wear her out and she was fast asleep by the time Mr Williams got the 'classic' car to start.

Before we reached the house, Sarah began to shudder like she was freezing and she was mumbling. Her fists clenched so hard her knuckles cracked and she began thrashing about.

'Is she having a fit or something?' I'd never seen anything quite like it before and was starting to think she was having a stroke or a heart attack or something. 'Maybe we should get her to a hospital.'

'No,' Mr Williams said. He was surprisingly calm considering the racket the girl was creating. 'She is having a premonition by the looks of it. I've dealt with prophets before and it's always like this when a vision comes to them. The prophecies reach their minds while they sleep. She'll wake any moment now.'

Sarah's eyes shot open and she sucked a sharp breath as she lurched forward.

'Are you all right?' Cathy asked, putting her arms around the girl and hugging her tight. 'Was it a nightmare?'

'Yes,' Sarah sobbed. 'It was horrible.'

'What did you dream about, love?'

'I dreamt about *the tin man*.'

'Who?' I asked her.

'The tin man. He's coming to kill us all.'

'Who is this tin man?' Mr Williams asked her. His voice had remained calm, but I could see it in his eyes that the prophecy had him flustered.

'I don't know. He's going to come after us and kill us. He's going to kill all your friends too.'

'The tin man …' I said, wondering what she was describing. 'Is he made of metal or something?'

'No, no,' Mr Williams scoffed. 'She must be referring to the character from the Wizard of Oz.' He looked back at the girl. 'Is this man looking for a heart?'

'I dunno,' Sarah said. She slouched into the seat and stared vacantly out the window.

'It's just a dream,' Cathy told her. 'Just a dream. The tin man doesn't really exist.'

Peter Williams and I exchanged a glance and it was enough to tell me that *he* believed this premonition.

We hardly spoke again for the rest of the journey. We reached the house soon after and tried to calm Sarah down. Nothing worked and she cried for almost an hour straight. At first I thought she was upset because of the vision she'd had, but after a while she told us how she'd been forced by Zalech to watch as he killed her foster parents. Cathy and I didn't know what to say to her. We just stood there listening to her story. Mr Williams spoke with her at great length and his wise words had a soothing effect on the young girl. He and Cathy brought her to her new bedroom and stayed with her until she fell asleep. I spent some time at Romand's grave and went to my room about 2am. When I finally climbed under the covers all I could think of was who the tin man from Sarah's vision could be …

I awoke to find myself strapped tightly to a bed and a dull pain throbbing in the back of my skull. I tried to get up but the thick leather straps across my chest, waist, wrists and ankles allowed for no movement. I tried to use my gifts to loosen them, but could not summon any strength.

I found it impossible to focus my eyes for a few

moments. When my vision finally cleared I realised I was in a hospital room and there were tubes and wires attached to my face, neck and chest. There were machines all around me bleeping and flashing. Fear surged through me. I concentrated as hard as I could on summoning some psychokinetic power so that I could break free, but the more my mind sharpened the more physical pain I experienced.

What had happened to me? Who had strapped me down? Did they know of my crimes? Why were my powers not working?

I made one last attempt and pushed myself forward, but the straps gave no sway.

'The restraints are for your own good, Edward,' a gentle voice said from across the room. 'You will only do yourself harm if you leave the bed. Trying to force them while in your condition could cost you your life.'

I tried to speak, but could not. There was some sort of contraption covering most of my face and there was a wide tube filling my throat and prodding at the inside of my chest when I tried to form words.

'Try to remain calm,' the woman spoke once more. 'I know it's natural to want to free yourself of these ugly machines but they are keeping you alive. You must remain calm, Edward.'

She was lying. She *had* to be lying. What had they done to me?

Suddenly I became still. I remembered what happened. The panther. It had mauled and bitten me in the neck and before I blacked out it had torn away part of my throat.

'Don't try to move and don't try to speak. Try to calm down. You have suffered horrific injuries but we can repair you. Your powers remain, and you will use them again in time. We have injected you with a specific sedative that numbs your control over true gifts.'

She came closer to the bed and the faint light in the room caught her face. She was younger than her voice suggested and had a softness in her eyes that calmed me when I looked into them.

'My name is Janet Walters and I will be your doctor while you are here. My goal is to help and protect you, Edward. Soon you will be back on your feet again.' She sat next to me on the bed and smiled as she adjusted a nozzle on the drip attached to my left arm. 'I'm going to put you to sleep now. You'll be going into surgery soon. You'll feel a little better tomorrow and I'll be here when you wake.'

CHAPTER FOURTEEN

Your Only Friend

I awoke at dawn and went outside to sit on the bench in the cool autumn air. I used to be able to sleep all day, but my time with Romand and Hunter had changed that and now I instinctively got up at daybreak. Being an agent for the Guild of the True meant you could never truly relax. You never knew what the day ahead had in store and it was probably for the best to be getting up early so you wouldn't be caught napping if you were called upon by the mysterious people who sat on the Council.

'Still thinking about the tin man?' Cathy asked.

I turned to see her standing by the back door with her duvet wrapped around her. Her hair was in tangles and her eyes were puffy with tiredness. She was still a vision of heaven to me.

'He had crossed my mind once or twice.'

'Come off it, Ross. I bet you haven't been able to get him out of your mind all night. I know I haven't!'

'It's the type of thing that's hard to forget. You think it was just a nightmare?' I asked.

'Peter didn't seem to think so. And he's the wisest person I know. He looked freaked out about it. He didn't even say goodnight when I went to bed last night. Just disappeared into his study.'

'I know. I went into the kitchen for a glass of water in the middle of the night and overheard him on the phone. I wonder who he was talking to.'

'I have no idea.'

'What could Sarah have meant by *tin man*? Does it mean a man made of tin? Something to do with the Wizard of Oz?'

'You have to remember that she's only eight years old, Ross. She can't articulate what she's seen like you or I can. I'm sure Peter will make some sense of it. Or at least someone in the Palatium will.'

'You ever been to this Palatium?'

'Never. I don't even know where it is. It's top secret. Big time top secret!' She left the doorway and sat next to me on the bench and stretched the duvet over my shoulders and wrapped her arms around me. 'This was meant to be *our* time. I thought we'd have endless hours to spend together with nothing important to talk about. Just chit chat about music and our gifts and each other and stuff.'

'And stuff?' I laughed.

'Yeah. Stuff,' she giggled. 'Don't underestimate the importance of stuff.'

I leaned over and kissed her softly while holding her tight around the waist. I could have sat there all day with her. It was one of those perfect moments.

'Such a lovely picture. It almost makes me want to puke.'

Hunter stepped out into the garden holding a steaming cup of coffee in one hand and an unlit cigar in the other.

'We're just chatting, Hunter,' Cathy said to him. 'Normal human beings do that from time to time.'

'Human beings do lots of pointless things, my dear.' He lit his cigar and blew a cloud of smoke above his head. 'So, did I miss anything while I was sleeping?'

'Not much,' I replied. 'Only a prophecy of doom. We're all going to be killed by a man made of tin apparently.'

'How delightful. The little girl scaring you again, Bentley?'

'Not just me. Mr Williams looked like he'd seen a ghost when she said it.'

'He's an excitable old geezer, is Williams. He's probably been on the phone half the night to Sterling about it.'

'Jim Sterling?' I asked. I remembered meeting the man at Romand's funeral, but I never got the chance to talk to him.

'Yeah.'

'Is Jim Sterling the head of the Council?'

'None of your business, Bentley. The less you know about Jim Sterling the better it will be for you.'

I couldn't determine what he was trying to get at by being purposely vague. I didn't bother asking because I knew he'd just fob me off like he always did.

'Mr Sterling has always seemed like a lovely man whenever I've met him,' Cathy said with a smile. 'I remember my dad spoke very fondly of him.'

'Yeah, that makes sense.' Hunter took a long pull on the cigar and flicked into the dewy grass. 'Well, I got business to attend to. You two lovebirds enjoy your down-time.'

'Don't leave until Mr Williams is up,' I said.

'What?'

'He said he was going to the Palatium with you.'

'Like hell he is. He'll only insist on travelling in one of his dinosaur cars. I'd like to get there this century so I'm out of here before he gets up.'

He stomped back inside the house and left the two of us wondering why he was so uptight about Jim Sterling. His dismissal of Sarah's latest premonition had eased my anxiety a little and I was able to enjoy the peace of the morning in Cathy's company, something I had longed to do during my exile in rural Scotland. We didn't discuss the Guild or what had happened in the north-east. We simply chatted and kissed as the sun climbed into the pale blue sky. It was a bright spot in an otherwise dark time of my life.

Mr Williams appeared an hour later and was furious to learn that Hunter had gone without him and spent the next couple of hours cursing under his breath. At 10am Sarah appeared and she sat right next to Cathy at the table and slowly picked at a bowl of cornflakes. Mr Williams called me into his study for a quick chat before he left for the Palatium.

'I know you were looking forward to having time with Cathy, but you have the rest of your lives ahead of you. I could be gone for a few days. So, I'm asking you to put your budding relationship on hold for the moment and look after Sarah – she's been through a lot lately and you must both keep a close eye on her.'

'I can live with that,' I lied. 'I'm sure all this will blow over in a few days anyway.'

'Yes,' he smiled without confidence. 'In the meantime, I have photocopied some pages from that book I told you about. I would like you to read them and practice the techniques outlined.'

'Why not just give me the book?' I asked. 'Why go to the trouble of photocopying one section?'

'I don't want to lay too much on you at once, Ross. You need to take time to digest each technique properly.'

'Mr Williams, are you sure the Guild trusts me?'

'Of course. Why do you ask?'

'They never fully trained Edward Zalech because they didn't trust him or thought they couldn't control him. I'm getting the vibe that I'm drip-fed information about the gifts I have. And I'm starting to believe I am being purposely held back.'

'They *are* holding you back,' he admitted openly and with no shame, 'though not for the same reasons as in Edward Zalech's case. We know you have great power, Ross, and you have so much potential, but you are a little reckless and tend to rush into things too much for our liking. Some of the techniques are very hazardous and we would like to wait until you're a little older for you to learn everything. That's all it is. You already have enough knowledge to defend yourself and this,' he handed me the sheets of paper, 'will strengthen your control. Be patient.'

'I guess I'm being a bit too eager.'

'You are. You have a lot of time to know all there is to know about the true gifts.' He handed me a card. 'My mobile phone number. Use it only in an emergency. Stay vigilant while I am away.'

I slipped the card into the back pocket of my jeans and took the sheets to my room and started reading ...

CHAPTER FIFTEEN

'The Dual Shield'

~~~~~~

Rudolph Klein (Der Orden der Befähigten)
The Unlimited Gift. (1978)

~~~~~~

*O*ne of the mistakes made by many novices when using psycho-kinesis in combat is that they think one-dimensionally. They think of either attack or defence and do not consider utilising both tactics simultaneously. I have seen this with my own two eyes; powerful people who have become over-confident in the impact of their attacks that they neglect to protect themselves properly and pay the ultimate price for this oversight. Likewise, those with an overly-cautious instinct concentrate solely on defensive strategies and allow their opponent too much time to work out a way of bypassing simple shields. Too much effort on either is misguided. A master of any of the true gifts will always consider both tactics at the same time.

There are a number of ways to protect oneself while launching an assault, but in this chapter I will outline the most consistent and best, in my opinion. Of course others will prefer alternative methods which I will outline in later chapters of this book. I believe these methods all have weak points, but are nonetheless very effective. They are as follows:

~~~~~~

Chapter 16 - Ground Pulse System - Designed by Martin Washington in 1892. Chapter 17 - The Cube Rotational - Designed by Pavel Zorchan in 1918. Chapter 18 - The Vacuum Cycle - Designed by Ben Clarke in 1951. Chapter 19 - The Double Domino - Designed by Carla Robbin in 1974. Chapter 20 - Kinetic Fusion - (Theorised by Trevor Banks in 1976).

~~~~~~

In this chapter I will focus chiefly on The Dual Shield, which was first created by Angela Barnes in 1963 while she was working with the Guild of the True. Barnes was one of their top tutors at the time and in the early 1960s she began training two very promising psychokinetics and was developing new manoeuvres for them to practise. She was sparring with them when she found that being outnumbered by two skilled people required a new technique altogether, one that encompassed both offence and defence.

Her solution was simple, but ingenious. She created a globe shield, which is an old technique used for a number of centuries. It is essentially a circular shield of power that acts as a force field. Her variation was inspired. Barnes discovered a way of making the energy field impenetrable from the outside, while porous from the inside. In layman's terms: nothing could pierce the shield, but she could allow objects *and kinetic assaults to pass through it from the inside.*

Her talented protégés could not combat this technique. And in time she made improvements on it. In 1971 it became a requisite for all higher-ranking psychokinetics to learn. As always, the Guild never revealed their most important techniques to junior members.

Barnes died in 1973 and never lived to see the Dual Shield brought to maximised capability. It was later that year when Erik Okker created a dual shield with a one-kilometre diameter. It was a powerful shield too, speeding cars could not enter it yet he could still launch simple strikes like the slice or the spear from within.

Okker had studied and practised the dual shield for many years and it was he who was tasked with teaching his colleagues how to perfect this power. Okker claimed he had used a simple regime: a small room and a ping-pong ball. He would create the shield close to his body, and threw the ball through it at the wall. It would ricochet and then strike the exterior of the shield. It took him time to get it right, but within a month he had it perfected. After that he practised at expanding the shield.

The first couple of pages were intriguing. I had never fully considered both defence and attack with the one move. I read the rest of the pages, but they were very technical and more aimed towards people who did not have psychokinesis, so that they could fully understand what the dual shield was. He also explained how it was used by a couple of the Guild agents, and his own small group who were based in Germany from the late 1960s and were an ally to the Guild. They didn't actively work alongside the Guild; they had an exchange system of sorts for a couple of decades. Ideas and even pupils were passed from one group to another, thus both would benefit because the ideologies of the two were very similar.

It warmed the heart to know there was another group like the Guild. That the world wasn't simply filled with evil organisations who cared only for money and power. Perhaps there was hope yet for the gifted community.

I put the papers aside and went searching the house for a ping-pong or tennis ball. I couldn't find any so I settled for one of Mr Williams's golf balls and quickly returned to my room. I really wanted to learn how to create the dual shield. It sounded like the type of thing that could come in handy one day if I was to come up against an imposing enemy.

I woke to find the dull throb in the back of my head was no more. It was replaced by a tightness in my face and sparks of pain in my neck. I opened my eyes fully and saw there was a plastic tube feeding from a machine to the right of the bed and into my throat and there were still a number of wires connected to my body.

My eyes gradually focused on the figure standing by the end of the bed. It was the woman, Janet Walters, who had spoken to me when I first woke after I sustained my injuries. Her long white coat gleamed in the light pouring through the two windows to the left of the bed.

'Welcome back,' she said with a warm smile. 'I'm pleased to inform you that the surgery was a success. You're surely through the worst of this now.'

I wanted to talk to her. I had so many questions. When I tried to speak nothing happened, apart from a sharp pain zapping the base of my neck.

'You have questions,' she said, as she watched my mouth trying to form words. 'There's probably a lot on your mind.'

I tried to lift my head from the pillow, but could not. I simply blinked once and Walters was smart enough to know that meant *yes*.

'I can guess the two questions that you most want to ask,' she said. 'I'm sure you are wondering where you are exactly. I have some files on you and they say you are very intelligent so you have probably worked out that this isn't a normal hospital. Otherwise there would be an armed guard in the room and you'd have had a visit from a detective and not only a doctor. I can tell you that you were being monitored by the people who run this company. They witnessed what happened and decided to save you when the fighting subsided. This building belongs to Golding Scientific. It is the company's experimental division. I can see by the look in your eyes that you are familiar with Mr Golding's reputation and that, up to this point, you have probably considered him an enemy. You have to realise he saved your life and he is willing to give you a second chance at that life. You owe him a lot, Edward, and I'm sure he is going to call in that favour soon enough. Do you understand?'

I blinked once.

'The second and probably more pressing matter that's on your mind is the fate of you sister. I am so very sorry, Edward. Golding Scientific's surveillance team observed an attack on the apartment you were holed up in. The people responsible were members of this mysterious group that you were once a part of.'

I tried hard not to show emotion, but could not resist clenching my fists. I knew all too well how ruthless my old colleagues were.

Walters approached the bed and sat on a chair next to me. She then leaned forward and moved her face close to mine and whispered.

'You will be watched carefully. Every expression is monitored and analysed. I am your only friend here, Edward. If you show aggression towards me or any of the other staff here they will terminate you. What I'm about to tell you will be very difficult to hear, but you must not react. It may be the difference between life and death for you. Do you understand?'

I blinked.

'Your sister was murdered.' She said it coldly, as if it had no meaning; her eyes told me a different story. 'That is all the information I have for you right now. I will try to gain a more detailed account for you in time.'

I looked away from her as tears welled up in my

eyes. I fought back the wave of sadness and anger. My sister, that I had risked so much for, was no more. My entire world came crumbling down around me. My life instantly lost the meaning that it once had. I wished in that moment that I too had succumbed to the Guild's attack. I no longer wanted to live.

'You need rest,' the doctor said as she walked to the door. 'I'll check in on you again later.'

I lied there as still as a statue. Inwardly I was in the midst of a storm of emotion. The rage was overwhelming. I would kill whoever was responsible. But they would suffer first. I would unleash hell on all those close to the person responsible. All I had to do was to keep my cool until they allowed me to leave the clinic. Then I would exact revenge in the most vicious fashion imaginable.

I was smart enough to know they were keeping me alive so that they could use me to hurt the Guild. I hated being used as a pawn, but I was content with the situation – for as long as it suited me. Golding had endless resources and they would be able to get me back on my feet soon enough. I simply had to be patient.

My thoughts then turned to the emotions that I was experiencing. For most of my life I was able to contain my emotions, now I was overcome by them. A mix of anger and sadness filled me. They were natural feelings for someone in my situation, but there was something more … I was skilled at hiding and repressing my emotions. Now they were running wild inside me, as if some unknown force was fuelling them. Perhaps the medical staff had operated on my brain ... This was the experimental section of Golding Scientific after all.

The emotions were so alien to me. I had grown comfortable with imprisoning any feelings for others. So much so that I once took extraordinary measures to remind myself of what, and who, I was supposed to be loyal to. Some years ago I had tattooed a portrait of Ania on the palm of my left hand so I would not forget that I was to protect and to care for her. Tattooed on the palm of my right hand was a symbol. This was the crest used by the assassins of the Guild; it was a variation on the wolf head logo that the Guild used. This one had the face of a snake in its centre. I got that tattoo to remind me of my duty to those who had saved me from the Eastern Shadow. Both were now reminders of the loss I had suffered.

I spent the following hours thinking of little Ania. I had risked so much for her over the years. I had sacrificed everything so that she could survive.

I had carried out the massacre in Switzerland for her sake; she was being pushed too hard by Cramer during her training and I knew that pyrokinetics ran the risk of setting themselves on fire – particularly during their adolescent years. I asked Cramer to lighten the training, but my concerns were dismissed. I was not going to let any harm come to my only sibling and was planning to escape with her. Then the offer came from JNCOR and it seemed like perfect timing. It had all fallen apart. My actions led to Ania's death instead of preventing it ...

But the Guild could have captured her! She was nothing more than a child and should not have faced execution!

I wondered who had carried out the killing. Which of the cowards had killed my sister? There were many in the Guild, but only a cold-hearted killer could do such a thing. I guessed it was either Armitage or Sakamoto. They were the cruellest of all the Guild's loyal assassins. Whoever it was would pay a heavy price and I was convinced that Dr Walters would find out who was responsible and share her knowledge, simply because that's what Golding would want. He would want to use me as a weapon to strike at the heart of the Guild. That was Golding's way of doing business – he preferred others to do his dirty work.

The day passed by slowly and the loneliness was only broken once every hour, when a nurse entered and took readings from the many machines I was connected to. The first nurse did three checks before being replaced by a younger woman who went very pale when she looked at my face.

Most people would have been upset if their appearance inspired such terror. I was far from upset by it. I took pleasure from her reaction; I knew the only thing left in life was to be an instrument of vengeance and that would be easier if the mere sight of me struck fear into my foes. I had not yet seen my face since the fight with the Guild, but I was badly mutilated if the nurse's reaction was anything to go by.

At 5pm the timid nurse returned to take her readings and jot the results onto her clip-board. This time she was accompanied by Dr Walters who checked the machines then drew the curtains and switched on the lamp over the bed. She spoke to me only when the nurse had left the room.

'I don't know how you're still awake. Most people would still be under from the anaesthetic.'

Walters obviously had little experience of those with true gifts. If she had dealt with them before she would have known the anger and emotional pain that I was suffering would fuel my powers, which I could then use to strengthen my body and force the anaesthetic from my system. And that is precisely what I had been doing.

'I'm sure it's difficult to find sleep when you are enduring so much,' she continued. 'And when you're tied so rigidly to the bed. Let me loosen those straps a bit.'

Walters approached me, a little cautiously, then unbuckled the thick leather straps across my biceps then the thinner ones that bound my wrists.

'Can you move your hands at all?' she asked.

I raised my left arm then moved my fingers, but

the movement was languid, as there was still a narcotic of some form being drip fed into my body. Walters
crossed the room and took a notepad before approaching me once more. She took one of the two pens from
the breast pocket of her white coat and asked me to
raise my right arm, then wrote into the pad.

'Your reactions are slow. That's simply down to
the amount of sedatives that have entered your system
over the last twenty four hours. Honestly, I don't even
know how you're managing to have any control over
your limbs. Technically this is impossible.'

She continued writing as I raised both arms and
brought them together above my head and clasped my
fingers together.

'Remarkable. Your recovery should be relatively
short if you continue to improve at this rate. We will
be changing the mix,' she tipped glass jar with the end
of her pen, 'this evening and although you will still feel
a little nauseous, it should allow you more control of
your reactions. And you may able to use the gifts again
in a day or two. Although my colleague, Professor King,
believes it may take a week or two for it to–'

My psychokinetic power had been slowly returning
since waking, and now I mustered enough strength to
make the red biro in her jacket pocket float into the air.
I then made the notepad fly out of her hand. It rotated
slowly over the bed then hovered in front of my face.
The tip of the pen met the open page and I began to

write without the use of my hands. My control over the pen fluctuated and the writing was erratic, but legible:

I know nothing about Prof King and he knows nothing of Edward Zalech!

He should not underestimate ME!!

'It appears I am the one who underestimated you, Edward. I still don't fully grasp these gifts that you and others like you possess. I was told you wouldn't regain this power as long as you were sedated.'

You have no idea of the power I possess. Strong emotions make it even more powerful. There is no need for the sedative!

'Edward, you have very severe injuries. Despite your confidence I do not think it is wise to remove the drip. You may feel strong now, but you should not put yourself under such strain, it can leave you open to infection; that's our worst enemy right now. I've never come across someone like you before, but you are still human and vulnerable to many bacteria. Allow us to continue with the sedative, at least for another day.' She reached out and touched my hand and smiled. 'Trust me?'

What is the extent of my injuries?

233

'Where do I start,' Walters sighed. 'Well ... You've sustained serious wounds to the trachea, oesophagus and larynx. And there is extensive damage to the sternocleidomastoid, omohyoid and platysma muscles – these are the muscles at the front of your neck. You have hardly any teeth left and there is damage to the gums and soft palate. There is a very deep cut through both the upper and lower lips. There are four scars on each side of your head. The first runs across your temples and converge at the sides of your forehead, another above the ears and end at the side of yours eyes, another under the ears and across the cheeks, and one more across the jaw line and ending either side of your mouth. That cat must have gotten a real good grip on you. Oh, you also have no eyebrows or eyelashes – they must have been singed away by the heat of the blaze.

'The exterior wounds look terrible, but they can be fixed relatively easily. The wounds on the inside are the serious ones. You won't be able to lift your head properly because you no longer have the muscles to perform that movement or take the weight of your head. And then there is the voice. Your vocal chords were shredded during the attack so you cannot speak in your current condition.

'This is all probably coming as a great shock to you. I have dealt with people with injuries like this before and I will help you, Edward. I will do everything in my

power to undo this damage. And I know you will overcome this dreadful ordeal that has befallen you.'

It is nothing compared to the ordeal I will put THEM through for murdering Ania!!

'Be patient, Edward. You must focus now on your
recovery. You have the rest of your life to get your revenge.'

There is NO time! The Guild constantly moves their operatives around. In a couple of weeks Ania's killer could be on the other side of the planet! I need to start the hunt SOON!!!

'I honestly don't know when you will be well enough
to leave this place, Edward. You need a lot of work. We
will need to fly in a team of plastic surgeons to fix up
your face. And in terms of your neck injuries, it may
take dozens of operations to get you anywhere close to
a normal and functional level of movement. That may
take months upon months to do ... although Professor
King, who is the head of the experimental division, has
come up with an alternative. One that might see you up
and about a lot quicker.'

What is this alternative?

'We have machines here that can replicate human body parts. Even the most intricate ones. It's quite astounding actually and will probably revolutionise how we deal with injuries and disease. He says he can rebuild you with metal parts. This technique is far from perfected, however he believes that because you are psychokinetic, you may be able to use your gift to help in the movements that these parts lack. He wants to use you as our first human test subject. These precise parts would not usually work because the body would reject such a large amount of metal installments. Our scientific team has devised a lot of new drugs that aid the body in coping with the trauma of something like this. It may just work.'

WHEN??

'I'll speak with him later and you'll know tomorrow if a decision has been made. Are you sure you want to go through with this? You're going to be a ... metal man, so to speak.'

I think you could refer to me as the Tin Man instead, doctor.

'You can call me Janet, if you like,' she smiled. 'Why would I refer to you as the tin man?'

I have finally found my heart.

'I don't quite understand. Enough of this – I'll inform Professor King that you are prepared to go through with the procedure.'

Communication from Professor Jason King of Golding Scientific Experimental Division to Aubrey Pearson, acting head of Golding Scientific Security Division.

We have now completed the experimental surgery on Edward Zalech. The operations took a total of seventeen hours to complete and he has been returned to his room and is being monitored by Dr Janet Walters and her staff.

The surgery was carried out in three stages.

Stage 1: Installation of fabricated body parts. We have implanted a series of metal and mechanical parts that will allow him to move his head and upper body. Also implanted into his throat was a device that will enable him to speak. The device has sensors that will pick up vibrations and these will be translated digitally by a small computer inside it. Then an electrical mechanism will form sounds – words –

for him. This new voice of his will be crude; he'll sound like a cross between Stephen Hawking and Count Dracula, but will be effective enough for him to communicate properly.

Stage 2: External surgery.

We spent three hours performing surgery to his face and neck in an attempt to give him a relatively-normal appearance.

Stage 3: Injection of experimental narcotics.

As requested by Mr Golding, we have used a number of experimental drugs on Zalech. Two are to aid him in fighting infection and to relieve some of the pain he would naturally experience after such extensive surgery.

The third narcotic is HF9* (Hyper-furens Version Nine). Mr Golding was adamant that this narcotic be used. It will make the subject emotionally unstable, but should enable his powers to grow exponentially. This is necessary in order for him to replicate the techniques outlined in the works of Penelope Gordon, which have been given to Edward to read in the coming days.

* Sub note

(Taken from the Golding Scientific medical archives)

Hyper-furens.

HyperFurens was first developed by the Nalsanyo Group in 1997. Its original purpose was to increase the stamina of military personnel. It was successful in most cases, but the adverse side effects ultimately rendered it useless. Each subject suffered nervous breakdown from uncontrollable waves of emotions. The program was shut down in March 1999. The serum (HF1) was deemed a failure.

The drug reappeared in 2001 when a Swiss medical company experimented with it. Their goal was to create a surge of emotion in order to bring those in comas to full consciousness. This version (HF2) was again seen a failure. There was a strange side effect: the lab rats tested with HF2 became tremendously aggressive when injected with even minuscule amounts.

In 2004, a pharmaceutical giant based in Japan manufactured HF3 and HF4. They believed they could alter the previous versions of the drug to make humans almost impervious to pain. Most of the test subjects died within hours of the experiments and testing was discontinued in 2005.

Golding Scientific bought all patents regarding Hyperfurens in 2007. Over the last five years they have created five new variations of the drug, the most successful to date being HF7. This version helped the human body to fight off infection – and even regressed serious disease. The same problem of uncontrollable aggression remained, as did the serious physical degradation.

In 2012 Golding Scientific Experimental Division devised HF9. It is the first ever drug to be fully self-replicating. Once injected with the substance, the subject will forever be under its influence. The substance uses red blood vessels to duplicate itself.

HF9 Results: Increased physical strength and stamina, heightened emotions, increased levels of violence.

Side Effects: Hemolytic Anemia.

Results: All test subjects have died due to heart failure within one month of being exposed.

CHAPTER SIXTEEN

The Real Deal

I was sitting in the centre of my room facing the wall as I prepared yet another attempt. I'd been trying to create the dual shield described in Rudolph Klein's book for hours. I'd had some success, but the cocoon of energy was unstable and more often than not the golf ball rebounded off the wall and passed through the kinetic barrier and hit me. It was frustrating and I was determined to master this technique. Over and over I tried until Cathy stormed into my room and stood there with her hands on her hips staring at me.

'What's with you?' I asked. She looked irate and her face and neck were glowing red, as they often did when she was angry.

'What's with me?' she said. 'Ross, you're really starting to bug me with that ball. You've been bouncing it off the wall for five hours straight. Do you realise how annoying it is?'

'Oh, I didn't think you could actually hear it from downstairs.'

'I would hear that racket all the way down the street! Are you that bored?'

'Not exactly.'

'We haven't seen each other in months and we're in the same house yet you decide to stay in your room all day, bouncing a damned golf ball off the wall. I don't understand you sometimes.'

'Exactly.' I climbed off the floor and walked to her and kissed her on the tip of her nose. 'It's a misunderstanding. I'm not doing this out of boredom. It's a training technique. Mr Williams gave me some extracts from a book on psychokinesis and told me I should start practising. And you know me, if I start something I rarely stop until I finish it.'

'I don't see how bouncing a ball is training.'

'It's complicated, but someday it might save my life.' I gave her the puppy-dog eyes. 'Isn't my life important to you?'

'Don't give me that look,' Cathy said, trying to hide her smile. 'And you shouldn't be making jokes about you dying. Not after everything that's happened lately, *and* after Sarah's predictions!'

'You're right.' I kissed her again. 'Where is Sarah anyway?'

'Asleep on the couch in the sitting room. We were watching a movie together and she drifted off, despite putting up a heroic effort to stay awake.'

'Seems like you've found a little sister.'

'Yeah. I've always wanted one actually, but her timing is deplorable.' She leaned in close to me and kissed my neck. 'I don't want anything to come in the way of us spending time together.'

I used a slight burst of power to nudge the door shut behind her. Then I carefully used my gift to unzip her hoodie and to peel it off her shoulders.

'Hey, you snake!' She gave me a playful slap across the chest. 'You're sneaky, Bentley. Real sneaky.'

'*I'm* sneaky! You're the one who switched your mind into a dog just so you could watch me getting undressed.'

'That was not intentional!'

'Yes, it was. And it was rather disturbing too!'

She suddenly pushed forward and I fell back onto the bed with her in my arms and we shared a long and passionate kiss. It became very heated between us until we both drew back at the same time then stared into each other's eyes.

'Are you thinking what I'm thinking?' she asked with an excited nod.

'I am if you're thinking that Sarah's left her diary unattended.'

'That's what I'm thinking.'

'Me too. Shall we?'

'Should we?'

'Shouldn't we?'

'I dunno. Seems wrong.'

'Wouldn't it be wrong *not* to look through it?'

'It's not exactly right to do it either.'

'Could be something important in it.'

'Might be nothing important in it.'

'In that case there's no reason not to look.'

'OK.' Cathy bounced off the bed and zipped her hoodie. 'We'll just have a quick look through it. Hurry, I don't want her to catch us, not now that she thinks of me as her best friend.'

She took me by the hand and we tiptoed across the landing to the room that Sarah had moved into. I used my gift to switch the bedside lamp on as we stepped inside and we stealthily began our search for the precious diary. It didn't take us very long to uncover it; she'd kept it tucked inside the pillow case.

'I feel awful for doing this,' Cathy moaned . She brought it to the lamp, but resisted turning the first page. 'It's like betraying her.'

'Cathy, what if there's something in there that could save our lives? Or anyone's life for that matter?'

'I know, I know,' she sighed. 'I'm sure she trusts me and I feel bad breaking that trust.'

'She'll never know.'

I opened the diary and flicked to the first entry which was almost indecipherable. It was nothing but scribbles and doodles, and neither of us could make any sense of it. We went from one page to another and I was starting to think Hunter was right about it being the simple notebook of a troubled child. There wasn't any indication that what she had written were premonitions. Some of it was simple descriptions of houses or people, and a lot of it was illegible.

'Her handwriting is atrocious,' Cathy pointed out as we sifted through the pages.

'I know. How did she get away with this in school?'

'She's been moved around a lot, remember? Probably hasn't spent any length of time in one school, or with one teacher.'

We went on and on until we found some notes about a bus crash. There were nine pages all dedicated to this one event and I recalled the newspaper article that had led us to her in the first place. It said she had predicted a school bus colliding with a car. A few people had died and this seemed to be a perfect description of it.

'I'm not convinced by this,' I told Cathy. 'There's no evidence that this was written before the crash took place.'

'Keep turning the pages. Perhaps we'll find something that might prove that her gift is genuine.'

We went on and there were more erratic notes on various subjects that had little relevance. Soon enough, though, we came across the second disaster that was mentioned in the newspaper article. We identified sixteen pages full of notes and even a sketch relating to a fishing trawler that sank in the North Sea. Again there was no concrete proof that these notes were made before the ship actually went down. But I felt there was something to this prediction. It didn't seem like a clever fake because one of the notes was written from the perspective of a crew member, and this person had become trapped in the engine room after he injured his back. We took the diary to Cathy's room and looked up the stories on the internet about the tragedy and there was some mention of this man, but no details of how he died.

'Still doesn't prove anything,' I sighed. I walked away from the laptop and rubbed my eyes. 'Maybe we should leave this to Mr Williams. We can't tell from this diary if she has the true gift of prophecy.'

'Maybe you're right.' Cathy continued turning pages. 'Hey, have there been any volcanic eruptions recently?'

'One in Iceland a couple of years ago.'

'I mean one that killed a whole load of people.'

'Not that I know of,' I said, shaking my head. 'Don't think there's been one like that for over a decade.'

'Come here and look at this,' she said, waving her hand frantically through the air. 'Does any of this look familiar?'

I looked over Cathy's shoulder and saw a very dramatic drawing of a volcano exploding with fire, and black smoke surrounding it like a vaporous wreath. There was some text alongside the sketch but it was cryptic and neither of us could understand it properly.

Cathy turned to the next page and there was more on this vol-cano. This time though the drawings were more detailed, the writ-ing remained mysterious. There were also some odd diagrams. They were line drawings and looked like a fried egg to me, but Cathy caught on much quicker than I did.

'You know what these drawings are?' I asked.

'They're aerial maps. This is an island from above and it appears the volcano is so powerful that it breaks the land-mass in two.'

'There definitely hasn't been any volcano like that recently so this still doesn't give us anything to go on. She might simply have an over-active imagination.'

We sifted through the erratic entries until we finally found a drawing that Cathy recognised straight away. It was the silhouette of a man standing in front of a terrible blaze and wielding a long, swirling whip of fire.

'That's Edward Zalech. Jesus, this is very odd.'

'Obviously.'

'No, I mean that this is how *I* saw Zalech, just before I attacked him. It's almost as if Sarah had seen this happen through my eyes.'

'Maybe that's how premonitions work. If I remember correctly, it's the emotions that people experience during a traumatic event that trigger the whole thing. The person's emotions travel through time because they're so potent.'

'Yes, and part of the imagery and thought processes travel with the emotion. Prophets are the only ones who can catch these time-travelling memories. Only the skilled ones can interpret them clearly.'

'I think Sarah did quite a good job on this considering her age.'

Cathy flipped the page and there was a long note about the *fire-girl* fighting with *gifted soldiers*. I read through it and there was no doubt this was an account of my battle with Ania Zalech.

'I think her gift is genuine,' Cathy said. She handed the diary to me and shut down her laptop. 'That would mean the *tin-man* may be coming to kill us all.'

I took her hand and gave it a reassuring squeeze. 'It might also have been a nightmare – a bad dream that's not connected to her gift.'

'I hope you're right.'

I looked through the last few pages of the book then stopped when I saw a series of drawings. Each depicted a man in a long coat killing a different person. The words 'Tin-man' were scribbled under each. There was no doubt in my mind that this murderous individual did exist. I had a strong feeling that we would meet him very soon.

I decided not to show Cathy the drawings. She had been through too much in the last few days and I didn't want to upset her with this. I continued flicking pages as if I hadn't noticed anything important.

I paused when I saw a simple drawing. Something about it caught my attention and I took a closer look at it. The sketch was a stick man wearing a top hat, and he was leaning on a walking stick. There were two lines of text scribbled above the rudimentary portrait.

He stands tall and his shadow remains on the world.

He waits for the other shadows to rise.

This seemed to be what Sarah was talking about in the car the previous day, but it was like so many of the entries; it was cryptic and virtually impossible to know what it meant – if it meant anything at all.

Just as I was about to close the diary I spied a word just beneath the drawing of the man. The writing was tiny and I had to lift the diary close to my face just to read it.

'What is it?' Cathy asked.

I said nothing. I could not draw my eyes away from the word.

KEMATTAN

This was one little detail that I could not keep from her.

🖙 🖙 🖙

We sat facing each other at the kitchen table. Cathy clung to a glass of white wine while my hands were clasped around a mug of black coffee. We had tried to find out if Sarah had a gift and it had been confirmed to us. She was a prophet and that meant all the trouble we had gone to was not in vain. We had snatched her from the clutches of evil so that her visions of future events could not be manipulated by our enemies. That all sounded great; it also meant that we had to deal with what she was seeing, and that was becoming more and more disturbing by the day. I was beginning to think we'd be better off not knowing what was coming.

She had spoken of the threat to our lives. This tin man that she dreamed about had us all on edge but that had now faded into the background. Such a threat paled in comparison to the one that James Barkley represented. He was known by many as the Kematian – Indonesian for 'death'. I had very little knowledge of the actual man, and the story behind him, but I knew enough to be frightened. Cathy went white as a sheet when I showed her the word written in the diary and only now was the colour seeping back to her face.

'His shadow remains on the world,' she recited the first line from the prophecy. 'You know, the more I think of it, that doesn't really mean he's alive. It could be that his reputation, and his crimes, remains enshrined in our memory. Like it's a scar that will last for a long time.'

'He waits for the other shadows to rise,' I replied. That was the second line of the prophecy and the one that had me worried so much. 'That would seem to indicate that he is alive and that he's waiting for something, or someone. Do you know much about Barkley?'

'Not a great deal.' She took a sip of wine and swept her red hair back over her shoulder. 'I know that he supposedly achieved the sixteenth gift. I know that he killed a lot of people. I know that he disappeared.'

'Didn't your mum or Romand ever talk about what happened to him?'

'Mum never really mentioned him. Romand did say a few things from time to time but nothing that expanded on the story that we both know. I do recall that he and Hunter, and a couple of others, were constantly looking for Barkley. They travelled the globe over the years, following up on any leads that came to the Guild's attention. But that was a long time ago and then the search stopped all of a sudden. About ten years ago it came to a stop and there was a release of the tension that they were all under. It seemed as though they'd gotten some news, maybe his death was confirmed, I don't know ... They never went looking for him again after that.'

'I wonder what happened …' I muttered. I took a gulp of coffee and shook my head. 'Why is the Guild always so bloody secretive?'

'They've survived for a very long time because they keep their secrets to themselves.'

'Well, we can't keep this to ourselves. We'll have to tell them what we've learned.'

'I'll ring Peter.' Cathy reached for her phone. 'He'll know what to do.'

She made the call from her mobile and put it on loudspeaker so we could both hear what he had to say. Cathy told him we'd looked at Sarah's diary and that she was confident the girl had the gift and then told him about the entry concerning the Kematian. There was a long silence on the other end after she mentioned that word.

He went on by saying this was most unexpected and that it made no sense at all. But he was flustered by the news and said that he and some other senior members of the Guild would come to the house the next day. Mr Williams also told us that Hunter had left the Palatium some hours earlier and that we would probably arrive at any minute. This gave me some comfort, and Cathy was visibly relieved to hear it. I never thought I'd be dying to see Hunter; I'd been only to happy to get away from him for a while and now I was counting the seconds to his arrival. There was an air of fear in the house and we'd both feel better once he returned.

I carried Sarah from the couch to her bed and she didn't even stir. I carried her in my arms and didn't use my gift, like I often did. I felt the same as Cathy; we'd betrayed her trust by looking in the diary, and I wouldn't betray her again. We were meant to look after her. I suppose I started seeing her as a little sister, not just a disturbed child that I didn't want any contact with. She needed support. It was bad enough reading her prophecies, but she actually experienced them. She never even knew when the next one was coming. I couldn't imagine the agony that would cause. Especially for someone so young.

It was way past midnight when Hunter pushed open the hall door and stomped into the hallway with a mist of cigar smoke in his wake. Cathy and I were waiting for him in the kitchen. I had a fresh mug of coffee in my hand and Cathy was drinking another glass of wine and was starting to tire.

'What are you two doing up?' Hunter asked, with a frown. 'Look like you've seen a ghost or something.'

Cathy told him about the diary, but Hunter didn't seem too perturbed by the news. 'You don't have to worry about Barkley,' he said. He pulled a chair from under the table sat with us. 'He's long gone. *But* the story of the Kematian is not well known. Only members of the Guild and the higher ranking folks in some other groups know of it. If this girl is aware of who and what Barkley was, it would mean she is a prophet. And if she is, then that would mean there is someone out there hell bent on killing us all.'

'The tin man,' I said.

'Yeah,' Hunter nodded. 'I wonder who he is.'

'I can't make any sense of it.'

'It probably does make perfect sense,' Cathy added, 'but Sarah is too young to explain clearly what she saw.'

'Hopefully Williams might be able to figure out what she saw. I'd like to be prepared for what's coming after us. I don't like the sound of it.'

'What the hell is that?' I said as I leaped from my chair.

There was banging and shouting coming from upstairs.

'It's Sarah!'

The three of us raced through the hallway and up the staircase to find her thrashing under the covers. Hunter held me back when I tried to wake her and Cathy paced the room frantically. He wanted to allow her to fully experience the prophecy and let her wake by herself. It was the right thing to do, it was nonetheless disturbing to watch.

Sarah woke with a start and almost fell out of the bed. Cathy went to her and held her tight while asking her what the nightmare was about.

'The tin man is going to hunt us down. He is looking for one of us!'

'Who is he looking for?' I asked.

'He's looking for …' Sarah paused and stared right into my eyes. 'You!'

I woke to see the nurse adjusting the drip. She did not dare look at me and took her clipboard and quickly shuffled across the room to the door. She must have increased the amount of sedative and within seconds I felt the effects of it. I struggled to keep my eyes open and I felt a strange floating sensation.

Before I lost consciousness I noticed a stack of pages on the table near the windows. Next to them was a white envelope. I used my gift to lift the pages but I was too weak and they fell and scattered across the floor. I focused on the envelope and was strong enough to make it float across the room and to open it when it landed on the bed. The page unfolded and was lifted into the air. There was one short line of text typed on it.

Somewhere beneath the calm waves of sedative was a storm of anger. Somewhere within the storm was a breeze of contentment.

I now knew the name of the person who would be the focal point of all my new-found bitterness and rage. There was some joy to be had in knowing that name.

Ross Bentley killed your sister.

CHAPTER SEVENTEEN

An Awakening

There was an uncomfortable mood in the house the next day. Hunter spent the majority of the morning pacing the grounds and smoking cigars. The girls watched TV shows for a couple of hours then Cathy gave her new best friend an impromptu make-over – with bizarre results. It was all very girly and I ended up alone in my room practising the dual shield again. I still couldn't perfect it but I found that I could create a shield that allowed objects to enter it while preventing anything from escaping. The opposite of what I was trying to achieve. I christened it a *reverse dual shield*. It didn't seem to have any practical applications so I simply put the day's training down as a failure. I hated failure and I grew frustrated and used my psychokinesis to crush the golf ball to the size of a pea before shooting it out the open window and across the sprawling grounds of the Williams estate.

After that I read more of Rudolph Klein's writings, some of the techniques he described were extremely complex and would probably take months to learn. They weren't the sort of manoeuvres one could practice in a bedroom anyway; they were lethal if you didn't get them right. One was called the *Vacuum Cycle* and it involved spinning energy around you then sucking it into your body, which if not done correctly could result in instant death. Needless to say I wasn't very eager to try it out.

At 6pm I left my room and went downstairs. Cathy and Sarah had gone for a walk to the nearby lake. Hunter was sitting by the back door, which was slightly ajar, picking at a bowl of pasta. I stood next to him and the sudden caress of cool evening air made me shiver.

'Winter's not far away,' I said as I zipped up my hoodie. 'I can feel it in the air.'

'Wow, that's so perceptive of you. Perhaps it's a gift the Guild never knew about – you could be the world's first *season predictor*.'

'You're a real funny guy, Hunter.' I shut the door and sat next to him at the table. 'You don't seem worried about the predictions that Sarah keeps making.'

'You'll have to get used to people trying to kill you, Bentley. This is what life is like in the Guild. There's always going to be some nasty git hunting you down, or you'll have to hunt them down. Either way, your life is always on the line.'

'I accepted that months ago. It's the way she described the tin man that has me on edge.'

'I'll admit it is unusual – sinister even – but Cathy was right when she said that the child can't accurately articulate the visions she's having. This isn't what you want to hear, but we'll just have to wait and see. This person will show up sooner or later and we'll just have to wait for him. We can't go looking for him as we have no clue to his identity.'

'I don't know how you're so calm about it all.'

'Worrying solves nothing.'

'Doesn't mean I can stop myself from doing it.'

I wanted to continue the conversation, but the door bell interrupted us. Hunter didn't budge so I left the table and plodded along the hallway to the door. I was expecting to see Cathy and Sarah returned from their evening stroll by the lake, instead I was looking out at five rather sombre faces.

I stood back and fully opened the door to let them in. Peter Williams was first, followed closely by two elderly women. One had a walking stick and looked about a hundred years old. The other was a heavy woman with serious eyes. Behind them were Angela and John Portman, whom I'd met at Romand's funeral. Angela smiled and said 'hello'. Her husband was dour and simply nodded as he passed me in the hall.

I followed them into the kitchen where they sat at the long dining table with Hunter, who didn't look too pleased to see them. They asked him where Sarah was and Hunter simply said, 'Gone out.'

'Could you be more vague?' Angela Portman said sarcastically.

'Probably could if I wanted to,' Hunter replied. I tried hard not to laugh; his quirky sense of humour and argumentative attitude were actually quite funny when they weren't directed at me.

'Is Cathy with her?' Peter Williams asked as he slumped into a chair at the head of the table.

'No, I let her leave the house on her own – of course she's with Cathy!'

'Your social skills need a lot of work, Hunter,' John Portman said dryly. 'And a pinch of respect wouldn't go amiss.'

'I could give you the same advice.'

'Enough!' Mr Williams snapped. This was the first time I'd ever seen him lose his cool. He had the look of a man under immense pressure and his face appeared even older than it normally did. 'Hunter, could you please go and look for the girls. Now is not a good time for them to be wandering the countryside without an escort.'

'Yes sir.' He got up and saluted the older man before storming away from the table. 'That's what I'm here for.'

I was left standing under the arched entrance to the hallway not knowing what to do with my hands. They were all looking at me, which happened a lot since The Million Dollar Gift competition. It always made me feel awkward.

'Ross, would you come sit with us for a moment?' Mr Williams asked.

A chair slid from under the table on its own. I didn't know which of them was psychokinetic, but the manner in which the gift was used only heightened my unease. I reluctantly sat in the empty chair and felt like a frog about to be dissected by a group of overzealous biology students.

'You've met the Portmans before, right?' Mr Williams continued. 'Yes, at poor Romand's funeral … such a dreadful day that was. Sitting next to you,' he indicated the ancient-looking woman with the walking stick 'is Clarissa Yenver. She is the oldest member of the Guild, she's retired now of course but she remains the wisest of us all. And to my right,' he held his wrinkly hand out to the dark-skinned woman, who had been watching me very carefully, 'is Pamela Powell. She lives in Florida, and travelled here when she got word that we were tracking a prophet.'

'I have a lot of experience with prophets,' Powell said to me. A smile grew on her face, but her eyes remained serious. 'The Guild always notifies me when they find one.'

'How does anyone become an expert in that field?' I asked.

'Being a prophet helps.'

'You see into the future?'

'Not much anymore. But when I was young I had a lot of premonitions. That particular gift diminishes with age and as you can tell, I am in the autumn of my years. No one can ever be an expert on such an unpredictable power, but I've learned how to cope with its unpredictability, which is very important because I can teach what I've learned to younger people who have this gift.'

'I've heard most prophets go nuts and end up killing themselves.'

'Can you blame them?'

'No, not after spending a few days with Sarah. These visions she's been having about the tin man are totally freaking me out.'

'She's had another?' Mr Williams butted in.

'Yeah, last night.'

'About the same man?' Yenver asked, her voice was very dignified, but a little shaky.

'The same. She keeps referring to him as "the tin man" and she insists that he's going to kill us all.'

'So, it was the same premonition?'

'Not quite. There's been one addition that I can't say was very pleasant to hear.'

'What did she add?' Mr Williams asked.

'She said that this killer was coming after one person in particular – me.'

There was silence for a moment. Not because they were speechless; each of them looked like they wanted to say something, just not in front of me.

'Hunter thinks it's a pile of crap,' I explained, 'and Cathy thinks the girl is misreading what she is seeing.'

'And what do *you* think?' Powell said to me.

'I don't know what to think.'

'I find that hard to believe.'

'Why? You don't know me, so how would you know what way my mind works?'

'When someone tells you that a man made of tin is going to kill you, it's hard to dispel that sort of thing from your mind, no matter who you are. It's the sort of thing that would keep you up at night.'

'All right, all right. Personally, I think she's genuine. So, that means there *is* some lunatic out there who's going to try to kill me. And I have no idea why he's after me.'

'Why …' Yenver sighed. '*Why* is the most important question we have to ask ourselves. If we can deduce *why* this tin man is after you, we may be able to uncover his identity.'

'Agreed,' John Portman said. 'Why would someone want to kill Ross?'

'Maybe it has something to do with The Million Dollar Gift,' I suggested. 'I think Paul Golding would love to see me dead.'

'Paul Golding wants to kill all of us,' Angela Portman replied. 'I'm sure he'd love to see Ross suffer, but he wouldn't be hunting him exclusively. Golding thinks like a business man, his mind is a financial one and there's little room for sentiment of any description. He'd only come after Ross if he thought he posed an immediate threat to his empire.'

'Perhaps he does.' I said.

'Angela is right,' Mr Williams said through knotted fingers. 'There must be something else behind this.'

'Ross has only been involved in three incidents,' Angela continued. 'It must be related to one of them.'

'That would make sense,' her husband said. I noticed he only agreed with the others' comments, and didn't voice any opinions of his own. Now I realised why Hunter wasn't happy to take a lecture from him.

'The Million Dollar Gift,' his wife said. 'I would rule that one out, for the reasons I just gave. Golding was the only person to lose out because of what happened but it wasn't serious enough for him to have some sort of vendetta against Ross. Then there was the death of Marianne Dolloway.'

'Marianne was a complete loner,' Mr Williams said with a shake of his head. 'She had no family or friends to avenge her. The closest person to her was Golding.'

'That only leaves the death of Ania Zalech,' Angela said.

'She was much the same as Marianne,' Mr Williams replied. 'She has no living relatives now and had little contact with the outside world, apart from her time with the Guild.'

'There is one other explanation,' Powell interrupted. 'This vision could be of a time far into the future. It might be years from now that this tin man comes after Ross. I'm sure he will make some enemies in the years ahead.'

'True,' Mr Williams sighed. 'We'll only know after we've probed the girl's mind properly.'

'I don't want to spend the rest of my life looking over my shoulder for a metal killer,' I said angrily. 'Now I know why most people don't like prophets. Sorry,' I raised my hands to Powell. 'No offence, but being able to see into the future doesn't make dealing with it any easier.'

'No one ever said it did.' Powell's smile had faded. There was something about her that made me nervous. Anyone with the ability to hold a stare for as long as she could was to be avoided. 'But sometimes it can save lives and Sarah's gift may save yours in time.'

'Or it might give me a nervous breakdown.'

'Young people,' Yenver giggled. 'Such a wonderful sense of humour.'

None of the others saw the funny side of it and the tension in the room remained.

'We'll question the girl tomorrow,' Powell announced. 'Let her have a rest this evening. It will be easier if she's feeling fresh.'

'Very well,' Mr Williams replied. 'It's been a long day for us all and I'm sure we'll prefer to tackle this after a good night's sleep.'

'Amen,' Powell said. Finally she drew her eyes from mine and left the table.

Mr Williams showed the others to the spare rooms where they'd sleep for the next few nights. After that he invited me to his study, saying he wanted to talk some things over. It was a small room in a part of the house that was rarely used. It was cluttered with books and towers of paper, old video cassettes, and some ancient-looking papyrus scrolls. There was a small desk in the centre of the circular floor and Mr Williams sat behind it. I dragged a chair from the corner of the room and sat opposite him. We chatted about

Rudolph Klein's writing on psychokinesis and I told him I couldn't get the dual shield right, but he was very impressed that I had created an inverted version of it; apparently it was an extremely difficult thing to do. I still couldn't see how it could be of any use, but praise was hard to come by and his kind words made me feel a little better about myself.

He went on to explain that Yenver and Powell would try to decipher Sarah's puzzling visions. Apparently, they'd gotten to the bottom of things like this many times before. I responded by telling him I wasn't sure if I really wanted to know what the cryptic visions meant.

'You are under the protection of the Guild now,' he said. 'No one will get to you.'

'That didn't stop Marianne from tracking me down.'

'Mistakes were made. We have learned from our mistakes, have we not?'

'Yes ...' He said it like he was talking about the Guild, but I knew he was really asking me if I'd learned from the mistake that led to Romand's death.

'You need something to get your mind off this dark business.' He started looking over the many shelves. 'Some reading will be a healthy distraction.'

'Not more of Klein's work,' I moaned. 'It's all very informative, but it's boring as hell!'

'Yes, he was a tad wearisome at times.' He unlocked a drawer under his desk and took out some pages held together with a large steel clip. 'However, it is necessary for you to familiarise yourself with his teachings.'

I took the stack from him. It looked like I had a tedious couple of days ahead of me.

I drifted in and out of consciousness for a number of hours. Dr Walters and her team spoke to me, but their words were no more than echoes at first. As the day grew old the voice of Dr Walters became coherent and she told me what had happened. She said the operation did not go smoothly and that I almost died at one point. The surgery had taken seventeen hours to complete and a further thirty-six hours had passed before my eyes had opened.

It was only when the sedatives eased off, and the medical team had left me alone in the room, that I became aware of the buzzing coming from my throat every time I took a breath. It sounded like someone running a plectrum up and down a steel guitar string when I inhaled and exhaled. It was a coarse and unnatural noise, one that would send a chill up a person's spine. I smiled as I listened to the electronic scraping sound as my chest rose and fell. I needed to be feared if I was to contend with my enemies, and the noise of my breathing would help me in that respect. I would also need to move my head if I was to make a start on my recovery and I concentrated on lifting myself off the pillow

There was another sound as my chin fell to my chest and my head slowly rose up. This was like drawing a sword from a sheath. It was a smoother and more seductive noise, but just as unnatural as the sound of my breathing.

The operation had indeed been a success. I was able to lift and turn my head; not like I once had, but it meant I was functional again, and that's all I needed. My gifts would do the rest. My face felt very tight when I moved my head around, as if the skin was wrapped too tightly across my skull. It was unsettling, but there were more important matters to deal with. Getting out of bed was my first mission.

I wrapped my hands around the guard rails on either side of the mattress then tried to physically pull myself forward. My strength quickly gave out and I fell back. I would have to use my gift of psychokinesis if I wanted to leave the bed.

It took almost ten minutes to create enough energy to push my body up off the mattress. I hovered above the bed then slowly rotated in the air, like an astronaut in zero-gravity. My bare feet tensed up as they met the cool tiles, my legs shook as they took my weight. I used my power to straighten myself and to remain steady.

It had taken a monumental effort just to stand up, but it would get easier once the sedatives wore off. I could feel the drugs in my system. They made me weak – the one thing I hated more than anything. I had to rid myself of this parasitic poison that flowed through me!

I summoned my gift of mageletonia and used it to force some of the debilitating drug from my body, by pushing it out the pores of my skin. I felt instantly stronger and was now able to stand without the use of psychokinesis. I still needed it to walk forward and had to create kinetic crutches to stop myself from falling over. I was up and moving about at last.

It was only then that I detected the other drug in my system. It was deeper and stronger than the sedative. I was clever enough to know I would require some cocktail of narcotics to help my body cope with the implants, and that is what I was feeling. But there was something more ...

This new drug was coming to the fore now that the sedative was forced out. It was coursing through my veins and it was having an unexpected influence on my brain. I was feeling intense anger. It had no direction. I was angry with everything. I wanted to kill everyone. I wanted to destroy the world and all in it. It was overwhelming me. I was very good at suppressing my emotions, but now I could not contain them ...

I dropped to my knees and threw my hands over my face. The anger was too much. It felt like my head was going to explode. This anger was drawing in too much energy and I was becoming *too* powerful. If I did not quench the fury I would literally explode – and the entire building would go with me.

I quickly used mageletonia to pull the sedative back through my pores and into my bloodstream and within seconds I began to calm down. I sucked in deep breaths and managed to climb back to my feet after a few moments.

Weakened by the sudden surge, I staggered to the window and sat on the wide sill. I did not recognise the city I was gazing out at. I looked down on busy streets either side of a wide river that had two bridges spanning it. One was old fashioned, made of stone, and the other, which was a half mile downstream, was modern and metal and abstract. There were tall glass towers in the distance and ghosts of mountains beyond. I had no idea where I was, but it mattered not. Golding's people would take me wherever I wanted to go once I was well enough to fight again.

I watched the people on the streets hurrying along and I wished to be with them. I wanted nothing more than to be free of the clinic and to begin the pursuit of my enemies. I would start with Ross Bentley, the person who had murdered Ania. I had never met him but was very familiar with his reputation. Bentley was a thoughtless teenager who had been at the centre of the controversy surrounding The Million Dollar Gift contest. The Guild of the True had gone into turmoil when videos of Bentley using his power surfaced on the internet. He had come close to ruining all the decades of hiding the gifted from the outside world.

Bentley was a troublesome teenager, but that did not mean he was to be underestimated. I had heard how Bentley fought Marianne Dolloway and survived – something no one else had ever managed. He was immensely powerful and would pose quite a challenge to me.

'Not powerful enough,' I said aloud.

My voice ... it was inhuman. It sounded like a fusion between an electro-larynx and a taser-gun. Some remnant of my old voice remained, but it was cloaked by the buzzing sound from my throat. Strangely, I found it amusing. Even more strange was my inability to control my amusement. My laughter was like a robotic hyena chattering.

I pushed myself from the sill and slowly staggered to a mirror hanging on the other side of the room by the door. This was an even bigger shock than hearing my new voice.

I had four deep scars on either side of my face. My eyebrows and eyelashes were no more. My face was deathly pale and darkness ringed my pale eyes. I opened my mouth to see two rows of shining metal teeth. I lifted my chin to get a better look at my neck, and saw it was wrapped in bandages and I pulled them down to see metal plates underneath. My appearance now matched my inner self: inhuman.

I moved closer to the mirror to inspect my gleaming metal teeth when, over my shoulder, I spied a bundle of paper lying on the table. I had tried to levitate it to the bed before the operation, but failed – only managing to move an envelope that had been placed next to the stack of paper.

I slowly made my way to the table. When I got closer I saw there was a new envelope lying on the tabletop and I took it in hand then returned to the bed and tore it open. There was a handwritten letter inside.

The tone of the message was friendly, despite being from Paul Golding, a man I had seen as an enemy for so many years. It was intriguing to say the least.

Hello Edward,

I hope you don't mind that I refer to you by your Christian name. I've watched you for so long that I feel as if I know you. I have spies all over the world and I have read so many reports on you over the years. When I learned that you had joined the Guild I had you earmarked as a potential threat to my organisation. Possibly even the greatest threat we would ever face. I am pleased that you have turned away from them, yet saddened by the manner in which they tried to capture you. The loss of a sister is a pain I know only too well. My sister, Sarah, was my only family and I had to endure a great loss when she was murdered. My thoughts are with you in this most difficult time. However, I am confident that you will overcome this tragedy. I am confident because I see in you a great determination.

I am sure you will want revenge for what happened. You want to destroy the Guild for murdering Ania, and also for disfiguring you so cruelly. You also want revenge against those who murdered your parents and who set you on this dark path that has taken so long to escape. I speak of The Eastern Shadow.

I have information on both groups that will help you find and kill their highest-ranking members. I offer this information to you freely. All I ask in return is that you follow my advice.

I suggest you should attack the Guild first. They are your greatest and most dangerous enemy and must be anni- hilated before they realise that you are alive and that you have my support. After they are gone, you can then focus on the more elusive yet less resourceful members of The East- ern Shadow. When both groups are no more, you can con- tinue to work alongside Golding Scientific if you wish. You will want for nothing for the rest of your days.

I am prepared to offer you unlimited financial resources in your quest for vengeance. All departments of Golding Sci- entific are at your disposal and I hope you see that this will be a healthy relationship for you to engage in. We are your friends. I am your friend. I wish only to help you.

I have helped you by rebuilding you physically but I am also prepared to aid you in improving the control you have over your gifts. On the table you will find some papers. It is part of the thesis written by Penelope Gordon in the 1980s. As you know, these writings are universally banned but I offer them to you as a gesture of goodwill. It will help you attain a power that you could have only dreamed about until now.

You are about to become the most powerful man on earth, Edward. No one will ever hurt you again.

Your friend,
Paul Golding

I had heard rumours of Penelope Gordon's work, but I never believed I would ever actually read what was contained in this rare piece of writing. Cramer mentioned it a couple of times, when he was very drunk, and said that one of the techniques she invented for mageletons was astounding, but too hazardous to teach to others. One technique in particular was, in Cramer's own words, 'deadly enough to destroy entire nations in an instant.'

I lifted my arm and the pages flew across the room into my hand. I looked upon the bold heading on the first page and grinned.

~~~~~~~~~~~~~~~~~~~~~~~~~~~~~~

Mageletonia - Part 3
The Wave of Destruction
by Penelope Gordon - 1983

CHAPTER EIGHTEEN

Forbidden Words

The door swung open before I could read past the heading and I slowly turned my head to see Walters entering the room with a tall and very muscular woman by her side. Walters smiled pleasantly as she always did. Her companion was apprehensive. There was only loathing in her eyes. She stood at the end of the bed with her arms folded and I looked her up and down, noticing a handgun in a waist holster, which was unclipped.

'Hello, Edward,' Walters said. 'I hope you're feeling well today.'

'I feel fantastic, doctor,' I said with my electric voice. 'You could say I feel like a new man.'

'I bet,' she replied. I could see in her eyes a mixture of surprise and horror at the power of my new voice. 'This is Aubrey Pearson,' she continued. 'She's the head of security.'

'Good day, Ms Pearson.' I smiled and pointed at her waist. 'There is no need for that in future.'

'Excuse me?' she frowned. 'What do you mean?'

'The gun. Do you think you can harm me with bullets?'

'As long as I don't aim for your neck, yes.'

'Very good,' I could not contain my amusement and laughed loudly. 'I like your sense of humour.'

'How are you feeling, Edward?' Walters asked softly. 'Are you experiencing any prolonged pain? Dizziness?'

'Neither.'

'Good. I can't believe you managed to get out of bed so soon.'

'I don't quite feel one hundred percent yet, but then I am *not* quite one hundred percent, am I?' I tapped the metal plates where my throat used to be. 'You did well, doctor. You did what said you would. I like people who follow through with their promises.'

'It was touch and go for a while.'

'That does not matter. I am here. I breathe.' I sucked in a deep breath and the room was filled with a buzzing sound. '*I live!*'

'Indeed you do.' Her eyes met the bound paper on the bed and she stepped away, a shade of fear ran across her face as if she knew what was contained in it. 'I see you're catching up on your reading.'

'I am indeed. This,' I pointed at the papers, 'was an unexpected, but *most* welcome surprise.'

'A present from the corporation,' Pearson interjected. 'One that should not be forgotten.'

I turned and stared at her. I had excused her remark about my neck, but would not allow her to interrupt me.

'Wait outside,' I said. 'You are making me feel uncomfortable and I do not want the room destroyed with your innards.'

'I'll have you know I'm in charge of looking after you,' Pearson replied sharply. 'One word from me and this little experiment is over.'

'I am surprised that someone in your position would be so naïve, Ms Pearson. You do realise that I am much more important to Golding Scientific than you will ever be. And you should also realise that I can crush your heart without lifting a finger.'

'I can look after myself—'

I reached out with my psychokinesis and gripped her heart. Pearson hunched over and clawed at her chest. She tried to reach for her gun, but I used my powers to press her arms against her ribs. I gradually bent her fingers backward, almost to breaking point. I then used mageletonia to make her saliva pool in the back of her mouth, preventing her from drawing air into her lungs.

I flashed my metal teeth at her and said, 'Are we getting the picture?'

Pearson nodded frantically and I released her from the invisible grip. She wasted no time in leaving Walters and I alone in the room. The doctor was terrified by the power I had, that was obvious and natural, but she seemed drawn to me for some reason. Perhaps she was the type of person who liked to take in stray animals, but I wanted to believe that she was attracted to me on some level. I did not care much about anything, but I was still a man and felt the need to be wanted. She would not talk openly, though. Not while Pearson was nearby. I looked across the room at a jug of water on the table and suddenly its contents floated up into the air then began to spread out and form a watery cocoon around both of us, which muffled our voices so that no one could hear what we were to say.

'How are you feeling?' she whispered as she sat next to me on the bed. 'How are you *really* feeling?'

'We both know there is something very unusual coursing through my veins, doctor. Beneath the sedative is a narcotic that makes me violent and strengthens the emotions I am feeling.'

'I expected this. It's one of the drugs they've given you.'

'You have used it before?'

'A couple of times. It's still at the experimental stage, like every thing we do here. It's called Hyperfurens. Those who were injected with it become very aggressive and erratic.'

'It is not wise to make a gifted person so aggressive.'

'I know that. I told them not to use it.'

'But they dismissed your opinion.'

'They did.'

'They want to make me as violent as possible. That way I will do more damage to their competitors.'

'They're only using you, Edward.'

'They *think* they are using me, but the opposite is the truth. It is *they* who are being used. I will ally myself with Golding only for as long as it suits me.'

'Don't underestimate him.'

'I know full well what he is capable of.'

'The sedatives will wear off within a couple of days. After that, the Hyper-furens will overpower you. Edward, you may not be yourself from that point onward. The person you are will be drowned in an uncontrollable rage.'

'I have a lot of experience in controlling rage.'

'This is not like anything you will have ever experienced. No one can suppress it.'

'Do I have any alternative?'

'I will try to get some tablets for you, to counter the effect of this rage. But you must not tell anyone that I gave them to you. It could get me killed.'

'No harm will come to you while I live.' I almost reached out to her but drew back my hand. One small part of who I once was had remained but now was not the time to become infatuated with a woman, especially one who worked for Paul Golding. 'Why do you want to help me, doctor?'

'You're alone. Nobody should be alone. Everyone needs a friend.'

'I have survived without help for a long time.'

'Surviving isn't living.'

'The option of having a life was taken from me long ago. I am not the type of friend you want.'

'At least let me help you,' Walters pleaded. 'I will smuggle some tablets to you. Please take them. Help me to help you.'

'I am tired,' I said. The conversation had gotten too personal for my liking. I was not used to people genuinely wanting to know me. 'I would like to be alone now.'

'Very well,' she said. 'Just don't push yourself too hard, Edward. Your enemies will wait. As will your *friends*. Try to get some rest.'

I was beginning to feel fatigued and as the evening sun faded I lay back in bed and threw the cotton sheet over my body. My strength had faded fast, but I kept my eyes open long enough to read the papers I had been given.

'*Mageletons have a powerful gift and are therefore coveted and feared by all those who are aware of their existence. They are coveted because they are feared. Those who wish to be feared seek out mageletons.*'

Albert Galmard, founder of the Guild of the True.

Little has changed since Galmard's time. Mageletons are still amongst the most prized of all the gifted, and the fear they cause has not diminished. There has always been a belief that mageletons are instinctively violent and therefore cannot be trusted. This is why most people fear to interact with them. The belief is not entirely true. But not entirely without basis either.

I started out by trying to vindicate the mageletons that have lived throughout the centuries but the results of my research may only compound the distrust of them.

In the two previous sections of this paper I have outlined how this gift can be used, both in everyday life and in combat. In this section, I will explain how far this gift can go and the immense threat it may pose if in the wrong hands. I have discovered a technique that could make a mageleton a threat to all humanity. For many months I have contemplated burying this report because I am unsure that this information should ever be shared. It could result in all mageletons being hunted down and murdered because of the potential risk they pose. It could also provide a malevolent mageleton with the knowledge to reach their full potential which could prove extremely perilous. The Guild has pressed me in recent months to complete the study so that it can be filed with the full investigations on all fifteen of the true gifts. I have decided on completing this paper, but will insist that only one copy exists and that it should be destroyed if the Guild deems this material to be unsafe.

Most mageletons have varying degrees of control over water. The strongest of our kind, those with the purest form of the gift, can manipulate any type of liquid. It can be impressive and has many practical uses, but this control is limited.

Even those with the pure gift can only control a certain amount of fluid at any given time. Most can only manipulate fifty gallons or so, or the equivalent of a bath tub of water. The strongest can control enough water to fill an Olympic-sized swimming pool. This amount of liquid can be dangerous if under the influence of a skilled mageleton, but it can be countered relatively easily by psychokinetics and electropsychs. What I set out to find was a variation of the gift that allows a person to control larger bodies of water. The variation that has never been reliably recorded, but rumours of its existence have persisted over the years.

I refer to the story of Tobias Deval. He lived in the fourteenth century and was said to have the ability to lift rivers out their beds then manipulate the water in any manner he wished. Most considered it to be nothing more than a yarn, but there is no smoke without fire and I spent three years trying to find any evidence that Deval and his unique power actually existed. It was 1968 that I found a story that appeared to match the old tale; it was an account from a French Military commander in the fourteenth century. He claimed to have witnessed an extraordinary event while on a tour of duty as a young officer. He said that he met a man named Tobias, who could raise rivers and move them across the land as if they were 'giant watery snakes'.

It was not definitive proof, but deep down I knew this was a genuine account, which meant the power to manipulate large bodies of water was possible. I immediately set out to achieve this power, but failed miserably. Then in 1973 I met George Watson, a teenager who had mageletonia and who was sent by the Guild to learn from me. We trained together for many months and in 1974 he began to aid me in my quest to replicate Deval's power.

In September 1975 we created something that was truly groundbreaking. We invented what has now become known as the Dual Wave

Effect.

I would never have discovered this without George Watson. I only have one gift, and it takes two specific gifts to create a dual wave effect, thus controlling large bodies of water such as lakes, rivers and even oceans.

You must have both mageletonia and psychokinesis to be able to do this. Mageletonia is required to control the mass of water and to fuse it into one single object, but psychokinesis is required to move this object. And even then, most psychokinetics could not move such a large object, and so the laws of gravity must also be employed. The ability to control a large amount of liquid requires you to create a wave effect. You must allow gravity to do the hard work, while using your gifts to influence the course of the water.

We first tested this technique in a swimming pool. George used his gifts to take control of the water then employed his psychokinesis to shift it slightly. When he relinquished his control, gravity seized the water and the natural reaction was for it flow back whence it came and it swept down to the opposite end of the pool. When this happened, George took control of the water once more and gave it a little nudge which started a see-saw wave effect. Eventually the water came right out of the pool and into the air. At that point he managed to make it float as if it were a solid object.

Throughout 1976 we practised this new and exciting technique with progressively larger swimming pools before moving onto something more ambitious; a lake in northern France. The results were astounding, but nothing prepared me for what happened in June 1977.

George was a naturally ambitious and curious young man, and he wanted to try the dual wave effect on an ocean. In the summer of 1977 we travelled north, to the island of Svalbard above the Barents

Sea. There, on the eastern coast, we tested the technique on the largest scale imaginable. George managed to create a rapid tidal effect that led to an immense wave being created. When he finally lost control of it, a tsunami took place and swept inland. I estimate the height of the wave to be more than fifty metres as it met the coastline. It would have killed many thousands of people if we had done this in a populated area, but the remoteness of Svalbard meant that no lives were lost.

I believe that this power poses too much of a risk to the world. It should never be replicated; George shared my opinion. We never repeated the test and have never documented the results until now.

The reason for my apprehension is that there is no limit to the dual-wave effect. The rocking motion involved continues to grow and grow as long as the person wants it to.

It is virtually limitless and could be used, theoretically, to control the majority of an entire ocean such as the Atlantic or the Pacific. This is my greatest fear. To alter one of these oceans could lead to the destruction of mankind.

The door to a new world of opportunity had just been opened for me and I could not help but smile at the prospect of creating havoc with this new power. I was an impatient person and there was no way I could wait until morning to start practicing the dual wave effect.

I lifted myself out of bed then went to the window. It was well past midnight and the streets below were quiet. Only the odd car here and there, a few revellers heading for the nightclubs, a homeless couple sitting in a doorway sharing a bottle of cheap wine.

My eyes narrowed on the river across the street. I reached out and pressed the palm of my hand against the glass and it began to frost over as I started to use my gifts.

I employed mageletonia to take control of the water flowing lazily under the bridges, then sent out a heavy burst of psychokinetic power to make it run against its natural course and rise under the old stone bridge. When the water fell, it rushed downstream and I seized control of it once more and it rose up under the metal bridge about half mile downstream. Again I released my control and the river sloshed down violently and I pushed it back upstream and the stone bridge was consumed as more water was caught up in the see-sawing wave effect. I stood back from the window and swept my hand through the air from side to side, as if I were conducting an orchestra.

The river was rising fifty feet over one bridge then sweeping down and climbing high above the other. Cars slid to a halt and people stood by the banks to watch this incredible event. And it *was* incredible. I could hardly believe I was doing it. Just before I released my grip on the water I sent out a wall of kinetic energy so that the tower of water fell to one side and splashed down on the crowd of onlookers. A little practical joke.

My laughter sounded like a wasp caught in a fly zapper.

'At what point does a man have the worship of a god?' I asked myself. 'For Poseidon himself would be envious of my power.'

My physical recovery went well over the following few days. Impossibly well. I was now able to walk without using my gifts, and the effect of the sedatives was gradually receding. My mind and reactions sharpened and I grew accustomed to the metal and electronic implants. The influence of the Hyper-furens was growing, though. I had to concentrate hard to keep my temper in check. It was as if the drug was tapping in some primitive aggression that had been lying dormant within me.

The only way to counter it was to take the tablets that Dr Walters smuggled into my room each morning. I took them the first day and the anger was quenched. But on the second day I spat them out on to the palm of my hand. I knew full well that anger was rocket fuel for any of the true gifts, and that allowing the Hyper-furens to affect me would make me so powerful that no one could match my strength. That was too much of a temptation to ignore. Raw ambition defeated common sense.

I looked at the three white tablets and used my psychokinesis to crush them into a fine powder that

I blew off the palm of my hand. Within twenty-four hours the sadness I had been enduring, along with the attraction to Dr Walters, had been eroded by a tide of rage that kept coming at me. With it came monumental power. I could feel it bubbling under my skin. I felt strong enough to conquer the world.

Each night I practised the dual wave effect on the nearby river, sometimes lifting large amounts of the water into the air, and other times just gently waving my hand from side to side and watching the river seesawing hypnotically. It was therapeutic in some way, and was the only thing that made me forget the rising anger. The rest of the time I had to concentrate to hold back my aggression. But the more I held it back, the more it altered my thoughts. Before long all I could think about was murder.

The monotony was severed when I awoke one morning to find a sheet of paper on the cabinet next to the bed. I picked it up and saw there was a name and address on it. I laughed for hours when I realised who this person was.

🕶 🕶 🕶

Seven days later I was almost back to full health and Professor King said there was no reason why I should remain at the clinic. He said I was free to leave but I was to accompany him to *Unit 2* first. Apparently there was someone important that I had to meet before beginning my rampage.

I followed him along the gleaming white corridor to an elevator that brought us into the bowels of the building. The doors opened to reveal what appeared to be a factory floor. There were workers shuffling around in white overalls and operating large machinery and there were thousands of vials on conveyor belts that rattled around them as we walked along the centre aisle of the room.

He brought me through a doorway to a hangar bay and there was a very well-dressed young man sitting on a large suitcase. Behind him a large object was covered with a black tarp and behind that a van was parked with two military types sitting in the front. Nearby was a young woman, around twenty years old, examining a long black cape; she watched me very carefully as I approached.

King hung back as I went to the man who stood and smiled, even though his eyes betrayed how afraid he was of me.

'My name is Henry Dragotto,' he said in an American accent. He held out his hand, that was quivering slightly, and I reluctantly shook it. 'I am the head of Golding Scientific's Advanced Weaponry Division.'

'Do they have a division for everything?' I asked. 'Incidentally, I do not require weapons of any kind; nature has already provided me with an arsenal of my own.'

'So I hear.' Dragotto chuckled. He stood and opened the suitcase. 'Weapons aren't the only things we develop.'

There was a heavy leather coat, black work boots, combat-style trousers and some sweaters inside the case. There were also very thin metal plates of various shapes and sizes.

'Are you a tailor?'

'Also a tinker, a soldier and a spy,' Dragotto winked. 'But in my heart I'm an inventor. Paul Golding hired me a few years ago to develop weapons for him, but twelve months ago I was invited to work on two new projects. Mr Golding first asked me develop clothing that would protect him and his closest bodyguards from psychokinetic attacks.'

'No clothing can withstand such attacks.'

'That's not entirely true, Mr Zalech.'

Dragotto picked up a small curved metal plate from inside the suitcase. It was wafer thin and had a strange hexagon pattern embossed on the front.

'This is Deflexus technology. It was partly inspired by stealth technology. You see, on a stealth aircraft there are no right angles for a radar signal to bounce off – and that got me thinking. I did many tests relating to psychokinetic energy and found that it has most impact when it strikes a flat and solid object. So, I came up with lots of different textured metals to see it could somehow be dispersed – or deflected – and this design,' he ran his hand over the surface of the metal plate, 'worked best. The energy seems to be scattered when it comes into contact with it. This was enhanced when we subjected this metal to radiation.' He put the plate back into the suitcase then lifted the long, black leather coat. 'It would work well if you wore a suit of armour made of this stuff, but I don't think that's very practical. Instead I designed very thin strips of Deflexus metal and lined clothing with it. This coat has plates for protecting the chest, ribs, back, and thin strips running the length of the sleeves. It won't make you immune to psychokinetic attacks but it could be the difference between a bruise and a broken bone.'

'Most ingenious,' I gave a complimentary nod. 'This will come in useful, no doubt.'

'As will this,' Dragotto nodded at the large object under the tarp. 'You've *gotta* see this! I've been working on it for almost a year. It was originally designed for another of Mr Golding's employees – Marianne Dolloway. She was a very impatient person and wanted us to develop a vehicle that could get her around quicker than your average sports car. I suggested a high powered motorbike but she demanded that I come up with something *unique* – which I did.'

He pulled back the tarp revealing an unusual-looking motorbike. It was longer than normal models and there were four exhausts, two slim ones and two wide ones that stretched from the engine to the back on either side of the rear wheel, which was very wide. The plastic casing at the front of the bike was elaborate and seemed more robust than normal. This casing was strangely moulded at the front of the bike and covered the handlebars.

'It can easily pass for a normal motorbike-'

'It is not a normal motorbike?'

'No. It's what I call a *Kinetibike*. This particular model is the GSK7 – short for Golding Scientific Kineti-bike Prototype Seven. It can run on petrol just like any other bike,' he turned the key in the ignition and revved the engine just to make his point. 'But it can also run on a different type of fuel. There are two funnels running from the opening at the handgrips and down through the engine and out the two wide exhausts at the back. The interior of these exhausts are lined with Deflexus technology.'

'I see. The rider channels psychokinetic energy through his hands into the funnels below the hand-grips and it powers the engine and is then forced out the back?'

'You have a keen intellect, Mr Zalech. That's pretty much exactly how it works. *But* the Deflexus metal is threaded around the interior of the exhausts rather than covering the whole lot of it. This has the effect of spinning the psychokinetic energy and making it more powerful, thus making the bike go even faster.'

'How fast can it go?'

'That depends on how powerful the rider is. Marianne clocked up a speed of 600kmph on one of the prototypes – the GSK6. This one is more aerodynamic than that model, so if you're as strong as she was, you could probably go faster.'

'I could get from one side of the country to the other in a little over an hour. No one could keep up with me.'

'Even helicopters couldn't keep up with this bad boy!' Dragotto slapped the leather seat of the bike. 'And the handling on this bike is second to none, even at extreme speeds.'

'Why am I not getting one?' the young woman who been closely inspecting a black cape said. 'Am I not important?'

'Ms Hofer, you do not need such a vehicle,' Dragotto said without turning. 'You're on security detail for the next six months, so why would you need one of these bikes?'

'It might be helpful ...'

'Forget it. This bike cost fifty million dollars to develop and you're not getting one.' Dragotto looked at me and snorted. 'Youngsters, eh? They always want new toys. Anyways, this bike is all yours, Mr Zalech.'

'You are quite the inventor,' I said, 'reminiscent of a James Bond character.'

'Yeah, except I'm working for the bad guys and not helping out the hero.'

'You will find that the villains always pay better.'

I took some of the clothes lined with Deflexus metal back to my room and spent the evening preparing for what was to come. I put on a pair of the heavy black boots, a dark blue pair of combat trousers, an armour-plated chest garment, the black leather jacket and a pair of the tactical gloves. I packed a number of documents into the case I had brought from the hangar and locked it. King had given me a house key that morning and I slipped it inside my trouser pocket. Golding had purchased a rural house south of Luton that I could use whenever I needed to rest. I would use it as a base to plan out each step in my masterpiece of revenge.

The mere thought of vengeance sent a ripple of power through my body and I almost passed out. I sat next to the window and drew in deep breaths until the devastating sensation abated.

'They're sending you into war,' Dr Walter said as she entered the room.

'I go of my own accord, doctor,' I said. 'Not everyone who goes to war dies at the hands of their enemies. There are always some who return.'

'Do you even know where you're going?'

'Yes. I will be driven to a private air strip a few miles north of here. There I will board Golding's private jet and two hours later I will have reached my first stop.'

'What is this first stop, Edward?'

'I have to pay a visit to someone in Ireland.'

'Please don't kill any innocents–'

A fit of anger overcame me and I lashed out. I held Walters against the wall with my psychokinetic power.

'Did they stop to ask my sister if she was innocent? Did they hesitate before killing her? Did they bother to ask me *why* I acted the way I had before they did this to me?' I ran my hands over the deep scars on the sides of my face. 'They did not care, my dear doctor! Why should I?'

I released her and she slid down the wall and hit the floor with a loud clatter. She had left the room before I returned to my senses.

CHAPTER NINETEEN

Argento

I'd gotten used to rude awakenings during my time in the Guild, but this was on another level entirely. It was the worst possible way to be dragged from sleep. Sarah was screaming from her bedroom. An intense, high-pitched sound filled the house and my chest with anxiety. I leaped from the bed, pulled on a pair of tracksuit bottoms and ran barefoot along the landing to her. Cathy appeared from her room and was right behind me as I barged into the young prophet's bedroom. I thought the girl was being butchered judging by the intensity of her calls, but found her to be the only one in the room.

'Run!' Sarah was screaming at the top of her voice. She didn't appear to be awake. Her eyes were closed and her body was rigid with fear. 'Run! He's coming for you! Lonely man! Run!'

I remained still, unsure of what to do. Cathy on the other hand rushed past me and jumped on the bed then proceeded to shake Sarah until she snapped out of the vision. When she did fully wake up, Sarah started crying and threw her arms around Cathy, who told her it was just a nightmare and that everything would be all right. I didn't think my girlfriend could ever be such a skilled liar; Sarah's gift was genuine and that meant something horrific was to take place, and everything was far from all right.

The older, and slower, house guests filled the room and surrounded her, and I could see my presence was of no use. I walked back to my room and got fully dressed, brushed my teeth and soaked my face in cold water, then went downstairs. The others had taken the young girl to the kitchen and the old ladies were mothering her, while Hunter and Mr Williams stood back with troubled expressions. An exhausted-looking Cathy was sitting at the table, a cup of tea beneath her chin.

The women asked Sarah what the dream was about, but her answers were as obscure as ever. She rambled on and on about *the sewer monster* then *the lonely man*. Then the tin man made another appearance. She wouldn't tell us what happened after that, though I guessed whoever the lonely man was, he met, or was to meet, with a sticky ending.

The two old women took Sarah outside for a walk in the fresh morning air, as if that would do her any good. The rest of us convened at the long kitchen table and discussed what we'd just heard.

'She has just described, in her own childlike manner, a person being murdered,' Mr Williams said. He looked dreadfully tired and I knew why. I'd heard him shuffling around in his study until the early hours. Something had him well and truly scared. 'It pains me greatly that I have no means to prevent it.'

'She didn't describe this person as gifted. Perhaps it's just a normal person. Why should we care if it is just a normal person?' Angela Portman said casually, and her husband nodded in agreement.

'You're a horrible little woman,' Hunter sneered at her. 'You're saying this doesn't matter if the lonely man is not gifted?'

'Our job is to protect the gifted, Hunter,' John Portman argued.

'Don't call me that. Only my friends call me by that name.'

'Enough of this bickering,' Mr Williams shouted. 'A man will be killed!'

'By whom?' Hunter asked. 'Who is this tin man? Until we find out, there is no chance of preventing this lonely man from getting killed.'

'I don't want to sit through this conversation again!' Cathy kicked back her chair and stormed out of the room and stomped noisily up the staircase.

'Neither do I.' I said getting up from my seat. I followed her upstairs and found her curled up on her bed, hugging her pillows, with eyes that were swollen with tears.

I shut the door and sat at the edge of the bed and rubbed her shoulder.

'Don't let it get you down,' I told her.

'It's impossible not to, Ross.'

I climbed onto the bed and wrapped my arms around her and held her tight to my chest. It was the first time I'd seen weakness in her since Romand's death. Usually she was so strong, and I came to take her strength for granted and forget that at times she needed a shoulder of support just like everyone else.

'I know this is a tough atmosphere,' I said, pressing my lips to her forehead. 'It won't always be like this. You know it won't.'

'It *is always* like this, Ross. And it's getting worse since we rescued Sarah. This house has become a prison and it feels like we're on death row, waiting for the end to creep up on us.'

'Hey, it's not that bad.'

'It *is*. There's a murderer lurking out there and he is going to come after you, Ross. How do you think that makes me feel?'

'Well, it doesn't make me feel too good either.'

'I'm worried that you'll be killed! This isn't a time for fooling around.'

'Let him come. Whoever this tin man is, he isn't going to get the better of me. I intend to live a long life and I also intend to share it with you.'

'I worry that we'll be torn apart by this constant struggle.' Cathy pulled away from me and sat with her back against the wall, a sudden distant expression on her face. 'I hate being part of the Guild. I hate that so much pain is caused by the gifts. I only want to use my gift to help people. Ross, as long as we are in the Guild we'll never be free of the fighting and the killing. I don't know if I want the rest of my life to be like this.'

'What are you trying to say?'

'Nothing.' She buried her face in her hands. 'I don't know what I'm trying to say.'

'You don't want to be a Guild agent?'

'No, I don't.'

'They need us.' I thought back to the conversation I'd had with Mr Williams the week before. He'd told me that the Guild saw me as a possible leader. They were dependant on young people like Cathy and me to secure their future, and to carry on the fight against the evils of the world. I liked that idea. I wanted to play a role in the future of the group. But I loved Cathy so much and staying in the Guild seemed to have her tormented. I could feel the first tugs of a titanic struggle coming on.

'The Guild will disappear if we turn our backs on it,' I said.

'Ross, this is all very new to you. I'm sure it's exciting right now, but I've spent my entire life around these people and I want to break free. I want to get away from all this. It's *always* like this! There's *always* some great threat that the Guild has to combat. If it's not the Kematian, it's Golding, then it's Marianne, then the Zalechs, now it's this tin man. And when he's finally caught it'll be someone else. Sooner or later the Guild will come up against someone, or some power, that they'll be unable to fight. They'll be wiped out and so will we, if we hang around.'

I reached out and slipped my hands under her arms and pulled her close to me. I kissed her very softly and stared into her eyes. 'Stop thinking like this,' I told her. 'You're the most beautiful and amazing girl in the entire world and believe me, no one is ever going to kill you, and no one is ever going to stop me from protecting you, and loving you. I'm not going away like your father or Romand. I'm here to stay.'

It was a risky thing to say, but it's what was on my mind and in my heart. I was half expecting her to slap me in the mush for mentioning the two fathers she had and lost, but instead she loosened up and hugged me.

I lifted her head off my shoulder and pecked the end of her nose and smiled. 'I think you need a break,' I said quietly. 'We need to get away from here for a while.'

'That's unlikely to happen. I could do with a distraction, though.'

'You wanna watch a movie or something?'

'I want to spend time with Argento. He always takes my mind off my troubles.'

'Argento?' I backed up, a sudden jab of jealousy made my arms fall from her waist. All I could think of was some smooth Latin guy that she might have a crush on. 'Who the hell is he?'

'A friend.'

'Sounds like a close friend to me …'

'He is.' She smiled fondly which did nothing to dispel my jealousy. 'He's magical, in a way.'

'He's a gifted person?'

'Not exactly. We should go visit him.' She climbed off the bed and took a jacket that had been draped over her open wardrobe door. 'I think you might like him,' she said as she punched her arms into the tight sleeves. 'In fact, you could learn a lot from him.'

'Really,' I said dryly as I followed her to the door to the landing. 'I can't wait to make his acquaintance.'

We didn't bother to tell the others we were leaving the house and slipped out the front door without anyone hearing us. Cathy said she didn't want to make the journey in the rain, so I used my gift to break into and start up the Portmans' car. Cathy, who was a very good driver, got into the driver's seat and started the engine. She drove out of the grounds and onto the winding country road leading west. It was the road I'd driven after Romand died and it was difficult to shake that memory.

'It's my least favourite road too,' Cathy said, without tearing her gaze from the rain soaked glass in front of her.

'Didn't know you could read minds.'

'I don't need to. It's impossible to think of anything else, isn't it?'

'Yeah.'

We didn't say much after that. We both would have said the

same thing: 'I wish Romand was still here. He'd know what to do.'

After a while I realised we were headed to the animal sanctuary owned by Peter Williams. Was she secretly in love with one of the staff members? Who the bloody hell was this Argento character? I'd struggle to hold my temper if he was the tanned Adonis that I was picturing.

We parked outside the main gate and the security guard waved us through from his tiny hut when we reached the entrance. A buzzer went off and Cathy opened the door and we strolled into the grounds.

'I'm not sure I want to talk to this guy,' I moaned. 'I can feel a bad mood coming on.'

'Oh, calm down, Ross,' Cathy replied. 'Argento feels threatened by men, especially aggressive men.'

'Can't expect me not to be aggressive if he's striking up a caring friendship with my girl!'

'It's not what you think. Are you going to be calm? Otherwise you'll have to wait outside.'

We were standing at the entrance to a small concrete building. I'd missed it completely when Mr Williams had given me the tour. It sure was an odd place to hang out, or work in, or whatever Argento did in there.

'Ross? Are you calm?'

'I'm cool.' I shrugged my shoulders. 'Totally cool.'

'Follow me and say nothing until I say you can.'

She unlocked the door to the small building and walked along a tight corridor. It was quiet and there was a strong odour in the air. I followed at a distance, not knowing exactly who I was about to encounter. Whoever he was, Argento wasn't normal!

Cathy slowly unlocked one of only two doors on the corridor. She looked at me and raised a finger to her lips before carefully turning the handle and opening the door. She took a step into the room and I followed her cautiously. There was only a single, naked bulb on one wall and the light from it was weak. The room around me stank and there were deep shadows in the corners. Cathy whispered to me to stand in the centre of the floor and not to move or speak. She then closed the door quietly before joining me.

A silent, and quite uncomfortable, moment passed. I knew from the instant she closed the door that we weren't the only ones in the room, and as the seconds passed I got that feeling of being watched.

'This is dumb,' I said.

The words were barely out of my mouth when a heavy grunt came from the shadows to my left. Something was lurking in the corner. Something very big.

'What the hell *is* this?'

'Ross,' Cathy hissed at me, 'be quiet.'

There was movement and I caught a very faint shape moving in the shadows. Not enough to define the thing, but enough to assure me it was there, and that it was bigger than I was.

There was another grunt. This one was loud and it echoed off the walls. It wasn't human ... I understood the meaning: I don't want you here!

'Cathy, I don't want to be here ...'

My words seemed to spur the *thing* into action. There was a heavy thump on the floor and it lurched forward. The aura of the dim bulb met its face, not exactly lighting it up, but giving it an amber sheen that helped to identify what it actually was. I slowly moved back as it loomed near, but Cathy blocked my way and within seconds I was face to face with it.

Deep shadows were cast on the gorilla's face making the creases on its leathery skin seem heavier than they were, and accentuating its irate expression. My heart almost skipped a beat as it moved its enormous face towards me. Its eyes were hidden under a heavy brow and were only given away by tiny sparkles reflecting the faint light. It seemed lifeless as it faced me, then it opened its mouth and roared at me. It was very much alive. Its fangs were as long as my fingers and could bite right through my neck if it managed to get hold of me.

I didn't sense danger, but didn't want to rely on my precognitive skills to evade any possible attack. I summoned my psychokinetic power and prepared to repel the giant ape.

Cathy stepped forward and stood in front of me. I wanted to drag her out of harm's way, but she moved out of my reach and then, to my surprise, sat right in front of the shadowy beast. She bowed her head, as if she was worshipping it. I knew this was the way mind-switchers transported their minds.

The broad-shouldered silverback seemed to be pacified and retreated a few steps and disappeared into the shadows. Cathy broke off the mind-switch and got to her feet.

'Sorry about that,' she said, turning to me. 'He's easily flustered, especially by strangers.'

'Are you still controlling its mind?'

'*His* mind, Ross. *His*. No, when he gets angry I have to step in and calm him down. It's like restarting a computer when there's a problem. He's gone back to his default setting now.'

'Why on earth did you bring me here, Cathy? This is dangerous!'

'We live dangerous lives, Ross. At least here I'm attempting to bring some good to the world.'

'That's what the Guild do.'

'No. What the Guild does usually ends up with death.' She turned her back on me and faced the shadowed ape. 'Argento, won't you come meet your visitor? He's a very close friend and means you no harm.'

The gorilla slowly emerged from the blackened corner of the room, the shadow slowly being peeled from its face. Its eyes were revealed for an instant and it nodded before disappearing into the shadow once more.

'Wow,' I breathed. 'That's one smart monkey you have there.'

'Don't refer to him as a monkey.'

'He doesn't like that?'

'*I* don't like it.' She turned back to Argento and held out her hand towards him. 'Come, don't stay in the darkness.'

He took her hand and she slowly coaxed him from the shadow to the relative brightness in the centre of the floor where they sat facing one another. The big ape watched her eyes very carefully and seemed oblivious to me now … or so I thought.

Argento's dark eyes rolled right and focused on me. He then held out his giant leathery hand to me. I felt compelled to put my hand in his and when I did he gave me light tug and I knew he wanted me to sit with him and Cathy.

'I'm sorry for calling you a monkey,' I said. I was half expecting him to say something but he returned his gaze to Cathy's face and all the aggression and uncertainty was now gone from his features.

'Argento spent most of his life in a private zoo in Italy, before his owner moved to England last year. The authorities raided the premises three months ago and most of the animals were taken from him. Argento ended up here. He'd been mistreated for years, kept in a darkened room with little or no contact with humans or other gorillas. He was so angry, and wild, and dangerous. The staff here had planned to euthanize him, but I pleaded with Peter to give him a chance. Just a few months to see if he could be helped.'

'How did you change him?'

'I read about how mind-switchers could tame animals and I was curious to see if I could do it. Argento was the perfect opportunity. The more I transported my mind into his, the fear and confusion he felt waned and some of my intelligence – a higher level of thinking and reasoning - remained with him. You see, Argento is no ordinary gorilla. He is a gorilla who has experienced human thoughts. I'd never been able to fully understand how mind-switchers tamed animals until this happened. They inherit a part of the human mind, and can think clearer and deal with their surroundings in a more measured way.'

'The world of the gifted never ceases to amaze me. Every day I seem to learn something new, something astounding, something that ordinary people would never believe is possible.'

'I don't even know what's possible,' Cathy breathed. 'I've only been working with Argento for two months and look at how advanced he is. I can't imagine how intelligent he may become if I spent a few years with him.'

'I'm glad I came here now. This is very different to what we've had to deal with lately.'

'This is what I want to do with my gift, Ross. I don't want to be out there fighting with other gifted people. I want to be here, working with animals, helping them. To think, I dragged the animal I had the closest bond with into our petty battle.'

'Nightshade?'

'Yes. Such a noble creature. I forced him into a fight with Edward Zalech, and he was broken into pieces because of it.'

'It does seem a little unfair.'

'A little? It was a great betrayal. I befriended him, taught him, and then killed him.'

'You didn't kill him.'

'I put him into that situation. I killed him.'

'You were following orders.'

'I'm not a soldier. I don't want to be following orders! My gift has to be used for good. Little Sarah and I are both gifted, and we have been thrown together, but we are very, very different. We offer two very different things. She brings fear. I bring understanding. They are not compatible and I feel drained when I'm around people like her.'

'You don't when you're around me.'

'I know. That's why I want you to leave the Guild with me.'

'So, you really are thinking about it.'

'I don't want to have the life my mother has had to endure. Would you want me to end up like she has?'

'No.'

'It breaks my heart when I think of what's become of her,' Cathy said. Tears rolled down her cheeks. 'I'm not following in her footsteps, Ross. Soon you're going to have to make a choice: me or the Guild.'

CHAPTER TWENTY

A Lethal Pet

It was late in the night and all was silent until a gurgling sound echoed from the shadows beneath the grate of the storm-drain. It got louder and louder until there were bubbles between the bars. Then a dark, putrid liquid overflowed onto the side of the road. The black water from the backed-up drain rolled along the curb then steadily flowed up into the air until every drop of it was elevated. It hovered for a moment, like a black cloak billowing in the breeze, then condensed into a slick sphere in front of my face. I could see a distorted reflection of myself in its rippling surface and I stepped forward and inspected my gleaming metal teeth. There were no remnants of the snack I had picked at on Golding's private jet.

I had finally been freed of the clinic and was driven to a nearby airfield, owned by Golding Scientific, where I boarded the Falcon 900. It had been a forty-five minute flight across the Irish Sea to south county

Dublin. An employee of Golding Scientific had driven me from the private strip to the lonely suburb of Maybrook. I kept a careful watch when I strolled from the open road towards the sprawling housing estate but to my surprise there were no Guild operatives stationed; I had expected they would have posted someone in the vicinity to keep watch over Bentley's father. The only opposition I came up against was a gang of youths hanging out on a corner by the edge of estate, who filed off the wall they were sitting on when they saw me approach. They blocked the pavement and had probably intended to mug me, or simply harass me, but when I drew nearer and they got a close look at me, they simply turned away and allowed me to pass unmolested. Not one had the courage to look me in the eye. The streets were now empty. I was free to do as I pleased.

I outstretched my right arm and the black orb moved ahead of me then gently fell to the pavement and rolled along before stretching out in a long line and slithering forward like a python. It would be my pet for the next hour. *A lethal pet.*

A storm of emotion was whipped up inside me, almost threatening to overwhelm me as I approached Maybrook Avenue. The Hyper-furens in my bloodstream constantly enhanced my emotions, particularly the negative ones, but I had a strong mind and was learning to prevent them from entirely dictating my thoughts and actions. That was when things were calm. In heated situations it would be very different and my emotions would run wild, and boost my powers immeasurably. I was beginning to feel excitement as I followed the slithering black shape towards the Bentley family home. A nervous tension and anticipation was climbing, and my mageletonia was tremendously strong. The low-hanging clouds over Maybrook were being drawn down towards me, the moisture within them attracted to me like a magnet. It swirled over the modest terraced houses like a dense fog and it formed a deep cloud above the Bentley home, sweeping over the rooftop and dancing around the upstairs windows.

I grinned when I saw the light from the TV pulsing behind the curtains of the sitting room window. My quarry was trapped. I drew in a deep breath and my electronic throat zinged as the cool evening air passed through it. It was time to unleash my power. It was time to land the first blow against the Guild.

I looked at the undulating and writhing black shape that swirled around my feet and I almost thought of it as a living being.

'Time for you to do your work, my friend,' I said with my buzzing voice. I pointed at the front of the house. 'Clear the way for me.'

The watery snake dashed forward, slipping through the bars of the garden gate then slithering beneath the old car parked in the centre of the paved garden. It oozed up onto the threshold and thinned out so it could slip into the gap around the front door. The water spread throughout the gap then pooled at the handle, putting immense pressure on the lock. The wooden door began to groan under the pressure then the metal lock gave way and broke apart. The door swung open as the rank liquid poured into the hallway.

I casually stepped forward, sending a shot of psychokinetic energy at the gate to open it. I strode through the garden then took a step inside the house. Mr Bentley was standing by the door to the sitting room frowning at the murky spillage on the floor of the hallway. He slowly looked up and took a step backward when he saw me appear in the open doorway.

'Mr Bentley, I presume?' My voice was booming in the narrow hallway and made sure I had his full attention. 'You must forgive this intrusion. I have come to talk with you about your son.'

'Ross ...?'

'Thank you for saving me some time by confirming your identity.' I chuckled as I shut the front door behind myself. 'Should we do this here,' I looked about the hallway, 'or shall we sit down, in relative comfort?'

Bentley simply bowed his head then turned despondently to the sitting room. I followed him inside, watching him carefully. He took the TV remote in hand and muted the speakers before he sat in an armchair by the fireplace. I stood in the centre of the floor and took a cursory look around the quaint room. A glass of water began to rattle on the table next to Mr Bentley. My powers were irresistible.

I turned to my reluctant host and smiled. 'A perfect picture of suburbia. Just as I imagined it would be.'

A chair rolled across the room and stopped behind my knees. I eased myself back into it and sat with my arms folded.

'I really expected more panic and screaming, fear and pleading, questions and begging – or perhaps just a measure of shock at my appearance, or surprise at my arrival.'

'It's no surprise really,' Bentley replied calmly. 'I had expected someone like you to appear eventually. The only surprise is that it took so long.'

'You expected someone like *me*?'

'I knew Ross would never be left alone once the world knew what he's capable of. I knew it from the instant I first saw him use his power. The power-hungry would want to control him and would stop at nothing to get their hands on him. But knowing Ross like I do, he'd repel them and refuse to be their pawn. And so they would finally send some weaker version of him, someone who is content to be a pawn; to hunt him down. So, the answer to your question is yes, I expected someone exactly like you. You're big and ugly and probably scare most folks, but not me. I used to be a boxer when I was young.'

'A strange comment.' I was intrigued by this seemingly fearless man facing me. 'Might I ask how is boxing relevant?'

'I was told when I started out as a lad that the fighter to be wary of is the one with the perfect face. He's usually the one who's so good that he's never taken a pounding. The guy with the flat face and the scars is an amateur and takes poundings regularly.'

'An inaccurate analogy,' I said, shaking my head. 'I had a perfect face until recently. That changed when I was outnumbered by a gang of gifted brutes. Oh, and you are probably not aware that your son is badly scarred too. Yes, he was cut up pretty badly in a fight recently. By all accounts he was lucky to live through it. That makes your comparison with fighters a little foolish, don't you think?'

'Doesn't change the fact that you're frightened of my son.'

'I am *not* frightened of him.'

'You are. I saw it in your face when you looked at that picture there.' Bentley pointed at a framed photograph of Ross standing above the fireplace. 'There's fear in your eyes.'

'I know no fear.'

'You're human – despite your appearance – and all humans know fear. You should wear sunglasses if you ever get to face my son, because he'll see it too.'

'You confuse hatred for fear.'

'Why would you hate him?'

'I have my reasons.'

'Jealousy?'

'I have been where he is now and it is not a place I would wish to return to. I have neither envy nor pity for Ross Bentley. Just anger. Loathing.'

'Yet you don't face him. You come here and act like a petty thug. That makes you a coward.'

'Do not misunderstand my presence, Mr Bentley. The only reason I am here is because Ross is hidden from me. But he will reveal himself to protect or avenge those he cares for.'

'You plan on killing me?'

'I thought that much was obvious.'

'I won't tell you anything that might hurt my son, or give you an advantage over him. I don't care what you do.'

'I have not come for information. I know you are not aware of his location. You have only one use to me.'

'I see.' Bentley leaned back in his chair and stared me. 'Why do you hate him so much?'

'He murdered someone who was precious to me.'

I projected calmness, but inside was a caldron of rage now that my thoughts dwelled on Ania. My eyes must have betrayed what I was feeling and Bentley could see it vividly. It probably terrified him to the core, but he did not want to give me the satisfaction of knowing it, and held his nerve.

'Your son murdered her in cold blood,' I continued. 'She was a child, but he did not spare her.'

'That's impossible,' Bentley argued. 'Ross isn't capable of murder.'

'I have no reason to lie.'

'Ross isn't a murderer,' he insisted. 'It simply isn't in him to do something like that. He's one of the few good guys left in this world.'

'Then explain why he dropped a car on my thirteen-year-old sister. Her body was smashed to pieces. *He did it!*' My inner fire was rising and I banged my fist on the arm of the chair. I had to concentrate hard to maintain control. 'I wanted to tell you what he did so that you could not go to your grave thinking your offspring is honourable in any way. He is *not* one of the good guys. He is as corrupt as everyone else.'

'If I am to go to my grave now, I will take only love for my son with me. Nothing you can say will change that.'

'How very valiant of you, Mr Bentley. In some ways you remind me of my own father. Would you like to know what happened to him?'

Bentley said nothing.

'Some merciless people had been trying to convince me to work for them. I refused. I did not want play any part in their *business*. Their response was to murder my father in a most brutal fashion. I find it fascinating that the father of my nemesis should share my own father's fate.'

'Do your worst,' he said defiantly.

I could not corrupt the father's love for his son and that frustrated me greatly. The conversation had been for nothing. It was now time to do what I came for. I allowed my inner defences to fall and the Hyper-furens began to influence my thoughts. All I could think of was murder. I sat back and laughed at the helpless man sitting across the sitting room.

'You will not have the honour of dying on your feet,' I said. 'Now, let me show you a glimpse of true power.'

The mass of filthy black water slithered into the room, guided by my invisible power of mageletonia. It snaked across the floor and rose up into the air like a gymnast's ribbon.

'Beautiful, is it not,' I said as I watched the thin strip of liquid twirling slowly between me and my prey. 'I give life to this stagnant water and through it I will take life from you. But before I do, I want you to know that I will find your son and I will give him a much slower death than the one I am about to give you.'

The watery serpent suddenly shot across the room. It hit Bentley hard on the bridge of the nose and splattered across his face and shoulders then dashed away in a thousand droplets and was brought together once more. Bentley was still in shock from the initial impact and he could not move as it came back at his face. This time it did not strike him. It arrowed into his mouth and poured into his throat. There it came to a stop. It did not budge no matter what he did. It could not be shifted. He crumbled to his knees clutching at his neck. The black water searched further inside and filled his lungs.

He crept off the seat and tried to reach me but I was blocking the way with a psychokinetic shield.

'I am sure you would like to kill me,' I said, 'but you cannot beat the devil at his own game.'

Bentley flailed wildly on the carpet in front of the fireplace. There was no way to save himself. I held the putrid liquid in his lungs and slowly he drowned. It was a horrible and drawn out death, but also an eerily silent one; there was hardly a sound as he died. I drew some pleasure from murdering Bentley's father. Ultimately, though, I was left unfulfilled.

It would take time for my nemesis to learn of what had just happened. I wondered what Ross's reaction would be when he got news of his father's death.

'I hope it makes you angry,' I said, as if Ross could hear me. 'I hope it makes you insane with anger. I hope that anger makes you as powerful as you can be. It will make it even more rewarding when I beat you when we are finally face to face.'

I left the lifeless figure on the floor, a pool a dark liquid pouring from his mouth and staining the carpet. I paced up the stairs and found the room that had belonged to Ross. I sat there for a long time. I wanted to get a feel for who Ross Bentley really was, but nothing in the room indicated he was anything other than a normal teenager. I thought that *I* might have had a room like this when I was in his teenage years if I had not been tracked down by the agents of The Eastern Shadow. Everything in my life led back to that moment, when they had smashed their way into my apartment and beat me up, shot my mother and father then put a gun to my infant sister's face. Even as a child I showed little emotion, but there was something in Ania's eyes that forced me to give into their demands. I went with them so that I could give Ania a chance in life. I then sided with the Guild for her. I killed Cramer and the others so Ania would not harm herself. I had hunted the young prophet down so Ania could have a future. My entire life was dominated by the connection with my sister. A connection that Ross Bentley had broken. Ross had made my life a pointless one. Was there a greater injury to suffer? Could I make my enemy suffer just as much?

'I will try,' I told myself. 'I will try.'

It was raining hard outside.

CHAPTER TWENTY-ONE

The Enemy Revealed

We stayed at the sanctuary the whole evening and didn't return to the Williams estate until around 4am. Argento had amazed me with his human-like intelligence and it was easy to see why Cathy liked to spend time with him. He even managed to play chess with me. Although I wouldn't play him again; he was a sore loser and smashed the board then chewed on my king piece. There was still a wild animal behind the intelligence he displayed.

When we got back to the house I thought this would be a perfect opportunity to ask Cathy to spend some time together. I didn't get the chance, though. Mr Williams appeared at his bedroom door when we reached the top of the stair and said, 'I hope you filled the tank with petrol. It's the least you could do after stealing Portman's car.'

He hadn't been serious and gave a tired laugh. He remained there until Cathy and I went our separate ways. I was asleep moments after my head hit the pillow and was grateful that I was not awoken by Sarah's screams. I woke up after midday, on hearing the door bell ring twice in quick succession. There were excited voices downstairs. Not excited enough to get me out of bed, though. I eventually rolled off the mattress around 1pm and went to the bathroom for a long shower. I took my time getting dressed then sauntered down the stair to find the house had fallen silent. I ducked into the sitting room then went through to the grand dining room. Both were empty. I walked to the kitchen then heard the muffled voices from outside. I looked out the small window above the sink and saw everyone gathered on the patio. Mr Williams was seated at the round outdoor table, most of the others were standing nearby, and Angela Portman had her arm around Cathy's shoulders – which I thought was rather odd. There was a sadness in Cathy's eyes and I knew something was wrong. The I saw the tall figure of Dominic Ballentine standing next to the Hunter by the steps to the lawn. It was obvious he had arrived with some bad news.

I went to the sliding doors and pulled them open; everyone went quiet and turned to me. They had a stunned look about them. They were watching me, yet no one wanted to make eye contact.

'What's going on?' I asked, walking from the house onto the patio. I looked at my girlfriend. 'Cathy, what's wrong?'

She tried to speak but couldn't get any words out.

Hunter then spoke up. 'Bentley,' his voice wavered slightly, 'there has been er …' His lips quivered and he raised his hand to his face to hide it. He sucked in a deep breath and cleared his throat, but didn't speak again. He looked close to tears. What on earth could have happened to reduce this hardened man to an emotional wreck?

'Do you remember me, Ross?' Ballentine asked. 'We met once before.'

'Yeah,' I replied. 'You were here when Romand was buried. Unfortunately I remember every detail of that dreadful day.'

'As do I,' he gave me a sympathetic smile that faded too fast for my liking. 'Could I ask you for a small favour?'

'What is it?' I replied cautiously. The entire scene was becoming surreal and I wanted someone to tell me what the hell was going on.

'I ask only that you would step off the patio and onto the lawn.'

'What for?'

'It will become clear in a moment.'

I reluctantly did as he asked and marched through the gathering and down the stone steps. Ballentine was right behind me. He remained at the top step and looked down on me as I reached the grass and turned to look up at him.

'What the hell is going on?' I asked, my voice rasping with annoyance. 'Out with it?'

'I came here today for two reasons,' Ballentine said evenly. 'The first to deliver some very bad news. The second is to protect my colleagues,' he nodded with the back of his head to indicate the others. It seemed strange that he didn't include me.

'Protect them from whom?'

'From you.'

'These people are my friends. Why in God's name would I harm them?'

'Unintentionally, of course.' He tried to smile, but it looked like pity to me. 'You see, Ross, I am also a psychokinetic and my particular forte is dome building. You may know this skill as defensive shields.' He raised his arms in the air and I knew from experience that he was creating a shield. I guessed he was building one around the patio in order to protect everyone who was standing on it. 'Unfortunately you are too powerful and too reckless to be around when you receive bad news. You will have to stand alone in your darkest hour. Tragically, this is one of the downsides to having a pure gift.'

'What is it, Ballentine?' I shouted. 'What's happened?'

'I received word this morning that your father has died.'

Those four words … your father has died … they hit me like four bullets in the heart. Time seemed to stand still and I found it near impossible to draw breath. I didn't want to believe it. I could not believe it. There had to be some mistake.

'No. You've got your wires crossed or something. My dad is still a young man. He's very healthy. He's strong as an ox. There's no way he could have died. You must have him confused with someone else of the same name.'

'There is no confusion, Ross. I am terribly sorry.'

'It can't be him!' I roared. My body began to tremble as my emotions ran out of control. One of the steps leading to the patio cracked in half. 'He was too young and healthy to die! How could he have died?'

The others backed up towards the house as the next of the granite steps shattered. Hunter sat by the table and held his face in his hands.

'We are certain it was your father, Ross,' Ballentine said. 'We are certain because of the way he died.'

'What?' I walked up the steps, but bounced off the invisible shield he had created. I stormed around the bottom of the raised patio. 'What are you trying to say?'

'This will come as a great shock. Prepare yourself.'

'I'm prepared, damn it. Tell me!'

'Your father drowned. He drowned, although he was in the sitting room of his home. There was little trace of fluid in the room.'

I looked at Hunter and he looked back and gave me a nod. It was the same fate that those poor souls in Newcastle had met.

'Hunter, is this true?'

'It is,' he replied solemnly.

'Zalech?' I asked Ballentine.

'We believe so. Somehow he has survived. He lives on – as do his murderous tendencies.'

I hunched over as the realisation of what had happened to Dad struck me. I had seen firsthand how Zalech's victims had died. It was a horrendous and excruciating death. A cowardly way to end a life and one that was not quick or merciful. Dad had probably suffered terribly at his hands before he died. I fell to my knees and dashed the tears from my eyes with the palms of my hands.

The evil bastard had killed the only family I had. My father. The most harmless man in the world. A lonely man … I slammed my knuckles against the dirt. Sarah's premonition made sense now. The lonely man was my dad and for some reason she had been referring to Zalech as the tin man.

My thoughts focused on the killer. My body became taut as I stood and roared at the top of my voice. The noise around me was deafening. The earth beneath my feet gave way. The last thing I remembered was falling.

🖤 🖤 🖤

I was lying on the bench next to Romand's grave when I came to.

For a couple of seconds I felt normal. I'd totally forgotten what had happened. Then Ballentine's words came rushing at me and I crumpled up inside like a collapsing house of cards.

I sat up and looked around and saw that I was alone. Hunter and Cathy were far off on the patio, watching me from a safe distance. The way they'd decided to inform me of my father's demise made sense to me now; the lawn looked like a meteorite had hit it. There was a deep circular hole about fifteen metres in diameter – if anyone had been standing next to me when I lost control they would have been crushed like a paper cup. That was why Ballentine had sent me away from the others. The fact that they still maintained the distance was logical. And I was thankful for it too. I didn't want anyone near me. I welcomed solitude.

For the first hour I couldn't stop crying. Then I went pacing around the grounds, trying not to get too angry, knowing I was a danger to everyone, including myself, when I flew into a rage. I managed to keep relatively calm for a while, but there was no fighting the aching feeling in my chest. My heart was shattered. I felt so empty. I was a shell of the real Ross Bentley.

I thought of the time I'd wasted when my father and I had that ridiculous rift. We'd hardly spoken to each other for two years solid. I hated myself for that. What I wouldn't give for one hour with him now. Even a minute so I could tell him that he was my hero … always. I had been so careless. Even when we'd mended our relationship I ran off to England and left him alone. I'd left him unprotected. He'd paid the ultimate price for my stupid ambitions.

I sat on the bench and stared at the dark patch of grass in front of me. Romand's grave. I had hated myself for causing my mentor's death, and now my dad was dead too. All because I wanted to enter a contest and win a million dollars. Two of the best and strongest people I'd ever known were killed because of my mindless greed. I might as well have killed them both myself.

When it got dark I sat hunched over with dried tears tightening my face. The lights were on at the house and I could see the others fluttering about the kitchen. Some were sitting sombrely at the table and others were pacing around, gesticulating wildly. It looked as if they were having an explosive debate. I didn't really care what they were arguing about. It all seemed pointless to me now. Life was pointless. I was surrounded by death and I was powerless to prevent those closest to me from being murdered. I couldn't draw my gaze from Romand's grave, thinking that my father would soon be buried, and I wouldn't even be able to attend his funeral. There was no way the Guild would let me leave. I would let Dad down one last time by allowing him to be put in the cold earth without his only son being there to say goodbye. The lonely man indeed.

'I'm a total asshole,' I said to the grave before me. 'Looks like I've failed yet again, Romand.'

'You haven't failed anyone,' someone said from the shadows. 'Stop thinking like that.'

I turned around and saw Hunter standing a few metres away puffing on a cigar.

'Still sneaking up on people I see,' I replied. I tried to make it sound humorous, but my voice was lifeless. He probably thought I was serious.

'It's past midnight,' he said. 'You've been out here almost twelve hours.'

'I hadn't noticed.'

'Time can play tricks on us at times like this.'

'I suppose so.'

He took a few steps towards me then paused, afraid to come too close. 'You calm, Bentley?'

'As calm as I can be.'

'I don't want to have my skull crushed if you lose your temper again.'

'I'm all right,' I said, holding my hand out at the empty part of the bench. 'You're safe.'

'You have every right to be angry,' he continued as he sat next to me. He took a long pull on the cigar before flicking it away into the grass. 'Nobody will blame you for being so angry.'

'I'm sure they're all terrified of me after what I did to Mr Williams's lawn.'

'Ah, he has enough money to hire a landscaping team to fix it. We expected you to lose your temper, that's why Ballentine hung around, so that he could protect the rest of us when you blew your lid. They don't think any less of you for what happened this afternoon.'

'I hope not.'

'Forget what they think.' Suddenly there was an urgency in his voice, and a genuine tone. 'You don't need to concern yourself with what other people think of you right now.'

'I don't know what to think. I feel like I'm going to explode, Hunter. I caused this whole thing. I wanna throw myself off a cliff.'

'You'll overcome it in time.'

'How can you even say that? This is not something that can be overcome. He can't be brought back!'

'You can't change the past, but you will live on and you will come to terms with what has happened.'

'I don't feel as confident about that as you do.'

'I've been where you are now, Bentley.'

I said nothing. I remembered what I'd read about him in Atkinson's journal, that his aunt had been killed when Blake tried to assassinate him. I didn't want Hunter knowing I'd snooped around his home while he was out and allowed him continue.

'I never really knew my parents,' Hunter explained. 'My father ran out on my mother before I was born, the lousy shit! He never returned. I have hardly any memories of my mother … just whispers of her voice, glimpses of her face.'

'What happened to her?'

'She turned to drink after my father left us. By the time I was three years old she was a raging alcoholic. Apparently she'd been drinking in a local pub one day. She got blind drunk and after she downed her last drink she staggered into the road outside. A car hit her. Died the next day in hospital.'

This was part of Hunter's story that I didn't know about. He really had had a tragic upbringing and somewhere in the swirling emotions I felt a great sympathy for him.

'My aunt was the only family I had after that. She took me in and raised me as her own. She was strict, and too religious for my liking, but she was a good person and kept me on the straight and narrow. By the time I was a teenager I thought of her as my mother.'

'She was killed by a gifted person?'

'Aye, she was.' A flicker of agony raced across his face. 'They came for me after I'd used my gift in public – I was showing off in front a girl I fancied. Gifted assassins arrived at my home and I was able to fight them off long enough to escape. My aunt wasn't so lucky. I'd run away and left her at their mercy.' He chewed his bottom lip and tried to hide his swollen eyes from me. 'Bloody killed her, they did. And I ran away.'

'Doesn't seem like you've overcome it, Hunter.'

'It still hurts. I still feel guilty. That never leaves me, but I haven't allowed the bitterness to eat away at me. I haven't lost sight of what's good and what's bad.'

'How did you keep going?'

'With the help of the Guild. Cathy's father brought me into the community and he helped to get my head straight. Then I lived with one of the most powerful members, Marie Canavan. She's my mentor. She taught me how to use the gifts I have and also taught me some very valuable lessons about life. Not allowing hatred to destroy me was the one of them.'

'I appreciate you trying to help me, Hunter, and I know it's not your way to be so candid about your past and your emotions. I really do appreciate it. But all I want to do is kill Edward Zalech. My life will be torture as long as he draws breath.'

Hunter looked at me and nodded slowly. 'All in good time, Bentley. All in good time.'

He didn't say in that usual condescending way of his. He said it in the way I needed to hear it. He was telling me to be patient and that the opportunity would come.

The night grew cold and Hunter convinced me to go inside the house. I was ready to apologise to everyone, but Cathy was the only one waiting in the kitchen. Hunter didn't hang around and left us alone. The first thing she did when Hunter left the room was to spring out of her seat and hug me. I slowly locked my arms around her and pressed my cheek on her shoulder.

'I'm so sorry,' she whispered. 'I can't imagine how this feels.'

'I'm too numb to feel anything. I can't seem to get it straight in my mind. I can't believe he's actually dead. I keep expecting to wake up and for someone to tell me it was all a big mistake.'

'This is my fault,' she sniffled. 'Your father would be alive right now if I'd made sure Zalech was dead.'

'No, Cathy.' I cupped her face with my hands and kissed her. 'This has nothing to do with you. I've had enough of the blame game for one day.'

'Come up to my room,' she said, taking my hand. 'I can't stand this damned kitchen anymore.'

We traipsed up the staircase to her room and she locked the door once we were inside. We lay on the bed and wrapped our arms around one another. There were no tears or kisses, words or sleep. There were only thoughts. The sadness was crushing, but I drew some comfort from being close to her. We hadn't spent all that much time in each other's company, but I felt like I'd known her my whole life. Without her I would truly be alone. It was on that awful night that I realised I never wanted to part with Cathy and that if she really wanted to leave the Guild then I would join her. The only thing that would keep me in the ranks for the time being was my desire to catch and kill Edward Zalech. I didn't much care for what the Guild intended to do. I wanted him dead and that's all that mattered to me.

Cathy eventually drifted off and I remained still in the blackness for what seemed like endless hours. My thoughts were darker than any of the shadows in the room. I held her close for a time, trying my best to forget my troubles, trying to find sleep. When the first signs of light appeared through the curtains I rose from the bed and went to the window. I drew the curtains back slightly and gazed at the deep purple sky stubbornly fighting off the dawn. My inner fire rose with the amber sun. I felt my powers strengthening. Edward Zalech would feel that strength when I finally caught up with him.

I stood by the window and watched the sun rising over the hills nearby. The chemical in my body, the Hyper-furens, had taken over when I murdered Bentley's father and still, even thirty hours later, it had barely waned. My anger was boiling inside me, my senses heightened, my powers at full tilt.

I had walked from the murder scene casually, lost in a mix of intoxication and rage. I saw the fear in the driver's eyes when I was picked up outside Maybrook and revelled in the effect I had on others. Oh, how it was good to be feared.

I boarded the Falcon 900 and when it rose to five thousand feet I heard the pilot shouting about a violent storm that had not shown up on his instruments.

I knew it was the moisture in the upper atmosphere being attracted to *me* – so powerful had my mageletonia become. The storm bounced the plane from side to side and at one point nearly took it out of the sky. I used my psychokinesis to counter the effects of the storm and we landed unscathed in England at 4am. Pearson was waiting for me in the small office on the private airfield. She had packed my Deflexus clothing into a backpack. She gave me directions to the rural house owned by the corporation. It was mine for as long as I needed it. She handed me a key to the GSK7 Kinetibike that was parked nearby.

I wanted to reach the relative safety of the country house without delay. I needed to lie low for a few days so I could plan my next move to perfection. There could be no mistakes. And besides, the Guild would have everyone out searching for me so it was wise to disappear for a while.

I pushed the bike to its limit on the way to the house. I had been told a prototype had been driven at 600kmph, but I managed to beat that speed. I did not care about cop cars or helicopters; they simply would not be able to keep up with me even if I came to their attention. And I could easily have used my gifts to stop them if they got too close.

I arrived at the isolated house as dawn was breaking. It was a renovated country house in a shallow valley with vibrant green fields stretching out to the horizon.

There were no other buildings to be seen and the only sound was the song of the finches whistling from the maples that lined the driveway. It was a clear morning except for the area surrounding the house. Moisture was being dragged from the atmosphere towards me and formed a mist above the roof of the house, which I found quite beautiful.

I walked the empty hallways, trying to suppress the anger caused by the Hyper-furens. It took hours, and when I did return to some normal emotional balance my mind went dull and I searched out a bed to sleep on. There were none. In fact, the large house was completely empty of furniture apart from an armchair in the front room. I made do with that. I slept right through the day and night. Now, as the new day was breaking, I was standing by the window contemplating my next move. All my thought was bent on avenging my sister. Every second was spent thinking of how to kill off the Guild members – especially Ross Bentley. *He* would be the icing on the cake.

I watched the sun climbing above distant hills and the cobwebs of slumber were banished completely. I walked to the kitchen and downed several pints of water then pulled open the fridge to find it bare. Strangely, I felt no hunger. I had not eaten anything in many days, but my stomach did not ache. I was not weakened at all.

My lack of sustenance did affect my appearance, however. I gazed at my reflection in the hallway mirror and saw a gaunt, vampirish figure staring back. Gone was the athletic young man I was used to seeing. He had been replaced by a sinewy stick insect with eyes too big for his emaciated face. I truly had become someone new. Someone to be feared.

Two days passed and the Hyper-furens regained sway over my emotions; the immense power returned with it. I had spent the previous forty eight hours plotting against the Guild and had finalised my plan. I envisaged my strategy over and over and over. It had to be planned to perfection. My every move had to be premeditated. That way Sarah Fisher would pick up on it easier. She would predict the hell I would unleash – she in turn would tell the Guild about it and they would send as many of their agents as possible to stop me. I laughed at how cunning my plan was. I would lead them into a trap. Hopefully Bentley would be with them when they walked into it.

My senses spiked as the drug in my body grew in influence. I could actually *feel* all the water nearby. I sensed the clouds that drifted high above the house. I felt a small stream cutting through the fields to the west. But overriding these was a much more substantial body of liquid. There was a nearby lake and it would be the perfect place to practise what I planned to do in the days to come.

I grabbed my coat and strode from the house, being led to the lake like a magnet. I walked along a narrow road that snaked into the hills then led me into a neighbouring valley. The long, wide lake came into view as soon as I reached the valley wall. Its surface was silverish and long reeds gave it a golden outline. A light breeze rippled the water and I lifted my arm and it became still, like glass. I had total control, but that was not quite enough. I had to be able to replicate what I had done to the river outside the clinic two weeks before. This would be a significant test for my new abilities.

I walked to the shore of the lake and swept my right arm from side to side. The water began to sway violently and I realised my power had grown since leaving the clinic. The lake rose up on one side then swooped back down and towered on the opposite side.

Then the entire body of water was lifted from the earth and began looping around in the air like a gigantic wheel of water. It was magnificent. My power was unrivalled. I slowed the pace and allowed the water to rest back into the lake bed. It sloshed around as if a hurricane was sweeping over it, yet there was hardly a breeze disturbing the quiet countryside.

'Hey!' A distant voice called. 'Hey, Mister! Did you just see that?'

I did not turn at first. I simply listened to the excited voices and the bushes behind me being shaken. I glanced over my shoulder and saw the two hill walkers in their matching outdoor clothing clambering down from the higher ground towards the lake. They were coming right towards me. I tittered and returned my gaze to the choppy waters.

'Hey, didn't you hear me? Mister?'

They were only a few metres behind me and had stopped. Probably stunned that I was not as excited as they were about the waters acting magically.

'Mister, you all right?' one of them asked

'He's probably in a daze after seeing that,' said the other. 'I know I am!'

'Bloody remarkable. And I caught it all on my camera phone here!'

'Ah, technology,' I buzzed. 'It seems to follow us everywhere these days.'

'What the ...'

They had never heard such a voice. Even my strange voice did not prepare them for the shock of seeing my deformed face when I turned to them in an ominous fashion. Their two pink, flustered faces went deathly pale and their smiles drooped into black ovals.

'What is wrong?' I asked sarcastically. 'You look like you have seen a monster.'

'Er ... no,' the older of the two said breathlessly.

'I must appear as a monster to two fine upstanding citizens like yourselves. A modern day Frankenstein's monster.'

'Just a wee surprise is all,' the younger man said. He had not even blinked since I turned to him. 'We'll be on our way now.'

'Have you ever watched the movie?' I asked. '*Frankenstein*? The old one with Boris Karloff?'

'Can't say that I have.'

'You should have,' I grinned. 'It is one of those movies you should see before you die.' My grin became a buzzing chuckle. 'It might have saved your lives if you had watched it. You might have learned not to approach a strange-looking man by the side of a lake.'

The hill walkers tried to back away, but I had trapped them both in an invisible web of psychokinetic energy.

'I *am* a monster,' I said to them as they struggled to escape. 'But unlike Frankenstein's monster, I have no master. In fact, it is *I* who am the master.'

I reached out with my psychokinetic powers and lifted the helpless pair high into the air then flung them far out into the lake. They hit the water with a loud clap and went under for a moment before remerging. They flapped about, trying to swim back to shore, but the water around them came to life. I created two giant watery hands either side of them and pushed them below the surface. Birds fluttered into the air on the opposite side of the lake and darted into the shadow of the nearby trees. All was silent in the valley apart from that. I smiled and strolled back to the house. I had total confidence in my power now. My technique had developed enough

to pull off something truly monumental.
Within days I would change the world.

CHAPTER TWENTY-TWO

Guy Fawkes

Each day blended into the next. That week was nothing more than a blur of tears and sadness. Every time I found myself alone I collapsed inward and was reduced to weeping into my pillow or sleeve or whatever was at hand to muffle the sound. It was days since I'd gotten the news of my father's death. He'd probably been buried by now, in the family plot by the graves of my mother and my grandparents. He was a quiet man, mostly, not one for socialising, not the life of the party, just a simple man who liked to keep himself to himself. It must have been a low-key funeral. Some of his former colleagues, a few of the neighbours, my friend Gemma and some of her mates, distant relatives. I couldn't think of anyone else who'd have cared enough to interrupt their day to attend a ceremony for one of the Bentleys. I didn't care about other people, though. All I cared about was that *I* wasn't there. How can you miss your own father's funeral? How can you miss the final farewell to your only family?

A sudden surge of anger rose in my chest and part of the window-sill I was leaning on cracked. This was why I was spending so much time alone. I couldn't allow something like that to happen when I was hugging Cathy, or chatting with Sarah or one of the others.

The cracked sill could easily be a cracked skull. I was a danger to everyone around me.

The house had quieted down a bit since the day Ballentine arrived to inform me of Dad's death. He'd left with the Portmans the next morning. Yenver and Powell went the day after. Their absence had made things a little easier; having the eyes of strangers focused on my weary face and feeling pity for me as if I was a helpless victim had irritated me and I'd lost my temper quite a few times. They shouldn't have been staring at me like I was helpless because nothing was further from the truth. They should have been looking at me and fearful of the rage within, the rage that made me stronger than anyone they had ever encountered before, the rage that made me a ticking time bomb. I would explode when I got hold of Edward Zalech.

It was clear in my mind that I would go in search of him. There was no alternative. I was loyal to the Guild, but the allegiance I had to my father superseded all other responsibilities. He had to be avenged, and I wasn't going to stand back and allow anyone else to do the job for me.

There was a tap on the bedroom door and Cathy poked her head in. 'You want to come down to the animal sanctuary with me?'

'Yeah,' I replied and walked from the window. 'It's only midday and I'm going nuts being cooped up in this place.'

We made daily visits to Mr Williams's enclosure. It was the only way to stave off madness. And I had thought living in Hunter's cottage had been maddening! This was excruciating. Waiting in silence. All of us. Waiting. Sleepless nights spent wondering what the next day would bring. When would death visit us again?

Being with the animals, in particular Argento, was a welcome distraction. He was a perfect example of a mind that had been through unimaginable torment yet had endured and remained dignified and beautiful – in his own way. Did I have the inner strength that this gorilla had? I couldn't help thinking that I didn't. I couldn't help thinking Argento made a better human than most humans. There was more good in him than in most people. It was then that I noticed that I was changing. It was only in calm moments, out of the eye of the storm, that I could assess myself, and I didn't like what I found. I was becoming the bitter man that Romand and Hunter warned me about. I was fast becoming a liability. Someone who was innately violent and hellbent on revenge. I should have been concerned about protecting those loved ones who still remained in the world of the living, yet I was focused solely on avenging those who had passed from this world into the endless darkness that lay beneath or beyond it.

Argento reached out to me and ran a finger across my cheek. I hadn't even noticed the tear rolling from my eye until he smudged it into my skin. I looked into his mysterious black eyes. They were like an abyss at first, but the longer I stared into them the more I saw of the intelligence within.

'He doesn't pity you, Ross.' Cathy said quietly. 'He's worried about you.'

'Why?'

'Because he knows what I know.'

'And what's that, Cathy?'

'He knows your heart is set on stepping up this conflict. He knows someone has pulled you into this endless cycle of death and destruction. And once you're in, you never get out.'

'Spare me, please.'

'You go your way, Ross. But know that if you do, you go a different way than I do. I won't be waiting for you to find your way back.'

'What do you expect me to do? Forget that he filled my father's lungs with water and slowly drowned him in his own home? *My father!*'

Argento backed away into the shadows, becoming one with the wall of darkness on the far side of the room.

'Way to go, Ross.'

'I'm sorry. Argento' I turned to the shadows where he had disappeared. '… I'm sorry, buddy.'

'I don't want you to become cold and bitter,' Cathy began to sob. 'I can't be with someone like that, Ross.'

'Just because I want justice for my father doesn't mean I'm like that. I'm not really like that.'

'You might not change back to the person you once were.'

'Cathy, why are you making this so difficult for me? You know I can't let this go. That fiend murdered my father and I'm going to make him pay for it. I'm not going to sit back and let the Guild deal with it while I stay out of it. I've seen how they've dealt with Zalech before and I've no confidence in them!'

'Ross, you've only met a handful of the Guild's agents. There are some who are lethal killers, people who enjoy killing just as much as Zalech does. They'll be the ones who are sent after him. They should be the ones to do it because they are already ruined souls who won't be damaged any further by having another death on their conscience.'

'Was Romand ruined?'

'Why do you have to bring him into this?'

'Was Romand a heartless killer?'

'No.'

'Yet he realised that he was the one who had to deal with Marianne. It was his fight. He didn't allow any of these Guild assassins you speak of to do his dirty work for him. Even after all that, he was a good and honest man that you loved. Why can't I be like Romand? This is *my* fight. I'm not backing down. I'm sure as hell not running away from it now.'

'It almost destroyed Romand,' she raised her voice. 'And he didn't hunt her down. He accepted that one day she'd find him and he lived his life as best he could until that day arrived.'

'You don't understand me.'

It was a pointless argument. I left her and went to the car outside the enclosure. She joined me half an hour later, when we'd both cooled off. I apologised, not because I thought I was in the wrong, but because I thought that's what she wanted to hear. It didn't work.

'Say it like you mean it next time.'

'God,' I sighed. 'Why are women so difficult?'

'Why are men so stupid?'

'We're not stupid. We're just misunderstood.'

'Stop trying to lighten the mood.'

'Sorry.'

'And stop saying you're sorry. You're not in the slightest bit sorry.'

'I'll stop talking, shall I?'

'That would be better.'

I didn't bother speaking for the rest of the journey to the Williams estate. Not because Cathy was angry with me. I had very little to say and talking simply deflected my thoughts from where they wanted to be: on killing Edward Zalech. How could I find him? Where was he hiding? What would his next move be?

Then a terrible thought flashed into my brain. What if he didn't reappear? What if he moved on and disappeared into the big wide world never to be heard from again? I should have been content with that idea; he wouldn't harm anyone close to me again if he disappeared, but that would rob me of the revenge I wanted so much.

Where are you, Edward? I thought. Under what stone do you hide? *Why* do you hide?

I thought of a thousand challenges I could put to him. I thought of a hundred ways to kill him. I thought of a million dramatic lines to speak as I ended his life. I could think of no way to find him. I was nothing more than a bystander until he made his move. This was Edward's game and he was calling the shots, but I was going to win. He would not beat me!

'You recognise the car?' I asked as we passed between the tall gates and took to the long driveway. There was small red hatchback parked outside the garage door that I hadn't seen before.

'No.'

Cathy didn't care about the car. It was probably another Guild member and Cathy had had her fill of them. Her desire to escape the Guild grew each day. I couldn't blame her; the situation we found ourselves in was maddening

I parked next to the hatchback and took a glance inside when I stepped onto the gravelled path. It was meticulously clean and gave no clue to the owner's identity. Apart from being a clean person and one who didn't like to drive fast.

Cathy pushed open the front door and stomped up the staircase without a single word to me. Hunter was lingering in the hallway like a guard dog and he watched her climbing the steps with a smirk.

'What's up with her?' he asked, grinning at me. He appeared to take some joy in other people's bad moods. 'Lover's tiff?'

'It's complicated,' I told him as I pulled shut the front door.

'It always is with women.'

'I'm beginning to see why you chose to be single.' I stood next to him as the house rattled when Cathy slammed her bedroom door.

'You must have done something pretty foolish to get her that worked up.'

'I'd rather not talk about it,' I replied. 'We got a visitor?'

'You noticed the car.'

'I did. Who owns it?'

'A senior member of the Guild. She's practically retired now.'

'She come to stick her beak into our trouble?'

'No. Just a friendly visit. This woman is like family to me so make sure you show her some respect, got it?'

'Family?'

'Pretty much.'

'At least you have some. I seem to be the only one without a family around here.'

'Now don't get all cranky again.'

'Hunter, my dad—'

'I know! I told you the time would come to beat your demon. Now is not the time to be cold and angry and to be alienating yourself from those who can help you.'

'I can't help it.' I leaned against the wall and pushed out a long and weary breath. 'Can't get it out of my mind. Not for more than a few minutes.'

'Try to keep it together, lad.' He raised his hand and almost patted me on the shoulder, then realised we weren't supposed to be close so he stuffed it back into his pocket.

'Have you spoken to the Council?' I asked. 'Is there anything being done to track Zalech down?'

'There are a lot of Guild operatives on the move around Britain and Ireland right now. They're scouring the land for any trace of him and they are the best trackers around. We have some spies – non-gifted – who are watching Golding's activities, there's been precious little to report. There's not much more we can be doing. We have limited people at our disposal but I'm sure they will pick up his scent sooner or later.'

'I hope so,' I said. 'So, who is this illustrious guest?'

'Marie Canavan. She's the most powerful light-tuner alive. She trained me when I joined the Guild. We have a tradition each year that we never miss, no matter what's going on.'

'What tradition?'

'You'll see tonight.'

We walked into the sitting room to find Canavan and Mr Williams sitting on one of the couches and deep in discussion. I knew I was the topic of conversation by the way they went silent as I entered. Canavan was about sixty years old, had short grey hair, her clothes were formal and she that hardness in her face that Hunter shared. Her bright green eyes were sympathetic without being condescending.

'The infamous Ross Bentley,' she said, turning in her seat to face me. 'I've heard so much about you that I almost feel we've known one another for many years.' She smiled and held out her hand towards me. 'My name is Marie, and I have been looking forward to meeting you. Although I would have preferred if it had been under less stressful circumstances.'

I shook her hand and forced myself to smile. I didn't want to appear rude, but the last thing I wanted was to meet someone new, to discuss my gifts, to have yet another Guild member probing my feelings. To her credit she never directly mentioned my father, nor Edward Zalech. She did refer to *the recent trouble* a few times as we chatted that afternoon, but I didn't take any offence. Mostly, she talked to me about the training I had done and my knowledge of the true gifts. She had a school teacher vibe about her and I got the feeling she was very knowledgeable about the fifteen true gifts and the history of the Guild and all the battles it had gotten involved in down through the years. In the couple of hours that I talked with her, she revealed that the Guild had started out in the year 988AD, in central Europe. A group of gifted people had come together and often held secret meetings and dealt with potential threats to their survival. They of course would have been viewed as devils or evildoers by the general public and the authorities and so they masqueraded as a Guild of craftsmen. This was how they became known as a *The Guild*. So much had changed in the years since then, but the Guild had remained.

'What's this tradition I've heard about?' I finally asked her.

'Ah,' Canavan chuckled, 'Hunter mentioned it, did he?'

'He did, but as always he failed to elaborate.'

'He does that a lot,' she chuckled again. 'Oh, he was such a difficult teenager – and he's not much easier as an adult. We have had a tradition for many, many years. The light-tuners of the Guild put on a light display on the Guy Fawkes Night. Hunter and I always meet this night each year and try to out-do the other with our light-tuning abilities.'

'Sounds like fun.'

'It is. You'll see once the sun sets, which will be soon enough. I would like to have my dinner now. One should never extend one's self too much on an empty stomach.'

All the occupants of the house convened in the kitchen at six in the evening for a grand dinner. Cathy reluctantly joined us. She didn't speak to me; she hardly even made eye contact. I didn't say much either, and was happy for Sarah to get the attention for a change. The others focused on her over dinner, and kept talking to her; trying to keep her mind off the horrible things she saw each time she slept.

At 7.30pm a few of bottles of wine were uncorked and everyone enjoyed a couple of glasses, except Sarah and me. The mood in the house was jovial for the first time since I arrived and even Cathy was smiling. I tried to join in and act like everything was rosy, but inside I was still caught up in the pain caused by my dad's death. That would never go away and would remain immediate until Zalech was either captured or killed.

After the wine bottles had been drained we walked out to the patio and we watched Hunter and Canavan descend the steps, around the huge hole in the lawn and walk down close to Romand's grave. We were then treated to the most spectacular fireworks display imaginable.

Hunter began by creating a small blue light-orb that shot out of his finger and swirled high over the lawn. It came to a stop about a hundred feet above him and hovered in the chilled night air. It grew in size and began to flash different colours. Red to green to blue to white. It was quite a sight, but this was merely the beginning.

Canavan pointed at the night sky and five orbs came from her hand. They rose up fast and surrounded the initial orb, spinning fast around it and changing colour from red to white and back again. They then grew in size, to dwarf the one Hunter had created then became star shaped and shifted from blue to yellow to purple.

'Ever wonder what all those UFO sightings really are?' Mr Williams said to me with a wide grin on his aged face.

The six orbs collapsed into one immense disk of light that swelled and became so bright I couldn't look directly at it. We shielded our eyes as it gained in size and strength, until finally it burst into a gazillion tiny flickering lights that danced through the air like a swarm of fireflies. The swarm shimmered every colour in the spectrum and I became mesmerised by its movement and by the lazy shift in its colour. Then the entire cloud of light became gold and was transformed into a giant eagle that circled the house. Sarah and Cathy cheered when it swooped low over the patio.

The immense bird glided over the lawn then spun fast and became a single orb of light that flickered.

I noticed Canavan moving her arms erratically as if she were trying to swat a fly. She was actually shaping the large disk of light into a new shape; this one was a shimmering shade of silver. It took a few moments before it became clear what this shape was. It was the distinctive wolf head of the Guild. The same one I'd seen on Romand's study papers, the one carved into porch posts at Hunter's house, and the same as the medal attached to the cover of Jonathan Atkinson's journal.

It was truly spectacular and perfectly formed, even its eyes glowed crimson, giving it a lifelike quality. Hunter threw out a number of light orbs from his open arms and they slowly rose and became six-pointed stars that revolved around the wolf's head. Fifteen of them in all. Each of them symbolising a true gift. It was a tradition I was happy they had continued. It was one of those moments that stay with you for the rest of your life.

The lightshow lasted more than two hours and some of the tricks Hunter and Canavan produced were astounding. They rounded it off by mimicking traditional fireworks. This was also the most surreal of the tricks; I'd never watched silent fireworks before.

Canavan appeared to tire at 11pm; her light tricks became more modest and were dwarfed by the grandiose explosions that Hunter continued to produce. She did, however, bow out with great style. Her body became surrounded by hundreds of tiny orbs that glowed bright orange, and when they faded, Canavan was nowhere to be seen.

'She disappeared!' Sarah cheered, her eyes looking ready to spring out of their sockets. 'Where did she go?'

'I haven't gone anywhere, my darling.' Canavan was standing behind us by the back porch smiling devilishly.

'Are you a magician?' Sarah asked.

'No, not at all.'

'But you can do magic. You're really special!'

'All of us here are all very special people,' Canavan said to Sarah as she stooped in front of her and kissed her forehead. 'That includes you. I think *your* gift is like magic.'

I didn't agree with what the old woman was saying. She was rambling on like Sarah's gift was a thing of beauty and wonder, when in truth it was a terrible affliction that caused the girl, and those around her, a lot of torment.

I went to my room alone before Hunter brought a conclusion to the light show. I had wanted to be with Cathy, but thought it best to give her some space. I tried to block out all the trouble and the great sense of loss that had dogged me for over a week.

I sat in the centre of the room and summoned energy to me. I felt it surge within me then I allowed it to radiate from my limbs, so that it formed an invisible but powerful sphere that shielded me on all sides. I concentrated hard on making it as strong as possible, a shield that nothing could pierce. Focusing all my energy and thoughts on a shield allowed me remove myself from all the negativity that surrounded me, almost like meditation. I'm not sure how long I held the shield in place – hours maybe – but when my power finally blinked out, the house had gone silent and everyone was asleep. I ambled to my bed, too drained to even get undressed. As soon as my head hit the pillow I was out cold.

CHAPTER TWENTY-THREE

Facing the Devil

I awoke with a start. Yet another disturbing dream about my dad. I sat on the side of the bed and wiped the sweat from my brow with the back of my hand. I'd been having the nightmares all week and found myself pacing my room at the break of dawn trying to forget the dreadful things I'd seen. This night was different, though. This night I wasn't the only one waking from a horrible dream.

I heard quiet sobbing and walked out of my room to the landing. The weeping was coming from Sarah's room. Did I really want to go in there and find out what she'd seen? My nightmares were a nuisance – Sarah's nightmares came true. I couldn't go back to bed and leave the child alone when she was obviously upset. I wasn't that cold hearted just yet.

I quietly walked to her door and eased it open. She was sitting at the top of the bed with the duvet pulled up tight to her chest by strained knuckles. The lamp was on and I saw in her eyes the same fear I'd seen in her after her last premonition, when she'd predicted Edward Zalech murdering my dad.

'Another nightmare?' I asked as I stepped onto the soft carpet in her room. I shut the door and went to the bed and sat.

'Uh huh,' she whispered. 'It was very scary.'

'What was it about?'

'It was the tin man again ...'

Suddenly I was very interested to hear what she had to say. The tin man was Edward Zalech, the person I was desperate to locate. Perhaps her premonition might shed some light on his whereabouts. Perhaps it might help me find and confront him!

'What was he doing in the dream?'

'He was killing lots of people.'

'Dear Lord ...' I breathed. He had to be stopped as soon as possible. I could not allow this monster, partly of my creation, to continue his rampage. 'Where was the tin man, Sarah?'

'By the sea.'

'On a boat? On a beach or something?'

'No,' she shook her head, sending her blonde hair clapping against her cheeks.

'Where?'

'In a city by the sea.'

'Do you know which city it was?'

'Nope. There were lots of buses nearby ... is that important?'

'Most cities have bus stations but it might help me to pin-point him if I can identify the city. Were there any signs on the road?'

'I don't remember.'

'Damn it,' I hissed in frustration. I quickly composed myself, not wanting to scare the girl. 'Was there a sign? Was there anything unusual?'

'Just the big tower.'

'Blackpool tower?'

'I dunno.'

'Can you describe the tower for me?'

'It was a big tower …'

This was of no use to me; most towers were big, particularly to an eight-year-old. I rummaged through the drawers in the room then under bed until I found a coloured pencil and a copy book. I handed them to Sarah and asked her if she could draw what she'd seen.

She took the copybook and weaved her hand across it over and over again. I watched the rough lines slowly taking shape until there was coherent image – a purple rendering of a tower. I took the copybook from her and stared at the childish image before me. It was the Spinnaker tower in Portsmouth. I was sure this could not be a rendering of any other tower in Britain. Edward Zalech would strike next in Portsmouth. I almost had him in my grasp. All I needed to know now was *when*.

'Sarah, I have to ask you a very important question.'

'OK.'

'Do you know when he's going to go this city by the sea?'

'No.'

'Are you sure? Was there *any* clue to when it was?'

'No. I never see the dates in my dreams. I just see stuff happening.'

'Think hard, Sarah. Think about the dream for a minute. Was there anything in the dream that would suggest when it was happening?'

'No…' she shook her head and frowned. 'Only …'

'What is it, Sarah? Tell me, please.'

'I saw the city before the tin man started hurting people. There were two old women outside a café, drinking tea. One of them said she didn't sleep well.'

'Right ...'

'The other said that she hadn't slept well either. The fireworks had been too loud and had been going off late into the night.'

'Fireworks the night before ... Guy Fawkes Night ...' I said to myself. 'Could it be? Was this to happen today? The tin man would strike Portsmouth today!

'You were there too.'

'I was?'

'You were talking to the tin man on an empty street.'

'I bet I was!'

I wasn't letting this opportunity pass me by. I couldn't tell the others, at least not Cathy or Mr Williams. Cathy would implore me to stay at the estate and allow someone else deal with Zalech, Mr Williams would insist that I not get directly involved. There wasn't a chance in hell that I would allow the other Guild agents deal with Zalech. He would have to pay for what he did to Dad. My powers would be the instrument of retribution.

'Try to get some sleep, Sarah,' I said as I tore the sheet of paper from the copy book and folded it. I got up off the bed and gazed down at her. 'Don't worry; I'm going to stop the tin man. Just don't tell the others about the dream, not until tomorrow, right?'

'OK,' she said. 'Ross ...'

'Yeah?'

'I saw you in the dream ...'

'I know, you told me that.'

'In the dream you couldn't stop the tin man. He was too strong for you …'

'We'll see about that.'

She lay back in her bed, not convinced. She said nothing and pulled the blanket up to her chin. I ruffled her hair then quietly paced back to my room and got dressed. There was no time to waste. If I got going soon I could be in Portsmouth in time to stop him from killing any more innocent people.

I pushed my hands through the sleeves of my jacket and pulled on my runners. I didn't need to bring anything else. I only needed my anger. I closed the bedroom door and took to the staircase but paused halfway down. Trepidation perhaps, common sense maybe. Sarah had said Zalech might be too much for me to handle by myself. Telling the others would mean I would lose out on the chance to face him. I slowly went back to the top of the staircase and looked along the dim hallway at the door to Hunter's room. He was just as reckless as me. Would he be so reckless as to keep it from the others and join me? Would he support me in that way? Were we that close or was he just the cold hearted swine that had tormented me for so long in Scotland?

'Hunter, are you awake?' I whispered as I went to his bed.

'What are you doing in my room, you oddball?'

'Shut up!' I whispered. I turned on the lamp and he shielded his eyes from the sudden brightness. 'Keep your voice down.'

'Bentley, I am sorry for your predicament and all that, but if you don't get out of here I'm going to hit you with a thousand volts!'

'I said keep your voice down!'

'What do you want?'

'Sarah just had a vision and she described it for me.'

'This better be good, Bentley.'

'She just told me where Zalech will be this afternoon. Now you listen up, Hunter, I'm going after him. Don't try and talk me out of it and don't try to stop me. I only came here to see if you wanted to join me.'

There was a long silence and our eyes locked. He never gave away what was on his mind and as he rose from the bed I had no idea if he planned to stop me or not.

'Well?' I asked.

'Go out to the car and make sure to roll it out onto the road before you start the engine. Leave the headlights off too. I'll join you in five minutes.'

I did as he said and took the old Mercedes and used my psycho-kinesis to roll it out of the driveway and onto the road. When I was fifty yards or so from the main gates I turned the key and started the engine. I sat there with the headlights off. The sun was visible in the eastern sky and I just hoped it wasn't too late. It was easily a four-hour drive to Portsmouth.

I glanced at the clock on the dash when Hunter eased himself into the driver's seat. It was 8.09am. We'd still get there by midday if we didn't make any stops. Hunter lit a cigar before pulling on his seatbelt.

'Now,' he said, cigar smoke dancing around his face, 'I've just done you a favour and I want you to also do yourself a favour.'

'How do I do that?'

'By sticking to the plan.'

'You haven't told me what the plan is yet … if you even have one.'

351

'The plan is that you follow my lead and don't go off on some insane solo mission.'

'I want to be the one who—'

'I know you do. There's more at stake here than your thirst for revenge, Bentley. Remember that. We'll do this together, right?'

'Right.'

Hunter shifted the gear stick and pressed hard on the accelerator. We barely spoke for the next couple of hours. I felt like I couldn't speak. I was far too nervous to hold a conversation. I got the feeling that my companion was nervous too; his fingers were tapping the steering wheel constantly, and he was chain smoking.

'We should be there soon,' Hunter announced. 'Did the child say where exactly he would be?'

'No. Just that he was by the sea … killing lots of people.'

'He's a real barrel of laughs this guy. When we do find him I want you to hang back and allow me to take the lead. I'll try to take him out with one hit.'

'And if that fails?'

'Then you move forward and we hit him in rapid succession. We have to be relentless and try and wear him down. The one thing we can't do is give him any breathing space. We'll be in big trouble if we get put on the back foot. Mageletons are difficult to stop once they gain momentum.'

'We *can* beat him, right?'

'Of course we can but don't be expecting this to be easy. This guy is very strong, he's very clever and he's pure evil. He'll probably enjoy the challenge and would love nothing more than to kill a couple of Guild agents.'

'You think he's working alone?'

'I can't say for sure. He doesn't seem to be operating at the behest of someone else, but I have a nagging suspicion that Golding has had a hand in all this, someone with a lot of money has to be providing him with a means to travel, and a place to lie low.' He flicked his cigar end out the open window. 'That's not important for the moment. Let's deal with Zalech first. After that, the Guild can fully investigate how he managed to recover so swiftly from his injuries.'

We continued along the motorway for what seemed an eternity. We spoke about our tactics, but there was no coherent plan; it was impossible to predict what would happen when we encountered Zalech. Finally, we took the road approaching Portsmouth city centre. I concentrated on how I would tackle Zalech when the time came. I ran over my repertoire of psychokinetic assaults *and* defences. I could create sturdy shields and could generate a lot of force with my attacks, I knew I was still a novice compared to Zalech and Hunter though. They had both spent years learning from the gifted veterans of the Guild and would be more creative, and unpredictable, than me. Still, I remained composed and confident, despite the flutters of nerves in the pit of my stomach.

'Here we go,' Hunter growled as he took an exit from the road and dead ahead was the city centre. 'This route should lead us down town, towards the bus station.'

'I hope we're not too late.'

'So do I. How are you feeling?'

'I'm up for this.'

'You know, it seems like I might have been wrong about you, Bentley.'

353

'Oh?'

'Yeah, if you survive today then you might gain my respect.' I saw the hint of a smile creeping onto his face. 'You *might*.'

'You won't get rid of me that easily, Hunter. Although I am bit worried about you. You're no spring chicken and you might not have the vigour for combat these days.'

'I've got many a year left in me and I fully intend to see out this day.'

The road led us through some of the suburban housing areas then into a busier and more built up system of streets with shops and businesses. It seemed like everything was as it should have been, but as we approached the bus station on the quays it was very obvious that something was not quite right.

'Look,' I said pointing ahead.

'It seems Zalech has arrived before us.'

There was large crowd of people running from the main street. The traffic on the road became backed up and Hunter brought the car to a stop.

'They're all running away from that one street,' I said. 'I'll bet that's where he is.'

Hunter didn't bother replying. He turned the steering wheel and drove the car up onto the centre island of the road then cut across onto another road. Soon we were brought to a halt again. The people were flooding out onto the road and blocking our way. Then we saw two police squad cars appear, the officers inside speaking on their radios. They left their vehicles and were directing the crowd and trying to bring some order to the chaos. The streams of frightened people bustled them our way and one of them turned his attention to us.

He pointed at Hunter and began shouting, 'Get this car out of here, you're blocking up the road!'

Hunter didn't obey the order at first, but the cop wasn't taking no for an answer. He came marching towards us and started shouting his head off.

'I'll have to back off,' Hunter said as he shifted the gear stick into reverse. 'We'll dump the car on a quieter road then – Bentley, where do you think you're going?'

I'd opened the passenger door and was halfway out before Hunter had even noticed. 'I'm sorry, Hunter,' I said over my shoulder. 'There's no time to waste.'

'Bentley!'

I jogged away from the car and into the oncoming crowd. People were screaming and jostling each other, a few people fell and others tripped over them increasing the panic amid the heaving mass. I should have been swept along with the crowd, but I created a small psychokinetic shield around my body that people simply bounced off and it allowed me to pass through them with ease.

By the time I reached the road by the bus station it was virtually empty. The locals had managed to get away and I could see clearly why they had run. Far off down the street was a man surrounded by lifeless bodies. There seemed to be a dozen or more bodies on the roadside, mostly police officers judging by their yellow hi-vis jackets. He was too far away to identify but in my heart I knew it was the man who had murdered my father. It *had* to be him.

I picked up the pace, striding along the centre of the road, and I felt my anger rising as I approached the lone figure with his back to me. My power was increasing. I felt strong. I felt ready.

The man turned slowly and faced me. We were thirty yards apart but I could see him clearly enough to identify him. It was Zalech … but not as I remembered him. His face was horribly scarred, his neck seemed to be made of metal and when he smiled at me his teeth reflected the sunlight like a mirror. The 'tin man' was exactly how a child would describe him. He looked thinner than before and his eyes were even crazier than they had been when I saw them in north-east some weeks before. It was his reaction to seeing me that was most shocking, though. He wasn't surprised or startled as I thought he might have been. In fact, it almost seemed like he'd been expecting me. I stopped dead in my tracks, knowing that somehow he had planned all this, and that I had walked into his trap.

We stood in the centre of the deserted road watching one another. My heart was pounding hard and beads of sweat were leaking out of my face. I'd wanted this for many days – it had been all I'd thought about – but now that the time was at hand, I wasn't so sure that I could take Zalech on. He looked so confident.

'Well?' he shouted to me. His voice was bizarre, like a robot from a sci-fi movie. 'Are you not going to say something, Bentley?'

'I didn't come here to talk.'

'I admire your bravery though I see in your eyes that it is quickly deserting you.'

There was an arrogant smirk on his horrid face that confirmed that I had indeed walked into a trap. Somehow he knew I'd show up. I wanted to tear him limb from limb, but I kept my distance. I didn't want to make this easy for him. I now realised I'd made a huge mistake by coming alone and wanted to keep Zalech talking until Hunter showed up.

'I had expected you to be full of blood and thunder,' he shouted, his voice echoing off the buildings on the empty street. 'Yes, to come rushing at me with all your power and venom. Yet you stand there with the eyes of a lamb, realising that you have stumbled into the wolf's lair.'

The entire situation, particularly Zalech's appearance, was odd to say the least, but I noticed something awfully peculiar: Zalech was gently waving his hand left and right, in a slow and hypnotic type of way. Was he totally insane or was this some new technique that I knew nothing of?

'Come on, Bentley!' he shouted again. 'Are you not going to say something?'

'I'm the one who's going to kill you.' I felt a sudden wave of courage in me and also a clever lie came into my thoughts. One that would surely wipe that grin from Zalech's face. 'The girl – the prophet you kidnapped – she predicted that I would be the one to kill you.'

I said it with enough assurance that Zalech's air of confidence fizzled away … momentarily.

'You are a skilled liar,' he said, smiling again. 'Yes, a very skilled young man indeed. I have heard so much about you and your many talents. Yet you lack the one talent that would save your life.'

'What talent is that?'

'Surfing.' He laughed wildly and his arms stopped swaying. 'Although, I doubt you could surf your way out of this no matter how talented you are.'

A shadow gradually crept over the buildings on the street and the sun disappeared. At first I thought it was a figment of my imagination or a passing cloud, but when I looked behind Zalech, towards the coast, it was as if a vast mountain was rising from the depths.

After a couple of seconds I came to my senses and saw it was no mountain. It was the sea that was rising. It was hundreds of feet high. It didn't look to be moving at first, but as the seconds passed by I knew it was hurtling towards the shore at a phenomenal speed.

I looked back at Zalech. He was smiling and his eyes were wild.

'I am sure you would like to kill me,' he shouted over the deep rumbling sound, 'but you cannot beat the devil at his own game.'

I sent two volleys of psychokinetic energy at him. The first had no impact and was simply deflected away. The second did strike him. I saw his body shake as the shot met his chest but he was only pushed back a couple of steps and was virtually unharmed. I stood there staring at him, dumbfounded that he took the brunt of an energy spear.

'You missed your chance, Bentley!' he roared at me over the terrible crashing sound of the approaching wave. 'Now you will see what true power really is!'

The immense wave was coming at us fast. It sounded like a jet engine powering up and now that it was close I saw the white foam at the crest and the deep mix of brown and blue beneath. I even spotted a boat that was caught within it and cars and buses were being sucked up off the road and were swallowed instantly.

There was a terrible crash as the wall of water fell forward towards the city. There was a rumble under my feet and it swept inland as fast as a bullet. It consumed the buildings as it rolled forward. Everything that lay in its path was swallowed. Then it hit the far end of the street. Fifty-foot high white explosions at the side, becoming black in the centre. The speed and ferocity of the wave was awesome and there was no escaping it.

It consumed Zalech, but I was wise enough to know he was surely immune to its force thanks for his mageletonia. Panic rose inside me and an awesome force came to me. I hunkered down and blasted a sphere of energy out of body and a solid shield protected me from the impact. Everything went black around me. Cars and debris swirled past. Everything was utterly vanquished by the wave. All except for the small circle around me.

It took all my strength to maintain the shield in place and I knew I couldn't hold out with such immense pressure hitting me from all sides.

CHAPTER TWENTY-FOUR

Retaliation

When I regained consciousness I was dangling like a lifeless dummy over Hunter's shoulder as he kicked his way through a flooded road. For a moment my mind was blank but the fog in my head soon cleared and I started to remember what had happened.

I recalled the mountainous wave sweeping inland and gobbling up the buildings beside the sea. I remembered Zalech disappearing into it as it smashed along the street. Then the rushing water hitting my defensive shield. The force of the wave pressed on the cocoon of energy from all sides and put a titanic strain on my hold over the shield. The spherical barrier shrank under the weight of the water and eventually it gave way. My only protection from the flood was gone and I was sure I was a dead man.

But, unintentionally, I had saved myself when I created the shield. Not only had it protected me from the impact of the terrible wave, it had also trapped air around me, and when the shield gave way I was in the middle of a large bubble of air that shot upward. I was carried inside it and when I reached the surface I was blasted up into the air. I spun like a rag doll tossed by an unruly child then came back down with a heavy thud. I'd hit my head off something, probably the roof of a vehicle or a phone box that had been pulled along in the torrent. I managed to keep it together for a while but I was dazed and struggled to use my gifts. I latched onto a long piece of timber and was carried away along the avenue of water.

I was dragged along until the floodwater dispersed onto some side streets. At this point I realised it had not been a tsunami like those I'd seen on the TV, it was a localised tidal wave that razed only a small part of the city. The other roads had not been flooded as badly and soon the water level fell rapidly. The wave had been summoned by Zalech to kill me. But only me. The vast majority of locals had avoided it because they fled when Zalech killed the police officers. That was the only positive to take from the whole disaster. The damage had been confined but the area had been obliterated by the water.

I felt cowardly that I hadn't rushed Zalech as soon as I laid eyes on him. I should have killed him when I had the chance and not thought of my own mortality. No one person should command the power to cause such devastation. Especially when that person is a raving lunatic. A known mass murderer.

At some point I lost my grasp on the piece of timber and floated into one the side streets and blacked out. The next thing I knew Hunter had picked me up and carried me away from the epicentre of the devastation. He didn't stop or even look back over his shoulder until he reached dry ground. He lifted me onto the bonnet of a car then took a few steps back and sucked in deep breaths.

After a moment I summoned the strength to lift myself up on my elbows. Hunter looked relieved when he saw I was awake, but his comfort was short-lived.

'What the bloody hell were you thinking?' he snapped. 'How could you go rushing off like that, you bloody fool?'

'I'm sorry, Hunter. I don't know what came over me.'

'You almost got yourself killed!' he shouted at me. 'Man, the Guild is going to be pissed off. They might expel us both for this.'

'You knew that before you came down here with me.'

'No! The plan was for both of us to attack Zalech and kill him. If we'd stuck to the plan we'd have been seen as heroes. Look at what your foolishness has caused. Half a city's been wiped out!'

'I'll tell them I acted alone.'

'I know you will! What in the name of God happened down there?'

'It was Zalech,' I panted – I was still finding it hard to catch my breath and my head felt like a balloon. 'Somehow he created that huge wave. He just lifted his arm and the sea climbed over the buildings. I never thought anyone could be that powerful.'

'I told you he was strong!'

'No. Not just strong, Hunter. He was immeasurably powerful. He'd make Dolloway look like a novice. Something has changed in him. By all accounts he was always a strong mageleton but he didn't have a power like this the last time we encountered him.'

'There's evil at work here. Zalech was never taught how to create waves like that. Someone very influential is aiding him.'

'He's not the Zalech you remember. He's changed. He's full of scars and metal plates.'

'A fight with a panther will do that to you.' Hunter pushed himself off the car and looked up and down the street. People were rushing around; others wandered from one street to the next, aimlessly.

'We've got to get out of here. Let's hotwire a car and get on the road. This is not a good place for us to linger.'

'He's not dead, Hunter.' I mustered enough strength to get back on my feet. 'He's still somewhere in the city.'

'Forget it, Bentley. We're not going looking for him. Not while he's right beside the sea. He can't be beaten in a place like this.'

'He'll disappear again,' I demanded. 'This might be our only chance.'

'A man who's looking for a fight rarely stays hidden for long. We'll face him again, Bentley. But next time we'll do it on more even ground. And besides, you look ready to keel over. *And* I wouldn't be surprised if Zalech is lurking these streets looking for you. We can't waste any more time. Let's go.'

'I wonder how many people have died,' I said, looking at the flooded streets. 'Is there no end to this hopeless darkness that surrounds us?'

'There is always the light of defiance, Bentley.' Hunter raised his arms and above the buildings I saw a vibrant rainbow appear gradually. 'Darkness can't chase it away.'

Hunter helped me along the pavement and we tried to find a street without cops. This wasn't easy; every cop in the county must have arrived in Portsmouth. I started to feel an intense anxiety when we turned each corner, thinking that Zalech would be waiting for us. We didn't see him again, though.

Hunter found an old van and broke the driver's window and had the engine going in less than a minute. I climbed into the passenger seat and took off my soaking jacket. Only then did I notice my t-shirt was covered in blood. I pressed the palm of my hand on the side of my head and felt a long gash over my right ear. It hurt like hell now that I knew it was there.

'Damn it,' I hissed. 'I must have bumped my head harder than I thought.'

'Yep, that's another scar to add to your collection. A few more years and few more fights and you'll look like me.'

'What a horrible thought …'

'We'll get it seen to when we reach Williams's place. That's if they don't kill us.'

'I'll take the flak. You can say that you saw me sneaking out of the house and followed me or something like that.'

'No, I'll own up to my part in this disaster. We'll take the grilling together.'

🖝 🖝 🖝

The drive back to the Williams estate was an uncomfortable one, not only because of the head wound I'd gotten in Portsmouth, but also I was dreading what Mr Williams would say to us on our arrival. Facing Cathy was an even worse prospect.

The last thing we wanted to do was arrive in a stolen vehicle, so Hunter parked the van a couple of miles from the house then we walked the rest of the way. Our pace became quite laboured once we passed through the tall gates at the end of the driveway and saw Mr Williams standing by the front door.

The old man was silent for a moment and I watched his face slowly growing pink until he started shouting at us.

'A rogue mageleton is on the loose, you two disappear in the middle of the night, the next morning there's a tsunami in Portsmouth, and there are all sorts of bizarre eyewitness accounts on the news. For some strange reason I have a hunch that these random events are linked. *Please* tell me I'm wrong!'

'We were in Portsmouth,' Hunter admitted, 'and yes, Zalech was there too and it was he who created the wave. He created it to kill Bentley. Now, could you please get out of the way and let us in? Bentley needs stitching.'

'He might need more than stitching when Ballentine gets here,' Mr Williams said as he stood to the side and allowed into the hall.

'What's he coming here for?' Hunter asked.

'What's he coming here for – he's coming here because I called it in when you two went missing, and while I was on the phone the first report of the tsunami came on the radio. Ballentine knew immediately that the pair of you were somehow involved. You seem to be very relaxed about all this, Hunter. Do you know how many people died today?'

'I'm not relaxed,' Hunter snapped. 'How many died?'

'Over a hundred confirmed already. Many more are missing and presumed dead.'

'That loony has to be stopped, Peter.'

'Damn right he does,' I added. 'The Guild should be assembling an army to fight this guy.'

'They are,' Mr Williams said coldly. 'An emergency call has been put out and there are operatives currently flying in from all corners of the world.'

'Good,' Hunter grunted. 'I'd prefer to be part of a team if I have to fight Zalech.'

'You'll be lucky if you ever get another assignment from the Guild! They might even force you into retirement because of this little stunt.'

'They'll forgive me.'

'I'm not so sure. Hunter, you are in deep you-know-what because of this.'

'Shit, Williams. It's called deep *shit*.'

'Please don't use language like that in my home.'

We went to kitchen and I placed my head under the tap over the sink. I ran some cold water and winced as it loosened up the cut behind my ear. Cathy and Canavan arrived at the house soon after and came straight to the kitchen. Canavan looked relieved when she saw us but that quickly turned to anger and she scolded Hunter for being so irresponsible. Cathy came to me when she saw the blood on the side of my head and neck.

'Are you OK? Jesus, look at your head!'

'I'll be all right,' I assured her. 'Just bumped my head is all.'

'It's more than a bump, Ross. You'll need it stitched right away.'

Mr Williams and Hunter continued to bicker amongst themselves about the disaster in Portsmouth while I was brought to my room by Cathy. Canavan followed us up and she began to stitch my head – without any anaesthetic. It hurt like hell but it was mild considering what Zalech had done to those poor unfortunate souls who had crossed his path in Portsmouth. Canavan took her time, saying she didn't want to do a rush job because the scar would be worse. She went on to tell me I was an extremely foolish young man.

When she snipped the last stitch she said, 'I suppose you're also brave in your own way. Just try not to allow your bravery to guide you all the time. Try to use your brain more often. Cathy has told me that you're quite intelligent behind all your bravado.'

'*Quite* intelligent?'

'You're not exactly a genius, Ross,' said Cathy.

'I know.'

She finally hugged me when Canavan left the room and descended the staircase.

'You had me worried sick, you know that? When you weren't in the house and then I heard the news. I thought…' she shook her head and frowned. 'That really was a stupid thing to do, Ross. I know you wanted revenge for your father's death, but you should have told the rest of us.'

'It wasn't just about revenge. I went down there so he couldn't hurt anyone else. I thought … I dunno … I thought it would have been the same as facing Marianne. I thought that he would rush into a fight with me and now that I was more skilled I could capture him, or even kill him. He was nothing like Marianne, though. He was so in control. I wanted to kill him – I still do – but I was stunned by what I found down there. I didn't know how to fight him. I hesitated and he took full advantage of that. I guess I am lucky to be alive. I know I won't hesitate next time I face him. No way.'

'There won't be a next time.'

'He's not dead and he's not going away. There will *have* to be a next time.'

'I realise that but next time it should be the Guild that faces him and not just you.' She pulled away and got to her feet. 'Speaking of the Guild, they'll be sending someone here soon.'

'Ballentine is already on his way.'

'You'll be in trouble for this.'

'I know. Maybe they'll expel me from the Guild.'

'I hope so.'

'You haven't changed your mind, have you?'

'No. If anything this episode has made me more determined to get away. Ross, will you join me when this is all over? After they catch that maniac?'

'Everything will change once Zalech is in the ground.' I stood and reached out to her, pulling her to me by using my gift. I held her tight and told her she was more important to me than the Guild could ever be. I meant it too.

🖛 🖛 🖛

Ballentine arrived a couple of hours later. He didn't say much at first, but if looks could kill, Hunter would have been stone dead at first glance. After having a conversation with Mr Williams in private he came to us and said he needed to speak to us all about what was to come. Mr Williams, Hunter, Canavan and I joined him in the study. Cathy said she didn't want to get involved and sat out in the garden with Sarah. This raised a few eyebrows from the others, but I knew all too well how she was feeling.

I was half expecting Ballentine to read the riot act on Hunter, instead he remained calm and asked us both to give a very detailed account of the events of the previous night and that morning. Hunter went first and Ballentine never once interrupted him. He simply took notes. Then it was my turn. I described Sarah's vision then the journey to the south coast before retelling the moment I saw Zalech on the main street. Ballentine asked me to describe his appearance in as much detail as possible, but his real interest was in how the wave had been summoned. Ballentine left the room after I finished telling my story, and I heard him on the phone in another part of the house, obviously relaying the events to the Council. When he returned his mood was almost indifferent to what had happened, almost like he'd taken our side all of a sudden. I got the feeling that he was very much like Hunter and I: impulsive, living on his instincts, a man with a taste for excitement, adventure and a fight. He also seemed to understand my desire for vengeance, although he didn't condone it.

'As you would probably expect,' he said after returning from his phone call, 'you are both officially off the Zalech case. And that does *not* mean you can remain on it unofficially.'

'Come on, Dominic!' Hunter moaned. 'We've invested a lot in tracking him down. None more so than young Bentley here. If anything, he deserves to land the killer blow against Zalech.'

'I understand that,' he said to Hunter before turning to me. 'I certainly understand your desire to kill him, Ross. But your actions have forced the hand of the Council, and we're seeking justice instead of revenge. You can't be part of the team in charge of tracking him down. There's too much emotion involved and that normally gets in the way of an efficient investigation.'

'Who will be tracking him down?'

'A hit squad has been called in. They're being briefed at the Palatium as we speak. That does not, however, mean you cannot be involved at some level.'

'What do you mean?' Hunter wondered. He had a suspicious

frown on his forehead. 'At what level exactly?'

'I have a lot of influence in these matters and that means I can conduct my own investigations as long as they don't directly impair those being run by the Council. It does not mean I have *carte blanche* but I won't have to even report directly to the Council.'

'Since when do you have privileges like this?' Hunter asked.

'Since I became a senior agent and the Guild are stretched too thin. There's lots of trouble around the world at present and some of us have been granted the freedom to operate autonomously.'

'I'm just as senior as you,' Hunter said, growing increasingly insulted. 'Why wasn't I notified?'

'You weren't given this freedom because you've spent the last twenty years rubbing the Council up the wrong way.'

'You want to start a parallel investigation, don't you?' Mr Williams interrupted, intrigued by Ballentine's admission.

'Perhaps. Zalech represents a great threat – to the Guild and to the public in general – but I am fascinated by how he recovered so soon after what were, allegedly, life threatening injuries. What interests me is who repaired him. Whoever repaired him is backing him. Whoever is backing him is directing him. Whoever is directing him will know where he is.'

'So, we squeeze his secret benefactor for information?' Hunter asked.

'In a way. I am hoping we might be able to force the mysterious benefactor into handing Zalech over to us.'

'We have to find out who it is first.' Hunter replied. 'That might not be too easy.'

'How many realistic suspects are there?' I asked. 'Not many

would have the means to do this, would they?'

'And to teach Zalech new tricks,' Hunter added.

'It has to be an organisation that has a long involvement with the true gifts,' Ballentine said thoughtfully. 'Only three spring to mind: The Jin Assassins – JNCOR – The Eastern Shadow, and Golding Scientific.'

'You can rule out JNCOR,' Mr Williams said flatly, sweeping his hand over his desk. 'Their ethical code wouldn't allow them to involve themselves with someone as deranged as Zalech.'

'You could have said the same about the Guild,' I replied.

'Edward wasn't deranged when we took him under our wing.'

'I would have my doubts about the Eastern Shadow.' Ballentine leaned back in his chair and clasped his hands over his chest. 'Not because they lack the means, but simply because they don't care enough about their operatives to invest so much time and money in them.'

'True,' Mr Williams nodded. 'They've always been a heartless crew.'

'Come on, why are we even debating this?' I asked. 'We all know Golding is behind it.'

'He *is* the most likely suspect,' Hunter nodded. 'Golding Scientific has the perfect set up to take Zalech in and to operate on him. They have an extensive library on the true gifts; somewhere in that library must be a lot of writing on mageletonia. Maybe they even have a copy of Penelope Gordon's study on the unlimited nature of that particular gift.'

'I wish it wasn't Golding,' Ballentine said. 'His organisation is impenetrable. We've been trying to place a mole in that company for years and have got nowhere. And only the high-ranking employ-ees are privy to any useful information.'

'There are always *alternative* methods of attaining information,' Hunter smiled deviously.

'Such as?' Ballentine asked.

'Kidnapping one of the high-ranking employees you mentioned.'

'Then?'

'Torture the hell out of 'em.'

'You are so obvious, Hunter.' Ballentine sighed. 'Far too obvious.'

'I'm direct. There's a difference.'

'How about getting Golding to give up Zalech,' I suggested.

'You mean Golding himself?' Ballentine asked, almost laughing.

'Yeah.'

'Impossible.'

'There has to be something that he values,' I replied. 'There has to be something that will make him play ball.'

'Even if there was something he valued,' Ballentine said to me, 'there's no way we could communicate with him.'

'Not true,' Mr Williams said. The room went quiet and everyone turned to him, waiting for him to elaborate.

'Don't sit there in silence, Peter,' Hunter said loudly from across the room. 'Out with it!'

'There is a way,' the old man said. 'We have a direct line to his personal assistant. It's only ever been used once before. I have a device here that allows me to make calls from a mobile phone with-out any chance of the call being traced. That's how we can commu-nicate with Paul Golding.'

'But we need to make him want to talk first,' Ballentine said.

'That's the tricky bit.'

'We need to have a direct approach if he's to talk,' Hunter added.

'Oh, I think I'm a little too long in the tooth for field work such as this,' Mr Williams admitted. 'All I'm good for at my age is paper work.'

'I know, Peter,' Ballentine said sympathetically, but he was looking at Canavan when he said it.

'I don't know why you're looking at me like that,' she said. 'I'm still fit as a fiddle and I've no problem doing the legwork.'

'What does Golding value more than anything else?' I wondered aloud. 'There has to be something that he loves.'

'Money,' Hunter snorted.

'I'm not one for economics,' Ballentine said. 'I don't know how we could hurt him financially.'

'I do,' I said. 'He's very proud of that big, fancy hotel of his. It has his name on it and it would be a very public way to stick it to him if we destroyed it.'

'The Golding Plaza?'

'Yeah. How about we demolish it … the five of us here have the power among us to bring any building to the ground.'

'Do we really want to start bringing down buildings in the centre of London?' Mr Williams asked. He turned and looked directly at Ballentine. 'And will such drastic measures be within our remit?'

'I think the Guild can stomach almost anything after what transpired in Portsmouth,' Ballentine said confidently. 'The Guild is determined to avoid anything like that happening again. Too many people are dead because of Zalech. If destroying some concrete monstrosity gets us what we want then the Guild will accept it.'

'There are a lot of people staying at the hotel,' Mr Williams replied. 'Not to mention the staff.'

'Getting them out of harm's way is the easy part,' Hunter shrugged. 'We can call in a bomb scare – the entire hotel and all the surrounding buildings will be cleared in fifteen minutes.'

'But there would be an army of police at the scene within no time at all,' Canavan argued. 'I don't want to get into a quarrel with the authorities.'

'We have to be on our way into the hotel as the staff and guests are on their way out,' Hunter said to her. 'We take down the building before the cops even lay out their plan to search the place.'

'This will be very dangerous,' Mr Williams said, as he contemplated the destruction of the building. 'Very dangerous indeed.'

'And probably very complicated,' Canavan added. 'It is a very big building.'

'It's not all that difficult,' Ballentine said. 'Ross and I could do it. We'd have to be *inside* the building – side by side. He could use his power to crack the supporting pillars while I create a shield around us both to protect us when the floors begin to topple down on one another. Canavan, you can create a maze of mirrors on the surrounding streets to buy us more time and Hunter can keep watch if any seriously unwanted attention comes along. Peter you will have to be the getaway driver.'

'A getaway driver!' Hunter roared with laughter. 'Maybe if we're being chased by Miss Daisy!'

'I don't enjoy driving fast,' the old man said proudly. 'It might be wiser to have Cathy as your getaway driver. Or perhaps we can call in the Portmans.'

'Not them,' Hunter moaned. 'Please not them.'

'I'll speak with Cathy,' Mr Williams said. 'The only decision left is when to do it.'

'I'd rather we didn't waste any time,' Ballentine replied. 'We should get it done as quickly as possible.'

'Bloody right!' Hunter cheered. 'You're started to sound like your old self, Dominic!'

'I've spent too much time in your company of late. You're a bad influence on me.'

CHAPTER TWENTY-FIVE

To Have a Heart

I went into an emotional meltdown after creating the tsunami. As the wave swept over me I simply created a kinetic shield which, unlike Bentley's, held firm despite the immense pressure bearing down on it. I simply waited until the initial wave had flowed inland before releasing my shield and rising to the surface of the water. I searched for Bentley, but he was either dead or had escaped. I was confident the former to be the case. My nemesis had been dealt with – quite easily – and now it was time to lie low for a day or two. The Guild would be out in force after my dramatic display of power. Many people had died, along with one of their most promising protégés, and they wouldn't be taking it lying down. Every agent and foot soldier that they had available would be scouring the land for me.

I had mounted the Kinetibike and was at my temporary abode in a little over an hour. Then, in the silence of the country house, the Hyper-furens kicked in. I had been using it that morning to build up my power, but had been able to hold back the insatiable fury that went hand-in-hand with it. I had been almost calm when I faced Bentley, but now that I was alone and all was quiet, the narcotic overwhelmed me. But not in a way I expected. The anger the drug induced seemed to have been eaten up when I created the monstrous wave, and now other emotions were coming to the fore. There were no distractions now. No searing hatred of Bentley to occupy my thoughts.

There had first been joy. As I rode along the motorways from Portsmouth on the GSK7 I could not contain my relief and subsequent elation at having killed Bentley, and at having created a wave of such magnitude. But as I fell into the single chair in the front room the happiness drained away. It left all the negative emotions behind. I raised the palm of my right hand and stared at the ink rendition of Ania. Tears ran down my scarred cheeks and dripped from my chin, some worked their way onto my lips and into my mouth, the unusual salty taste deflecting my thoughts for a few seconds.

I was thinking like a normal person for the first time since the evening the Eastern Shadow broke into my home all those years ago. I experienced an intense fear and despair when one of the thugs had put a gun to my infant sister's temple. I had been a special, but relatively normal, boy up until that evening. From then on I had been nothing more than a murderous puppet, incapable of relating to the people that crossed my path. Incapable of understanding the fear in the eyes of my victims before I ended their lives.

'You cannot beat the devil at his own game.'

What was I now that I too could feel sorrow and fear like my victims? Can the devil be sad? Can he be remorseful and afraid? The devil had been chased out – albeit temporarily – by a side effect of the drug that stubbornly remained in my body. What does a person who has been possessed by the devil for most of their life do when that dark force has been exorcised? What is the first thing they do? What could they do if they were aware that the demon would reclaim their body again soon?

Sitting alone in a dark room and staring out the window at black trees dancing lazily in the autumn bluster was not the answer. No, there was a different answer: to be with someone who cared for me. That was the only answer. In this fleeting moment, when the tin man had a heart, I could indulge those same feelings that I had taken for granted when I was a child. I could simply be next to another human being and talk. I wanted to tell someone that beneath the madness, the rage, the power, and the clandestine existence was a real person and I was free for the moment from all the walls that had imprisoned my original and natural self.

I left the house and took to the Kinetibike, then shot across the countryside like a silent missile. It took over two hours to reach the river where I had practised my wave techniques, the one that the Golding Scientific experimental clinic overlooked. I parked the bike in an alleyway and strolled along the waterway then stood on one of its many bridges and watched the main door to the clinic. She appeared twenty minutes later, shuffling awkwardly in the wind trying to keep the dozens of files under her arms from flying away like great white bats.

'Allow me to carry those for you, doctor.' My voice could not be mistaken for any other. Its deep buzzing almost seemed to give Walters an electric shock, and she froze on the pathway of the bridge and was visibly shaking. 'Do not be alarmed,' I continued. 'I have not come here to harm you. What happened before I left was a moment of rage, not my own, but of a synthetic kind that I could not control. It was not me – not the real me. But right now, the person I am, the person who I *truly* am, has broken through the narcotic fog. I wanted to see you while I could think straight and feel what all *normal* people feel.'

'I know what you did this morning,' she replied, the shock still identifiable in her voice. 'Do you know how many people lost their lives, Edward?'

'No. I felt compelled to create it. The wave was a weapon, you see. It was created to destroy the person who murdered my sister. The rage I have been experiencing left me with no choice but to kill him.'

'Could this not have been done without killing so many innocent people?'

'Perhaps.' A shudder ran through me as I thought of the people I had killed before Bentley arrived. I had murdered them just to attract Bentley and the agents of the Guild. I did not share this with the doctor. Stopping a car in the middle of the main street and crushing it with the driver and passengers inside, waiting for the police to arrive then systematically executing each and every one of them. No, I could not share that information with the doctor. It would be too much for her to accept.

I used psychokinesis to make the files under Walters' arms spin out of her control. They swept up over her head and floated lazily into my steady grasp.

'At least allow me to carry these to your car for you. It is the least I can do. After all, you were the one ...' my sentence trailed off as a young couple sauntered past, each hugging the other tightly. They were people who knew nothing of the true horrors of the world and would not have reacted well to my unusual voice – not to mention my appearance.

'My apologies,' I said when they were a good distance away. 'This voice you and your colleagues have given me draws unwanted attention.'

'It was the best we could do,' Walters replied distantly.

'I know you did your best.'

She started walking and asked me to walk with her. She did not look at me directly, but I felt no insult at this, not after what I had done to her in the clinic before I left for Ireland.

'Why did you come here, Edward?' she asked as we passed along the pavement towards the town centre. 'When you left I thought you were nothing more than a cold blooded killer.'

'But you thought more of me before that outburst, am I right?'

'You *are* more,' she admitted, almost ashamedly. 'Although it's hard to forget your tantrums when you have been on the receiving end of one.'

'I have apologised.'

'And I haven't run away.'

We reached a corner and Dr Walters told me to wait there while she fetched her car. I was suspicious at first, but she explained that the car park attendants would stare if I came with her.

She reappeared a few moments later and drove across the street and parked the car. I retrieved the Kinetibike and followed her to the house she rented in one of the suburbs. I scanned the house, and the street, before climbing off the bike and following her to the front door.

Walters was even more nervous when we were alone and in a confined space. She brought me down the short hallway to the sitting room, then flicked on the lights and sat on a chair near the blackened fire-place. I sat on an identical seat opposite her and was reminded of the night I killed Bentley's father. The seating arrangement. The room. The house. The family portraits. The similarities were very striking. Even the mood in the room was tinged with fear like it had been on that night in Maybrook.

'I have worried about you,' Walters admitted, fidg-eting with an imaginary object in her hands. 'I was wor-ried about what you'd do, but also worried *for* you. I hear whispers in the corridors of the clinic about people like you – the gifted – and how they have a secret war. That they hunt each other.'

'I would rather not discuss it.' I leaned back in the chair. My right knee was twitching. Fear was as new as sorrow to me and I felt it every time I thought of the Guild's hit squads and what they might subject me to if I was caught.

'You're struggling with the new emotions, aren't you?'

'Struggling with the sudden lack of anger.'

'It will return soon enough. Somehow you used up all the Hyper-furens in your brain, but the drug is self replicating and right now your system is being flooded with it once again. The rage will return very soon.'

'Then I must leave you very soon, doctor. I would not risk a repeat of what happened before I left the clinic. I simply wanted to speak with you while I could reason properly, and feel the emotions that have been so often hidden inside me.'

'What do you feel, Edward?'

'Regret mostly. I cannot remain here for much longer even though I wish I could. I would like you to know, doctor, that I am not simply a monster. I am not only a tin man without a heart. I was once more than that and perhaps I can be again.'

'You'll have to avoid your enemies until I can find a version of the Hyper-furens that suppresses the anger.'

'How long could it take?'

'I have no answer to that question. I am not a chemist and I don't even know if it's possible to create a strain of the drug tailored to your specific requirements. But there may be a formula stored in the vaults that might work. It'll take me some time to find out. Here,' she hopped off her chair and went to the table her handbag was lying on. She delved into it and took a mobile phone to me. 'Take this. At least that way I can contact you when I have found another formula.'

I stood and there was just a fleeting hint of a smile as I looked down on her pretty face. It felt so good to be close to her. I felt human as I watched her eyes portray her genuine concern. Perhaps it was more than just concern ... It did feel good to be human.

It was nothing more than a dream, though, and could not last for much longer. There was a good chance this would be the last time I would ever feel such emotions. The drug they had injected into me would not be going away and the most skilled killers on the planet were probably already searching for me. I decided to end the dream in the nicest possible way and kissed Walters with my scarred lips. She did not flinch. That was the best part.

I took the phone from her hand and thanked her before walking to the door. I paused on the porch for a moment and scanned the street before walking to the bike. I hit 500kmph as I reached the first of the motorways leading away from the city.

Walters was correct when she said the Hyperfurens would renew itself and once it did, the anger would re-emerge. I was seething as I reached the country house. All I could think of was the Guild and how they had murdered Ania and disfigured me. The anger was so potent that it made my body shake and my brain throb inside my skull. I began to pace from one dark room to another, thinking of my next attack. One that would strike deep into the heart of the Guild.

CHAPTER TWENTY-SIX

Demolition Squad

We passed the rest of that night discussing our plan to demolish the Golding Plaza hotel. I spent the next morning trying to convince Cathy to get involved, even just as a getaway driver. She refused at first, but by midday she relented and we had our five-person demolition squad. Ballentine was calling the shots and he decided we should hit the hotel just after nightfall – approximately 7pm. The timing was decided on mostly because light-tuners operate best in darkness, but also because London would still be very busy at that time and it would take the authorities longer to get organised after we called in the bomb scare.

Mr Williams seemed to be an expert on every subject, and destroying a building was no exception. Hunter and Ballentine had brought down buildings before, but on a much smaller scale. Between the three they had a fairly solid and detailed plan to weaken the structure enough for it to collapse under its own weight. I provided them with all the details I could remember from my time in the hotel, none of which were pleasant to recount, and it was decided that the underground car park would be the focal point of our attack.

We would have to knock out as many of the smaller pillars as possible, then find one of the main support pillars and break it. That would be enough to make the hotel fold inward like a giant accordion. Once that was done, Cathy would make a phone call to the house and Mr Williams in turn would make a call to Golding's people. What would happen after that was anyone's guess.

We hit the road at 5pm, taking one of the unmarked 4x4s from Mr Williams' animal sanctuary. Cathy drove while the rest of us checked and double checked all the details of the plot. At 6pm, as we were approaching London, a phone call came through to the one mobile that we had with us. It was from Mr Williams and he informed us that he had called the police and told them that a massive, thousand-pound bomb was in one of the rooms of the hotel, that it was remotely operated, and to get everyone, including police, out of the area before it was detonated. The wheels had been set in motion and there was no turning back.

We reached London half an hour later and couldn't get within two miles of the hotel. Dozens of police officers were turning away any vehicle trying to approach, which had been expected. Police cars were tearing through the roads and siren-blasts mixed with panic-stricken voices filled the evening air. It was chaos with hordes of pedestrians hurrying away from the scene. I thought of the harrowing scenes I'd witnessed in Portsmouth and felt a pang of anxiety in my lower chest. I was hopeful, though, that this time there would be no nasty surprises and that no innocent people would get hurt.

Hunter began directing Cathy through the side streets and eventually we came to a small car-valet garage that was hidden from view of the main streets nearby. The staff had bolted as soon they heard about the bomb and Cathy parked up on the deserted forecourt and the rest of us disembarked.

'Cathy,' Hunter said, leaning into the open window next to her, '7.30pm and you're out of here. You leave with or without us.'

'I'm not going to leave without any of you,' she retorted. 'Maybe that's the way you operate – it's not my way, Hunter. And it wasn't my dad's way.'

'I'm not debating this with you, young lady,' he snapped. 'We don't know what we're going to run into at the hotel. It wouldn't even surprise me if Golding guessed we'd do something like this and had a few assassins stationed around here.'

'You're just being paranoid.'

'Don't wait a second past 7.30. I mean it.'

He stormed away from the vehicle and we followed him along the narrow, cobbled street towards the hotel I said I'd never return to, even if my life depended on it.

'You don't really think he'd place assassins in the hotel, do you?' I asked him as I moved to his side.

'We're dealing with Paul Golding,' he replied with a shake of his head. 'I thought you'd have a fair idea of how devious he is by now.'

'He won't be expecting us to hit the hotel,' Ballentine boasted. 'Cathy was right; Hunter's just being paranoid.'

'Whatever you say, Dominic. You're the one who'll be in the firing line.'

'Let us keep our minds on the task at hand,' Ballentine said. 'This is a civilian hotel, full of tourists, and I don't see any reason for there to be trouble apart from some security guards, and they will not be stupid enough to hang about after a bomb scare. Golding doesn't pay his employees handsomely, remember.'

'I hope you're right,' Hunter said. 'I really do.'

We cut through a maze of narrow alleyways as we made our way to the hotel. They were all empty apart from one. A cat watched us passing and the hair on its back stood on end when I met its gaze. I found this very odd, seeing as though Canavan had us cloaked.

'You sure we're invisible?' I asked her. 'That cat just looked me dead in the eye.'

'Body refraction doesn't work on cats,' she replied. 'That's the first lesson light-tuners learn during their training.'

'Quiet,' Ballentine whispered. 'Both of you.'

We soon came to the broad street that the hotel was on. I found myself only yards from the spot where Romand had been standing when he first made contact with me. I wished he was still with us.

'Right,' Ballentine said. 'Hunter and Canavan, it's time for you to work your magic.'

The light-tuners didn't waste any time, and from the entrance of the alleyway they built a maze of towering mirrors. This was to delay any police who tried to enter the hotel. Basically, when anyone approached the hotel they wouldn't see it; they would see the reflection of another nearby building. It would delay them long enough for Ballentine and me to do our work. When the light-tuners finished creating the house of mirrors, and had blocked off all approaches to the Golding Plaza, it was time for us to move.

'I'll cloak you both as you enter,' Hunter said to us. 'You'll be invisible until you get inside. After that, you're on your own.'

Ballentine allowed me to lead the way as I knew the hotel all too well. We moved forward with no hesitation, knowing that Hunter's ability to bend light around us would keep us safe. I darted across the eerily quiet street and headed for the entrance ramp that led to the large underground car park.

Once inside, the cloak gave way and we were visible again. We moved amid the lines of vehicles at a cautious pace, watching for any movement. Once we were sure there was no one left in the car park, Ballentine took control of the situation and he pointed out certain pillars that I would have to crush. We wouldn't get started until we'd decided which of the main load-bearing pillars were to be broken; these were the pivotal ones that would collapse the many floors above us.

'There,' he said pointing at wide, grey pillar that was about six feet wide on all sides. 'That one should be enough, as long as we can take out a handful of the smaller ones surrounding it.'

'Shall I begin?'

'I think it would be wise to wait until I create a shield strong enough to protect us from a thousand tonnes of concrete, don't you?'

He smiled at me and I was just about to smile back when I felt a stinging sensation in my brain; my precognitive gift was suddenly in riot.

'Something isn't right,' I said to Ballentine. 'We're not alone.'

He didn't even have time to respond to my warning. I felt an attack and I turned to my left and released a wave that deflected a volley of automatic gun fire. The bullets cracked off the wave and ricocheted around us, some striking the high ceiling, others dashing the bodywork of the cars.

We scrambled for cover. I ran into the shadow of the large pillar and Ballentine backed up against a car and crouched low. The gun fire kept coming. Thankfully we were unharmed; my colleague created one of his impenetrable shields and the bullets sparked brightly as they bounced off it. He emerged from his hiding place and marched forward into the face of the gunfire. He was unscathed and I followed him into the fray.

Then our attacker was revealed. He was positioned behind the pillars on the far side of car park, nothing more than a shadow at first behind the bright flashes from the muzzle of the gun. Ballentine's defensive shield enveloped me as it grew. Cars were pushed away by it as he moved towards the assailant.

'I'll protect us,' he shouted over the loud echoing gun shots, 'you take him out once you build up enough strength.'

'Got it,' I shouted back.

Then the assassin made what appeared at first to be a costly error. He dashed forward from his position of cover towards a line of cars. I reacted swiftly and fired a dart of kinetic energy at him. He was struck flush in the chest and was knocked off his feet. The impact should have killed him, but to my horror he rolled across the dusty floor and then bounced up onto his feet and began firing again.

'What just happened?' Ballentine roared at me.

'I don't know. That shot should have broken him in two!'

Ballentine halted his approach then backed away. It wasn't wise to keep pushing on when we didn't know what we were actually dealing with. Our retreat spurred the shadowy figure to move towards us. I got a good look at him, and realised it wasn't a 'he' after all. He was actually a she. She was tall and slender, had a very elegant way of moving – almost like a cat – and was wearing long grey boots, black leggings, and a long, black cape with a neck cowl and a hood that was covering her head and hiding her face.

She kept firing at us; the bullets were unable to pierce the shield and she ceased firing. I watched her taking some small objects from under her cape and she threw them in our direction. Suddenly there were loud bangs and a blinding light. Ballentine was taken by surprise and his shield gave way.

Bullets whizzed by my ear as the assassin began shooting once more. Ballentine and I darted for the cover of one of the large pillars and crouched low to the ground.

'I've never seen anyone capable to taking a psychokinetic hit like that before,' I panted.

'Neither have I,' Ballentine said. 'I'll have to take more heed of Hunter's paranoia in future. We have been delayed too long as it is. Let's show this assassin what agents of the Guild are made of, shall we?'

'Hell, yeah.'

He didn't waste any time and got to his feet and built a new shield around himself. Bullets bounced off the invisible barrier and Ballentine took a moment to pin-point the assassin. She was trying to flank us and was out in the open, away from the cover of the lines of parked vehicles. Ballentine pumped his fist into the air and the assassin was knocked off her feet. Just as before she was relatively unharmed and was quickly climbing off the floor. This time, however, she felt the full force of Ballentine's psychokinesis and was blasted into the air and was sent smashing into the windscreen of a car.

I was about to send a volley of energy at her, but she lobbed a flash-bang grenade in our direction and momentarily stunned Ballentine. I had sensed the attack and made a dash to another line of cars as the bright flash went off. I summoned as much power as I could then threw my arms in the air. Cars on both sides of me were dragged off the ground and tumbled forward. The assassin dropped her gun instantly and raised her arms. The cars struck a shield she had created and spun around the floor. Car alarms were going off all over the place and I could barely hear myself think. The noise distracted me and I was almost killed when the attacker lifted and threw a motorcycle at me.

I leapt out of its way and pushed energy out of my hands and aimed it at a car in front of me. It was bumped into the air and I hit it with another wave that propelled it across the cavernous room. It came down with a loud crash and I believed I'd put an end to the duel.

I was wrong, and narrowly avoided an energy spear that crushed a car right next to me. I retaliated and the assassin was knocked to the ground yet again. This time I heard her moan. She'd finally been hurt, and tried to make a run for it.

She was all out of luck. Ballentine managed to bring down part of the ceiling that fell right on top of her as she fled. We held a quick search of the car park; there were no more mysterious assassins, then we went to the body of our attacker and stooped over her. On closer inspection we saw that it was not simply a cape that she was wearing. It was almost like chain mail with a nylon fabric covering it to make it look like it was a normal garment.

'So, that's how he did it,' I said under my breath.

'Zalech?'

'Yeah, he must have been wearing something like this when I

fought him in Portsmouth. That's why he wasn't hurt when I attacked him.'

'We should take this cape with us,' Ballentine said. 'The Guild will have to know more about technology that renders basic psychokinetic attacks impotent. Golding has been a busy bee of late.'

Ballentine ripped the unusual cape from the assassin and her face was revealed. She was quite young and very beautiful, nothing like I had expected her to be. Her green eyes stared vacantly at us and her mouth was open and full of blood.

'Irena,' Ballentine said. 'You foolish girl.'

'You knew her?'

'Yes. Her name is Irena Hofer. We tried to convince her to join the Guild two years ago, she refused because there was no money in it for her. We warned her that others would try to recruit her, but she was dismissive and said that if they paid well she would work for them.'

'Golding must have come calling.'

'Indeed. Almost every gifted person he comes into contact with ends up like this.'

'Aren't I the lucky one,' I smiled.

'Lucky that Marcus Romand thought you were worth risking his life for.'

'I know.'

'Come,' he said, draping the cape over his shoulder. 'If we delay any longer we will never get out of here alive.'

He created an invisible shield around us. No ordinary shield, this was the dual shield that I couldn't manage to conjure after days and days of training. It would protect us both from anything outside it but would allow me to fire out energy from within it. I shot out ten of the small pillars easily with energy spears then focused my attention and all my power on the large, load-bearing one. I fired a powerful slice and it crumbled at its centre.

'That's enough,' Ballentine said. 'Let's make a hasty retreat.'

'Shouldn't we make sure that it will collapse?'

'Ross, my shields are magnificent, but I'd rather get out of here than test their solidity under the weight of a crumbling hotel.'

'Point taken.'

The ceiling creaked above and the lights flickered. We quickened our pace to the exit ramp. By the time we reached it the ceiling was folding, huge chunks of concrete were flattening the cars and silencing the screaming sirens. We raced into the street and I turned briefly to see the immense tower breaking apart, dark clouds bursting through the walls and windows as it stuttered downward. The noise was tremendous and the ground shook and I nearly lost my footing. Ballentine maintained his shield and ran straight to Hunter and Canavan. There were sucked inside and all four of us were protected from the dirty wall of debris that rushed into the street in all directions.

Ballentine released the shield when we entered the first of the alleyways leading away from the ruined hotel. There were no cops this time; they had all run for cover once the building began to implode.

Hunter suggested breaking into the first car we came across, which he seemed accustomed to doing. I insisted we go back to the car valet place, though, to see if Cathy waited. Hunter said she was probably long gone because Ballentine and I had taken so long inside the hotel and we began arguing. Canavan quickly defused it - she appeared to have some influence over Hunter – and we reached the narrow side street to find Cathy sitting in the 4x4 with the engine running.

'Bet you're glad I don't listen to you,' she said to Hunter as he climbed into the seat next to her. 'Eh?'

'Shut up and drive, smart arse.'

Canavan cloaked our vehicle for the return journey and Cathy pushed it to the limit. We reached the Williams estate just before 10pm and when we convened in his study he told he had made the call and that there had been an answer. 'Call back in two hours. Mr Golding will speak to you then,' was all that was said.

That wasn't the only call he'd made in our absence. As soon as he knew that Golding was willing to talk, Mr Williams contacted the leadership of the Guild and they told him the hit-squad that was specially assembled to kill Zalech were released from the Palatium.

'They will be based here tonight and make their move before dawn,' Mr Williams explained.

'That's if Golding gives up Zalech,' Hunter almost cut him off. 'He's just as likely to declare full-scale war on us after we turned his prized hotel into a mountain of dust.'

'He won't,' the old man said confidently. 'I have an ace up my sleeve if Mr Golding starts issuing threats.'

'Never fancied you for a poker player,' the big Scot snorted.

'I'm happy to inform you, Hunter, that you don't know everything about me. I managed to survive decades as an agent for the Guild before you came along.'

'I'm sure the pace was a little slower back in the good ol' days.'

'Will you two stop the bickering for a while?' Cathy moaned. 'Sometimes I forget which of us are veterans and which of us are beginners.'

The squabbling ceased and was followed by a debate on who should do the talking. Everyone wanted the job because they all had a beef with the evil billionaire, but Mr Williams remained determined that he should be the negotiator and eventually the others gave up and we all sat in silence, watching as the clock counted to eleven. It was like time had stood still and the ticking of the old antique timepiece seemed deafening in the cramped room.

Hunter slapped the table as the clock struck eleven and demanded Mr Williams make the call. He was not in a patient frame of mind and the older man told him he'd have to leave the room if he couldn't keep his temper in check.

'Make the damned call, will you.' Hunter snarled. 'We shouldn't have to go by Golding's schedule! We're in the driving seat here!'

'Hunter's right,' Canavan said. 'Let's not dally, Peter.'

'Right,' Mr Williams sighed as he punched a number onto the screen of his cell phone. 'Here goes nothing.'

He placed the phone on his desk, set it to speaker, and we all listened intently to the dial tone over and over until it was silenced.

'Paul Golding here,' I recognised his cold, calculating voice from the video I watched on You Tube before I entered The Million Dollar Gift contest. 'To whom am I speaking?'

'We spoke once before,' Mr Williams answered evenly.

'I don't recall your name.'

'I never gave you my name. Please, we aren't children. Let's not waste our time with silly games.'

'My apologies. I was under the impression I was dealing with a group of reckless children who have no idea of how much time, money and effort goes into building a hotel like the Golding Plaza.'

Hunter couldn't contain himself and shouted at the phone, 'Do you know how much time went into building Portsmouth? A hell of a lot more than your bloody hotel!'

'Please tell that ignoramus to be quiet, or else Ill hang up.'

'He's not an ignoramus, you cold-hearted swine!' I hadn't been able to contain myself either.

'That could only be the arrogant brogue of Ross Bentley ... oh, how I detest that name.'

'Get used to it,' I spat. 'I'm not going anywhere until I take you down!'

'My word, you are an angry young man. I suppose it's understandable seeing as you're in mourning. Incidentally, I heard they put on a lovely service for your father. Shame no one turned up.'

'One day, Golding,' I replied bitterly. 'One day, I'll make you pay for all the pain you've inflicted on me and those around me.'

'Come, did you go to all this trouble just to hurl empty threats at me down a phone line? I expected a much more intelligent and meaningful conversation.'

'We want to talk about what happened on the south coast yesterday,' Mr Williams said to him calmly.

'Ah, yes. Your former colleague is certainly ... making waves lately.'

'It's no laughing matter.'

'Quite. Yes, I must admit what happened in Portsmouth was a tad overzealous.'

'Overzealous?' Mr Williams gasped. 'Do you have any idea how many people are dead because of what Zalech did?'

'There are seven billion people in the world,' Golding said, 'a few hundred won't make much difference in the grand scheme of things.'

'You sound like you're proud of this abomination that you've created.'

'I didn't create him. I merely refined him. As did you.'

'We tried to *help* him.'

'You taught him how to kill. That was just fine as long as he was on your side, and now that he's on the opposite side, you deem him a monster.'

'He was a troubled young man while he was with us. Edward was difficult and challenging, but not what he is now. He left us as a killer, yes, but not as someone who could destroy an entire city.'

'Our training techniques are superior to yours. I won't apologise for being better than you nor should you expect me to.'

'You didn't train him! You somehow gave him this power then set him loose to wreak havoc on the world. You're a fool, Golding. Sooner or later he'll turn his anger and his power on you.'

'Do you honestly think I would empower anyone to such an extent without being able to control them? I may be many things but a fool is not one of them.'

'Edward Zalech cannot be controlled. Not even you, with all your resources, can make such a claim.'

'I don't claim to have control over him. Edward is living on borrowed time so I don't *need* to control him directly. All I have to do is sit back and watch him destroy you before his time runs out.'

'What do you mean by borrowed time?'

'I saved his life and gave him a new one. Alas, this second life that I have given him will be a short one.'

'Don't try to tell me you're planning on killing him. That's simply not logical and I doubt you have the manpower to contend with him.'

'I don't need hired muscle to outlive Zalech,' Golding laughed 'Edward Zalech is already dead. He just hasn't realised yet.'

'Stop speaking in riddles.'

'We have devised a new drug,' Golding admitted. 'It gives even modestly gifted people exceptional power. This is how Edward has become so strong. There is a downside, though. The drug is still at an experimental stage and comes with some very serious side effects. Death being one of them. It's essentially a poison and sooner or later it will kill our troublesome young friend.'

'How long has he got?'

'I can't say for sure. Originally we believed he'd hold out for a month. But he is a very determined individual and his powers of recovery made us reassess our initial projection.'

'Go on.'

'He could hold out for three months.'

There was a collective sigh around the room.

'Zalech could wipe out millions of lives in three months,' Mr Williams said. 'He cannot be allowed to live on for that amount of time.'

'Not my problem.'

'He would also have time to turn on you.'

'I'm quite a ways down his list. I'll take my chances.'

'Then it's war. Everyone connected to us will be unleashed upon you and your organisation. We will not stop until you're dead.'

'You people do have a flair for the dramatic. You wouldn't risk a war with me because there's a chance that you'll lose. Besides, you can't get near me, or the heart of my operation. You don't even know where I am!'

'You have been given a warning, Golding. There won't be a second one.'

'Save your warnings. This conversation is over.'

'Hang up and we will immediately send every gifted person we have to Iceland … to an area known as Sudavik.'

This was obviously the ace Mr Williams had up his sleeve. There was a long silence on the other end of the line.

'Perhaps I have underestimated you,' Golding finally said.

'Do you want to cut a deal?'

'Right,' Golding said, as the first hint of aggression had crept into his tone. 'I will give you Zalech and you give me time to move my operation out of Iceland? Then we can restart our game of cat and mouse.'

'You have a deal as long as the information you supply is one hundred percent accurate.'

'It's accurate. In fact, I know exactly where he is right at this moment. I put him up in a house owned by the corporation. He'll be hiding out there for a few days after his recent antics on the coast.'

'Where is his hideout?'

'I'll send a text in a few moments with the GPS coordinates. Make sure you keep up your side of the bargain.'

The line went dead and there was a few seconds of silence in the room as we all quietly made up our minds if Golding could be trusted or not.

'It's a wind-up,' Hunter said. 'I don't believe a word out of that snake's mouth. He probably won't even send the text message.'

The words had hardly left his lips when the mobile buzzed twice.

'Ye of little faith,' Mr Williams chuckled as he lifted the phone. 'GPS coordinates, just as Golding promised.'

'It's more likely to be a trap. We'll be sending our team into the arms of a hundred of Golding's assassins.'

'Unlikely,' Ballentine said, shaking his head. 'Golding knows we have his new location pinpointed and he also knows that if he double-crosses us his new facility will be under attack within twenty-four hours. He won't risk that for the sake of Edward Zalech. Remember, he is a man who knows no loyalty … he even sent his own sister to her death!'

'Well, I don't trust him,' Hunter replied. He leaned back in his chair and folded his big arms. 'He'd do anything to put the hurt on us.'

'It's not our decision,' Mr Williams added. 'Sakamoto will lead the attack and he hand picked those who will go with him. It should be up to him to decide whether this lead is genuine or if it's too much of a risk.'

'When will they get here?' I wondered.

'Shouldn't be too long,' William answered. 'Within the hour I would say.'

Hunter kept going on and on about it being a trap. The others disagreed and didn't entertain his wild assertions. I tended to agree with him, but held my tongue. I was selfish in my silence; I wanted Sakamoto and his team to go to that house even if there *was* the possibility of an ambush. I didn't want them to miss out on any chance, even a slim one, of killing Zalech. I wanted nothing more than to know he was dead.

'Isn't anyone going to back me up?' Hunter shouted. His eyes searched every face in the room but none would side with him.

I got up and went to the kitchen, content in the knowledge that Zalech would be dead within a few hours. The only thing that took the gloss off of my mood was that I wouldn't be the one to finish him. The others emerged from the study moments later and all except Hunter joined me at the long kitchen table. There was relief amongst us, but the air remained tainted with tension. We all knew that Zalech would die, and that didn't bother any of us, but it was quite reasonable to believe he would bring a few of the Guild's assassins down with him. It would be a hollow victory if that happened. How much did I want my revenge? What price could I accept? My emotions were too strong and too many to find the answers.

CHAPTER TWENTY-SEVEN

The Assassins

I sat at the kitchen table listening as Ballentine and Mr Williams talked about the assassins who would soon arrive at the house. From what I could gather, each assassin worked alone, except in times of great peril when they banded together to ensure the safety of the Guild. There were three of these loosely-connected groups: one that operated in the Americas, another based in North Africa, and one in Europe. Soon we would meet the European outfit, and they were the most feared of the three. The reason they were feared more than the other groups was because of their leader – Sakamoto. He'd once been the Guild's top agent in their fight against JNCOR in the East. He then joined the ranks of the assassins after the Guild called a truce with JNCOR. Sakamoto quickly gained a reputation as a cold and flawless killer. A reputation that had been growing ever since. I felt uneasy – fearful even – in the knowledge that I would soon be in the company of such notorious killers.

'Doesn't sit well with me that people like Sakamoto are members of the Guild,' I said. 'Don't they go against what we stand for?'

'The gifted need an army to protect them, Ross,' Mr Williams replied. 'The Guild is that army ... but every army requires a Black Ops team to do the type of work that others cannot countenance.'

'If you say so.'

The doorbell clanged and we walked to the archway leading into the hall to get a look at who it was. Hunter, who had been sulking in the sitting room alone, pulled open the door and there stood a number of shadowy figures huddled together on the threshold. The nearest and tallest of them spoke to Hunter briefly before stepping inside. He lingered under the chandelier and waved to us. I recognised him the instant the light met his stern face. It was Jim Sterling, the mysterious leader of the Guild. Hunter gave him a wide berth as he entered. The others, nine of them in all, followed in Sterling's wake. This was a very different team to the one first assembled to kill Edward Zalech in Newcastle. This was a hardened crew of killers. I saw ruthlessness in their eyes as they marched into the kitchen, all of them dressed in black, and I felt confident they could handle what lay ahead of them. The last assassin to enter was Linda Farrier; she was the only one I recognised. She lingered in the hall with Hunter before joining the others in the kitchen and giving me *the* smile when she saw me.

'You all seem surprised to see me,' Sterling said, taking off his coat. His voice was deep and supremely confident. 'Didn't you tell them I was coming, Peter?'

'It slipped my mind,' Mr Williams replied. He was the only one who had remained seated. 'I've had quite a lot on my mind this evening.'

'Of course you have. An unfair burden for you to shoulder alone.' Sterling gave me a courteous nod as he strolled to the table where he took a seat. 'Come, everyone relax – relaxation clears the mind – and clear minds are needed in moments like these.'

We all took seats at the table, except Hunter, who loitered under the arched entrance to the hallway. He had an odd expression on his weathered face, almost fearful. I thought at first it was because he was worried for the assassins and Linda in particular, but the more I thought about it the more it seemed he was afraid of Sterling. It was probably my imagination because Hunter wasn't afraid of anyone, and certainly not a colleague.

'Did you make the call?' Sterling asked Mr Williams quite casually, as if nothing was riding on it.

'I made contact with Golding, yes. He wasn't very forthcoming at first–'

'He never is,' Sterling interrupted. A far from pleasant smile widened his thin face.

'His tune changed as soon as I mentioned Sudavik.'

'I bet it did.' Sterling broke into a hearty laugh. The assassins laughed with him, as did Ballentine. 'I bet he nearly crapped himself when you dropped that bombshell on him.'

'Quite possibly. He said he would give up Zalech if we stayed away from Iceland long enough for him to clear out.'

'Good.'

'I think we should attack his base as soon as possible,' Ballentine argued, '*before* he gets a chance to relocate. This is a golden opportunity, Jim. One that we shouldn't squander.'

'We can talk about that at another time, Dominic.' He turned to Mr Williams again. 'Where is Zalech now?'

'We were sent GPS coordinates of a house he's been holed up in. It's in Bedfordshire – a rural area. The location is very remote.'

'Perfect,' Sterling announced. 'That will make the job a lot easier.'

'There is more,' Hunter said from the shadowy archway.

'I guessed as much, judging by that bullish look on your face,' Sterling said to him. 'What vexes you, old friend?'

'Two things have me worried for your team, Sterling. First, that it could be a trap. Second, Golding said that Zalech is under the influence of a drug that gives him incredible reserves of power.'

'Ah, I was wondering how he managed to create that tsunami. Did Golding go into any detail regarding this narcotic?'

'It makes him very angry apparently. Angry enough to control an ocean is angry enough to kill nine assassins.'

'Hunter has a point,' Ballentine said grudgingly. 'We don't know how strong this drug has made him. Perhaps more of us should join the team?'

'No,' a tall, oriental man with a shaved head said. I guessed this was the infamous Sakamoto I'd heard so much about. 'My team is well versed and will operate as a cohesive unit. Late additions could jeopardise the mission.'

'Jim?' Ballentine said, turning to Sterling.

'There is logic on both sides of this argument. But I must side with Sakamoto. His team acts as a tight unit, and a false step from a newcomer could cost lives.'

'I think you're taking a huge risk,' Hunter added. 'Facing Zalech in his current condition is a step into the unknown. There should be more sent. I will offer my skills, as will Dominic.'

'I will,' Ballentine confirmed proudly.

'The decision has been made,' Sterling insisted. 'Only nine will go.'

'There is even more to tell you,' Ballentine said as he left his seat. He went to the counter and brought the long black cape that he'd taken from Irena Hofer to Sterling. 'Bentley and I encountered another of Golding's gifted assassins beneath the Golding Plaza hotel. She was wearing this.'

'And?'

'Both Bentley and I struck her with psychokinetic blows that should have killed her. Yet each time she survived, thanks to this. The fabric is woven over a very thin chain-mail type garment. It appears to deflect psychokinetic attacks – even relatively powerful ones.'

'I'm pretty sure Zalech was decked out with the same stuff when I faced him in Portsmouth,' I said. 'I hit him damned hard and he barely flinched. I couldn't understand it at the time, but as soon as I saw this material I realised he must have been wearing the same stuff.'

'Sakamoto,' Sterling said, staring across the table at him. 'You will need to take this into account before you make your attack.'

'I will.' He gave a single, sharp nod. 'We will not attack with psychokinesis alone. Zalech will face numerous gifts from expert assassins. Protective clothing will not be enough to save him.'

The other assassins became giddy with excitement. The prospect of killing such a noted enemy of the Guild should have had us *all* grinning, but something about the whole situation didn't feel right to me. Hunter felt the same, that much was obvious by glancing at his dull countenance. Mr Williams, Cathy and even Ballentine were also looking rather sober as the visitors spoke about how they would make their approach and how they would close the net on their prey, and how they would make the kill.

My trepidation did ease somewhat as the minutes passed by and I listened to them speak of previous assaults and kills. Sakamoto spoke to me for a while about my battle with Marianne and commended me for my bravery, spirit and skill. That awful night was never an easy subject for me to speak of so I diverted the conversation and asked him about a tattoo on the back of his hand. It was very similar to the wolf head logo used by the Guild, but this one had a snake head instead.

'The wolf head is used by the Guild as a mark of respect for its founder, who was a mind-switcher. He travelled with a wolf and switched his mind into the beast in times of danger. All assassins use a different emblem: the snake. You see, the first ever assassin employed by the Guild was also a mind-switcher. She placed her thoughts in the body of a snake and used *it* to kill those who threatened the Guild. And so we tattoo the snake on our hands in memory of her.' He raised his hand so I could get a better look at it. 'We all have identical tattoos. Oh, where are my manners? I never formally introduced ourselves to you. My name is Shinji Sakamoto. I am gifted in pyrokinesis, psychokinesis and pitch-shifting. Chief assassin for the Guild of the True since 1997.'

He then introduced Wolfgang Platz and Miranda Jacobs who were sitting either side of him. Both were in their early thirties and had the gift of psychokinesis.

Standing close by was Dylan Logan, who was very broad and spoke with an American accent. He was a precognitive and electro-psych, and according to Sakamoto, was an expert in both gifts.

Emilia Metz was in her late forties. She was quiet the whole time, and simply smiled when Sakamoto told me she was a brilliant light-tuner.

Josef Vorn displayed his pyrokinetic skill, by creating a halo of flames around his head, when his name was mentioned. He was the youngest, and probably the cockiest of the bunch.

Jennifer Jones was the next name to be announced, and I was surprised to hear that she was a mageleton, like Edward Zalech. 'I don't have his level of ability,' she said, 'but I know how to use what I've got.'

Li Fan had three of the true gifts. He was a talented mind-switcher and was partially gifted in psychokinesis and precognition.

That only left Linda Farrier, who I was already familiar with. Sakamoto told me she was both a psychokinetic and a siren. He also added that she was one of the most able assassins he had ever encountered.

Zalech was immensely powerful *and* psychotic, but could anyone truly contend with such a vast array of gifts, wielded by experienced killers? My concerns dissipated as the night wore on. As the hour approached 3am, the tension in the room spiked once more. The team wanted to get going because it was a two-hour journey and they wanted to hit Zalech just before dawn.

Sterling announced that he too had to get going, to London. He spoke to us before leaving the house.

'Hopefully the dawn will bring this terrible chapter for you all to an abrupt end,' he began. 'I would like to apologise for allowing such a small group to bear such great grief and danger all too often in recent times. I am well aware that you all lost a close friend and ally in Marcus Romand only a few short months ago, and that it has been difficult for you to conquer your sense of loss. And now, unexpectedly, you have had to face a new and sinister threat in the shape of Edward Zalech. The menace he has posed is now removed from you all. Although that will come as little comfort to some of you,' he glanced at me when he said it, 'tomorrow you should move on with your lives. Peter, you can now return to your well-deserved retirement and I swear it will not be interrupted again, under any circumstances. Cathy, I have learned that you wish to leave England for France, so that you can be with your mother to aid her in her recovery. I must admit I had hoped you would involve yourself more deeply with the Guild, but I respect your needs and you should take your leave tomorrow. The Guild has already booked you on a flight to France. The flight will leave Gatwick at 10pm tomorrow.'

She didn't look at me even once and I felt crushed that she'd made these plans without consulting, or even informing, me.

'Ross,' Sterling continued. 'I know you want nothing more than to travel to Ireland to visit your father's resting place. I believe it would be wiser if you were to remain out of sight for a few months more. You should return to Scotland with Hunter. Spend the winter there, practise your skills, and then come see me in the spring. I would like to discuss your future with you at great lengths. After that, you can take some time for yourself and mourn your father properly.'

It didn't appear that my future was up for debate, which made me very uncomfortable. I valued my freedom and independence too much to have someone I hardly knew dictating what I should and shouldn't do. I wanted to tell him to shove his orders, but there was something about Sterling, an assurance, a confidence, a great power behind his steely eyes that stopped me from objecting. Not even Hunter had dared question him, and I felt it best to follow his example and keep my opinions to myself.

Sterling wished Sakamoto luck and left with Canavan, who hadn't said a word for hours, and little Sarah Fisher, who had been napping in front of the TV the entire evening. Moments later the team left the house one by one and gathered around three dark-coloured, saloon cars that were parked at the front of the house.

Hunter stopped Farrier as she walked to the hallway and they talked for a moment. The only words I caught were Hunters: 'Linda, just be careful and don't be too proud to run if it goes bad. This will not be the same Zalech we faced in Newcastle.'

She said something to him and placed her hand on his shoulder before smiling and walking away. It pained me to see the worry in Hunter's eyes, but I had my own drama to deal with. Cathy was due to leave within twenty-four hours and we had barely spoken in days, since our argument at the animal sanctuary. I still loved her with all my heart and didn't want us to part on such bad terms. I waited for a quiet moment then asked her to come with me to the bench on the patio out back.

'Thanks for letting me know you're leaving the country,' I said, sitting on the edge of the frigid wooden seat. 'I can't believe you're just going, without so much as a single word.'

'I decided after what happened in Portsmouth,' she admitted. She took a seat on the other end of the bench – as far away from me as possible – and rubbed her arms to chase away the chill of the night. 'I did tell you I'd had enough. Then a few hours later you just went off on a solo run against Zalech. Did you say a single word to *me*? No. You just went. You might never have come back. How do you think that made me feel, Ross?'

'It was a stupid thing to do. I realise that now.'

'It might have been too late to realise that. You could, and probably *should*, be dead right now!'

'I said I was sorry.'

'Sometimes sorry isn't enough.'

I used my psychokinesis to lift the other end of the bench and she slid along the seat into my waiting arms. She struggled for about half a second before hugging me. I didn't blame her for wanting to escape the chaos that had besieged both our lives since that dreadful night when Marianne Dolloway found us. We'd both been in limbo ever since and in the fog of confusion we were losing one another. That true and instant love we shared was under far too much strain, and only now could I see that she'd been right all along. Our budding relationship could not survive on the battlefield that was life in the Guild of the True.

'Seems we won't be seeing much of each other for a while,' I sighed. 'Life just grows more and more complicated.'

'It'll keep going in that direction ... For you anyway.'

'Why do you say that?'

'You heard what Sterling said. He wants you to visit him in the spring. That means he wants to draft you in as a fully-fledged Guild agent. You're being set up as one of their key soldiers. You'll be thrown into every major conflict that comes along from then on.'

'That's only if I choose to stay.'

'You think they'll give you a choice?'

'I choose my own destiny, Cathy, and I want it to be with you. Being part of the Guild has already cost me my father and I'm not sure I can watch others around me die like Romand did. And,' I glanced over my shoulder to make sure no one could hear me, 'I get the feeling we won't be seeing some members of Sakamoto's team again.'

'They'll kill Zalech,' Cathy said sombrely as she gazed at the darkness beyond the patio. 'You don't know how relentless they are.'

'They don't know how strong *he* is.'

'I don't want to think about him.' She shook her head and grimaced as if the mere thought of Zalech caused her physical pain.

'Neither do I.' It was the truth; I didn't *want* to think about him. But it was also true that I couldn't *stop* myself from thinking about him. He would travel with me the rest of my days even if he were dead. That was his curse. Once you cross paths with someone as evil as Zalech or Golding or Dolloway they leave their mark on you. One that does not fade with time and cannot be washed away. 'I'd rather look forward to a future with you than spend my life fighting for the Guild. I hope that doesn't make me sound like a coward.'

'It makes you brave.' She kissed me on the cheek. 'You don't have to make your mind up now, Ross. You'll have a lot of time on your hands when you go north. Take that time and do what you think is right. I'll wait for you. Promise.'

'I don't even know where you'll be. How will I contact you?'

'You don't need to know where I am, Ross. I know where you are.' She smiled and that sparkle in her eyes that had been absent for so long returned momentarily. 'All you need do is watch the skies for large eagles.'

'I'll do that,' I smiled. 'And I'll look forward to your letters.'

'Enough of the canoodling, Bentley! I'm not hanging about here. Let's get a move on.'

'Christ,' I cursed. 'I cannot believe I have to spend the next six months listening to my own name being shouted at me all day every day.'

'Stop acting like a sissy. I'll be out front.'

I left Hunter waiting and spent almost half an hour kissing Cathy, without speaking. We just wanted to be close to each other now that the great pressure that had been on us was removed. The constant danger had fizzled away and we could act like human beings again. Sadly it was not to last. Our time together was short and we would spend the long winter apart. It was all too familiar. I was to leave her in the wake of a tragedy again, just like I had a few months before.

Hunter yelled at me again and I went back to the house with Cathy by my side. I said farewell to Mr Williams then shared an embrace with Cathy before leaving. I climbed into the passenger seat of the old Mercedes that Mr Williams allowed us to borrow, and Hunter pressed the accelerator before I could close the door. All too familiar indeed!

'Can't wait to get home!' he barked. 'Clean air, no phones, no politics, and no problems. I've had a bellyful of that lot,' he pointed over his shoulder with a thumb, 'a right bellyful!'

'I know what you mean.'

I thought about spending a winter in that flimsy old cottage. I was destined for punishment. At least Hunter and I had buried the hatchet and had become friends, and I wouldn't have to argue with him every day like we had during our previous period of exile.

The isolation was daunting, yet even that did not keep my mind from wandering back to Edward Zalech. The team would reach him within an hour or so and then his reign of terror would be brought to a violent conclusion. It was a horrible admission, one that I would not make aloud, that I was frustrated because I couldn't be there to see him take his final breath. Still, if I had been there I don't know how I really would have felt or how I'd act. There was a deep fear of him inside me. I'd hated him after I learned of my father's murder, but once I set eyes on him in Portsmouth I was scared of his power and of how demented and homicidal he was. One good thing he had done was to turn me away from death. I'd had enough of death and fighting and murder. I doubted I could ever take another person's life. I doubted I could ever walk into a situation like that again. Killing Ania Zalech had been a costly lesson: I was not a killer and never would be.

'You all right?' Hunter asked. 'Very quiet over there.'

'This feels like we're running away from a fight before the final round.'

'Nothing we can do about it, is there?'

'I guess not. I just wish I hadn't tried to fight him alone the other day. I should have waited for you. We should have fought him together and killed him when we had the chance.'

'We blew it.'

'*I* blew it.'

'Yeah, you certainly did. The most important thing is that the Guild are about to kill Edward Zalech and he'll never be able to hurt anyone ever again.'

'I have a terrible feeling he'll survive this assassination attempt,

Hunter. I know I'm being paranoid so don't say so. It's just a nagging feeling in my gut.'

'You're probably just being paranoid.'

The stillness of the night was shattered when the cell phone buzzed. Walters had saved her own number into the contacts and it was flashing onscreen.

'Doctor?' I answered.

'Edward, thank God you answered.' Her voice was trembling and her breathing loud and rapid. 'You're in great danger.'

'This is not news to me,' I replied. 'I have been in danger my entire life.'

'No! Pearson called me to the clinic a few moments ago. She's ordered me to destroy all documentation relating to you. I asked her why, fearing you had been overwhelmed by the Hyper-furens and died. She said that Golding had sold you out to your enemies. He told them where you are, Edward!'

'When will they come?'

'I don't know. I really don't. She wanted everything, all the paperwork and all the computer files, gone by morning. That makes me think they'll come for you before dawn. You don't have much time,

Edward. Run!'

'Thank you, doctor. I owe my life to you a second time.'

CHAPTER TWENTY-EIGHT

The Hidden Gift

I slid my arms into the coat lined with Deflexus plates and zipped up the front right to the point of my chin. I went to the window and stared out at the dim surroundings. There was no movement in the garden or amid the trees that lined the pathways of the nearby hills. The shadows of the landscape were frozen and not a sound could be heard. I still had time.

I went upstairs and turned on the taps of the sink and bath in the bathroom, then did the same for the sink in the kitchen before hurrying to the back door. I pulled it open by an inch and watched the hedge that ran along the back of the lawn. All was quiet and now was the time to make a run for it. I stepped into the pouring rain and gently shut the door behind me. I took another glance at the dark surroundings before bolting for the gate at the end of the garden. I did not stop until I had reached the crest of a hill nearby, one that overlooked the property that Golding had allowed me to use. From the hilltop I had a panoramic view of the area. I could see the house, both the front and rear gardens, and the two pathways as well the narrow road that led to the property.

I eased down on my stomach, with my face just above the overgrown grass, and watched for any movement towards the house. Sheets of rain were sweeping in from the north, but I remained dry; water simply rolled off my clothes thanks to my gift of mageletonia. I was quite comfortable lying there, waiting for the Guild's assassins. The rage had been building all day long, and now it was in full flow because of the excitement and the danger inspired by the call from Dr Walters. My power was rising to an entirely new level. This is why I was not fleeing into the night. I was waiting for the assassins. I had already set up an ambush that they would walk straight into.

For almost an hour I waited in the grass, motionless and barely blinking, before I noticed a shadow creeping towards the house. It appeared on one of the little winding pathways that cut through the fields to the east and it quickly disappeared into the trees near the front garden. Then another followed it. More came from the pathway to the west. I counted nine in all. I was too far away to identify any of them but I was confident that they were the cream of the crop. Some of the best killers in the service of the Guild were down there, sneaking to the house and surrounding it. Walters's warning had been accurate. Golding *had* betrayed me.

I slowly crept forward, moving through the grass like a giant snake. The assassins had surrounded the house and were moving to the doors at the front and back. I slithered all the way to the bottom of the hill, into long grass mixed with weeds and small bushes. There I waited until the assassins made their move.

They burst through the doors and marched into the house, leaving only two outside; one at the front and one at the back. I got to my feet slowly and shuffled forward as quietly as possible. When I reached the rear garden I identified the lookout. It was Josef Vorn, a very talented pyrokinetic who had once given Ania a few lessons. I knew him not as a teacher, but as a man who had killed dozens of people over the years. But for all his experience and skill and power, Vorn could do nothing to save himself.

I pointed at him with my index finger and fired two small but very precise darts of psychokinetic energy at him. Vorn's heart seized up and he fell onto his back without as much as a whimper. I was scouting around the side of the house before Vorn even hit the dirt, and gradually made my way towards the front lawn. I could hear a racket from the other side of the wall as the assassins in the house pulled the rooms apart looking for me. The clamour made my approach easier than it should have been.

Standing under a tree at the end of the garden was

Miranda Jacobs, who I had met on a few occasions over the years. She was a gifted assassin, but too inexperienced for a mission like this. She seemed strangely complacent, leaning her shoulder against the trunk of the maple, watching only the façade of the house, and paying no attention to the flanks. She failed to see the decapitation slice coming. I was moving to the front door before she hit the ground.

I kept close to the wall and slid along it to the open doorway. There were voices inside, and the sounds of feet slashing through water. The entire house was flooded from the taps I had left on which meant I had an advantage over the seven remaining assassins. I focused on my mageleton gift before taking my first step inside. When I used the gift I could actually feel the water around me, as if it were a part of me and now with his my heightened powers I could manipulate every last droplet within the house.

The water rushed from the bathroom floor and the landing, pouring down the staircase as if it had a mind of its own. Then the water from the kitchen was lifted off the floor and was channelled through the doorway into the hall where the stream from upstairs flowed directly into it. The hallway was filled from wall to wall, floor to ceiling with icy water and the unfortunate figure of Emilia Metz was caught in it. I watched her struggling for a moment. I would have liked to see her drown slowly, but I had not the time for that, and I used my gift to force the water into her mouth until her chest practically exploded.

'Three down, six to go,' I whispered.

I summoned the water to me and it surrounded my body on all sides as I strode to the sitting room. There I found Jennifer Jones, a veteran mageleton. She attacked me on sight, but her efforts were weak and she could not tear open my watery shield no matter how hard she tried. I stunned her when I shot a portion of the water at her face. She stumbled backward and I used psychokinesis to crush her heart. Her death was instantaneous.

I then moved to the door leading to the kitchen, but was attacked from behind before I reached it. Someone fired a powerful blast of energy at me and my shield collapsed momentarily. Water dashed the sitting room floor and created a thunderous crash.

I saw a sleek figure pass in front of the window then raise a hand above her head. A shot of energy struck me in the shoulder and knocked me straight through the door and onto the kitchen floor. It should have been powerful enough to kill me but the coat lined with Deflexus padding deflected most of the force and saved my life.

I drew the water from the sitting room and struck the woman with it, knocking her off her feet. I then summoned it through the doorway and it surrounded me once more, and just in time. Wolfgang Platz entered from the hallway and fired a wave of energy at me that almost broke the shield of fluid once more.

This time it held fast and I sprang forward and ran straight at my attacker. The water consumed Platz and I grabbed hold of him, countered his psychokinetic power with my own – rendering him powerless. I held him within the giant glob of fluid until he drowned.

By this time I was under attack again from the female assassin. She was close to the sitting room door and was using her energy to pull my shield asunder. I held it long enough to muster my psychokinetic powers once more. I allowed the water to collapse then fired an energy spear through the wall. A part of the brickwork was obliterated and the assassin was thrown through the air and smacked violently into the granite fireplace. She was still alive and was groaning quietly. She would pose no threat to me now so I moved out into the hallway again. The real test of my strength was still to come. I recognised all the assassins so far and although they were very skilled, they were not master assassins and none would be given the job of leading an attack on him after what I had done in Portsmouth. I was sure there were even more able killers upstairs, but I felt no fear in facing them.

'Prepare yourselves as best you can,' I shouted from the hallway. 'Or simply pray to whatever god you worship.'

I heard hurried footsteps from above as they got

ready for me to make my move. I waited in the hallway as the water wrapped around me in coils until I was enclosed in it completely. I allowed more of it to flow up the stairs ahead of me. When it reached the landing I formed it into numerous walls that skated forward like pawns to block his enemies' assaults.

As I climbed the stairs I saw a shadow moving behind one of the walls of water. I used mageletonia to lash the figure with water. The assassin remained unharmed but was forced back into one of the empty bedrooms.

Suddenly a bright flash went off to my right and blue fingers of electricity spread across the walls and consumed my shield of water. The electricity scattered across the outside of the shield and pulsed around me. I was unhurt, but if the shield gave way, even for a fraction of a second, I would be electrocuted and my Deflexus clothing would not aid me.

There was a loud blast from above and part of the ceiling came down and smashed into the shield. Then another blast that shattered part of the wall next to me, sending pieces of plaster spinning rapidly through the darkness.

The shield was hit directly from someone else and the force of it sent me backwards and I almost lost my footing on the staircase. I was under constant attacks now and my shield was being stripped away gradually by two of the assassins.

I felt panicked and the power within me surged. I gathered the water in the house around me and fired it onto the landing, knocking everything out of his way. I paced upward and reached the landing while weaving an energy shield around my body. I was hit from one of the doorways, but I remained unscathed. I reacted instantly and sucked energy towards me and the assassin was drawn out and rolled across the landing.

'Ah, Mr Fan,' I laughed at the figure sprawled on the floor at my feet. 'How appropriate that a trick you once taught me should prove to be your undoing.'

Fan tried to speak, but was crushed by a layer of energy that snapped his bones then the floorboards beneath him.

I mustered a terrifying amount of energy and sent all of it towards the back bedroom. This was where the electro-psych had been hiding and the room was totally destroyed, even the heavy joists from the ceiling came crashing down and no one could have survived it.

Only one assassin remained. The master.

'I counted you and your colleagues as you approached the house,' I said as my gaze crossed each doorway on the long hallway. 'I've downed eight assassins, leaving only one. You are alone and you are going to die. Save us both the bother and come on out here so I can give you a warrior's death.'

There was only silence.

'Who am I talking to I wonder. Mendez? Carrizo?

Sakamoto? Armitage? I would be insulted if Jim Sterling sent any lesser than one of the big four. Surely he would not send a mere foot soldier. Surely he recognises how dangerous I really am. Come, it is not befitting for a warrior to hide from his quarry. Are you afraid?'

'I am unafraid.'

I stared down the landing at the tall figure of Sakamoto. I would have preferred someone else. Sakamoto was an extremely dangerous assassin, possibly the most lethal the Guild had available. Sakamoto was a pyrokinetic, psychokinetic and a siren. Three deadly gifts and he had mastered all known techniques. He was more skilled than I. Did he have the raw power that I had?

'Finally,' I buzzed, 'someone who is deserving of my respect.'

'The respect is not mutual,' Sakamoto replied coldly. 'You have used a sacred gift to maim and to kill innocent people. For this you must be executed.'

'That is easier said than done, old friend. If you have not noticed, I have killed your entire team in less than five minutes.'

'I noticed.' Sakamoto fell into a very dramatic stance. One arm was pulled tight against his ribs, the other extended fully in front. 'You will find killing me much more complicated.'

'I am sure you would love to kill me, Sakamoto.' I grinned at the challenge and readied myself for the duel. 'But you cannot beat the devil at his own game.'

Sakamoto closed his fists and the walls on either side of them were instantly set alight. I reacted by cocooning myself with a wall of water, thinking it would protect me from the flames. Sakamoto was undeterred and moved his hands about in circles, and the fire on either side of him leaped from the walls and spun around my shield, covering it completely. The blazing cocoon became more and more intense and started to evaporate the water that was protecting me. The hallways filled with boiling steam and I lost sight of my enemy. All there was to be seen was the circle of fire that raged on, brighter and hotter as each second passed, until suddenly the sphere of liquid burst spectacularly and doused the flames.

I was defenceless and Sakamoto tried to take advantage of this momentary vulnerability. He fired two shots of kinetic power along the hallway that severed the cloud of steam. One shot hit me in the arm and the other went askew. The Deflexus armour had saved me once more, this time from having my arm cut off.

I replied by firing a wave along the hall that tore up some of the wooden boards of the floor and scratched the charred walls. Sakamoto had a protective shield in place and had hardly broken sweat. I tried to hit him again but with no success. Sakamoto's response was to strike me so hard that I was knocked through the window at the end of the hallway; I fell face-first into the grass at the side of the house.

I scrambled to my feet but by the time I turned around Sakamoto was standing right in front of me. I threw up my arms and water from the sodden ground shot up and deflected what would have been a killer blow from the master assassin.

Sakamoto then employed the use of his third gift. He was a siren, more commonly known in the Guild as a pitch-shifter.

'Die,' the assassin said softly. As the word left his mouth the pitch heightened to a deafening scream. The sound was so strong it penetrated the watery orb and almost crushed my ear drums. It then became a hum that seemed to split into every note imaginable and my mind began to numb. I knew I would fall into a coma within seconds if I did not react.

The water collapsed to the ground and left me open to attack. Sakamoto reacted instantly by launching a strong shot of energy at me. My newfound strength enabled me to actually catch the energy in mid flight and take control over it. I spun around and shot the energy back at Sakamoto, who could not respond quickly enough.

He was blasted into the air and smacked the side of the house. He was badly injured, but still he tried to get to his feet to continue the fight. I gathered a dense ball of energy in my hand as he rose then fired it at his chest. The infamous Sakamoto fell silently into the grass – dead.

I took some moments to gather myself then walked to the front of the house. There was still one assassin alive – the woman I had thrown against the fireplace.

I strolled back inside the house and through to the sitting room only to find one body. That of Jennifer Jones. The other woman had gone. I quickly paced through the hall then to the kitchen and to an empty room at the back of the house. Frustrated I ran back to the sitting room and to the window. As I scanned the front lawn I heard a faint scratching. It was coming from the fireplace. The chimney of the old house was big enough for an adult to climb through and that was where the last assassin was hiding. I drew water from around the house and allowed it to slowly fill the chimney. The level rose sharply and enveloped the fleeing killer.

I kept the water at a high level for over a minute before relinquishing my control over it. The water came crashing down on the hearth and flowed out across the floor. With it had tumbled the assassin, chocking and coughing, writhing in agony as she tried to suck air into her sizzling lungs. I grabbed a handful of her long raven hair then dragged her across the floor and threw her into the armchair.

'Take the weight off your feet, Ms Farrier,' I said mockingly. I stood in front of her, watching as she coughed and hunched over. 'I remember you were kind to me once. Back when the others in the Guild treating me in a most cruel fashion. For that I thank you. For your part in this plot I must kill you. A gesture of kindness is not enough to save you.'

'Stick it, Zalech,' she panted.

'Mind your manners!' I slapped her across the cheek and loomed over her. 'Be nice now, as you once were, and I may grant you a swift death.'

'Save your speeches and get it over with.'

'You spent too much time with your Scotch brute of a boyfriend. You used to be quite an eloquent woman, but it would appear you have inherited his foul tongue. *And* his lack of respect.'

'I have absolutely zero respect for you, *murderer*!'

'We are all murderers, Ms Farrier. Even you.'

'Why are keeping me alive?'

'Oh, do not worry; it is not for the conversation, Ms Farrier. No. You will prove most useful before I put you to death.'

'I won't tell you anything. Even if you torture me.'

'Torture is too time-consuming. And I know you would not *spill the beans*.'

'Then kill me!'

'Right after I look into your mind.'

Now I could complete my masterpiece of revenge by revealing my third gift. I had kept it hidden my entire life. Not even Ania had known about it. I pressed my hand over Farrier's mouth and the other I clamped on the top of her skull. I took a firm grip then used *my hidden gift*. The gift of time-scanning.

I scanned into Farrier's past and saw all that she saw that evening, heard all that she heard. I saw her entering a large house with the other assassins. Inside were more people from the Guild, including Ross Bentley. I was stunned that Bentley had survived the tsunami, but there would now be an opportunity to rectify that. Also present was Cathy Atkinson, who looked very close to Bentley. It dawned on me that she must have been the one who controlled the panther that had done so much damage to me in the north-east. I then listened to Jim Sterling's speech in its entirety. I now knew my enemy's plans in fine detail.

I released the scan then snapped Farrier's neck before walking to the front of the house and climbing onto the Kinetibike. I waited before leaving the garden. Would I go north or south?

I could go north after Bentley and gain the revenge I desperately desired. I could go south to the Williams house, kill the girl who had disfigured me, then time-scan Williams who would know the addresses of all the leading members of the Guild. I would even find out the location of the notorious Palatium where the Council gathered. The same Council who had sent the assassins to kill me.

I drove out onto the narrow road and soon I reached a t-junction. Left would lead me to a motorway to the north. Right would take me to the south road. I spent five minutes pondering the dilemma before turning the bike and accelerating fast.

CHAPTER TWENTY-NINE

Knowledge

The clock on the centre of the dashboard read 4.30am and I was still wide awake. I should have been fighting to keep my eyes open, but my mind was too active with all that had happened to find sleep. Hunter's speeding didn't help either. We were travelling at over 120kmph on a narrow road in driving rain.

I watched the glistening road ahead clear every time the wipers squeaked across the windscreen only to be drowned by streams of rainwater again. It kept reminding me of what Zalech had done in Portsmouth. A clear road being destroyed by a wall of water. Dozens of people dead. I definitely would not have peace of mind until we got word from the Guild confirming his death. A part of me, though, doubted that word would come.

'I have a real bad feeling about everything the Guild has planned, Hunter.'

'Give it a rest, Bentley. I've told you four times since we left the house, I understand that you wanted to be the one to kill him, but it's best to leave all this to the Guild! Sakamoto knows what he's doing. He will not fail.'

'I'm worried for Cathy. Really worried.'

'She'll be out of the country tomorrow so she's the last person

433

you need worry about.'

'What if Golding was lying? What if Zalech wasn't at that house? You know, the more I think about it the more I fear that Golding was tracing the call Mr Williams made and sent Zalech there.'

'Shut up.'

'No.'

'You're making *me* paranoid.'

'Let's go back, Hunter. Just to be certain. We can stay the rest of the night and leave for Scotland again tomorrow evening when we're sure the others are completely safe.'

I knew Hunter hadn't trusted Mr Williams's plan right from the start, and he certainly hadn't trusted what Golding had to say. It was written all over his face that he shared my fears for the others.

'Come on, Hunter,' I pleaded. 'For the sake of a few hours. This could be something we'll both regret for the rest of our lives. It's too much to leave to chance.'

He lifted his foot off the accelerator and the car gradually slowed. He steered onto the side of the lane then brought the car to a stop.

'Williams will think I'm a right tool.' Hunter banged his head off the head-rest in frustration. 'He'll think I'm going soft in my old age!'

'You know it's the right thing to do.'

'You're starting to sound like an ol' granny!'

'You know it's the most sensible thing to do.'

He turned the steering wheel and the car spun on the slick tarmac when he pressed his foot on the accelerator.

'You better not be doing this just so you can cosy up to your sweetheart for one more night before the winter!'

We drove the quiet stretch of road for almost twenty minutes before I got a pang of anxiety in the pit of my stomach that instantly shot through my chest. It was my precognitive gift telling me danger was approaching.

'Something's not right,' I breathed. 'I'm sensing an attack.'

Before Hunter responded we both saw a single headlight in the distance. It was nothing more than a speck of light passing under the glow of the street lamps at first – it was travelling incredibly fast and within two seconds it was right on us. I caught just a glimpse of it as it approached and realised it was someone on a motorbike. That was all I registered before our car was struck by an invisible force.

The front of the car rose up then banked right and skidded across into the opposite lane. There was no way to alter its course and I watched helplessly as we left the road, careered into a lamp post then spun into a deep ditch on the edge of the road. There was a heavy thump as the car impacted the bottom of the ditch and then it rolled a number of times before finally coming to a rest.

I saw that the vehicle was an absolute wreck when I gathered my senses. Most of the windows were smashed or shattered and the doors were battered and had pushed in on me. I was relatively unharmed, probably because I released a lot of energy on the initial impact. It had protected me from the force, but my head was spinning and my ears ringing. I looked across at Hunter and saw that he hadn't quite been so lucky. He was still fixed into the chair by the safety belt, there was blood on his face and his legs were crushed by the dashboard of the car that had been bent backwards when the front of the car hit the ditch. His head was slumped forward and his body was limp.

'Hunter,' I shouted as I shifted over to him. 'Hunter, don't you die on me!'

I grabbed his head and lifted it up, my hand searching under his jaw for a pulse. 'Hunter, please!'

'Bentley, get your damned paws off me!' he said in a low and very angry voice. 'What the hell are you doing?'

'I thought you were dead.'

'Well, I'm not.' He tried to move – then let out a cry in agony. 'Damn it! My legs are broken.'

'I'll get you out of here.' I released the safety belt and used my powers to push the dashboard back off his legs. 'You'll be all right.'

'Forget about me, you fool. That was Zalech on the motorbike. He's going to kill both of us unless you get back on that road and fight him!'

'Hunter, I can't fight him. I can't match his power.'

'Bentley, get up there and fight him with everything you've got. It pains me more than my legs to say it, but I believe in you ... just like Romand did.'

'You hang on in there, Hunter.'

I turned and forced a pulse of energy out of my hands that bent the frame of the car out of my way. I stepped out onto the wet ground and took a deep breath before I clambered up the slope on all fours until I reached the roadside. Zalech was standing at the centre of the road, about ten metres away. He had his hands stuffed into his coat pockets and looked very calm. He watched me carefully as I paced into the road and faced him.

'Like Lazarus of old he rises. I must hand it to you, Bentley,' he said in that spine-chilling voice of his, 'you are *most* difficult to kill.'

'I intend to stay alive long enough to see you in the ground.'

'The best-laid plans of mice and men often go awry,' he tittered. 'Oh, I've been meaning to ask you something. How did you feel when you learned of your father's death?'

'The opposite of what I felt when I crushed the life out of your little sister.'

Zalech's grin began to twitch and his face became taut with hatred.

'And the opposite of what I felt when Sarah Fisher prophesised your death.'

'You are a terrible liar, young man. I told you that the last time we met.'

'See if I am lying now. Golding sold you out to us and when he did, he told us that there's a drug in your body that's nothing more than poison. You only have weeks to live. Even if you beat me – even if you beat the entire Guild – you're a dead man walking. You can do nothing to prevent it.'

'I am ahead of yet again, Bentley. I know all about the substance that flows in my veins and I know exactly how long I have left on this earth. I must take maximum pleasure from my final days.' His hands came from his pockets and he took a couple of confident strides forward. 'And nothing gives me more pleasure than killing.'

'You don't scare me.'

'That is why you fail. Bentley, you *should* fear me. Instead you desired revenge and that is how I lured you out of hiding. It was easy enough. All I had to do was find something you cared for. You see, that which you love can always be used to destroy you. In your case, your love for your father.'

'And you'll pay for what you did to him.'

'You are going to make me pay?'

'Too right I am!'

'I have my doubts,' he said with a twisted smile. 'I do not think you are powerful enough to represent a real challenge for me. Perhaps I am wrong.' Zalech walked to the roadside and gazed down at the wrecked car. 'Let us test your strength. To see if you are worthy of fighting me.'

He raised his hand above his head, turned to me and winked, then lowered his arm very slowly. As he did, the roof of the car drooped and the entire upper frame bent inward and threatened to crush the life out of Hunter.

I quickly summoned as much power as I could and concentrated on pushing the metal outward. There was a loud bang as the roof popped back out, then snapped back down as Zalech exerted more pressure through his psychokinesis. I pushed as hard as I could and so did he, but neither of us could gain a clear advantage over the other. I was under immense strain and Zalech had hardly flinched. He was so powerful – almost impossibly powerful – but I could not allow another mentor to die before my eyes. I refused to let him claim Hunter's life and pressed every vestige of strength into keeping the roof from collapsing.

'Getting tired?' Zalech laughed. His crazed stare was fixed on me. It seemed so easy for him and I was practically exhausted. 'You look like you are about to snap, Bentley.'

'You're just good at hiding the strain, Zalech. If you were able to overpower me you would have done it by now.'

He lowered his arm further and the car began to crumple like a paper cup. Panic flooded my senses and I was able to tap into a reserve of power that I did not know I had. The car was shaking and the bending metal cracked noisily, but still it did not fold. Hunter remained safe inside for the moment.

Zalech frowned and his nose wrinkled with the effort he was putting into the crush layer. It was the first time I'd seen him under pressure and it filled me with confidence.

'Getting tired?' I shouted to him and I managed a wink. 'You look like you're ready to snap, Zalech.'

'Enough!' He roared as he spun towards me. The car shook as the two opposing forces were released from it. Hunter was no longer in peril. It was now my turn to face Zalech's wrath.

How would he attack? Which gift would he use? Should I go on the offensive? So many questions. No time for answers.

The raindrops above the road froze in mid-air. Then they moved lazily – some were lifted, others fell slowly – until they formed one thin level of water as far as I could see in all directions. A ceiling of water was above us and the man before me had total control over it. I would face his mageletonia first.

'Oh, how I love the rain,' he said.

I wasn't waiting for him to make the first move and shot a psychokinetic bolt right at his face. Zalech raised his hands and created some form of shield that took the brunt of my attack, but he still slid a few metres backwards on his heels. I didn't get disheartened and fired two slices at him. One at his upper body and another at his knees.

Zalech swung both his arms through the air and the road was

torn to pieces in front of him as my attacks were deflected downward. I was relentless and shot a flurry of energy spears at him. The first few were deflected, but one clipped his arm and spun him fast through the air and the last hit him in the stomach and sent him skidding along the road.

I launched an outward wave as he picked himself off the ground and he was knocked onto his back once more. I sprinted forward and prepared for the kill ... Then I was out-manoeuvred. The ceiling of water condensed into an enormous cube that completely surrounded Zalech. When I fired another bolt at him it simply rippled the surface of his liquid shield.

I could see Zalech within the cube, nothing more than a rippling shadow, and he was uninjured as he nimbly got to his feet. I backed away, not really understanding this gift that he had. I had no clue as to what he would do next, and very little idea on how to counter the mageleton gift. I remembered Hunter telling me that kinetic energy did not travel effectively through water which meant there was little chance of killing him while he was surrounded by so much of it. I would have to choose my moment carefully.

The cube rotated then broke down into a star shape that opened up like an accordion to reveal my enemy to the open air again. There was blood dripping from his mouth, but his grin remained and he appeared more confident than ever.

The water broke up into square sheets that revolved at different speeds and floated off the ground at varying levels. I was dazzled by the control he had over his gift, but tried my best to stay focused on him, knowing he was trying to distract me.

'Beautiful, is it not?'

'It would be if you didn't use it to kill innocent people.'

'Innocent people?' he laughed. 'Which of my victims was truly innocent?'

'My father was.'

'Your father allowed his only son to travel to a foreign land in search of riches. He thought more of wealth than of your wellbeing. He would still be alive if he had been more innocent.'

'The reporters in the north-east!'

'Vultures who used a disturbed child to gain profit. They deserved what they got.'

'And the people who died just so you could prove that you could create tidal waves, did they deserve what they got?'

'Some of them probably did. The others are simply victims of chance and of the aggressive nature of all men. I too am a victim of it, as are you. Neither of us should have become what we are now.'

'You like what you are now, Zalech?'

'Indeed I do.'

Suddenly the sheets of water combined above his head and formed a fast-spinning sphere that came hurtling at me. I tried to break it apart using my powers. I managed merely to dent it before it smashed into me. I was hit hard and rolled across the road. Before I could get my bearings I was consumed by the sphere of water and couldn't catch a breath. My lungs began to burn and I released a wave, but the orb of liquid refused to release me. I shot out more energy in all directions – every time I created a hole in the sphere it was instantly flooded over and there was no way to find air. Panic set in as water crept into my nostrils and I drew as much energy from my surroundings as possible. I sent the energy out of my body in all directions and the sphere was blasted apart. Within seconds it began to reform around me; I was smart enough not to fight the weapon, but the person who wielded it. I focused on the panic and built up one immense shot at Zalech.

This time his armour didn't help him much. His leg gave way under him and he howled in agony. I moved forward while he was down, determined to bring the battle to a conclusion. I was outsmarted yet again. The water that covered the road thickened beneath my feet and rose at a sharp angle and I slid to the side and came crashing down hard on my shoulder.

We both took some time to get to our feet. Zalech seemed worse off. He took longer to stand up and I noticed his left leg couldn't bear much weight. I knew from experience that his physical injury would not impair his ability to control his gifts. Often, it seemed, the gifted were more dangerous when in physical pain.

'Where's that stupid grin of yours now, Zalech?'

'Right here,' he smiled. 'This is more like the fight I expected in Portsmouth. To think, if you had been less of a coward that day you might have saved all those people. Does that bother you, Bentley? Or are you just like the rest of us messed up freaks who cannot feel for the normal folk?'

'I won't take the blame for what you did, Zalech. You did that all by yourself.'

'You were afraid then like you are afraid now. You should have shown your anger and you might have saved them. And you might have saved your friends who died tonight. Anger will not be enough to save you. You see, it is knowledge that you lack.' He raised his arms above his head. 'Knowledge is king, Bentley, and you do not know enough!'

Waves rose on either side of the road and came crashing down on me. I was thrown up into the air then hit the road with a heavy thump. Another wave smashed me in the face and flew backward only to be hit from the side and I skidded across the road. I lashed out with my psychokinesis wildly, in the hope that it would stop the constant attacks, but I was lashed from above and almost lost consciousness. I could not take another blow to the head and fired one desperate bolt at my enemy.

I saw Zalech collapse to the ground and I staggered forward and hit him with a direct, though weak, attack. He fell back, then countered and knocked me in the ribs with a psychokinetic blast.

He had an answer for my every move. Maybe he was right. Maybe I simply did not have the knowledge to contend with him. What did I know that someone like him did not …?

Then it came to me. There was one thing that I *could* do. Something that Zalech had never heard of before, because I was the only one who could do it. I was the one who invented it.

I created a large reverse-dual-shield. It was dome-shaped and spanned a twenty-metre diameter. It would allow any object to pass inside it, but nothing would escape it. Zalech hadn't noticed what I'd done and taunted me from the opposite side of the road. He was totally unaware that I was shrinking the shield around us both. Rain was pounding down and entering the dome and as it became smaller, the water level began to rise. I intended to drown Zalech.

The dome got smaller and smaller and the water was up to our knees. Zalech used his power to chase it away from himself – that would not be enough to save him. The shield just got smaller and the water rose higher.

'You said you always loved the rain, Zalech. Be careful about what you love because it can be used to destroy you – your own words.'

I released the shield for an instant – no more than a fraction of a second. It was just long enough for me to escape. Once outside I hastened the shrinking of the dome. Within seconds Zalech was up to his chest in rain water. Panic was etched into his ghostly countenance as the true horror of his situation dawned on him. He was about to meet the fate that he had inflicted on so many others. I shrank the invisible sphere quickly and the water passed over his face and he began to thrash wildly. His arms pounded at the shield and his legs kicked in a futile attempt to free himself. Not even Zalech, with all his powers, with all his anger and hate could break this new and obscure form of psychokinesis that I had stumbled on by accident while training alone.

I watched as his movements became languid and air bubbles escaped his mouth and nostrils. His eyes were large with fear as the water entered his mouth and started to fill his lungs.

I held the shield as long as I could before my strength faltered and I had to break it off. Water sprang out in all directions and washed across the broken tarmac. Zalech fell onto his back and coughed out a mouthful of water. He was barely conscious, but still a major threat so I took my chance and hit him with a powerful blast of energy that tore through his protective clothing and snapped his spine in half.

He lay there motionless and I kept a safe distance until I found the strength and courage to stagger forward and stand over him.

Our eyes locked and that familiar grin stretched his wicked face one last time. He coughed and hissed in a breath before laughing weakly at me.

'You find this amusing?' I asked. 'You're stranger than I thought.'

'I do not find my own death amusing, but I do find victory rather fulfilling.'

'I fail to see how this is a victory for you.'

'All you need do is watch the skies for large eagles …'

Those were Cathy's final words to me before I left her. How on earth could he have known? A dreadful chill ran through my heart when I realised he must have gone to the house before he tracked me down. Had he killed Cathy? Had I lost the last person that I truly loved?

'What did you do?' I grabbed his collars and shook him violently. 'What the *hell* did you do to her, Zalech?'

'Very little. In fact, Peter Williams is the one who will kill her.'

'Peter would never hurt her!' Zalech's eyes were rolling back in his skull and his mouth fell open. 'Zalech, what did you do?'

'I killed all the assassins, but used my hidden gift on one of them. I am a time-scanner and I saw all that she saw this night. That is how I found you. And that is how I found Cathy Atkinson before I chased you down.'

'You *liar!*'

'You lose, Bentley,' he whispered before a long breath passed between his scarred lips. 'You lose.'

He was in his dying seconds, but I could still get answers even if he was unwilling to give them to me. I pressed the palm of my hand over his face and used *my* time-scanning abilities. I saw through his eyes and ran back through our battle, through his journey on the bike, to the little road outside the Williams estate. He was dragging Cathy and Mr Williams across the tarmac and into a nearby field, all the way to the small lake where, to my horror, he killed Mr Williams, then tied his ankles with a length of rope. After that he tied the other end of the rope to Cathy's right wrist. Then he tied her legs and left arm together, behind her back.

'Don't let your friends bring you down!' he laughed at Cathy, before kicking Mr Williams into the water. Cathy had slid right to the water's edge then managed to lift her right arm a little and fought the weight on the other end. As soon as her strength gave out she would slide into the water, dragged below the surface by Mr Williams's body, and with her limbs tied she would not be able to swim. She would die. Mr Williams would kill her, just like Zalech said. He'd walked away laughing, believing that I would never know, or if I did beat him in the fight, that I would be too late to save her ...

My mind went blank when Zalech finally died. I stood up away from him and heaved in breaths of the damp night air. Was there time to save her or was she already dead? It was two hours by car to the lake. She would never have been able to hold out that long. I had failed her.

Or had I ...?

I saw in Zalech's mind that he travelled at phenomenal speeds on that odd looking motorbike of his. In his thoughts he had referred to the bike as a *GSK7*, short for *Golding Scientific Kinetibike Version Seven*. He'd been pushing psychokinetic energy into it, somehow propelling it as fast as a bullet. Perhaps there was still time.

I dashed down the hill and looked into the wreckage of the car to see Hunter was conscious.

'I have to go without you,' I panted. 'If I don't leave now Cathy may die. Will you be all right?'

'Get out of here, Bentley,' he managed to say. 'I'll live.'

'You better!'

I raced up the hill and leaped onto the saddle of the bike then wrapped my hands around the grips of the handles. I kicked off the stand and turned the nose of the bike south.

'Right, GSK7, let's see what you can do.'

My thoughts were filled with the vision of Cathy being slowly dragged into the icy waters of the lake and my body surged with emotion. An awesome power exuded from me and I forced all of it into the front of the bike and suddenly I exploded onto the road. The speed was incredible and I struggled to steer the bike for a few moments. I almost drove straight into an oncoming truck then managed to dodge it at the last second. I was risking my life by travelling at such a speed but I couldn't slow down. I had to get to that lake as quickly as I could.

I saw the digital counter reading 500kmph. I looked back to the road ahead and increased the speed.

CHAPTER THIRTY

The Last Straw

I jumped off the bike when I reached the iron gate at the edge of the road. I kicked it open then raced through the field leading to the lake. Driving rain lashed my face as I ran through the long grass and my heart was pounding like crazy. I kept running until I spotted Cathy by the lake. My pace slowed for a moment and I felt a weight in my stomach. Her head and shoulders were under the water. The rest of her body was motionless.

I sprinted to the shore and dragged her away from the lake. I used my power to sever the rope that dragged her into the water. She lay there with her eyes bulging and her mouth gaping. Bizarrely, I was reminded of how Zalech looked just after he died. Cathy had that same ghostly appearance.

'No!' I screamed. I would not, and could not, accept this fate. I had lost too many loved ones and refused to let Cathy become one of them.

I sent a cloud of energy into her stomach and pushed it upwards which emptied her lungs of frozen water. It spilled out of her mouth then I fired a dart of energy into her heart. This was a technique that was normally used for killing, but I thought that somehow it might stimulate her heart.

Nothing happened. Again I shot at her heart then pressed my lips on hers and blew air into her body.

Nothing.

I tried again.

Her eyes twitched.

Her chest lurched forward and she wheezed in a deep breath then reached out and grabbed hold of me. Water spurted out of her mouth and she coughed and wheezed, her body jolting and shivering. She was alive.

'Ross ...' she tried to speak.

'Don't talk, Cathy. You're going to be all right.'

'Ross ... Ross, he tied me to Peter. Ross ... he murdered Peter ...'

'I know.'

I pulled her close then wrapped my arms underneath her and carried her back to the road. I sat her down on the bike then jumped on and got it moving. My instinct was to bring her to a hospital, but that was dangerous for us both. The others always told me to avoid hospitals at costs. I had to find help and I had no idea where the other Guild members were.

I was taking a risk, but I had little other choice. I drove to the animal sanctuary knowing that there were people there who were loyal to Mr Williams, and there was always medical personnel stationed there at night in case any of the animals were unwell.

The security staff, who all knew Cathy personally, helped me to bring her into the central building where we found the medical officer on duty. He insisted he was only a veterinary physician and was not qualified to treat a human who had almost drowned and was suffering hypothermia. I showed him the ligature marks on

Cathy's wrist and lied that there was a killer on the loose, and that she couldn't leave the safety of the building until he was caught. Eventually he relented under pressure and agreed to look after her.

One of the security guards brought me to a small cafeteria on the first floor of the centre and sat me down with a blanket over my shoulders and a cup of hot, black coffee in front of me on a table. My body was aching now that the adrenaline was wearing off. I had pains everywhere after the fight with Zalech but that was the least of my worries and I felt selfish even thinking of myself. I would have some bruises, maybe another scar or two to add to my growing collection. That was unimportant considering how many people had died earlier in the night.

I went to the sink and vomited when I thought of Peter Williams. My friend and protector had met with a terrible death, one that he didn't deserve. His body had been used in a sick and twisted game to kill the girl I loved. The only positive was that Zalech's murderous rampage was over. He would never again hurt innocent people and would never again kill the gifted members of the Guild of the True.

I was called into the room just after dawn; the vet told me Cathy would pull through. Apparently I had gotten to her just in the nick of time. I asked to be left alone with her, and after they left the room I climbed onto the examination table next to her and held her tight until I fell asleep.

❧ ❧ ❧

Cathy was gone when I woke up. I climbed off the table and saw the tall figure of Jim Sterling across the room, by the door.

'Stay seated, young Bentley,' he said. 'Cathy is fine. She's been brought to a proper doctor who is employed by the Guild. He will examine her injuries and will medicate her accordingly.'

'I thought she was gone … I don't know what I thought …'

'I'm not surprised. You look as though you've taken quite a beating. You're black and blue and I wouldn't be surprised if there's a fractured bone or two in your body.'

'Who cares? He killed Peter Williams.' I held my face in my hands and roared into them out of frustration. 'He killed your entire team. He time-scanned Linda Farrier to find out where the rest of us were. Then he killed her!'

'So, that's how he did it.' Sterling crossed the room and sat next to me. 'I found out what happened a couple of hours ago, but I couldn't quite figure out how he'd managed it. I still can't … how on earth did he have time to kill the hit squad then travel down here before catching up with you and Hunter? All in the space of a couple of hours.'

'The bike that I came here on – I don't know where the hell he got it – it runs on psychokinetic energy and can move like a fighter jet. That's how he managed to get from one place to another so fast.'

'Golding and his toys,' Sterling said distantly. 'I should have allowed for something like this.'

'You're wrong, Mr Sterling. Your plan was almost perfect.'

'My team should have been able to kill him. He must have been told we were coming.'

'Hunter said we couldn't trust Golding and it seems he was right. That bastard betrayed us and ten people are dead because of it.' I pushed myself off the table and shuffled to the counter and ran my head under the tap before taking a mouthful of water. 'I had to leave Hunter on the side of the road. He was badly injured.'

'Hunter's alive. He turned up at a hospital a couple of hours ago. He'd been brought there by a trucker who came upon the crash site. I don't know what his injuries are, but he'll get through this. He's a strong man.'

'And Zalech?'

'Our moles in the police service have confirmed he is dead. The police will conduct an autopsy on him. He'll be an oddity to them with his metal parts, but he can reveal nothing about the gifts or about the Guild. His treachery is over. Now it's time to rebuild.'

'I don't think I can be a part of it anymore.'

Sterling didn't seem surprised or offended. 'I understand. You have to rebuild your life first before you can think of the Guild. I trust you will make the right decision in time.' He walked to the door and held it open for me. 'Come, I'll take you up to the house. You can take a proper rest and Cathy will join you tomorrow.'

'I don't know if I want to go to that house alone. Not after what happened to Mr Williams.'

'Where else would you go?'

I had no answer to his question. For the first time in my life I had nowhere to go and no one to turn to. The only place for me was that big empty house and now I had to act like an adult. I had to stand on my own two feet. There was no Romand or Mr Williams to watch over me. I now had to be as strong as they once were.

'There is no need for fear, Ross. You have faced and defeated the deadliest of villains and you lived. You are victorious. In this moment your mind is confused and your heart is torn with grief, but in time you will see how monumental your achievements truly are. There are very few people walking this earth who can contend with you now. Fewer still who would dare challenge you. Go to the house and rest. Trust me, you *are* safe.'

He had spoken the truth and Cathy did come to the house the next day. She was quiet, and often stared off into the distance, much like her mother had in the aftermath of Romand's death. There were tears too that first day. Lots of them. There were less the day after, and within three days she was showing fleeting signs of her old self. The Guild had kept their distance, but on the fourth day Sterling returned and shared a pot of tea with us. He told us that Mrs Williams would be back from France the next morning, along with Cathy's mother, and that we could stay in the house with them or move to an apartment in London that the Guild had used as a safe house for many years. We opted for the latter after the funeral. Peter Williams's ashes were to be planted with an oak sapling next to the one that stood over Romand's final resting place.

The house, that seemed so big and empty and cold now, would see a second funeral service in the space of five months. No one would have ever guessed that two of the wisest, strongest and most loved members of the Guild would meet such cruel deaths in such a short space of time.

Sterling also mentioned Golding's betrayal, and spoke of revenge. I understood why he needed to get even, but also why he would not rest until the great threat posed by Golding was banished forever. I didn't commit to his plans, and Cathy downright refused. She told Sterling that she was done with the Guild. Never again would she expose herself to the dangers of that way of life. Sterling didn't argue with her and seemed prepared to let her go.

He took a different attitude with me. He was insistent that I take part in the attacks on Golding Scientific, when the time came. I appeased him by saying I needed a couple of months to recover and would join him after that. I had no intention of doing so. Cathy wouldn't hear of it. As soon as Sterling had gone we talked about running away from England altogether and never returning to the Guild of the True and the long war they had been fighting. I didn't like the idea of running away, but I liked the idea of her suffering a lot less. We made the decision that night to leave together after the funeral was over.

🖝 🖝 🖝

Cathy's mum arrived at the house early the next morning with Mrs Williams, who seemed quite composed considering what had just happened to her husband of so many years. She was probably still in a state of shock and I couldn't blame her for that; we all remained stunned by the events of that horrible night. By late morning there were over twenty mourners hanging about the house, including Hunter. Some people associated with the Guild had smuggled him out of the hospital two days earlier. He was sitting rather uncomfortably in a wheelchair. He said both his legs were broken, but he would be back walking soon enough. His face was still bruised and there was a deep scar above his right eye. He looked a right mess, but I was sure the emotional wounds would be harder to recover from. I told him I was sorry to learn of Linda Farrier's death. He just pretended he hadn't heard me and looked away.

At 4pm they planted the sapling with Peter Williams's ashes and some of those closest to him spoke briefly. After that we reconvened at the house and most took a drink, and everyone spoke of their memories of their departed friend.

Jim Sterling announced just before nightfall that he was leaving. Before he left the house he came to me and handed me a key and a piece of paper with an address written on it.

It was the key for the apartment in London where Cathy and I would stay for a month or two, until I recovered enough to rejoin the Guild's activities. He then gave me another key, this one for a lock-up that was at the rear of the apartments. Sterling had left the Kinetibike there for me. He told me to contact him in December then went to his car.

The evening seemed to go on forever. It was long past midnight before the last of the guests left. Mrs Williams went to bed right after that, and Cathy then told her mother of our plans. June didn't argue. In fact, she seemed genuinely pleased that we were getting away from the Guild. I left her and Cathy to talk and went to bed.

I didn't sleep a great deal and was up and dressed by 7am. We were on the road an hour later and by early afternoon we had retrieved the Kinetibike and were heading west for the port of Pembroke. We boarded a ferry at 11pm that docked on the south-east coast of Ireland four hours later. From there we rode the bike north to the small cemetery near Maybrook.

I didn't know what I expected to see or feel when I reached my father's grave. There were no tears shed. All I felt was resentment that his life had been taken by a brute like Zalech. I couldn't even focus on any sense of loss because my anger was too potent.

I spent no more than ten minutes by the grave. My father was gone and a slab of stone didn't make me feel any closer to him. I would mourn him in my own way and in my own time. Visiting the grave hadn't been a good idea and it took hours for my anger to ease off. By that time we had reached the north-west coast of the island, thanks to the GSK7.

We had organised the entire escape two nights before. Cathy had transferred her considerable inheritance to an Irish bank account, under an assumed name, and we had searched the internet and found a small cottage by the coast that was available to rent. Cathy had contacted the owner and he was waiting for us when we arrived. We were free at last.

CHAPTER THIRTY-ONE

A Visitor at Christmas

Many weeks passed peacefully and we grew to love our quaint, little home. It was a basic cottage with a bedroom, a small sitting room and a kitchen not much more spacious than the cramped bathroom. It was safe and it was ours though, that was all that mattered to us. Neither of us would ever get over the incredible losses we suffered at the hands of Edward Zalech, but after a time we learned to live with the awful things we had experienced. Life goes on, as they say.

We even fell into a routine: Cathy liked to run along the cliffs to the north in the morning and then she'd make breakfast for us both. I had got used to waking up late again, and I often spent the afternoon practising on my skateboard that I bought in a nearby town. In the evenings we would spend time together doing simple things that all normal couples do. At night I would get a fire going and Cathy would sit on the couch in front of it, reading a book. I would walk the beach, which was just ten minutes walk from the cottage, and on my return I would always find her sleeping with her face on the arm of the chair.

As I made my way home one night, in late November, a stray, black cat followed me. It was a bitterly cold night and I couldn't bear to leave her outside in the freezing temperatures. I took her into the cottage and Cathy insisted that she be allowed to stay. I knew how fond she was of animals, particularly cats, so I agreed that Nightshade, as we called her, would be our first pet.

At Christmas we bought a few glittering decorations and a short pine that we placed next to the window of our sitting room. We both bought some presents for one another and had them wrapped and placed under the tree. The ones I bought were the ones that looked like a monkey had wrapped them. Cathy's were picture perfect.

The night before Christmas was very much like any other, apart from my constant begging to open my presents early. She hadn't let me. When she started reading in front of the fire I told her I was going for a stroll along the beach.

I was contemplating the previous year and all that I had learned and lost. I thought of my parents mostly and how I missed them both so much. Anger and deep regret still tainted every memory I had of Dad. I also thought of Romand and of Peter Williams and how dull the world was without them. Hunter, too, occupied my thoughts now and again, and I found that I really missed the big grump.

Zalech crossed my mind once or twice and the certain devastation that had been avoided by his death. I wondered if another villain similar to him, or Dolloway, would emerge from some corner of the world and would the Guild be able to deal with them. Part of me felt guilty for having run away, leaving them to deal with the sinister forces of the gifted world. They probably needed me, but I had made my decision and I didn't see any way of going back. I chose Cathy over the Guild. I chose normality over adventure. I chose a life full of love rather than a life circled with death.

I reached the cottage later than usual that night and I was shaking with the cold when I got to the front door. Nightshade was standing the steps outside the door and the hair on her back was raised.

'What's up with you?' I said to her. She usually pawed at the door when I returned from my walk. 'Stupid cat.'

Nightshade hissed wildly and backed up against the door.

'What's got you so spooked, Nightshade?'

'Cats can see through body refraction. Don't you remember?'

I spun around – no one was there. I had recognised Hunter's voice, though, and a second later he became uncloaked, right next to me.

'What are you doing here?' I asked. 'How the hell did you know where I was?'

'Bentley, you can't hide from the Guild of the True. We have ways of finding people and you didn't do a very good job of covering your tracks. I was sent to find you and then to inform the Guild of your whereabouts. I've been hanging around this area for two days. I spotted you this morning, but needed to come down here for a closer look to be sure it was you.'

'Now you know it's me.'

'Yes. That doesn't mean the Guild has to know.' He came closer, limping slightly. 'I guess you deserve a quiet life more than anyone. As does Cathy.'

'I would be very grateful if you tell them you never found us.'

'Found who?' He turned away and slowly headed along the path to the gate. He paused before he opened it, but didn't look back. 'If we ever get in too much trouble,' he said, 'if the Guild is in danger of being totally destroyed, I will have to come back here. Not to demand anything from you. But to you ask you as a friend, and as a respected former colleague, for your help.'

He opened the gate started off along the road. I waited a few seconds then went to the end of the garden and out onto the road.

'Hunter,' I called after him, 'ask for my help and you'll have it. Just don't ask any time too soon.'

'All in good time, Bentley,' he shouted over his shoulder. 'All in good time.'

The first Ross Bentley book

HE HAS THE GIFT, BUT HE'S NOT THE ONLY ONE.

MILLION DOLLAR
GIFT

IAN SOMERS

Million Dollar Gift
by Ian Somers

Ross Bentley has a gift – he can move things with his mind.

Ross has always known he was different, but he's kept his talent secret, even from those closest to him. Everything changes when he hears about a contest called The Million Dollar Gift – a wealthy businessman has pledged a million dollars to anyone who can prove they have superhuman powers. It's too good a chance to miss ...

But Ross finds himself drawn ever deeper into a world of corruption and peril. His gift puts him in danger from powerful foes, but also introduces him to people and talents he can hardly believe exist ...

A fast-paced ride into a hidden world of extraordinary gifts and deadly enemies.